NOT IN TIME

BY SHAWNA SEED

————————

G ENEVIEVE MCKENNA REALIZED – too late, as usual – that she'd made the wrong call.

She'd seen the traffic on the 10 freeway backing up and debated with herself for the last quarter-mile before the exit, then decided against the side streets at the last minute.

Now she was stuck.

She'd be late to work.

Normally, the unpredictability of Los Angeles traffic made the concept of "late to work" somewhat elastic. Ten minutes past the hour was essentially on time; 20 minutes was still within the margin of error.

But late on the day the boss had requested her presence in his office at 9 a.m. sharp?

Late on the day she was probably getting laid off?

Even LA's elasticity on tardiness would not stretch to cover that.

Just thinking the words "laid off" made her feel sick. Her skin, normally pale, flushed from her chest to the roots of her hair. She concentrated on breathing – in through the nose, out through the mouth. She reminded herself that no, she was not having a heart attack and no, she would not die.

She'd been having these panics since the first rumors that the grant funding her job was in jeopardy. She'd be busy with something else, and out of nowhere, terror would grip her. Her vision narrowed, her pulse raced, and her stomach dropped. It was a little like a roller-coaster ride, but without the comforting restraint of a harness.

Now she knew what people meant when they said "my heart sank."

Genevieve surveyed the sea of idling cars and reviewed the mistakes that had brought her to this point in life.

Should have set her alarm 15 minutes earlier.

Should have circulated her résumé the minute she heard the rumors about the grant.

Should have pursued her doctorate. Should have majored in something more practical than Art History. Should have chosen a more prestigious college instead of settling for one close to home.

She could see an endless string of mistakes stretching from her childhood in Wichita Falls to this moment on the 10.

People were always stressing the value of a positive attitude, and she supposed they were right – she shouldn't be thinking these thoughts. But the habit was comforting in its own destructive way, like biting her fingernails.

Suddenly, traffic began to flow, like a drain unclogged. She glanced at the Camry's dashboard clock. 8:38 a.m.

She wouldn't be late after all.

❑

Genevieve's employer – for the moment, anyway – was the Hilliard Museum, a private institution firmly stuck in the middle tier of the LA cultural hierarchy. It had an excellent collection of Etruscan funerary art that almost no one came to see and an eclectic (some would say poorly curated) assortment of European and American paintings, mostly from the 19th and 20th centuries.

She'd been hired six years earlier, fresh off a professional triumph at a small Pasadena museum. A painting there had a puzzling gap in its chain of ownership – provenance, in art-world parlance – and Genevieve solved the mystery. Her discovery earned a mention in a professional journal, and the Hilliard had come calling.

Leaving the freeway well before she reached the touristy part of Santa Monica, Genevieve drove past the public face of the museum, a white stucco modernist structure, and into the parking deck. She waved her security card in front of the electronic gizmo and waited for the gate to lift.

As she parked and shut off the car, it hit her that she might be going through this routine for the last time. She took a deep breath, swung her bag out of the passenger seat and started up the ramp toward the employee entrance.

She'd been so excited when she landed this job. It wasn't the Getty, sure, but she knew she'd never get a spot there, not with her diploma from Texas Tech and no Ph.D.

At the time, the Hilliard desperately needed someone to straighten out its provenance files, which had been neglected for years. Like a lot of museums, it had come under pressure to scour its collection for anything that might have changed hands during World War II and make sure those pieces had been transferred legitimately, not looted from their rightful owners and then sold to unsuspecting – or unquestioning – museums.

Genevieve was supposed to make sure the chain of possession for each work of art was documented. She thought she'd be sort of an art detective, helping avenge old wrongs.

But the project hit snag after snag, and she never really did any detective work. It had taken forever to get the records organized, and she'd only recently begun to identify anything that had changed hands during the war and enter those pieces in an international database. She hadn't even made it halfway through the collection.

And now it seemed that whatever urgency the Hilliard once had on the topic had dissipated. Genevieve wasn't sure why. She knew the museum's endowment had shrunk with the economy, and her slow progress probably didn't help with donors.

Rumors had been swirling that the Hilliard had lost a big grant and that provenance research would be cut. Then, she'd received a memo asking her to report to the museum director's office at 9 this morning, no further explanation offered.

She paused at the employee entrance, juggling her coffee and bag so she could show her museum ID. The security guard, Bill, patiently held the door.

"Good morning, Miss Jenny."

Bill, unfailingly pleasant, always mangled her name. She'd given up correcting him.

"Morning, Bill."

"Hang in there," he called as she headed down the corridor toward her cubicle.

The security guard who couldn't even get her name right seemed to think she needed encouragement. That couldn't be a good sign.

She dropped off her purse and coffee at her desk, took a minute to compose herself, and then headed to the office of Malcolm Stewart, the museum director.

Malcolm, a hotshot with an Ivy League pedigree, was hired a year before Genevieve. He was an expert on the Etruscans with an international reputation and a mandate to elevate the museum's profile. She got off on the wrong foot with him almost immediately, when her proposal for digitizing the provenance records and creating an internal database sat on his desk for months. Then, after finally approving the project, Malcolm halted it midway through because he found a process he thought was better. She'd been forced to start over and had been playing catch-up ever since.

As it turned out, Malcolm wasn't in his office when Genevieve presented herself at 8:59. He was running late.

Carol Gladstone, Malcolm's assistant, apologized for the delay, as if it were her fault. She said she would call when he arrived.

Genevieve went back to her desk. Five minutes passed, then 10, and she was so nervous she could barely stay in her chair. To distract herself, Genevieve decided to sign on to her computer and see whether there were new listings in the international provenance database.

She typed her user name and password.

"INVALID PASSWORD" flashed on the screen.

She tried again, making sure the caps lock key was off. Another error message. Her fingers were poised to try again when it hit her: They'd already disabled her login.

The phone rang. It was Carol. Malcolm was ready for her.

◻

Or almost ready for her. Malcolm was on the phone when she was shown into his office, tilted back in his ergonomic chair, nodding along as he listened to whoever was on the other end. He waved Genevieve into a chair opposite his desk.

She perched nervously on the chair's edge. She had no idea what to do with her hands, which were shaking. She wished she'd brought pen and paper, something to make her feel less naked.

An unmarked manila folder, closed, sat precisely in the center of Malcolm's desk. It seemed very thin. If he truly were laying her off, wouldn't there be reams of paper involved? Maybe that was an encouraging sign. Maybe this would be another situation where she anticipated the worst and things turned out just fine. Borrowing trouble, as her grandmother used to say. Catastrophizing, her best friend called it.

On his laptop, she could see an email Malcolm had begun but not sent. The subject line said MEMO TO THE STAFF. Malcolm loved sending memos – in fact, he communicated almost exclusively through memos, something his employees mocked mercilessly. Genevieve wondered what this one would be about.

Malcolm caught her eye and angled the laptop screen away.

Oh. Of course. The memo would be about her.

Feeling her chin begin to tremble, Genevieve turned her head away. She focused on a family photo on Malcolm's credenza – him, his (much younger, very beautiful) wife and two adorable children on a beach, posed in the shade of a palm tree.

They'd gone somewhere tropical for Christmas, Genevieve had heard. Fiji? Tahiti? She refused to be drawn into office gossip about Malcolm's lifestyle. His wife supposedly came from money; how they spent it was none of Genevieve's business.

"I apologize for keeping you waiting."

Genevieve lurched a little in her chair. She took a deep breath and turned toward Malcolm. He pushed back a shock of blond hair that had fallen over his forehead. Although he was at least 50, Malcolm cultivated a certain boyishness. He pulled a pair of rimless reading glasses from his desk drawer and opened the manila folder on his desk.

"Due to a recent drop in funding, your position with the museum is being eliminated, effective immediately," he began.

It was a script. The folder held a script, and he was reading it. Word for word, Genevieve supposed. He wasn't even making eye contact.

"You are entitled to eight weeks of severance pay and to continue your health insurance under applicable law. Those benefits..."

Malcolm stopped. "This is awful," he said, finally making eye contact. "The HR people insisted I recite this as written, but that seems inhumane."

He shoved the folder across the desk to her. "Do you want to just read it?

Genevieve accepted the folder and began silently reading where Malcolm left off.

"...will begin once you've signed the necessary paperwork, although you are not required to do so today. Once you've cleaned out your desk – boxes will be provided to you – you can leave your badge with the security desk. Only personal items should be taken. Anything relating to your work is the property of the museum and must remain. The museum thanks you for your contributions and wishes you well."

He removed his glasses, setting them carefully aside. "Any questions?"

Numb, Genevieve shook her head.

"Carol will have the details on the paperwork," Malcolm said. "And I'm going beyond what I'm authorized to say here, but of course we'll give you a good reference, one that will put the progress of the provenance project in the best possible light, given the obstacles."

Obstacles. That was one way to put it. The false start on the database. The year she'd done Carter's job while he was on sabbatical in Ravenna. The nine months spent covering for Samantha during her maternity leave. The endless requests that she pitch in here, pick up an unrelated duty there. *Obstacles.*

Malcolm stood, signaling that the meeting was over. "Do you think you'll go back to Kansas?"

"*What?*" It came out a little sharper than Genevieve intended, but she resisted the temptation to apologize. The man had just fired her, after all.

"I thought you were from Wichita," Malcolm said. "I could check my contacts, see if I know anyone there..."

"I'm from Wichita Falls," Genevieve said. "Texas."

Malcolm slapped his hand against his forehead. "Of course. I've only lived on the coasts. I'm shamefully ignorant about the middle of the country."

He offered his hand. "I'm not supposed to say this, either, but I'm sorry to see you go."

Genevieve felt she had no choice but to shake it.

CHAPTER TWO

GENEVIEVE WALKED BACK to her cubicle, head up, eyes focused on the distant wall. It was only 50 feet from Malcolm's office to her desk, but it felt like a mile.

She did not want to cry in the office.

Fortunately, her colleagues seemed keen to avoid her. One picked up his phone as she walked by. Another pulled open a drawer and began a frantic hunt for something. A third seemed engrossed by the faux wood grain of his desk.

At Genevieve's cubicle, Carol was dropping off a stack of flattened boxes.

"I'm so sorry," Carol said, waving at the boxes. "This must seem heartless." Why did the coldest bosses always have the nicest gatekeepers?

"It's fine, Carol. I'm not mad."

"You'll land on your feet. I just know it." Carol patted her reassuringly on the arm. "Malcolm said you don't have to sign the papers today, right? I really recommend waiting."

"Thanks," Genevieve mumbled. "I think I'll do that."

Carol took the hint and left.

Genevieve knew the best thing was to get out quickly, but she couldn't fathom where to begin. She opened drawers, then closed them without moving anything.

The shaved head of Thomas Monroe, her favorite co-worker, popped over the cubicle divider. His eyes narrowed at the sight of the boxes on her desk.

"Damn," he said, drawing the word out to the two syllables it merited in his native North Carolina.

He came around the divider and sat on her desk. "How can I help?"

Genevieve began folding one of the boxes into shape. "Some help packing would be great."

Thomas opened a drawer and began lifting out files.

"I can only take personal stuff," Genevieve told him.

Thomas began scanning files. "What else did Malcolm say?"

"I get eight weeks of severance, and I can pay to keep my insurance. There's some paperwork, but I don't have to sign it today. Everyone wishes me well and thanks me for my contributions. I can leave my ID with security."

"That's it?"

"There was a script, but he felt awful doing it and just gave it to me to read instead. I think if he could have figured out a way to lay me off by memo, he would have," Genevieve said, hating the way her voice trembled.

"Oh, Malcolm. Genius on ancient cultures, dolt dealing with live humans," Thomas said, clucking his tongue. "Good thing he has that wife to schmooze the donors."

"Maybe she should be in charge of cutting the deadweight," Genevieve said.

Thomas pushed his glasses up on his forehead. "You know this isn't about you, right? It's just money. It's nothing to be embarrassed about."

Genevieve took a deep breath, trying to maintain her composure. "Tell that to everyone else. They're avoiding me like I have a communicable disease. Don't they know you can't catch 'fired' from casual contact?"

"You're not fired," Thomas said. "You're laid off. Huge difference." He held up a piece of paper. "ARTnews is offering you 30 percent off a subscription. Keep or toss?"

"Toss."

Ten minutes later, they had cleared the last drawer.

"Thanks for helping me. I want you to know you've always..." her voice caught. She couldn't finish.

From the day she started, Thomas had been her biggest champion and best resource. He always seemed to know where to look for the file no one else could find, and more than once he'd run interference for her with Malcolm, who respected his opinions. Somewhere along the way, he'd become one of her best friends.

People sometimes called Thomas "Mayor of the Museum," because he seemed to know everyone and everything. He'd been the one who warned Genevieve her job might be in jeopardy.

Thomas put his hand on his hip and gave her a mock-stern look. "No farewell speeches. It's not like you're never going to see me again. In fact, you could have dinner with Philip and me tonight if you're up for it."

He shoved the last drawer closed with the heel of his hand, but it caught.

Frowning, he yanked the drawer all the way out and extracted a battered 8 x 10 manila envelope that was wedged in the back. He opened the envelope and read the title of the weathered pamphlet inside.

"A 1939 catalog from the Galerie de l'Étoile in Paris? Where'd you get this?"

"I forgot I even had that," Genevieve said. "It just showed up in the mail one day."

Thomas began to leaf through the catalog, his art historian impulses momentarily trumping everything else. "I bet there's some amazing stuff in here."

"I wouldn't know," Genevieve said. "I was so worried about not meeting my deadlines that I set it aside. Figured I'd look at it later. And now I guess I have to leave it, because Malcolm specifically said I could only take personal items."

Thomas flipped over the envelope. "It's addressed to you," he said. "That makes it personal, I'd say. And it's a pretty cool souvenir."

Genevieve weighed the decision. "Oh, the hell with Malcolm. I'm taking it."

"That's right," Thomas said. "The hell with him. You should take it."

Thomas held out his arms, and Genevieve burrowed into the hug, aware that it was inappropriate for the office but not really caring.

With that, she walked out of her cubicle for the last time.

□

Genevieve was surprised to see Bill still working the employee entrance. Glancing at the clock, she realized she'd been at the museum only an hour.

"Let me help you with those boxes," Bill said. His tone was kind but urgent.

"That's OK. They're not... Oh. You're supposed to look through them, aren't you?" She put the boxes down and opened them.

"Sorry about this," he said, poking quickly through them. "Memo from the boss."

When he was done, Genevieve handed him her badge and electronic access card.

Bill took them, but instead of ushering her out, he nodded toward the door that led to the galleries. "Would you like a walk-through? I don't think anyone would mind – the doors open in a few minutes anyway. I'll watch your things."

The Hilliard was rarely mobbed, but Genevieve loved being alone in the galleries. It reminded her of afternoons as a little girl spent paging through art books with her mother.

She wound her way past all of her favorites – the Kandinsky that she and Thomas debated endlessly, the Van Gogh that reminded her of the Texas plains where she'd grown up.

Her last stop was a drawing called *Study for Tristan and Iseult*, by Théodore Lazare.

It wasn't the most famous thing in the museum. In fact, it wasn't even always on display. It was just a sketch, something the artist did to work out ideas.

Lazare had died young, leaving fewer than 20 finished works. He'd attained a bit of success near the end of his life with paintings inspired by a trip to Morocco, pieces now considered second-rate. The drawing was part of his earlier output, which featured themes from literature and was influenced by the romanticism of Delacroix.

The drawing showed Iseult in profile, her hair obscuring her face. Genevieve had always been moved by the way Lazare conveyed so much emotion with so few strokes. She could imagine the torment of a woman about to be ripped away from her true love.

There was another reason Genevieve liked the drawing: It had a mystery attached to it. The finished painting *Tristan and Iseult* had disappeared during World War II. There weren't even photos of it. The drawing was all that remained.

Voices floated toward her, alerting her that the museum had opened. She took one last look at poor, doomed Iseult and headed for the exit.

□

Genevieve budgeted two hours for wallowing in self-pity.

Hunkered down on her sofa in a pair of yoga pants and a Texas Tech sweatshirt, she flipped through the TV channels, but home improvement shows could keep her anxiety at bay for only so long.

She decided a dose of Texas can-do optimism was required. She muted the TV and scrolled through her cell phone for the contact that said, simply, D.

D Jones was Genevieve's former roommate and still her best friend. On move-in day their freshman year, Genevieve made the mistake of using D's given name, which was in the letter Genevieve had received from the dorm. She'd learned right then that D might as well stand for Don't-ever-call-me-anything-else.

"What do you recommend to counteract the effects of unemployment?" Genevieve asked when D answered.

"Aw, Gen," D said in her Dallas twang. "You caught me at airport security. Are you cratering or can I call you back in five?"

Five turned out to be 15.

"Sorry about that," D said when she called back. "I was tussling with TSA. I told them all I had on under my jacket was a cami and I wasn't parading around in my frickin' underwear. I think that guy just wanted a free look. Not that there's much to see." She paused to take a breath. "OK. So, you're canned from that job that made you miserable. Tell me everything."

Genevieve gave her a short recap. "So, those are the high-lights. Or lowlights," she said. "So, the question is, what do I do now?"

D was ready with an answer. "Get your butt out to Vegas and meet me at this stupid sales meeting! Even unemployed, you'll be way more fun than anybody else there."

Genevieve laughed, for the first time in days. It was just like D to come up with something outrageous. "I don't think I should spend my severance in Vegas," she said.

"You can share my room. Free!" D said. "I have miles and can book you a ticket. Free! Drinks in the casino are, say it with me: Free!"

"D, that's really generous of you, but ..."

D would not be derailed.

"I'm eating on the expense account, so we'll order lots of courses and share – you don't eat much anyway. Now, you will have to pay cab fare from the airport, though I guess if you really wanted to economize you could take a bus or, I don't know, walk."

She paused for breath, finally, and Genevieve seized the opening.

"I really was just hoping you could help me brainstorm my next move."

D was ready for that one. "You know I strategize better over cocktails."

Genevieve had to admit this was true. Parties, crowds, noise – they all seemed to make D sharper. She fed off other people's energy.

Genevieve began to waver. She hadn't seen D in months, and that was at her grandmother's funeral – hardly a fun occasion. But her conscience reasserted itself. "That just sounds like running away from reality."

D laughed. "No, you are running to reality! The reality where you and I dream up your next career move and have drinks and maybe even meet some hot guys!"

And this was why D was in sales. She could make the most outrageous idea seem perfectly reasonable, even smart.

Genevieve knew when she was defeated. "OK, Viva Las Vegas," she said. "But it's only a couple hundred miles. I'll drive."

"Yesss!" D whooped. "I am liking that answer."

"I feel so much better knowing I've made the responsible decision."

"Gen, this is going to do you a world of good," D said. "How are you doing, anyway? Still having the panic attacks?"

"One in the car this morning on the way to work."

"Are you sleeping OK? Did you talk to the doc about getting something for anxiety and insomnia?"

D sold pharmaceuticals and thought her sample case held the solution to any problem. It surprised Genevieve how much she honestly believed in her wares.

"He gave me the sleeping pill you told me to ask for."

"Any side effects? Because..." D was suddenly drowned out by a boarding announcement.

"Gen? Gotta go. That's my flight and I need to pee. See you there! Oh, and Gen? Pack fun clothes."

D hung up before Genevieve could respond.

❑

Talking to D energized Genevieve. She emailed several contacts, asking them to keep an eye out for job openings. She did laundry and tidied her place. It didn't take long – she lived in a converted garage that had less than 400 square feet.

She balanced her checkbook and paid bills and tried not to think about money.

Thomas called to check up on her. He promised to have leads by Monday. "I'm networking like a fiend – gay grapevine, black grapevine, every damn grapevine I have," he said. "I am a one-man rainbow coalition working for you."

She told him about the Vegas trip, dreading his reaction. But he surprised her.

"You should go and have fun," he said. "It's not costing you anything." He even offered to feed Mona, her cat.

At 5 p.m., 7 back in Texas, she called her father. She knew he'd be in his recliner, digesting his dinner (supper, he called it), watching TV.

He was concerned, as she knew he would be. He offered money, which she declined. He asked several times how she was "handling all this." She told him she was "handling it just fine."

She wished they didn't have to speak in code.

Are you losing it, like your mother?

No, Dad, you aren't going to have to institutionalize me.

But they were too careful to speak that way to one another. More than 25 years later, her mother remained a topic that they talked around, not about.

CHAPTER THREE

GENEVIEVE HAD NEVER been to Venice; she knew it from Canaletto's paintings. As she pulled up to the Venetian hotel in Las Vegas, she laughed out loud at the ersatz Rialto and St. Mark's Square. She supposed her artistic sensibilities should be offended, but the sheer audacity of the fakery seemed fun, like an outrageous Halloween costume.

After parking and dropping her bag at the bell desk, she wandered around the casino and the shopping area, trying to kill time until D was free. For once, she'd overestimated LA traffic.

Genevieve didn't know how to gamble and couldn't afford it anyway. She did know how to shop, but she couldn't afford that, either. Finally, she spotted a coffee shop, entertainment in her price range.

She ordered a latte and took a book from her bag, a Matisse biography her father had given her for Christmas.

One chapter in, a voice interrupted her. "Hey there. Excuse me?"

Genevieve looked up. A man was setting up his laptop at the next table.

"Could I plug into that outlet?" He pointed to a spot behind her chair and flashed a smile.

The smile was killer, and the rest of him wasn't bad either. The man was tall, over 6 feet. He wore jeans and a wrinkled blue-and-white striped shirt, untucked, the sleeves rolled partway up. His hair was brown and on the long side – hovering somewhere between fashionable and messy.

She scooted forward to give him room. He unspooled a power cord and plugged in the laptop. She caught a whiff of something as he leaned past her, a scent that made her think of clean shirts on her grandmother's clothesline.

"All set," the man said. "Will you watch this for me while I grab a coffee?"

That smile again.

"Sure," Genevieve said. She found herself smiling back.

"Get you a refill while I'm up?"

"No thanks."

Genevieve studied his back, admiring his broad shoulders. Fashionable, she decided on the hair.

Then, worried that he'd catch her staring and think she wanted conversation, she went back to her book. Talking to new people made her profoundly uncomfortable. She never knew what to say, and so she often ended up saying something that made her cringe every time she remembered it.

The man returned with a coffee and folded his frame into the small cafe chair. She heard the distinctive tone of a computer starting. "Thanks for watching my laptop," he said.

"You're lucky I had an opening in my schedule," Genevieve said. "I usually can't take walk-ins."

The man gave her an appreciative nod and chuckled. Just then, a 20-something woman in an electric blue micro-mini shuffled past, her silver stilettos clutched in one hand. Her hair was squashed on one side, and her black eyeliner was smudged.

"Must have been some party," the man said.

"Late in the day for the walk of shame," Genevieve said.

"Even by Vegas standards," he added.

This conversation was going to end with her tongue-tied and embarrassed. Genevieve knew that, and yet she didn't really want to shut it down.

"Not often I see someone reading a real book in Vegas," he said. "Very impressive."

"Well, the Chippendales matinee was sold out."

The man threw his head back and laughed, and Genevieve allowed herself a smile. She'd managed to say something funny! Twice!

At the counter, the woman in the micro-mini swiveled unsteadily and scowled at them over her croissant.

The man leaned over. "Uh-oh. Miss Walk-of-Shame is annoyed," he said, his voice throaty and low. "Better use my inside voice."

More like your bedroom voice, Genevieve thought, then began to blush furiously.

"And he didn't even get her breakfast? Very bad form." The man caught Genevieve's expression. "I'm sorry – am I embarrassing you?"

Genevieve shook her head.

"It's just that you're blushing," he said.

As if she didn't know. Blushing was Genevieve's special curse, the flashing sign that told the world she was embarrassed or upset. Controlling it wasn't possible, so she'd learned to make light of it.

"It's an evolutionary defense," she said. "Now my face is red to match my hair. Camouflage. Like a lizard."

He nodded thoughtfully. "I see," he said. Something pinged on his computer, drawing his attention. Genevieve took advantage of the moment to study his profile.

He typed for a few seconds, then turned back to her.

"Don't your eyes pose a problem?"

"My eyes?"

"That blue. They do stand out," he said. He tipped his head to one side, a smile creasing his face. "In this light, they're almost violet."

Before Genevieve could attempt a response, her phone chirped to let her know she had a text. She snatched it up from the table, grateful to have a chance to look away.

D's meeting was wrapping up, and she wanted Genevieve to meet her.

"My friend," Genevieve told the man, gesturing vaguely with her phone. She drained her latte. "Her sales meeting is over."

"Big plans for the evening?"

"She's determined to teach me to play craps."

He smiled again, and again Genevieve returned the smile in spite of herself.

"Craps is fun. You'll like it," he said. "You hitting the tables here or somewhere else?"

With a jolt, Genevieve realized he wasn't just making conversation. He was trying to find out where she might be later.

"I... um..." She could think of nothing to say. "Um, I should get going."

The man leaned back in his chair, his smile dimming a bit. "Have fun!"

Then he cut his eyes toward the woman in the mini, who was waiting for her drink at the counter. "But maybe not as much fun as her."

"Thanks," Genevieve said, edging toward the exit. "You too."

Genevieve shook her head as she walked away. *You too?* Had she really said that? She was such an idiot sometimes.

◻

D was waiting near the bell desk with a drink in each hand. She gave Genevieve an awkward hug, thrust a martini glass full of icy pink liquid into her hand and said, "Let's go!"

She grabbed the handle of Genevieve's suitcase and set off briskly – despite her heels – toward the elevators.

"Hope you weren't waiting around too long," D said over her shoulder as Genevieve hustled to keep up.

"Not too," Genevieve said. "I got a coffee and read for a little bit."

D flashed a room key at a security guard near the elevators, led Genevieve to the correct bank and pushed the button while managing not to spill her drink.

"Only you would come to Vegas and sit around reading a frickin' book."

Genevieve usually didn't mind being the foil to D's life-of-the-party persona. But occasionally she felt the need to prove she wasn't *entirely* boring.

"Actually this guy sat next to me and we started talking."

The elevator arrived, and D blocked the door with her hip so Genevieve could board.

Genevieve told D about the conversation as the elevator began its ascent, pausing at the end of her story to sip the drink. It hit her mouth icy cold and warmed as it traveled down her throat. "What's in this?"

"No idea," D said. "But it's tasty, isn't it?"

The elevator dinged, and D started down the hall toward the room. "You told me everything he said, but you didn't tell me what he looked like! Was he hot?"

"Definitely. Tall. But rangy, you know, not like a linebacker. Dark hair, kind of longish. Nice eyes. Brown. Great smile." Genevieve blushed a little, remembering.

D inserted a key card into a door, waited for the electronic signal and pushed the door open. She maneuvered Genevieve's suitcase into the room. "Movie star?"

It was a game they'd played since college. Genevieve was supposed to come up with the actor who most closely resembled the man she'd just met.

Kicking off her shoes, D perched on one bed and motioned Genevieve toward the other.

Genevieve put her shoulder bag down, thinking. "Oh, I know," she said. "The guy in *Troy*, the one who played the older brother."

"Never seen it," D said. "You know I hate high-brow stuff like that."

"Really? Not even for Brad Pitt? In a skirt? It's on cable all the time."

D grimaced as she rubbed her toes, and they made a disconcerting cracking noise. Genevieve had never understood why D, who was 5-11, insisted on high heels.

"And he was single, right?"

"I hope so. He was kind of a flirt for a married guy," Genevieve said.

"Well, did he have a ring?"

"I didn't look," Genevieve confessed.

"Really, Gen? Really?" D rolled her eyes. "And is that what you were wearing?"

It was a rhetorical question; obviously Genevieve hadn't changed. She stood and looked at herself in the mirror: black turtleneck, jeans, ballet flats. "You don't like?"

"Well, the jeans are cute," D said. "But a turtleneck? You're hiding your light under a bushel. If I was built like you, my going-out clothes would all be cut down to here." She pointed in the general vicinity of her navel.

D's envy of Genevieve's curves was a longstanding theme. "Most women would kill to look like you, no body fat *anywhere*," Genevieve told her, not for the first time.

"Yeah, well, that's the women. Men like curves," D said. "Did you get his name?"

"No," Genevieve said. "He seemed like he was trying to figure out where we were going tonight, and I just kind of froze."

D laughed. "God love you, Gen, but you are hopeless sometimes. You finally got a live one on the line, and you didn't reel him in. How long has it been since what's-his-name, the one who moved to San Diego?"

"Luke," Genevieve said. "And it was San Francisco. Silicon Valley, actually."

D waved her hand in exasperation and took another sip of her drink.

"Two years, OK? I haven't been on a date in two years," Genevieve said. "But I thought we were strategizing on finding me a job, not a man."

D stood and walked to the closet. "I met a guy at a session today," she said.

"And he would be played by?"

D pulled a black sheath out and held the hanger away from her, sizing up the dress. "Dark hair. Blue eyes. Strong jaw. I'm going to say Jake Gyllenhall."

"Nice," Genevieve said. "Only taller?"

"No," D said. She tossed the dress on the bed. "And he's from Akron frickin' Ohio."

"Oof."

"Well, sometimes a girl has to make do," D said. "Let's get you into some cuter clothes and get some dinner, and then we'll go find some fun."

She nodded toward Genevieve's glass.

"Drink up, Shriner."

□

As anticipated, D rejected most of the clothes Genevieve had packed. She eventually signed off on a pair of black pants ("your butt looks cute, at least"), a jade-green vintage silk shirt ("undo another button") and, sighing, the ballet flats.

Over dinner, they tackled Genevieve's next career move.

"It's a do-it-yourself economy right now," D said. "What if you set up as a consultant on this World War II art thing? Worst case, you wouldn't have a gap on your résumé when people start hiring again. You'd look entrepreneurial!"

"A consultant? I wouldn't even know where to start," Genevieve said.

"Pick a company name, get some business cards, and then network, network, network," D said. "Write yourself a press release announcing your business and send it to everyone in your contacts."

Genevieve groaned.

"Or I'll write your frickin' press release and then you can go through and fix all the grammar mistakes," D said. She took a healthy slug of her wine. "What should we call you? The Art Detective?"

Genevieve shook her head furiously. "That sounds dumb. Maybe something with investigations?"

"What do people call this World War II art thing? Isn't there a name for it?"

"You mean looted art?"

D wrinkled her nose. "Looted sounds like people boosting flat screens after a disaster or something. That's no good."

"Lost art, then," Genevieve said.

"Ooooh," D said. "I'm liking that."

Genevieve pushed away her plate. "Lost Art Investigations?"

CHAPTER FOUR

GENEVIEVE DIDN'T WANT to play craps, but D insisted gambling alone was no fun and Genevieve's company was worth the cost of staking her.

They had been playing about 30 minutes, and miraculously Genevieve was up $14, when another player slid into the table's only empty spot, right next to D.

"Chippendales sold out tonight, too?" He leaned around D to smile at Genevieve.

By means of exaggerated eye movements and furtive gestures, D established the identity of the man next to her. Then she turned on her Texas charm.

"So you're the coffee break I've heard so much about. I'm D," she said, offering her hand. "And you know Gen. Pleased to meet you."

He shook hands with D, then reached across to Genevieve. "Jay," he said. "Nice to see you again – Gen, is it?"

D mouthed the words "no ring" to Genevieve. Then she squared her shoulders, and with a let-me-show-you-how-it's-done look, turned her attention to Jay.

"What brings you to Vegas, business or pleasure?" she asked him.

"Client meeting," he replied.

He'd changed shirts and shaved since she'd seen him last, Genevieve noticed. The sleeves were rolled up again, baring tanned, muscular forearms.

The dealer pushed chips toward him, and Jay stacked them in the tray in front of him. "How's the table been?"

"So-so, but I have a feeling things are about to heat up," D drawled. Genevieve had been watching her work this routine since college, but it never ceased to fascinate her. D, who had three brothers, had an easy way with men that Genevieve could only envy, never emulate.

"So, Jay, what kind of clients do you have?"

"Satisfied ones, I hope," Jay said. He straightened to his full height and studied D. "Now you, I'll bet you're in sales." He smiled at Genevieve as he said it.

D's mouth opened wide. "How did you..." then she caught his smile. "Oh, Gen told you." She punched Jay on the arm. "No fair."

Jay leaned around D to address Genevieve. "But you never said what you do."

Genevieve was at a loss. What to say? "Unemployed?" "Between projects?"

D motioned Jay closer and lowered her voice. "Hip-hop mogul. But keep it quiet. Once people hear her name, they'll start giving her demos and we'll have to leave."

"It's true," Genevieve said solemnly. "Everybody thinks they're the new Kanye."

"Your disguise is good," Jay said. "I would have guessed something in the visual arts. A gallery, maybe."

Genevieve turned to stare at him, but suddenly there was a chorus of groans around the table, and dealers started raking in chips.

"So, Jay," D drawled. "Where you from?"

"LA," he said.

"Really?" She raised an eyebrow at Genevieve. "Gen lives in LA."

"Yeah?" Jay asked, obviously intrigued.

"New shooter comin' out," one of the dealers called, pushing the dice toward Genevieve.

She looked at D, eyes wide. "Am I supposed to roll?"

"You can pass," Jay said. "Do whatever you want."

"But it's good luck when a woman rolls," D said. Then she addressed the table at large. "Fellas, it's good luck when a woman rolls, right? Am I right?"

The dealer wielding the stick nodded.

Genevieve looked to D for reassurance, then shrugged. "What the heck."

Jay smiled at that and tossed a chip toward the center of the table, which a dealer caught. "Ten dollar yo," he said.

"Oh, I am liking that idea," D said to him. "Betting big on our girl's maiden voyage." She tossed two chips on the table. "Five dollar yo and one for the boys."

"Do I need to do that?" Genevieve asked.

"Nah, I'm making a bet for me and one for the dealers," D said. "Now, pick two of the dice, and your new friend Jay and I would really appreciate an 11."

"Just pick them up," said a dealer, "and toss them right down the center of the table, like a jet down the runway. Make sure you hit the wall at the other end."

Genevieve picked up the dice, closed her eyes, and tossed them. One showed five, the other six. Was that good or bad? Wait, wasn't that 11?

"Yo, yo, yo," the dealer called.

Jay clapped, and the dealers began paying off bets.

"You hit yo!" D said. "You made everyone a winner, but especially me and Jay." Out of the side of her mouth, she said, "You just made me 75 bucks and 150 for him."

Before Genevieve could respond, the dealer pushed the dice to her again. She flung them, then stood on her tiptoes to see the results – a three and a four.

Jay began clapping again, and the dealers began payoffs.

"I thought seven was bad," Genevieve whispered to D.

"Not in this case," D said. "You're doing great."

Jay threw another chip on the table. "Hard six and hard eight, two each, one for the boys."

He smiled at Genevieve. "Make me a winner again."

"Oh, you're already a winner," she said, not quite believing she was saying it. Genevieve was starting to see why Jay and D thought this game was so much fun.

Her next roll produced two fours.

"Eight, hard eight, the point is eight," a dealer called. Another dropped a stack of chips in front of Jay.

"You just made Jay a bunch of money," D whispered. "Now it's easy. Hit the eight."

"Eight," Genevieve said. "Got it."

She threw the dice again. One rolled down the table and landed, showing five. The other, to her horror, bounced off Jay and back onto the table. It landed showing three.

She began to stutter apologies, but applause around the table drowned her out.

"Winner, winner, chicken dinner," a player called from the other end of the table as the payoffs began.

"Hit me again if you want," Jay said, tapping his palm against his chest.

His smile was infectious. Genevieve couldn't remember the last time she'd had so much fun.

But the dealer made a grim face as he slid the dice toward her. "You need to hit the back wall," he said.

"Oh, leave her alone," D chided him. "She's doing great!"

Just like that, Genevieve was nervous and self-conscious. On her next roll, she threw one die off the table. Then she did it again.

"Down the middle of the table, like a jet down the runway," the stickman reminded her.

It seemed as though everyone at the table was staring at her, and Genevieve began to feel the familiar, creeping dread of embarrassment.

On her next roll, one die hooked and flew off the table, whizzing past Jay's head as he ducked.

"Calm down and do it like you did that first time," D coached quietly.

A blotchy flush spread over Genevieve's chest, up her neck and to her face.

"Can I just stop?" she asked D.

"No, Gen, you have to keep going until you roll seven. It's OK. You'll be fine."

Genevieve rolled the dice, taking care to keep the trajectory low. They died in the middle of the table. The dealers exchanged glances. "No roll," one of them pronounced.

"I don't know what I'm doing," Genevieve said.

"No shit," she heard someone mutter from the other end of the table.

Jay glared down the table, then turned to her. "You'll never see any of these people again. Who cares what they think? You're doing great."

Feeling slightly encouraged, Genevieve rolled again, landing the dice close enough to the wall to satisfy the dealers. One showed three. The other, four.

"Seven out, seven out," a dealer called, raking players' chips off the table.

Genevieve was never so relieved to lose so many people so much money.

"Good roll," Jay said. Genevieve assumed he was being sarcastic, but his smile said otherwise.

The dice came to D next. She rolled for 15 minutes or so, earning minor payouts but nothing big. When she hit seven, she said, "I need to powder my nose anyway."

She signaled to a dealer, who spread a small towel over her chips. Then she took Genevieve's arm and pulled her toward Jay. "Scoot this way so you can keep a better eye on my chips while I'm gone."

"You keep her from running wild," D said to Jay. Then she winked at Genevieve and sauntered away.

Jay draped his tall frame over the table, edging closer to Genevieve. "How long have you two been friends?"

Again Genevieve caught the scent she'd noticed at the coffee shop. She resisted the urge to bury her head in his sleeve and inhale, but only just.

A dealer pushed the dice toward him. Genevieve had noticed that many of the players studied the dice before rolling. Not Jay. He grabbed them and threw them expertly down the table, almost casually.

People around the table clapped, and the dealers began a round of payoffs.

"We were roommates in college and then a few years after," Genevieve said.

Jay dropped a stack of chips on the table and reeled off how he wanted them placed. Genevieve didn't catch all of it. She was playing only the pass line, which D had explained was the easiest and lowest-risk approach.

"And you have a history of running wild when she's not around?"

Their eyes met. Genevieve tried frantically to think of a witty comeback, but her mind was blank.

A slight tilt of Jay's head told Genevieve that she'd held the eye contact too long.

"You need to pick up your payoff," Jay said, a smile spreading over his face.

"What?"

Jay tapped the back of her hand with his index finger. "You need..."

Genevieve didn't hear the rest.

Her peripheral vision began to fade, and the table in front of her seemed to spin. The green felt, white lines and brightly colored chips began to blur at the edges, becoming indistinct bits of color, like pigment on a painter's palette. She gripped the table as the casino's light seemed to grow brighter. She tipped her head back and squinted against the white light. She thought, for a moment, that she glimpsed blue sky.

"Hey, you OK there?"

And just like that, it was over. She turned to Jay, who was staring at her.

"I'm fine," Genevieve said. "Just had a little..."

A little what? What had just happened to her?

Jay smiled. "Little too much to drink, maybe? Easy to get dehydrated here."

Genevieve shook her head. "Just one drink before dinner, and I didn't finish it."

Jay signaled a cocktail waitress. "Can we get water, please?"

She handed him a bottle of water, and he dropped a couple chips on her tray, then gave the water to Genevieve. "Do you need to sit?"

Genevieve opened the water and took a sip. "I'm fine."

The game had not paused. A dealer pushed the dice toward Jay. He threw them down the table, taking his eyes off Genevieve only briefly.

"Seven, seven out," one of the dealers called.

Jay barely seemed to notice. "You want to call your friend?"

"I left my phone upstairs," Genevieve said. "I'm sure she'll be back soon."

Genevieve wasn't sure this was true, not at all. D might have struck up a conversation with someone from her convention – or a total stranger – and lost track of time. It had happened before.

Jay wasn't convinced either, apparently. He stepped back from the table and pulled his phone from his pocket. "What's her number?"

Genevieve recited D's number.

"Hey, this is Jay at the craps table," he said when D picked up. "Your friend isn't feeling well. You might want to head back this way."

▢

D arrived a few minutes later, striding across the crowded casino like Moses through the Red Sea.

Jay stopped playing when his roll ended, and Genevieve had, too. She sipped her water and tried to avoid looking at him. Whatever had troubled her had passed. She felt perfectly normal. Completely embarrassed, but normal.

"What's up?" D asked, bending down to look Genevieve in the eye.

"She did this weird whole-body shudder," Jay said, "and then she rolled her head back and stared at the ceiling. She seemed kind of, I don't know, *gone*."

"I'm fine now," Genevieve said. She didn't want to make a big deal of the incident in front of Jay. Not that it mattered — his interest seemed to be waning.

"You want to go?" D asked.

Genevieve nodded. D put her chips on the table and signaled for Genevieve to do the same, suddenly all business. "Color in," she said.

The dealers stacked and counted the chips, then handed back the winnings in larger denominations.

Genevieve caught Jay's eye one last time as she and D left. "Nice meeting you," she said.

"Hope you feel better," he said. Then he placed a bet and went back to the game.

"So what was that?" D asked as they threaded their way to the elevators. "Panic attack?"

"It didn't feel like one. It was really weird," Genevieve said, pausing to take a drink of water.

D eyed the bottle suspiciously. "Where did that come from?"

"This?" Genevieve held the bottle aloft. "One of the waitresses brought it."

"Did you put it down uncapped? Did anyone touch it?"

"Jay handed it to me, but..."

D snatched the bottle away as Genevieve watched, astonished. "Haven't you heard of the date-rape drug? A guy can put it in your drink, and the next thing you know..." D rolled her head back and let her mouth hang open.

"If he was trying to drug me, why would he call you?" Genevieve said. "Anyway, he flagged the waitress down *after* the thing happened."

They reached the elevators; D stabbed the "up" button with her thumb, taking care to spare her French manicure.

"Well, that's a good point, actually," D said, handing the water back. "Let's rethink. Have you started any new medicines, even something over the counter?"

"Just the one sleeping pill the other night," Genevieve said. The elevator doors opened and they boarded.

"You might should avoid that," D said. "Anything else strange happen lately?"

"Other than the whole getting-laid-off-and-having-panic-attacks thing?"

D looked her up and down in the bright light of the elevator. "You seem a little flushed but otherwise you look OK," she said. "Tell me what happened after I left."

"Jay moved over closer, and we were talking, and everything was fine, except I had that thing where he would say something funny and I couldn't think of a comeback," Genevieve said. "And then he touched my hand, and, remember that time in college I had the allergic reaction and you had to take me to the health center?"

"You're saying it was like a bad case of hives?" The elevator opened, and D held the door for Genevieve.

"No," Genevieve said, keeping pace with D down the hall. "But they gave me an IV of something in the ER then and I felt it sort of swoosh through my veins. This was like that. I felt something swoosh through me, and the table went blurry, and then I looked up because there was this really bright light, and I thought I saw blue sky and..."

Genevieve took in D's expression and paused. "What?"

"Did a frickin' angel choir appear and go 'laaaaaa?' "

"What do you mean?"

"All this because that guy touched your *hand*?" D shook her head. "Pitiful, Gen. That's just pitiful."

Genevieve followed D into the room and sat on the bed. "Well, I don't really think that's it," she said. "Maybe I'm just tired. I guess I ruined your evening. Sorry."

D remained standing. "About my evening..."

"Oooooh, did you run into Fake Jake from Akron?"

"He wants me to meet him for Pai Gow poker," D said. "I told him I had to check up on my friend and then I'd text him. I'll just tell him you're not feeling well and see if we can switch it to coffee tomorrow."

D pulled her phone from her purse, but she didn't seem in a hurry to reply.

"I'm fine," Genevieve said. "You should totally go."

"You sure? I won't go if you're not OK."

"I'm fine," Genevieve said. "I'm just going to have a bath and go to sleep."

That was all the permission D needed. She took a few minutes to check her hair and fix her makeup, and then she was off for her Pai Gow poker date.

After D left, Genevieve ran a bath in the deep soaking tub and eased into it. Her apartment had only a shower; a bath was a rare luxury.

She tried to relax, but her thoughts kept returning to the scene in the casino. It didn't feel like any of her panic attacks, she was sure of that.

As the water cooled, she began to realize she'd done nothing to address the source of her panic: unemployment. The confidence she'd gained from strategizing with D began to leak away. Her own consulting business? Who would hire her?

Genevieve got out of the tub and wrapped herself in one of the hotel's plush robes. After she'd brushed her teeth, she discovered that she'd forgotten pajamas. She didn't even have a T-shirt that would stand in.

She dithered for a moment, then shrugged off the robe and slipped between the sheets. She knew D probably wouldn't care when she came in late and crawled into the other bed. That was, if D came back at all.

Bright sunlight pours through the windows. It warms her bare shoulders.

Her head is at an awkward angle; all she can see is the floor with its scuffed, bare planks.

Her hair covers her face, tickling her cheek. She longs to brush it away, but she knows she must hold the pose.

The only noise is the faint scratch of the pencil as he sketches. He doesn't speak, and she has no desire to force conversation.

They have nothing to say to each other. Not now.

CHAPTER FIVE

GENEVIEVE WOKE the next morning alone in the vast hotel room.

D's bed appeared to have been slept in; Genevieve wasn't sure whether that was a good sign.

She got up and belted the hotel bathrobe around her, then opened the curtains. Another sunny day in Sin City.

D had left a note on the desk:

Guess who's a whiz at Pai Gow poker!
Order breakfast and charge it! Call you later!

Genevieve ordered the cheapest thing from room service, which she still found shockingly expensive.

While she was waiting for it to arrive, Thomas called.

"How's Vegas?"

"Strange," Genevieve said. "How's Mona?"

"Frisky," he said. "A guy called, said he wanted to talk to you about a job. I wouldn't give him your number but I said I would pass his along."

"That was fast," Genevieve said, her voice rising in excitement. "I can't believe one of your friends came through already."

"Oh, I don't know him. He called out of the blue," Thomas said. "Don't know how he found me, even."

"Who is he?" she asked, her hopes deflating a bit.

"His name is Henry Lazare," Thomas said. "He didn't tell me much. You want the number?"

"Lazare like the painter? Hang on, let me get a pen."

Genevieve flipped over D's note and took down the number from Thomas.

"Did he say what kind of work? What's his story?"

"He was kind of curt. Why don't you Google him? I have to run. Let's have dinner when you get back."

Fortunately, D had left her laptop. It was password-protected, but Genevieve got the password right on her second guess – the name of D's high school boyfriend. She typed Henry Lazare's name into a search engine.

The first link was for a Beverly Hills law firm, Manning, Chalmers and Lazare. She clicked through a few links and discovered that Henry Lazare specialized in matrimonial law. What did a divorce lawyer want with her?

The second link took her to a *Los Angeles Times* story about a studio bigwig's divorce. It mentioned Lazare's "hardball tactics."

Next up was a magazine piece about the city's best divorce lawyers. It called Lazare a "pit bull." He did not sound like a nice person, but she supposed that was what rich people wanted in a divorce lawyer.

Her cell phone rang, startling her. It was D.

"Where are you?"

"In the room. I needed to get online," Genevieve said. "I can't believe you're using Vince for your password."

"You're supposed to pick something easy to remember, right?" D laughed. "And they say you never forget your first. Meet me for lunch at 12:30. I have a surprise!"

Genevieve thought the surprise might be a chance to meet D's poker pal, but she was wrong. D was alone at a table that looked out on the casino floor, sipping a glass of white wine. She'd ordered one for Genevieve, too.

As soon as Genevieve sat down, D demanded her phone.

"Is yours out of juice?" Genevieve asked as she handed it over.

"No, I want you to see what a genius I am!"

D fiddled with the phone, then handed it back with a triumphant grin.

Genevieve had a new contact: *Jay in LA*, with a phone number.

"I looked at my recent calls and realized I had his number," D crowed. "Now, I know what you're thinking. You're thinking, 'D, what am I supposed to do with this?'

"So here's what you're going to do," D said, tapping Genevieve's menu for emphasis. "Back in LA, you're going to call and say you appreciate him being so nice when you weren't feeling well la-la-la and can you buy him lunch to thank him!"

She beamed at Genevieve. "Is that genius or what?"

"D, you're a wonder."

"I know! So you're going to follow up, right?"

Genevieve hesitated. "Oh... I don't know. I mean, won't he think it's weird that I have his number?"

"He's not going to care how you got it," D said.

"It's just, I don't know, lunch? That could be an hour and a half. I could hardly think of anything to say to him last night."

"Coffee, then," D said. "That's more your style anyway. And in your budget!"

"Oh, I have news on that front," Genevieve said, eager to change the subject. She started to explain about Henry Lazare, but D interrupted three sentences into her story.

"So what did he say when you called him?"

"What did who say?"

"This Lazare guy. You *have* called him, haven't you Gen?"

"Not yet. I wanted to research him first," Genevieve said. "He's a divorce lawyer, which is strange, don't you think? What could he want with me?"

The waiter arrived to take their order, but D shooed him away. She placed both hands flat on the table. "Gen, it's time for a come-to-Jesus meeting."

Genevieve didn't look up. In their college days, D had called these "meetings" on a regular basis.

"I'm worried about you," D said. "I mean, you've always been shy, but you used to could cowboy up and do things."

She paused to take a drink of her wine before continuing. "I think you're being way too cautious, about dating, work, everything! You haven't been on a date in two years! Jay is hot, and he likes you! Why not ask him to coffee? Worst case, he says no, or he says yes and it's boring. You're looking for work! Why not call this guy about a job? What's wrong with you?"

Genevieve sat very still, then reached up with her napkin to dash at the tears that had begun to slide down her cheeks.

"Oh, Gen, I'm sorry," D said, softening her tone. "I know life's been kicking your ass lately."

"Mostly my own fault," Genevieve said.

D waved that comment off. "There's a difference between normal caution and being afraid to live your life. It seems like you are changing into this mousy person, and that is not the Genevieve I know."

Genevieve took a deep breath, gathering herself. She pushed away from the table.

D was startled. "Gen? Don't run off. I'm sorry. I'm just trying to help."

"It's OK," Genevieve said. "It's just that I have a phone call to make about a job."

"Well, now hang on. I don't want to miss this!" D hurriedly put some cash on the table, drained her wine and snagged her bag from the back of her chair.

□

Back in the room, Genevieve dialed the number Thomas had given her and reached Henry Lazare's assistant.

"And what is this regarding?" she asked.

"I don't really know," Genevieve fumbled. "He called me. Well, no, he called my, um, former colleague trying to reach me." She thought she sounded like an idiot, but D nodded her encouragement. The assistant put the call through.

"Henry Lazare," a gruff voice answered. "Ms. McKenna? I understand you were just let go by the Hilliard."

"Yes, well, the grant that funded... Wait, how did you know that?"

"And you were working on provenance research, correct?"

"That was my job description, yes, although..."

D was furiously shaking her head.

"I'm getting bogged down in details," Genevieve said. "Yes, I specialize in provenance research."

D gave her a thumbs up.

"I need an art historian for a project, and I think you're the perfect person. Interested?"

Genevieve felt as though she was being cross-examined on one of those TV courtroom dramas. She decided shorter answers were better, because Henry Lazare wasn't going to let her finish her sentences anyway.

"What do you have in mind?" she asked.

"The Hilliard has something stolen from my family. I want you to prove it. I'll put you on a monthly retainer," he said, naming a figure so far beyond her museum salary that Genevieve thought she'd misheard and asked him to repeat it.

"I'll also cover your expenses, within reason," Lazare said. "As a bonus, you get to stick it to the museum. What do you say?"

Genevieve wanted to ask for time to consider the offer, but then she looked at D. "OK," she said.

"Great. We have a deal," Lazare said. "I don't really know jack about art; my cousin's the one with the details. Julien Brooks. I'll have him call you. Any questions?"

"No. Wait, yes," she said. "The piece that you believe is yours, what is it?"

"*Study for Tristan and Iseult*," he said. "The artist is a distant relative. Julien will tell you everything."

Genevieve turned to D after she hung up. "I think Lost Art Investigations just landed its first client."

D offered her a high five. "I knew it was a good idea! Let's celebrate!"

CHAPTER SIX

A FTER AN ENTERTAINING DINNER with D and some of her fellow salespeople, Genevieve was back on the road to LA the next morning by 10.

She'd planned to use the time to brainstorm on the Lazare provenance project, but she found herself thinking instead of Jay.

Genevieve had never asked a man out, not even for coffee. Not that she thought there was anything wrong with a woman's taking the initiative. She'd just never had the nerve to invite rejection.

D, true to form, had been unwilling to let the subject drop. She'd offered to role-play the invitation with Genevieve, and at dinner, she'd surveyed her colleagues on whether a first move by a woman was appealing or a turnoff. Appealing, the assembled men agreed, but Genevieve suspected they were supplying the answer D so clearly wanted.

The last thing D said before Genevieve left was, "Don't chicken out!"

Genevieve stopped in Barstow for gas and lunch, discovering that everyone on the road between Las Vegas and Los Angeles had the same idea. As she idled in the drive-through line, she toyed with the idea of calling Jay. D had insisted, with her usual conviction, that afternoon was the perfect time to issue a coffee invitation.

"Morning implies you spent all night thinking about it," D said.

Genevieve ran through the script in her head. "Hi, Jay. This is Genevieve – we met in Las Vegas?"

No, no, no. That part wasn't a question. She needed to make her intonation lower at the end of that sentence. "Hi, Jay..."

Her phone rang in her hand. She checked the display.

Jay in LA, it read.

Genevieve laughed. D must have called Jay and offered Genevieve's number, unwilling to run the risk that Genevieve would lose her nerve.

She hit the answer button.

"Well, hi," she said. "I'm glad you called! I didn't really get a chance to say thanks for flagging down that water for me."

"Hello?" There was a long pause at the other end. "I'm trying to reach Genevieve McKenna?"

"Your timing couldn't be better," Genevieve said. "I'm in the drive-through line at In-N-Out in Barstow, and I've hardly moved in 15 minutes."

"Excuse me? Is this Genevieve McKenna?" He sounded slightly annoyed, and Genevieve felt foolish for adopting such a casual tone.

"Yes," she said, trying to sound more serious.

"Oh, good. I was worried for a minute that my cousin had given me a wrong number. Henry Lazare told you to expect my call?"

Startled, Genevieve nearly dropped her phone.

"Oh! I, uh, I thought you were someone else," Genevieve

stammered. "Obviously." She held the phone away from her face and took a deep breath.

"Sorry for the confusion," she continued in her most professional voice. "A friend programmed a new contact in my phone, uh, a number of someone we met, and she must have transposed a couple digits. Yes, this is Genevieve McKenna, and yes, your cousin told me to expect your call regarding *Study for Tristan and Iseult.*"

Silence stretched again on the other end.

"Did you say you were in Barstow?"

"Yes," Genevieve said. "I'm traveling. I'll be in LA later this afternoon, and..."

"Are you on your way back from Vegas?"

Genevieve, realizing that a midweek trip to Vegas sounded unprofessional, was instantly wary. "Yes," she answered, resisting the temptation to explain herself.

"And that's where you met this person your friend put in your contacts?"

What did that have to do with anything? Genevieve was starting to wish she'd let this call go to voicemail.

"Your cousin Henry said you could fill me in on..." she began, trying to steer the conversation back to business.

"And your friend is from Texas."

"Wait a minute," Genevieve said. "Who *is* this? Are you Julien Brooks?"

"Yes. And I guess we've already met, at the coffee shop," he said. "And then again playing craps. But I thought your name was Jennifer."

"Wait, what?" Genevieve's heart began to pound, and not in a good way. "Jay?"

The driver behind her honked. She put her car in gear and moved up 5 feet.

"Right, really only my family calls me Julien," he said, laughing. "How weird is this? So I guess the deal is Henry hired you? And I'm supposed to fill you in on what we know about the drawing?"

Now completely unnerved, Genevieve tried to think what to say next, how to get control of the situation.

Suddenly, she knew exactly what she needed to do.

"My phone's about out of juice and my car charger's in the trunk," she said. "I'll have to call you back later."

Once she had her food, Genevieve pulled into a shady parking place, turned off the ignition and made another phone call.

"Gen! Did you call him?"

"He called me," Genevieve told D. "Just now. And something here is totally not right, because it turns out Jay is Julien Brooks."

"He called you? That's awesome," D said. "But how did Jay get your number, and who's Julien Brooks?"

"He's the cousin of Henry Lazare, the guy who just hired me," Genevieve said. Sometimes she wondered how much D actually listened to her.

"Lazare said his cousin would call me about this supposedly stolen drawing, and now it turns out that the cousin, Julien Brooks, is Jay."

"So Jay's real name is Julien? I wonder why he doesn't use that," D said. "I like it. Kinda foreign and sexy."

"Maybe he does go by Julien, but he said Jay because he was hiding who he is," Genevieve said. "Anyway, that's not the point!"

"Oh, I get it! Now you don't have to invent an excuse to meet with him," D said. "That's even better!"

"Again, D, not the point," Genevieve said, beginning to feel exasperated. "This feels really wrong. First this Henry Lazare calls Thomas for my number, and somehow he knows the museum's fired me. Then his cousin just happens to sit next to me in Vegas and strikes up a conversation?"

"It's like when Meredith hooks up with that guy," D said, "and then the next day he turns out to be her boss. *And* married."

"That's a TV show, D! This is real life, and it's creepy," Genevieve said. "It's like they've been stalking me or something."

"Um, Gen? You sound kind of paranoid."

"You know, that's what Pete used to say, when I wondered why he had to work late so much," Genevieve said. "Or that time after I'd been home for Christmas and found that lipstick in our apartment, and he convinced me I bought it and forgot about it because I didn't like the color, and then he turned it into a fight about how I never returned things that were the wrong color or didn't fit because I was too embarrassed and I wasted money and..."

"Gen, slow down a minute," D said. "Take a deep breath."

Genevieve stopped. She inhaled and exhaled slowly.

"Sorry to trip your trigger," D said. "You never told me that lipstick story. But forget Pete for now, OK? One thing's got nothing to do with the other."

"I have to quit," Genevieve said. "There's something not right about this."

"Hang on now," D said. "Let's think about this. What motive would these guys have for stalking you?"

Genevieve considered D's question. "I don't know," she said.

"Maybe it just feels that way because you're really sensitive after everything with Pete," D said. "Maybe it's just a coincidence."

"A coincidence? You really think that?"

"I'm just suggesting you should think long and hard about quitting a job over this," D said.

Genevieve weighed D's point. "Well, it's true that I can't really afford to," she said.

"You can always quit later, right? So why don't you talk again with Jay or Julien or whatever the hell his name is," D said. "See what kind of vibe you get."

Genevieve was going to be late for her meeting with Julien Brooks.

She called when she got home, apologizing for the abrupt end to their earlier conversation. He suggested that they meet the next day for coffee, which might have been funny if she hadn't been so rattled.

When she walked into the coffee shop, 15 minutes late, she immediately spotted him at a corner table. A woman in running clothes – younger than Genevieve and in much better shape – was leaning on the chair opposite him, chatting. The angle of the lean seemed designed to show off her breasts.

The woman said something funny, and Julien laughed. Genevieve remembered that laugh.

He caught Genevieve's eye and glanced at his watch, a silent rebuke that put her on edge. He said something to the runner, who sauntered off, tossing a wave over her shoulder. Genevieve instantly disliked her.

Because she was wary about this meeting, Genevieve had prepared for it carefully. She was determined to be professional, to ask smart questions. She would volunteer no information and was ready to resign on the spot if anything seemed amiss.

She'd spent the previous evening reading everything she could find about Théodore Lazare. Her background file was tucked into her shoulder bag, the good leather one her father had bought for her 30th birthday. She was dressed in a gray turtleneck and black pants; her hair was gathered into a chignon. She walked purposefully to the table and offered Julien Brooks a firm handshake. "Sorry to make you wait," she said. "I ran into traffic."

He half-rose from the table to shake hands. He did not favor her with one of his megawatt smiles.

"Do you want coffee before we get started?"

Genevieve shook her head and took a seat.

Julien handed her a manila folder. "Paperwork from Henry," he said. "You're supposed to sign that and fax it to him, and then he'll give you a countersigned copy."

"Thanks." Genevieve put the folder in her bag unopened and retrieved her notepad and pen. "So, let's get started," she said. "*Study for Tristan and Iseult.* Tell me why your cousin believes it was looted."

Irritation flashed across his face, and Genevieve realized she'd struck exactly the wrong tone.

"We don't *believe* it was looted, it *was* looted," Julien said. "You worked for the Hilliard; where do they say it came from? That's the real question you should be asking."

Genevieve instinctively covered her notepad with her hand. She had a whole list of questions written out in advance;

Julien had apparently spotted them. The direct opening had seemed a good idea when she'd scripted it the night before.

"I don't have any inside information for you. Unfortunately, I left the museum in the middle of a reorganization and review of the provenance files, and I was only up to the letter I," she said. "The museum's website, which I checked last night, lists it as an acquisition from a private collection in 1979. Lazare drew it sometime in the 1840s. So we've got a 130-year gap to account for."

"Whose private collection did the drawing come from? Maybe they've got the painting, too," Julien said. "You know that disappeared, right?"

"I have no idea who had the drawing," Genevieve said, a little more primly than she intended.

"What *do* you know?" He crossed his arms over his chest.

"This is the first I've heard that there's any question of it's being looted," Genevieve said. "Have you approached the museum?"

"Henry thought we should have our facts together first."

The easy charm he'd displayed in Vegas was nowhere in evidence, which Genevieve found a relief. If nothing else, it made it easier for her to concentrate.

"If I'm going to help you, I need to know the basis of your claim."

Julien exhaled and uncrossed his arms. "You sure you don't want coffee? It's a long story."

CHAPTER SEVEN

————————————

"**J**UST TO WARN YOU up front: A lot of this is hazy. My mother didn't talk about this for the longest time," Julien said, "as hard as that is to believe."

Genevieve didn't find that hard to believe. Her family never talked about its most traumatic events, either.

"I knew she had a brother who died in the war, but I thought it was like my dad's brother who died in the war – his brother James killed in Holland and her brother David... well, I never asked. It seemed like I wasn't supposed to."

He broke off eye contact, staring out the coffee shop window.

"My mom died of cancer three years ago. A lot of this story, I got at the very end, sitting up nights with her. She'd drift in and out."

"I understand," Genevieve said. "Tell me what you know, and then we can try to fill in the blanks."

He took a deep breath and let it out.

"This started when I took her to an exhibit at the Hilliard. She was having one of her good days, and I thought we'd get out of the house and... Well, anyway. We saw the drawing, and she just about collapsed."

Genevieve nodded, encouraging him to go on.

"She said it used to hang in her family's apartment and she hadn't seen it since 1939," he said. "See, my mom was born in Paris, and her family..."

He paused, thought for a moment.

"This gets kind of complicated. Can I have your pen? And a piece of paper?"

Genevieve passed them across the table.

At the top of one sheet he wrote:

"Théodore and Henri Lazare"

"OK, Théodore, the artist, died fairly young. Whatever work he didn't sell – and that was most of it, especially the early Romantic period stuff – ended up with his brother, Henri. My cousin and I are descended from Henri. With me so far?"

Genevieve nodded.

He wrote "**World War II**" and underscored it.

"So, fast-forward a hundred years. You've got three Henri Lazare descendants. My mom, Regine, was the youngest. Her brother David was something like 14 years older than her, and he was running a gallery that the original Henri started 100 years earlier, Galerie de l'Étoile."

"Galerie de l'Étoile?"

"You know it?" Julien seemed surprised.

"I've heard of it," Genevieve said. She had the 1939 catalog sent to her at the museum; the connection to Théodore Lazare hadn't come up in her research. She encouraged Julien to go on. She didn't need to put all her cards on the table right away.

Julien wrote:

"Regine (my mother)
David (my uncle, Henry's great-uncle)
Georges (my uncle, Henry's grandfather)

"Still with me?"

Genevieve nodded again.

"So, this is the way my mother explained it to me. David was running the gallery, and he and my mom lived in an apartment above it. The family had owned the building a long time. Théodore Lazare's original studio was in the attic, actually."

"So David was raising your mom?"

"Yeah, their parents were dead," Julien said. "She was his half-sister, really. I think it was more like David was generally responsible for her, but a nanny or whatever was in charge of the day-to-day. They had servants and stuff."

"And the oldest brother, who was Henry's... grandfather?"

"Georges. He married some industrialist's daughter and went to work in her family's business," Julien said. "There was some kind of falling out between the brothers; I'm not really sure what that was about."

Genevieve was regretting that she'd handed over her notebook. She was going to have to get all of this background down quickly when Julien gave it back.

"They had a pretty extensive art collection in the apartment," Julien said. "*Study for Tristan and Iseult,* the painting itself, plus other stuff. My mom said they had a Picasso, but I don't know – that part might be drug-induced.

"OK, so everyone's getting nervous about Hitler. I think this was 1939. You're some kind of expert on looted art, you're probably better on the timeline than me."

"Some kind of expert" sounded dismissive to Genevieve, but she let it go. "Right. Keep going," she said.

"They knew about *Kristallnacht,* obviously. But even people who thought there would be a war didn't envision the Nazi occupation of France. And the Lazares were not religious. From what my mom said, they didn't especially think of themselves as Jews."

"I guess a lot of people didn't grasp the danger," Genevieve said.

"But David was very worried, according to my mom," Julien said. "He arranged for her to visit friends in England, had her travel with an American friend who was leaving France. Then Germany invaded Poland, and David refused to let her come back to France. And that's how my mother spent the war."

He took a sip of his coffee.

"France fell really fast. There was a huge panic to get out of Paris. You know all of this, right?"

"Yes."

"Georges went with his wife and son to her parents' place out in the countryside, in Unoccupied France. The son was my cousin Henry's father.

"I don't know exactly what happened to David. My mom said he died in Paris, probably in '41, but I don't know what that's based on."

Genevieve wasn't sure what to say, so she just sat quietly.

"When Georges made it back to Paris, he found that the Nazis had cleaned out the apartment and the gallery. All of the artwork was gone. Not just the artwork. They took everything: jewelry that had been in the family for years, furniture, even dishes. They stripped the place."

"I'm so sorry," Genevieve said. "There are so many horrible stories like that."

"And worse," Julien said. "We lost only one person. But my mother never really recovered from it. David was the one who'd always looked out for her."

Genevieve picked up her pen from where he'd left it on the table. He slid the notepad across, and she turned to a fresh page.

"And was anything ever recovered?"

"I don't think so," Julien said. "Although my mom dropped hints that she thought Georges might have screwed her out of some things. He was like that, apparently."

"And you didn't notify the Hilliard after your mother saw the drawing, but you want to pursue a claim now?"

Julien sighed. "Life got very complicated. Mom died and I was dealing with her estate. I took a buyout from the *LA Times* and started my own graphic design business. And... well, there was just a lot going on. Henry wasn't very interested. Then he read about some family getting a painting that was worth millions."

Now Genevieve knew why Henry was willing to pay her so well. "You should be aware that this drawing isn't worth anywhere near that much. Théodore Lazare's works aren't valued that highly, and this is only a study."

"Oh, I know that," Julien said. "Henry knows that, too. It's not really about the money. Henry mostly hates the idea that someone is getting the better of him."

Genevieve, reassured that the job hadn't evaporated before it really started, shifted back into art historian mode.

"Well, there are several ways to prove ownership. Is there anyone alive who would recall the drawing in the family's possession? What about your father?"

"He's dead, too. And he met my mother after the war."

"OK, so no contemporary eyewitnesses that we know of," Genevieve said, tapping the pen on the table. "It's possible the drawing was listed in someone's will or maybe they had their possessions inventoried for insurance at some point," she said. "Are there any old family photos? I know of one case where the family had a photo of their grandmother's apartment that showed their Pissarro hanging on the wall."

"I never saw any, but that doesn't mean anything," Julien said. "I've got some old stuff of my mom's in my garage. I could look."

"Do you have any idea who, specifically, did the looting?"

"What, like the names of the people?" His expression was incredulous.

"No, I meant which organization. The Nazis had several different groups involved," Genevieve said. "People took things for a museum Hitler wanted to build. Goering was building a collection as a tribute to his wife. The ERR, the Einsatzstab Reichsleiter Rosenberg, confiscated Jewish property in France. There was a lot of competition among them to get the best stuff, actually."

Julien drained his coffee. "So the Nazis had turf battles. Who knew?"

Genevieve began making a list – an action plan, as D would call it. "Here are a few ways we can proceed. It's worth going through your mother's papers, because you never know where clues are going to surface. I'll track down scholarly research on Théodore Lazare and see if there are any leads there. I'll investigate what kind of probate records exist. It would be good to get a family tree with as many names and dates as possible."

"Henry's first wife is a genealogy buff. I'll call her."

Genevieve checked the time. Her hour of free parking was just about up.

Julien Brooks had done nothing during the meeting to alarm her, and now she was intrigued by the Lazare family's story.

She would sign Henry Lazare's paperwork and fax it back.

Genevieve was home, studying the Galerie de l'Étoile catalog, when Thomas called.

She brought him up to speed quickly on the developments – Henry Lazare's offer and her meetings with Jay-who-turned-out-to-be-Julien.

"So, I'm working for them, but obviously, I have misgivings," she concluded.

"Well, I wouldn't worry about the *Hilliard*," Thomas harrumphed. "If the drawing is looted, the museum is in the wrong. Is there something else bothering you?"

"Don't you think it's weird that I met this guy twice in Vegas?"

"Oh, I don't know," Thomas said. "I ran into a college classmate in a cafe in Madrid once. Hadn't seen the man in 15 years. Coincidences happen. Is there anything else about him that makes you uncomfortable?"

"Other than he's devastatingly handsome?"

"You didn't mention that," Thomas said. "Do tell."

Genevieve pulled her feet up under her and coaxed Mona to the sofa. She described for Thomas her first meeting with Julien Brooks at the coffee shop in Vegas.

He whistled when she was done. "Oh, Gen. I have to say, he doesn't sound like your type."

"Well, I'm working for him, so it doesn't matter now," Genevieve said. "But why is he not my type?"

"Don't get huffy. I've just never seen you date someone outgoing."

"You've barely seen me date anyone," Genevieve said.

"True. But the computer guy – what was his name? – I could hardly get two words out of him. In fact, Philip worried he was too boring for you."

"Tell me about it."

"Ohhhhh," Thomas said. "Well. OK, then. Does this Julien Brooks seem devastatingly handsome in a dangerous kind of way?"

"Define dangerous."

"Genevieve, you know what I mean."

"I know," she said. "And the answer is, I can't tell."

Bright, white light. A man's hand grasps her arm.

Her fist is clenched. He tries to force it open.

Then, with a muttered curse, he relinquishes his grip.

She hears something clatter and looks down.

Lying on the floor, glinting in the bright light,

is a small gold heart.

CHAPTER EIGHT

G ENEVIEVE WAS GOING to be late to a meeting with Julien Brooks. Again.

He'd called to say he'd borrowed a conference room for the afternoon and wanted Genevieve to help him sort through his mother's papers. "I don't know what I'm looking for," he said. "You do."

Genevieve wouldn't be able to blame traffic; she'd used that excuse the day before. He was unlikely to believe she'd been lost, because he'd given her very explicit directions.

She was late because she'd slept poorly, hit "snooze" too many times and then dithered over what to wear, even calling D for advice. She'd settled on a black pencil skirt and a vintage twin set embroidered with seed pearls. D argued against the twin set, saying it sounded "schoolmarmish," but Genevieve thought its shade of lavender was one of her best colors.

She pulled up to the address Julien had given her, a cinder-block midcentury office building a few blocks from Culver City's downtown. Leaving her Camry in the visitor parking, she pushed through a glass door marked "Cohen and Associates."

She had no idea what Cohen and Associates did, or what Julien's relationship to the business was — he hadn't said.

The reception area was dark, illuminated only by the daylight slanting in the windows. A tiny woman with a mass of eggplant-colored curls turned from a filing cabinet to greet Genevieve. She wore an oversized white linen shirt, black leggings and black ballerina flats. A woman after Genevieve's heart.

"Are you here to see Jay? Come with me."

Genevieve followed the woman down a short hall to the conference room.

The room was done up in modernist style — polished concrete floor, metal table, chairs that looked vaguely uncomfortable. Cardboard boxes littered the table. A wall of windows looked out on a courtyard ringed with benches, a popular spot for coffee and smoke breaks, it appeared. The windows were cranked open; it was about time for the sea breeze to kick up.

Julien sat before an open laptop, talking on his cell phone.

"Sure," he said. "Me too. Looking forward to it. OK. See you then."

He ended the call and looked up at Genevieve. To her relief, he did not check his watch.

"Hey," he said. "I didn't label any of this stuff when I packed it, which I can't quite believe. This is going to be more of a scavenger hunt than I thought. Have a seat and pick a box."

"OK." Genevieve sat opposite him and opened the box nearest her. It was full of insurance and medical forms. Even though Regine Lazare Brooks was dead, Genevieve felt like she was violating her privacy. She put the papers back. "This is all health insurance forms and doctor bills. Paperwork."

"Which reminds me, I saw Henry this morning." Julien reached for a folder near his laptop and passed it to her. "That's your copy of the contract, or whatever he calls it."

"Thanks." Genevieve put the folder to one side.

Julien pushed another box toward her. "Try that one. There are photos here somewhere. And you might put the folder in your bag. Pretty sure there's a check in it."

Genevieve put the folder away. Julien, she thought, seemed to be studiously ignoring her. Which was fine.

"I might as well shred that stuff," he said, hefting the box she'd just poked through. "No need for it all now." He walked out and turned toward the reception area.

"Belle?" His voice carried back down the hall. "If your head's so bad you've got to turn the lights off, you should just go home."

"I have to wait for the mail, a client's bringing a check, and Manny's coming for a work order," Belle said. "I can't clear it with the boss because she's busy, and I don't know if you knew, but Erica can be a real pain in the ass."

"Really," Julien said, and even from another room, Genevieve could detect the sarcasm. "She can't be mad that you had a migraine. Just go. I'll cover things here."

A whispered conversation ensued. Genevieve opened the folder Julien had given her. He was right. It contained a check, one that would cover her bills for the rest of the month.

Julien reappeared in the doorway.

"Belle has a migraine and is going home," he began. "I'm going to stay to answer the phone and deal with the apparent *flood of people*" – at this he looked over his shoulder – "expected through the office doors this afternoon."

"OK," Genevieve said, confused.

"You're welcome to stay or go, it's totally up to you."

Taking in Genevieve's expression, he dropped his voice. "Belle's worried that you're uncomfortable being left here alone with me."

Belle appeared in the doorway and elbowed him. "Jay!"

She smiled at Genevieve. "Only because you girls can't be too careful. Jay's a prince. I'd let him marry my grand-daughter, but she's a lesbian and wouldn't have him."

With that, Belle hitched a giant raffia purse up on her shoulder and headed out.

Julien waited in the doorway. "Staying or going?"

Genevieve debated with herself for a moment. She didn't feel uncomfortable. "Staying," she said.

They'd been working about 45 minutes and had found nothing useful when the office phone rang.

Julien hit the speaker button. "Cohen and Associates," he said.

"Jay?"

"Hey, Erica."

"Why are you answering the phone? Where's Belle?"

"She had a migraine. I sent her home."

"So you're making executive decisions now?"

Genevieve glanced up from the box she was working on, which so far had yielded nothing but cruise itineraries and faded travel agency brochures. Julien's expression was untroubled, and Genevieve couldn't tell whether the woman on the phone was upset or whether this was just banter.

"I told her I'd cover the phone. Did you want something or is this some kind of spot-check?"

"There's a number on my desk I need," Erica said.

"Hang on." Julien hit the hold button and walked into an office across the hall.

Genevieve took advantage of the diversion to study him. He was wearing jeans, a long-sleeved olive T-shirt and flip-flops. Clearly, he'd put a lot less thought into his outfit than she had. And yet he was no less attractive for it.

D had asked her that morning why she was dressing up if she thought he might be gaslighting her. Genevieve had to concede that was an excellent question.

Julien had put the call on speakerphone again, and she eavesdropped as he found the number for Erica, whoever she was, and scolded her for not storing it in her cell phone.

"Hey, are you going to the thing at Brent and Sandy's?" he asked her as the conversation wound down.

"If I finish work soon enough," Erica said. "Are you bringing what's-her-name?"

A clue about Julien's social life? Genevieve tried to listen more closely.

"Meg? God, no," Julien said.

"Not Meg." Erica sounded exasperated. "The podiatrist."

"Mika? She's a pediatrician, not a podiatrist. And I haven't seen her lately."

"Ha. Called that! Why would I think you were bringing Meg?"

"Didn't you always call her what's-her-name?"

"I call them all what's-her-name," Erica said. "Jay, you and Meg aren't actually *on* again, are you?"

"No," Jay said. "Hey, I need to get back to this archaeo-logical dig through Mom's stuff. Thanks for the conference room. See you Friday, maybe."

He strode back into the conference room just as Genevieve reached the bottom of the box she was working on, where she found several stacks of photos. Most were still in the glossy folders from the processing center, but a few were loose – a badly lit luau, a lake flanked by snow-capped mountains, a group of people at a restaurant table.

She picked up the last photo and studied it more carefully. An elegant, silver-haired woman in a pale blue dress was at the center of the photo. To her left was a woman in her 30s with chestnut chin-length hair, dark eyes and a square jaw. She wore a green sleeveless shift that showed off tanned, toned arms. The woman on the other side was a decade or so older, blonde, and wearing a shade of caramel favored by Beverly Hills women of a certain age.

Behind the women, leaning forward, was a younger version of Julien. His hair was much shorter, and there were fewer lines around his eyes. One hand rested on the back of the older woman's chair, the other, on the chair of the woman in green.

"What have you got there?" Julien's question startled Genevieve.

She showed him the photo. "Is this your mom? Looks like a special occasion."

He glanced over. "That was her 75th birthday. We took her to Catalina for dinner. The blonde is Henry's second ex-wife, Sherry. He must have taken the photo. And that's Erica in the green – this is her office."

"Is she another of your cousins?"

Julien seemed to find the idea amusing. "No. Erica is not my cousin."

Clearly, Genevieve had said something stupid. She began to blush.

"Erica's my ex-wife," Julien said.

"Oh." Genevieve's face began to feel hotter. "Sorry. That was, um... that was really stupid."

For the first time since Vegas, Julien gave her one of his megawatt smiles. "No reason to deploy the camouflage," he said, gesturing toward his own cheek.

Genevieve ducked her head. "You guys are friendly."

"Amicable divorce is the way to go," he said.

"Not sure I've ever seen one of those in action," Genevieve said.

"Your parents went the ugly route?"

"What? No," Genevieve said, flustered. "I meant with my friends."

"So they're still together, your parents? That's cool."

"Until my mom died," Genevieve said.

Julien's eyes flicked to her face. "Oh. I'm sorry." He went back to the box in front of him. "Hey, look at this."

He showed her a photo of a man and woman standing next to a grinning boy wearing a shirt with loud stripes.

"Is that you?"

"Yeah, and my parents. Check out my coast-to-coast collar! Who dressed me?"

Flowers bloomed in a pot in the corner of the frame. His mother's hair was still mostly dark, although gray was showing at her temples. Julien's father was tall, with silver hair and a certain grace. He reminded Genevieve of Cary Grant. Several inches of daylight showed between him and Julien's mother.

"When was this taken?" Genevieve asked.

Julien thought about it. "I was 10 when my dad died, so maybe a year before that?"

"Oh," Genevieve said. "I'm so sorry. That's so hard when you're a kid."

She paused. Should she say more?

"It's all so awful: the creepy celebrity it gives you at school, kids who never liked you wanting everyone to see them being nice to you, not being able to talk to anyone about it, all of it."

Julien stared at her for a few beats.

"I was seven," Genevieve said.

Julien gave her a sad smile, a nod of recognition. "My dad had a heart attack. What happened with your mom?" He set the photo aside.

Genevieve suddenly wished she hadn't mentioned her mother, uncomfortable under Julien's steady gaze. "Fire," she said in a way that she hoped would shut down the conversation.

"Your house? That's horrible. Were you there?"

"No," Genevieve said. "It was in the garage, kind of a shed, almost. She smoked out there. I was at school. My dad was at work."

———————————

CHAPTER NINE

JULIEN'S LAPTOP DINGED, rescuing her, and he checked the screen. "I've been waiting for this," he said. "Helen, Henry's first ex-wife, said she would export her genealogy file to me."

He typed for a few minutes, then pushed the chair next to him out with his foot. "This has the names and dates you want," he said. "Come over and take a look. She's got photos, too."

Genevieve grabbed her notebook and a pen and slid into the offered chair.

Julien angled the screen toward her and scooted his chair a bit closer. She caught a whiff of the scent that she'd come to think of as his, the one that reminded her of clean laundry and blue summer skies.

"Let's start with the artist's brother, Henri. The stuff farther back really isn't germane," he said.

Genevieve flipped open her notebook to jot down the dates of death for Henri and his wife, Clothilde.

"You don't have to take notes. I'll send you a copy of the file," Julien said. He scrolled down. The photos started in the next generation, with a stiff portrait of Henri's son, Emile, taken late in life. Emile's son Daniel and his wife, Veronique, had posed for a portrait on their wedding day in 1878.

The file included wedding portraits for Julien's grandfather Laurent with both of his wives – Olivie, who had given birth to the boys Georges and David, and Esmé, who was Julien's grandmother.

On the next row of the family tree was a wedding portrait of Georges and his wife, a photo of David as a child, and a shot of Julien's parents when his mother must have been in her 20s. She was wearing a corsage and a hat with a small veil.

All of the photos appeared to be studio shots with the exception of the one of Julien's parents, who posed in an office. No art was visible in any background.

"Well, I guess that gives you names and dates, but not much else," Julien said, moving to close the file.

Genevieve reached out to stop him. "Wait!"

Julien paused. "Did you see something?"

"No," she said, abashed. "Sorry. I just wanted to look at what they're wearing. I like vintage clothes. But if you're sending me a copy, I can do that on my own time."

He slid the laptop toward her. "Go ahead."

Genevieve slowly scrolled up and down, studying the wedding photos.

"Your parents look so serious," she said.

"Not sure how happy they were," Julien said. "Shotgun wedding."

Genevieve turned to look at him. "You have a brother? A sister?"

He shook his head. "No, Mom lost the baby, kind of late. They thought she couldn't have kids after that. Imagine their surprise when she got pregnant at 41 or whatever."

"They must have been so happy," Genevieve said, glancing from the screen to Julien.

"I guess." He shrugged.

Genevieve scrolled back to the earliest wedding photo and then forward to the photo of Julien's grandparents. Something about the earlier pictures was nagging at her.

"Is your sweater vintage?"

Genevieve's hand went to her shoulder. The cardigan had a small tear along the seam that her dry cleaner had repaired. "Did you spot the place I had it fixed?"

"What? No. I just wondered," Julien said.

"I found it at a yard sale," Genevieve said. "Someone was unloading their aunt's work clothes from the 1960s."

"It's a great color on you."

"Thanks. The vintage thing is really just kind of defensive, because I have no fashion sense. I never know what's in, and even if I did I can't afford it, so I buy old stuff and pair it with cheap basics, and..."

Why was she telling him this? Julien Brooks couldn't possibly be interested in her shopping philosophy.

"I think you have a great look."

"Well, thanks..." Suddenly, the thing that had been nagging her became obvious. "Look," she said, pointing. "Aren't these three women wearing the same necklace?"

Julien pulled the laptop back toward him. "Yeah, they might be."

He pulled the photos out onto his desktop, dragged them into another program, and began to manipulate them.

"My mom told me there was some necklace all the brides in the family wore, but she didn't get to, because the Nazis snatched it. Supposedly Théodore bought it on a trip to Florence."

"I thought Théodore Lazare died single?"

Tapping away at the keyboard, Julien nodded once. "Yeah, that doesn't make sense, does it? Maybe that part was the pain meds talking." He paused to study his work. "You're right. It's the same necklace."

He turned the screen back toward Genevieve to show her the enlarged photos. Suspended around each woman's neck was an open-work, heart-shaped pendant of gold.

The door jangled up front and a woman's voice called down the hall. "FedEx!"

"Be right back," Julien said. He got up and headed toward the reception area.

Genevieve pulled the laptop toward her and felt an odd tingle of recognition.

Where had she seen that pendant before?

□

Two more hours of work yielded nothing. Genevieve was relieved to be down to the last box. Julien had gone quiet, and she had never been good at small talk.

In the last box, though, they did discover something promising – a cigar box full of black-and-white photos from Paris before the war.

"Now we're getting somewhere," Julien said, handing her half the stack.

Genevieve gasped as she pulled out a photo of a man who bore a striking resemblance to Julien. He had the same dark hair, the same eyes. "He looks like you. Who is this?"

"Probably David," he said, craning his head to look. "My mom always said I looked like him, only taller."

In the photo, a man and a young woman stood close together on a sidewalk. They weren't touching, but there seemed to be an intimacy between them.

"David was single, right?"

"Yes." Julien looked more closely at the photo. "Wonder who that is?"

"Her name is Vivian," Genevieve said. She showed him the faint pencil scrawl on the back of the photo: "David et Vivian. 1938."

Julien took the photo. "Never heard of her. That's not the French spelling." He turned the photo over again. "You know, I think that might be the gallery in the background. You can just see the last few letters of the sign."

"I think you're right," Genevieve said. "I recognize it from the catalog."

Julien's head snapped up. "What catalog?"

Genevieve silently kicked herself. "I have a 1939 catalog from the gallery," she said, trying to sound casual.

"Where did you get it?"

Was he angry? She couldn't tell.

"Someone sent it to the museum a couple years ago, I have no idea why. I've checked everything in it against the looted art database," she said. "No hits. I don't think there's any connection."

Julien turned the photo of David over a couple times, then set it aside. "Why didn't you tell me about the catalog yesterday?"

What could she tell him? *Hey, I'm not sure I trust you and your cousin?*

"Oh, I don't know. I wasn't sure it had anything to do with this."

Julien stared at her for so long that Genevieve had to look away.

"So," she said, finally. "Next steps. The Getty library has some reference material on Théodore Lazare that I need to check out, just to get a sense of what other archives might have. Unfortunately, my research credential was issued through the Hilliard, so I'll need to go through the whole rigamarole of applying for a new one, which can take a week or so."

"If you already have a credential, why not use that?" Julien's tone was impatient.

"Because it says I'm affiliated with the Hilliard."

"You're a legit researcher, so what difference does it make? I lost my *LA Times* badge at one point, and I got into the building for months just flashing my gym ID at the guards," Julien said. "Do they really check?"

Genevieve felt vaguely guilty that she'd withheld the gallery catalog and obliged to make a peace offering. "Well, I can see whether they'll let me in with it, I suppose. It *would* be good to get started as soon as possible. I know that some of the articles will be in French, and mine's pretty rusty, so it could be slow going."

"My French is pretty good," Julien said. "Why don't I come with you? Is tomorrow good?"

Genevieve hadn't seen that coming. "I have to warn you, it could be really tedious."

Julien merely shrugged, and it occurred to Genevieve that perhaps Henry wanted his cousin to keep an eye on her. She began to gather up her things to leave.

"Well, suit yourself," she said. "It opens at 10, I think. Do you know where the library entrance is?"

Julien walked her down the hall. "I'm basically on your way. Do you want to meet at my house and we'll drive together?"

Genevieve couldn't think of a good reason to say no. "How about 9:30?"

"Let's make it 9:15. I'll email you the address."

Genevieve had timed her exit from Cohen and Associates perfectly for sitting in traffic. She did what she often did when she had time to kill – she called D.

She knew better than to bore D with the art history stuff. She stuck to the details about Julien Brooks, telling her about his volunteering to cover for Belle, the receptionist with the migraine, and Belle's droll comment that the boss could be a real pain in the ass.

"And guess who the boss is?"

"No idea," D said, her attention clearly wandering.

"Julien's ex-wife."

"WHAT?" A thousand miles away, Genevieve could hear the wheels turning in D's head.

"How did you find that out? What did he say about it?"

Genevieve told her about the overheard phone conversation, finding the photo, her assumption that Erica Cohen was another Lazare cousin.

"What did she look like?"

"Dark hair," Genevieve said. "Great bones. Tan. Really buff arms."

"And how did he seem about her?"

Genevieve thought about that. "On the phone they were giving each other grief, like they were friends."

"Well, I think that's weird, but whatever," D said. "He wasn't worried about telling you. What should we read into that?"

"That he doesn't care what I think?"

D ignored that. "He's telling you about his personal life. That's good! And what's her name again? Erica? I'm thinking she's kind of snotty."

Genevieve laughed. "D, how can you possibly reach that conclusion?"

"I read people, Gen. That's what I'm good at. Now, tell me what he was wearing. Did he seem like he'd spiffed up for you?"

"We're working together, D. It wasn't a date."

"Humor me," D drawled.

"Jeans. Long-sleeved T-shirt. Flip-flops."

"I am liking that," D mused. "Comfortable in his own skin. When do you see him – I'm sorry – *work* with him again?"

"He's going to the research library with me tomorrow," Genevieve said. "We're meeting at his house and driving together. It's on the way. His idea."

"Oh, I'm liking that," D said. "You should definitely maneuver it so that he drives. Can you invent some reason he has to have a drink with you afterward?"

"D, this is work," Genevieve protested.

"Anyway," D said, "tell him your car is acting up or low on gas if you have to."

"D!"

"Now, another thing: make sure you get there on time. Because, you know, some men are sort of charmed by that 20 minutes late thing, it's a lady's prerogative and all that, but my gut tells me he's not one of them."

"Be on time. Let him drive," Genevieve repeated. "Anything else?"

"What are you going to wear? And please don't say a frickin' turtleneck or another one of your old-lady sweaters."

CHAPTER TEN

G ENEVIEVE CALCULATED the worst-case traffic scenario from her place to Julien's house. Then she gave herself an extra 10 minutes.

She got off the freeway at 8:55, a full 20 minutes early, which left her time to stop for a latte.

Julien lived just a few blocks from Cohen and Associates. Some houses in the neighborhood had obviously been expanded, and the late-model SUVs and luxury sedans in the driveways told Genevieve that the neighborhood was gentrifying. Other houses showed more wear and tear, as did the cars parked out front.

Julien's place, a Spanish-style house of caramel-colored stucco, had been fixed up but appeared to occupy its original footprint. It had not grown up and out like some on the block.

The real attraction was the landscaping. The front yard had no grass, just a collection of desert shrubs. Genevieve recognized rosemary and lavender but not much else. Even though it was the last day of January and little was blooming, she could tell a lot of effort had gone into the project.

She was grateful to find a parking spot at the curb out front. A silver Audi convertible was in the driveway, which hugged the side of the house and led to a detached garage in the back.

Genevieve was exactly 8 minutes early. She could see Julien through a big window, sitting at a table, drinking from a mug. He was talking on the phone with the newspaper spread out before him. He looked up when she shut her car door.

He opened the front door when she knocked and held up one finger, phone pressed to his ear. He was wearing jeans and a dark green T-shirt, his hair still wet from the shower. "OK, just email me the details and I'll get you an estimate tomorrow," he said into the phone.

He beckoned Genevieve in. "Uh-huh," he said into the phone. "OK. Thanks."

"You're early," he said as he hung up. "Come in. I just need a second. You want coffee?"

She hoisted her Starbucks cup. "I already stopped." She stepped over the threshold as Julien disappeared into another room, giving her an opportunity to check out his house unobserved.

The wood floors were buffed to a high sheen. On the wall opposite the door was a leather sofa in chocolate brown. The coffee table was covered with magazines and books. The long wall to her right was filled with floor-to-ceiling shelves of books, broken up only by a giant plasma screen TV.

D was definitely going to declare this a bachelor pad. Julien probably had nothing in the refrigerator but beer and mustard. But it was, Genevieve had to admit, cleaner than her apartment.

Julien reappeared, having added a black sweater and shoes. "Ready?"

On the porch, Julien took one look at her car and said, "I'll drive."

D will be so pleased, she thought, and I didn't even have to lie.

She paused when she noticed the Audi's spotless interior. He might be one of those guys who was fussy about his car. "OK to bring my coffee?"

"Sure. Why wouldn't you?"

Genevieve sank into the buttery leather seat. "Oh, you know, some people are funny about eating or drinking in their cars." She deposited her coffee in the cup holder and fastened her seatbelt. "And this is a really nice car."

"It's criminal how much I love it. It's a cliché, I know," he said, reversing out of the driveway. "Get divorced, buy a convertible."

"At least it's not red," Genevieve said.

Julien rewarded her with a smile. "No, but it is German. My mother would be furious."

Soon they were on the 10 freeway, crawling west.

"Sitting in traffic on the 10," Genevieve said. "I don't miss that about my job."

"You must really like your place to have put up with that commute," Julien said.

"Not really," Genevieve said.

"No? So why live there?"

"I needed a place in a hurry," she said, not eager to get into the details of that particular catastrophe. "I didn't have time to be picky."

"When's your lease up?"

Genevieve laughed self-consciously. "This summer? But I've been there six years already. I know; it's ridiculous. Something always happens right when I should be moving."

"So quit worrying about when you should have done it, and do it this year," Julien said. He glanced over his shoulder and changed lanes. "Just move."

"You sound like D," Genevieve said. "She's always on me to do something."

"So, tell me something about D," Julien said. "Was she hitting on me at the craps table, or was she just being friendly?"

Genevieve laughed. "Oh, that was her version of friendly. She's just very Dallas, and kind of larger than life. You'd know if she was hitting on you. When she does, your only options are submit, or run for your life."

"Good to know. So you're from Dallas?"

"Oh God no. I'm from Wichita Falls. Very much smaller than life."

Julien smiled at that. "I wondered about the accent."

"This is not a Texas accent," Genevieve said. "I hate it when people say I sound like I'm from Texas. I mean, I gave up all my 'fixin tos' and 'might coulds.' What else do I have to do?"

"Fixin to? Do people really talk like that?"

"It's a really handy phrase," Genevieve said. "Fixin to. Might could. Used to could."

"Might used to… what?" Julien shook his head. "Use them in a sentence."

"I'm fixin to go to the store, do you need anything? If I hurry, I might could make it before they close. I used to could get there in 10 minutes, but now we've got all this dang traffic."

Julien laughed out loud.

"See, I'm what you'd call a *recovering* Texan," she said.

"So how did a girl from Wichita Falls end up with a French name like Genevieve?"

"That's my mom's doing," Genevieve said. "Everybody back home thought it was really pretentious."

"I think it's pretty," Julien said, nodding once for emphasis. "And not pretentious at all. It suits you."

By 10:15, Genevieve and Julien were seated at a long library table plowing through information on Théodore Lazare.

Genevieve had been prepared for a complex negotiation over her research credential and Julien's presence. But he'd taken charge, waving her credential while pushing through the library doors, and no one had said a word.

They started with the books and journals Genevieve could pull from the library shelves. She'd save the items that required special requests until later.

After two hours of slogging through scholarly articles, most of which mentioned Lazare only in passing, Julien looked pointedly at his watch. "Let's get some lunch," he whispered.

They found a table in the sun at the museum's cafe.

Julien stretched his long legs in front of him. "It feels good to be outside." He gave Genevieve a long look. "So, do you write interminable essays like that? Because you don't *seem* that dull. But maybe I've misjudged you."

Genevieve laughed. "Don't say I didn't warn you. I told you that you'd be bored. To answer your question, I wasn't good at scholarly papers like that, not at all."

"So why did you choose this as a career?"

"That's a really good question," Genevieve said.

Julien said nothing. He just sat there with an amused expression on his face.

"Oh, you actually want me to answer?"

He laughed.

"I've always loved art. My mom and I used to look at art books when I was little. I took a bunch of art history courses in college, and it just sort of turned into my major," she said.

She turned her face from the sun and looked at Julien. "I didn't really have a plan."

"So what do you love about art?"

This was a question Genevieve could answer easily. "I like the way you can look at something an artist created hundreds of years ago, something that captures a moment of life, and that moment can still feel real centuries later. Passion, love, loss... So much of the world feels temporary, but a really great piece of art is timeless."

Julien didn't respond, and she suddenly felt self-conscious. "I guess that sounds dumb."

"Not at all," he said. "Although it doesn't seem to have much to do with the stuff we've just been reading."

"Sometimes I think I went about this all wrong," Genevieve said. "I should have had my dad take me to the gun range to teach me to shoot, and then I could have been a museum guard," Genevieve said. "You know, just stand around the paintings all day."

"Of course you were no good at writing boring papers," Julien said. "You're too funny."

The afternoon was not especially productive. Most of the references they found to Théodore Lazare were in larger articles about other artists, and Genevieve uncovered no footnotes that would lead her to other sources.

At 3:30, Julien leaned over and whispered, "I think I'm done for the day. I have plans tonight. Let's get out ahead of the traffic."

Soon they were on the freeway back to Julien's house, where Genevieve had left her car. The day of research had gone about the way she'd expected – perhaps a little worse – but still she felt the need to explain to Julien.

"I'm sorry; you must feel like you wasted a whole day."

His eyes were unreadable behind his sunglasses. He gave a little shake of his head, but whether that was directed at her or the SUV trying to force its way into his lane, she couldn't say.

"That's just the way research goes," she said. "I should have made it more clear."

"Oh, you were pretty clear about that," Julien said. "Don't do it, pal," he cautioned the SUV driver. "So, when are we coming back for round two?"

Genevieve was incredulous. "Oh, come on. You don't want to do this again."

"Sure I do," Julien said evenly. "I just said I would."

Genevieve found the blandness of his answer infuriating. She didn't get mad very often, but when she did, it tended to come on in a hurry. "You and Henry must *really* not trust me if he's going to make you watch me every day," she said.

Just then, the SUV made its move, and Julien accelerated and veered left to avoid a collision. Genevieve's purse tipped over, scattering her things across the floor of the car and angering her further.

"You OK? I *knew* that guy was going to try that," Julien said. "Now, what were you saying about Henry?"

Still strapped in her seatbelt, Genevieve bent over awkwardly and began rounding up her belongings.

"Does Henry think I'm goofing off?" She chucked her hairbrush, compact and cell phone back into her bag. "Is that why he has you chaperoning me every second?

"I don't even know why he hired me," she huffed as she tried to pry her lipstick from an especially tricky spot between her seat and the center console.

To her horror, Julien began to laugh. She stared out the window as a red flush crept up her face. "Well, I'm glad you're amused," she said, her voice tight.

"Sorry to laugh. It's just that the idea of Henry ordering me to do anything is pretty funny," Julien said. "He *wishes* he could, I'm sure."

"So why are you doing this?"

"Honestly?" Julien let out a sigh. "You can only design so many logos and websites before it gets monotonous, you know? Trying to track the drawing is interesting. It reminds me of the newspaper business, back when the newspaper business was fun."

He chuckled. "I can't believe you thought Henry sent me to spy on you."

CHAPTER ELEVEN

THE LIGHTS THAT LINED the driveway were off when Genevieve got home, a sure sign that the musician who lived in the house at the front of the property was away. She cursed under her breath. Her fellow tenant was fanatical about setting lights in his house with timers when he was out of town, and somehow he always managed to disrupt the programming for the outside lights. Genevieve would have to complain to the landlord again.

She goosed her Camry up the driveway's steep slope and maneuvered into her parking place. This move required first nosing the car up to the wall of her building, where the garage door had once been. Then she put it in reverse and executed a tight 90-degree turn onto a concrete pad tucked between a six-foot-high wall that sheltered the other tenant's patio and a shorter wall that created a small courtyard around her entryway, the former side entrance to the garage.

The first 50 or so times, this procedure had filled Genevieve with terror. If she'd been less desperate when she'd been apartment hunting, the parking might have put her off the place altogether.

She'd long ignored the warning signs in her relationship with Pete, but once she'd decided to leave, she'd grabbed her things and *gone*. Her landlord seemed to grasp the situation when he showed Genevieve this place, and, after a quick call to verify her employment, he'd rented it to her on the spot. She moved in right away and slept on the floor the first night.

Procrastination had kept her there for six years, but so, too, had a perverse sense of loyalty to her landlord. It was silly – Genevieve knew that. The neighborhood was trendy now, and the apartment would rent quickly if she left. For all she knew, the landlord was holding the rent down out of a perverse sense of loyalty to her.

Genevieve let herself in, turned on the lamp and petted Mona, who was curled up in her usual spot in the rocking chair by the door.

She dumped the mail and her bag on the bar that separated the living room and kitchen, and surveyed her apartment. If Julien's leather sofa and big TV screamed "bachelor pad" – albeit a clean one with really nice floors – what did her place say?

When the building was converted to living space, the side that had been the garage door had been walled in without the addition of windows. As a result, the front half of the apartment got natural light only from small windows on each end – one near the front door, and one over the kitchen sink.

Genevieve was forever trying to brighten up the space. The long windowless wall held white shelving units from IKEA with a few ceramic pieces she'd picked up, her TV, stereo, books and CDs. She had covered most of the floor with a rug in pale blue, lavender and green chevrons. It helped hide the pickled oak laminate that, as Thomas liked to say, "goes with nothing and looks terrible with everything."

Her sofa was a shabby chic thing in blue chenille originally owned by Philip. A recent move had finally given Thomas the chance to banish it. Above it hung a watercolor of the Santa Monica Pier, which Genevieve bought from a guy on the 3rd Street Promenade for $20 simply because she liked it.

The walnut rocking chair by the front door had belonged to Genevieve's parents, and she'd brought it from Texas in a U-Haul.

What did her living room say about her?

She owned very little of value. Like her lease, most everything in her life was a year-to-year proposition.

□

The earlier conversation with Julien about procrastination had left her feeling guilty. It was too early to do anything about a lease that was up in August. But she still hadn't signed her Hilliard severance paperwork. That was something she could quit putting off. She vowed that she would go to the museum the next day, no more excuses.

To keep herself from weaseling out, she called Thomas and made plans to have lunch after her paperwork errand. Then she'd go to the bank and deposit her check from Henry Lazare. Once it cleared, she'd take care of her bills.

What else had she been avoiding? Wasn't there something she could dispatch right now, something that would make her feel virtuous? She had yet to write a thank-you note to her mother's college roommate for her Christmas gift. That would do the trick.

Genevieve's mother had lasted less than a year at college back East, but Grace Knapp McKenna and Christine Kern Jensen had forged a strong bond. Even after Genevieve's mother had a breakdown and left school, Christine stayed in touch. She was there when Genevieve's parents got married, and she was there when Genevieve's mother was buried. She always remembered Genevieve at her birthday and Christmas.

Christine had sent amethyst earrings at Christmas and a copy of the book that had been produced for the school's anniversary, which she said had some pictures of Grace, even though she hadn't graduated.

Genevieve had put off writing a thank you because she thought she ought to say something about the photos, but then she couldn't bring herself to look at them. So she did nothing. And now February was nearly here, and Christine was sitting in Chicago undoubtedly wondering whether Genevieve had received the gift at all.

Genevieve hunted through her stash of art cards purchased from the Hilliard gift shop using her employee discount and found a Georges Seurat snow scene she thought Christine might like. Eliding the subject of the book, she thanked Christine effusively for the earrings, which she really did like.

Writing to her mother's college roommate gave her a flash of inspiration on the Lazare project. One of her grad school classmates wrote her master's thesis on Delacroix. She might know an expert on the French romantics who had done useful research on Théodore Lazare or could lead Genevieve to someone who had.

It took her nearly an hour of online searching, but Genevieve finally tracked down the former classmate. She was teaching at a small college in Illinois – much smaller than Genevieve would have expected, given the woman's outsized ego in grad school. Either she wasn't nearly as brilliant as she thought she was, or the academic world was tougher than Genevieve had imagined. Perhaps a little of both.

Genevieve emailed, explaining what she hoped to find, then went to the website of her favorite Thai restaurant. It was nearly 8 p.m., and she was famished. Would it be Pad Thai or Panang curry tonight?

Genevieve made her selections and clicked through to the payment screen, then reached into her bag for her wallet.

It wasn't there.

Slowly, she removed everything in the bag and ran her hand around inside. No wallet. She tipped the bag upside-down over the bar and shook it. Nothing came out but an old receipt from Starbucks.

She pawed through the mail, thinking perhaps her wallet was buried in the stack. No luck.

The trick to finding something that was lost, she knew, was recalling the last place she had it and working forward from there. So, where had she last seen her wallet?

She bought coffee in Culver City before going to Julien's house. Had she lost it at the coffee shop? No, because she and Julien split the lunch check at the Getty cafe later. Had she left her wallet on the table? Dropped it on the patio?

Genevieve sighed. She never carried much cash, so no great loss there, but she dreaded the thought of replacing her credit card, her insurance card, and most of all, her driver's license.

She knew she should call the credit card company right away, but first she had to eat. No way could she deal with that phone menu on an empty stomach.

In the refrigerator, she found two cans of Diet Dr Pepper, three bottles of Shiner and the remnants of a pizza she'd ordered the night before she'd been laid off. She cautiously peeled back the aluminum foil on the pizza. She wasn't *that* hungry.

Her phone rang, and Genevieve checked the display. *Jay in LA.* She really needed to edit that. She hit the answer button. "Hello there."

"Hey, I found your wallet in my car," Julien said.

"Oh, thank God," she said, exhaling. "I just discovered it was missing when I was ordering takeout from my Thai place, and I was freaking out."

"I guess it fell out when you dumped your purse over."

"That wasn't my fault! You *swerved*!"

Then, embarrassed by her display of temper, Genevieve hastily added, "I'm going to Santa Monica in the morning. I could swing by your house, if that works for you."

"Didn't you say you live in Silver Lake? I was just having a drink in Hollywood," Julien said. "I could run it by."

"I don't want to inconvenience you."

"I don't mind," Julien said. "Anyway, seems only fair, since I *swerved*."

It took Julien 20 minutes to get to her apartment, which gave Genevieve time to straighten up the coffee table, comb her hair, brush her teeth and put on lipstick – while telling herself she was being ridiculous, he was just going to hand her the wallet and leave and it didn't matter anyway because they were just working together.

When she opened the door, her first thought was, "Damn, he looks good." Since she'd seen him last, he'd changed into an off-white dress shirt and topped it with a black sport coat that had a subtle caramel-colored pattern.

That thought was immediately followed by a disappointing realization: Drinks in Hollywood. As in, a date.

He *had* said he had plans that evening.

Julien handed her the wallet and smiled. "Did I beat the Thai delivery guy here? I overshot your driveway the first time. It's really dark."

Genevieve, confused, blinked at him. "What? Oh, um, actually, I didn't order."

Mona strolled up to sniff his shoe, and Julien eyed her warily. "Should I be worried it's about to do something disgusting on my foot?"

"That's how cats say hi. Her worst habit is sneaking outside while the door is open," Genevieve said. She paused. "Would you like to come in?"

"Sure." Julien stepped inside, and she closed the door behind him, marveling as she did at how this was unfolding. D would be so impressed.

"How late does your place deliver?" He checked his watch. "Because I haven't eaten either."

Genevieve tried to mask her surprise. "They know me pretty well, so as long as I call by 9, it's cool. Do you want to look at the menu?"

They walked to the bar, where her computer was still open to the menu, and Genevieve pointed out the best dishes. They made their selections, and when she clicked through to the payment screen, Julien reached for his wallet.

"My treat," he said. "Because I *swerved*."

Genevieve felt her face grow hot. "Is this going to be a thing now? The swerve?"

"Your righteous indignation when you said it was pretty priceless," Julien said.

"In my defense, I was contemplating a day at the DMV to replace my license," Genevieve said.

Julien spread his hands wide. "Fair enough. So, I firmly believe Thai food goes best with beer. Any chance you've got one?"

Genevieve, who almost never had beer in her fridge, rounded the bar into the kitchen. "You're in luck."

"Interesting place," Julien said, wandering over to inspect her books. "Used to be the garage?"

"Yeah," Genevieve said. "Do you want a glass?"

"Bottle's fine."

When she came back to the living room, Julien was leaning over her sofa, staring at the watercolor of the Santa Monica Pier.

"Great use of color. Who's the artist?"

"Some scruffy dude who sells his stuff on the Promenade, down by the Apple Store," she said, handing him the beer. "Twenty bucks."

"Seriously?"

"Seriously. I just liked it. And the price was right."

Julien threw his head back and laughed.

Every time she earned one of those laughs felt like an accomplishment. She'd always disdained the girls in high school who slavered over the popular boys, and now she was basking in Julien's attention like Mona in a sunbeam. It was embarrassing, really. But he was so nice, so easy to be with. She couldn't quite believe she'd mistrusted him. D was right; she was too paranoid.

Once the food came, they sat side by side at the bar to eat. Julien nodded thoughtfully as she told him about her email to her classmate, her latest attempt to track down anyone with expertise on Théodore Lazare.

"What about this gallery catalog?" he said. "Are you sure it won't help?"

Genevieve took a swig of her beer. Julien was right – it did pair well with Thai food. "I went through it three times. Nothing in there shows up in the looted art database. There's nothing by Théodore Lazare. It's mostly 20th century stuff. The only connection is that it's from Galerie de l'Étoile, which was run by your family."

Julien pushed his plate away, and Genevieve did the same. His was empty; she'd save her leftovers for another meal.

He turned his bar stool toward her. "Tell me again how you got it."

"It just showed up at the museum one day," Genevieve said. "No note or anything. The *Times* did a story about looted art and the impact on local museums, and my boss – my former boss – was quoted in it."

She took another sip of beer. "He gave all these really pretentious comments about the 'tragedy' of looted art and how dedicated the museum was to making sure nothing in the collection was affected..."

She took in Julien's expression. "I'm just jabbering, aren't I?"

"A little."

"Sorry. I really didn't like him. He would give interviews like that, and then once, I got forwarded an email about a project he wanted me to help on, and at the bottom was the very first message from him, and it said, 'Use Genevieve, because she's not doing anything important right now.' "

"Ouch," Julien said. "OK, so this catalog showed up right after the article ran in the *Times*?"

Genevieve thought about that. "Actually, I'm not sure about the timing."

"Can I see the catalog?"

Was there any reason, really, to hold it back? Genevieve hopped down from her chair and dug around in the pile on her coffee table, extracting the catalog from its envelope and handing it to Julien.

"Give me the envelope, too," he said.

"The envelope?"

"You know more about art than me, and you say there's no connection between the drawing and the pieces in the catalog," he said. "So let's look at the envelope."

Genevieve handed it to him, and he smoothed it out on the bar.

She gathered up the plates and took them to the sink.

"OK, first question, were you mentioned in this article?"

"Me? No. Too far down the food chain." Genevieve put the leftovers in the fridge and began to wash plates. "Why?"

"The envelope is addressed to you," Julien said.

"Right. I knew that. I guess I forgot. Well, it could be that someone called the museum to ask who was working on provenance," Genevieve said.

"Possible," Julien said. "The envelope's torn, but there's part of a postmark with a date. I'll have a friend at the *Times* check the article's date in the archives."

Julien came into the kitchen, where the light was better, and tipped the envelope up so that Genevieve could look at it too. "We've got a zip code, too. What do you think, is that a four or a nine?"

Their elbows brushed. Genevieve tried hard to concentrate. "I vote four."

"Me too." Julien walked back around the bar. "So let's look up zip code 04578. Mind if I use your computer?"

Genevieve, busy with the dishes, waved her assent.

Julien typed. "Wiscasset, Maine. That mean anything to you?"

"Not a thing."

"So maybe it was a nine, not a four," Julien said. He began typing again. "Well, this is more interesting."

Genevieve dried her hands and came around to look over his shoulder. "It's the beginning of an FPO address," he said.

"What's that?"

"That's sort of the zip code for the military. See?"

"You're saying someone sent me this from a *ship*?"

"Does that make more sense?"

"Even less."

Genevieve liked the idea that they were a team, trying to solve problems together, but something still nagged at her.

"Can I ask you something?" Genevieve turned from the screen to look at him. "Doesn't it seem weird to you, how we met in Vegas?"

"A little," he said. "But stuff like that happens. When Erica and I had been dating about six months, we realized that we'd finished within seconds of each other in a half-marathon a couple years before. You can see me in the background of her finish-line photo." He grinned. "Yeah, she beat me. In my defense, I was coming off knee surgery."

He tapped the manila envelope impatiently on the bar. "So now what?"

"More research, I think," Genevieve said. "Back to the Getty."

"Another day at the Getty." He sighed. "You got that family tree I emailed you, right?"

"No. When did you send it?"

"When I got home this afternoon. Maybe it's in your spam filter? I used the address Henry had for you."

"Lost Art Investigations? I don't check it very often. I'll look later."

Julien stifled a yawn. "I'd better get going. I have a client call early. Call me when you're ready to make another Getty run?"

"Sure. Maybe Monday?" Genevieve walked with him to the door, scooping up Mona and depositing her in the rocker so she could keep an eye on her. "Thanks for bringing my wallet by. I hope it didn't tumble out onto your date's foot or anything. That would be awkward."

Julien glanced away, and just for an instant, Genevieve thought he was uncomfortable.

But then he met her eyes again, and he seemed his usual confident, breezy self. "We met up at the bar. Standard operating procedure for the low-risk, weeknight meet-for-drinks first date that might segue into dinner but might not. No harm done."

CHAPTER TWELVE

G ENEVIEVE WOKE UP the next morning bursting with energy. She wanted to attribute this to her newfound commitment to avoiding procrastination. But deep down, she knew she was buoyed because Julien Brooks had gone on a date that could have segued into dinner but did not.

In fact, he had dinner with *her.*

It had been too late back in Texas to call after he left; Genevieve had contented herself with sending an email. She had come up with this D-worthy positive spin all on her own, and she was rather proud of it.

In fact, she thought she might try living her whole day in a D frame of mind, just to see what it was like. For instance, the trip to the Hilliard to sign her severance paperwork was not a humiliating task to be dreaded. Rather, it would cut her last tie to a job that hadn't worked out.

Her good mood even seemed to have affected Mona. Instead of burrowing into the covers while Genevieve was trying to make the bed, the cat was tearing around the apartment in a playful mood.

Before the glow could wear off, Genevieve signed on to her new consultant's email to find the family tree information from Julien had arrived. He'd also scanned the photo of David Lazare and his friend Vivian on the sidewalk outside the gallery.

Then she clicked over to the email address she used most of the time, user name *GenwithaG*, and emailed Thomas to confirm their lunch date.

Mona began to meow piteously, and Genevieve turned away from the computer to see what the fuss was about.

The cat was stretched out on the floor beside the sofa, one paw extended underneath it.

"Are you in another of your blue periods, Mona?"

Mona went through intermittent bouts of intense devotion to a small blue toy mouse. She'd prance around the apartment with it in her mouth mewling, then drop it and bat at it until it flew under a piece of furniture. Once it did, she'd sit vigil and howl until Genevieve retrieved it for her. Then, mysteriously as it had begun, her blue period would be over.

Genevieve fetched the broom, inched the sofa away from the wall, and swished back and forth. Out came cat hair and an earring missing for months, but no blue mouse. She made another pass, and Mona pounced on something.

But it wasn't a blue mouse.

Genevieve bent down to investigate, snatching the bauble away from the cat.

It was an open-work, heart-shaped pendant of gold.

Genevieve sank to her knees on her living room floor.

She knew this pendant – a man gripping her arm, his other hand trying to force her fist open, then the pendant falling to the floor and rolling away.

As she stared at the pendant in her palm, she noticed four bruises in a row, each about the size of a dime, marring the skin of her forearm.

Her pulse quickened.

She looked at the other side of her arm. There was a fifth bruise there.

The day everything had blown up with Pete, he'd grabbed her arm, hard, and not let go. The next day, the imprint of his fingers had been on her arm.

But there was something more. The pendant was familiar from somewhere else.

She grabbed her computer and set it up on the coffee table.

She called up Julien's email and opened the file he'd sent her, the one with photos of generations of Lazare brides.

And there, around the necks of three of them, was an open-work, heart-shaped pendant of gold.

Which had been familiar to her, somehow, *before* she saw these photos.

□

Genevieve rocked back on her heels and considered the possibilities, none encouraging.

Could the pendant have belonged to a previous tenant and gone undiscovered in her apartment for six years? She was a bad housekeeper, but not *that* bad. And what were the odds that it would look exactly like the pendant worn by Lazare brides and that she would find it just days after dreaming about it and seeing photographs of it?

Genevieve leaned her head back against the sofa and caught sight of the cheap watercolor Julien had admired the night before.

Julien. In her apartment. For no good reason, really. He could have dropped off her wallet at the door and left. He didn't have to hang around for dinner. And he'd stood right by the sofa, looking at the painting.

OK. Another theory. Julien Brooks had come into her apartment and dropped the pendant behind her sofa when she wasn't looking because... Genevieve was at a loss. Because she'd noticed it in the photo? It didn't make any sense. And he couldn't possibly know she'd dreamed about it.

And that was another thing. Genevieve had been calling this thing a dream, but it didn't exactly *feel* like a dream. She'd felt the same way about the... whatever it was in Las Vegas, when she was staring at a bare wood floor, holding a pose. Both times, she sensed that she was in the same place. The light seemed the same, so bright, flooding in.

D had mocked her, asked had she heard an angel choir, but she'd had the same fleeting experience in the casino.

Genevieve carefully put the pendant on the coffee table and rubbed both palms over her face. There was one obvious answer, of course.

She'd done her homework – how could she not? She knew the warning signs of the major mental illnesses. Paranoid delusions, hearing voices, grandiosity... she scrolled through the checklist in her head. Schizophrenia usually manifested in the teens and 20s; once she hit 30, she'd thought she was safe.

Had some faulty bit of wiring deep in her brain, inherited from her mother, begun to spark?

Other kids in Wichita Falls grew up scared of tornadoes or Jason from Halloween or the Rapture. For Genevieve, mental illness had always been her bogeyman.

Maybe she'd skip signing her severance paperwork, cancel her lunch with Thomas, too. She'd spend the day in her dark apartment... doing what, exactly? Obsessively reading websites about mental illness?

If she weren't already crazy, that just might do the trick.

Genevieve presented herself at the museum at 11:27 and gave her name to the guard. Malcolm's secretary arrived a few minutes later carrying a thick folder. "Hello, Genevieve," Carol said. "You're looking well."

She ushered Genevieve toward a door marked "employees only" and swiped a plastic security card in front of an electronic eye. "There's an empty conference room on the second floor we can use," she said.

"How have you been?" she asked over her shoulder as they climbed the stairs.

"Fine," Genevieve said, ready with the answer she'd rehearsed on the drive over. "I'm doing some consulting."

"I heard that," Carol said. "I knew you'd land on your feet."

Genevieve silently cursed Thomas. She'd asked him not to tell anyone about her work for Henry Lazare.

The conference room was tiny and dim. Genevieve was struck, not for the first time, by the contrast between the museum's public spaces and the employee areas. The galleries were all white walls and beautiful, filtered light. The worker areas had worn industrial-grade carpet, scuffed beige walls and flat fluorescent light that flattered no one.

Carol urged Genevieve to sit and handed her the folder. "You need to sign all the places there's an X. It's long and kind of complicated, so I'll give you a few minutes. I have to go take care of something for Malcolm."

She left, shutting the door behind her.

Genevieve started reading the severance agreement and immediately felt overwhelmed. A part of her just wanted to look for the X's, sign, and leave as quickly as possible.

The last page spelled out conditions she must not violate, and she felt a rising panic as she read each clause. She must not discuss the terms of the agreement. She'd already told Thomas, and D, and her father. Surely she couldn't get in trouble for that?

She must not divulge any proprietary information she'd learned in the course of performing her duties. Did she have any information about Théodore Lazare's drawing that was proprietary?

The consequences were spelled out in capital letters at the end of each clause. She'd forfeit her severance. And the museum could sue her for damages.

Genevieve wished she had done more homework and had known what to expect.

Carol poked her head back in the door.

"Any questions?"

Genevieve swallowed hard, trying to unstick her tongue from the roof of her mouth. "There's a lot of legal stuff here. I didn't realize it would be so complicated."

Carol pursed her lips. "Do you want more time?"

"I think it might be a good idea for me to have someone take a look at this before I sign it," Genevieve said.

"Unfortunately, I can't allow you to take the paperwork out of the building. Malcolm was very clear on that," Carol said. She looked over her shoulder. "Although that seems like a pointless rule now that everyone has a phone with a camera."

And then she shut the door again.

It took Genevieve less than five minutes to photograph the clauses that concerned her. When Carol returned, she was ready.

"I think I need a little more time to think on this," Genevieve said.

"Of course," Carol said. "When you're ready to sign, just let me know."

She and Thomas had agreed to meet in front of the museum at 12:15. She'd jokingly asked him if he preferred to meet at the restaurant, to avoid the taint of being seen with someone who had been fired, and he'd jokingly reminded her that no employees used the front entrance anyway.

It was only 11:50, so Genevieve took a seat on the low wall that flanked the museum's entrance and called D.

"He blew off his date to have dinner with you? Tell me everything!"

Genevieve had almost forgotten the excited email she'd sent D the night before. "I think I'm kind of over that crush, honestly."

"Really?" D sounded incredulous. "What happened? Did he chew with his mouth open?"

"No."

"Burp and not say 'excuse me?' Fart?"

"D!"

"Because it wasn't even two weeks ago you heard the angels singing when he touched your hand."

"D, please stop," Genevieve said. That particular experience was not one Genevieve wanted to recall. "I need legal advice."

"Are you in jail?"

"What? Of course not."

"Dang. I was hoping you'd committed a *crime of passion*," D said.

"D, be serious. Do you think your sister-in-law could look at something for me?"

Genevieve explained that her Hilliard paperwork had a series of clauses that concerned her, in particular, the one about nondisclosure.

"I can get Marta to take a look," D said.

"I never did anything on the Lazare drawing when I worked for the museum," Genevieve said, "and I'm not using any knowledge that's not available to the public. But I really don't want them to cancel my health insurance."

Especially not if my brain's going on the fritz, she thought.

"Do you have a copy? That would be the easiest thing, rather than me trying to explain it all to her," D said.

"They wouldn't let me take it out of the museum, but I shot the key parts with my cell phone. Can I just email the photos to you and you'll forward them to her?"

"Look at you, breaking the rules," D said. "Sure, send it."

"Thanks, D, you're the best."

"Now, what's the deal with Julien? What did he do to cool you off so fast?"

Genevieve weighed her options and decided she didn't want to go down that path with D. It was simply too complicated.

"The more I thought about it, the more I realized it made sense to keep it professional," Genevieve said.

"That's the dumbest thing I ever heard. Where do you think everybody hooks up these days, Gen? At *work*! The main thing is, you just have to..."

"D? I'm meeting Thomas for lunch, and he's here now, so I have to go. Tell Marta thanks for me, and I'll call you later."

Genevieve ended the call and tossed her phone back in her bag. As she did, she noticed a man standing a few feet away, apparently engrossed in the screen of *his* phone.

It was Malcolm Stewart, her old boss.

How much had he just heard? Remembering the way Julien Brooks had breezed right past the front desk at the Getty Library by acting as though he belonged there, Genevieve cleared her throat.

"Hello, Malcolm," she said.

Malcolm looked up from his phone, startled. "Genevieve, this is a surprise. What brings you here?"

"I came by hoping to sign my severance paperwork, but I ran out of time," she said. "There was more to it than I anticipated."

Malcolm nodded thoughtfully. "And how have you been?"

"Fine," Genevieve said. "I'm doing some consulting."

"I heard that," Malcolm said.

Genevieve had always known Thomas was a gossip, and she'd benefited from his access to the inside scoop on more than one occasion. But she never really imagined he would gossip about *her*.

A black Mercedes glided to the curb in front of the museum. "I'm off to a meeting," Malcolm said. "Nice seeing you. Best of luck to you."

CHAPTER THIRTEEN

THOMAS BOUNDED DOWN the museum steps right on time a few minutes later, and Genevieve fumed as he made small talk for a few blocks. She would not make the mistake of discussing the Lazare case near the Hilliard again.

Once they were seated at the restaurant, though, she could no longer control her temper.

"How many people have you told I'm working for the Lazare family?" she demanded as Thomas unfurled his napkin.

He froze, the napkin held aloft, and stared at her. "No one. What are you talking about?"

"I told Carol I was doing some consulting, and she said she'd heard that," Genevieve sputtered. "Then I ran into Malcolm on the front steps, and he said the same thing."

"On the front steps? How weird." Thomas settled his napkin in his lap. "I haven't said anything about the Lazares, I swear. Carol was waiting at my desk to drop off some papers when I was on the phone with Philip, and I might have said something about your consulting gig, but I'm sure I didn't mention your client. Anyway, you're not doing anything wrong, so what's the problem?"

"There's all this stuff in my severance agreement about not divulging any proprietary information," Genevieve said. "But I don't think I even know anything proprietary about the drawing."

"So it's fine," Thomas said. "Don't be so paranoid."

Was she just being paranoid? Genevieve lapsed into silence, but Thomas hardly seemed to notice. He had his own agenda for lunch, his latest real-estate adventure. He and Philip had sold their house with the expectation of moving into something bigger, but then the market collapsed and mortgage lenders became very picky. They had spent months crammed into a one-bedroom condo downtown; most of their things were in storage or with relatives. But they'd finally found a house they wanted at the right price, and the deal was just days away from being locked down.

Genevieve picked at her salad and nodded along sympathetically. Thomas had strong opinions about who was at fault in the real-estate mess. His father was a professor; Thomas sometimes indulged a tendency to pontificate.

Finally, though, he ran out of steam, and Genevieve saw her opportunity.

"Thomas, I need to ask you for a couple favors, some help on this Lazare case."

"I can't disclose any proprietary information, either. You know that, right?"

Genevieve gasped. "I wouldn't ask you to!"

"What do you need, then?"

Genevieve decided to start with the easiest thing.

"At a gallery opening once, you introduced me to a *Times* critic, remember?"

Thomas nodded at her to go on.

"Can you call and ask him about Julien Brooks? Or Jay Brooks; I guess that's what he goes by, actually."

"You mean like, 'is he single, is he seeing anyone?' – that sort of thing?" Thomas grinned at her. "Of course I'll do it, Gen, but that's a little junior high."

"No," Genevieve said, and Thomas blanched. It came out more emphatic than she intended. "He runs a graphic design business, so maybe you could act like you were checking for someone thinking of hiring him? You know, is he trustworthy?"

A frown creased his forehead. "What's going on?"

"I need to be sure what I'm dealing with," Genevieve said. "Can you do that?"

"Sure."

Genevieve reached into her bag. The next part might be tricky to navigate.

She put a plastic bag holding the heart pendant on the table.

"Do you know anyone with expertise in jewelry?"

Thomas held the bag up to the light. Then he arched an eyebrow at Genevieve.

"What is this, *Antiques Roadshow*?"

Genevieve sighed. "Do you know anyone?"

"I know a guy at LACMA," Thomas said.

"I need to know the style, the age, the origin," she said.

"Got it," he said, pocketing the bag. "And you're not going to tell me why?"

"Let's just say I found it and I need to know where it came from," Genevieve said.

"Would this have anything to do with your rekindled distrust of Julien Brooks?"

"Something like that," Genevieve said. She waved down the waiter for the bill. "Let me get this, since I'm asking you all these favors."

"It's only two, that's not so many," Thomas said. "It'll give me an excuse to talk to some people I haven't talked to lately. Got to keep the network humming. Who knows? I could be out there job hunting next."

Genevieve paused in the middle of counting ones to cover the tip. "Is the Hilliard making more cuts?"

"Something is definitely up," Thomas said.

"They'd never let you go. The place couldn't function without you," Genevieve said. "You know everything and everybody."

"Well, that's true," he said, rising. "And I really should be getting back."

Genevieve put her hand on his wrist to restrain him. "I just need to ask you one more favor, and it's a big one."

Thomas sat back down, palms flat on the table. "If it's money, just name the amount and it's yours." He took a deep breath. "Within reason, obviously. But Philip and I have talked about this."

"I don't need money."

"Oh." Thomas visibly relaxed. "OK. What is it, then?"

"Thomas, what would you do if you thought I seemed like..." she'd rehearsed this in the car, but now she faltered. "What if you thought I was showing signs of mental illness? What would you do?"

He cocked his head to one side. "Are you serious?"

"Yes."

"Gen, is everything OK? Because if it's not, I don't have to go back to work."

"Everything is fine." Genevieve had never been a very effective liar, but she hoped she was pulling it off.

"Then why are you asking me this?"

"It's always in the back of my mind, because of my mom," Genevieve said. "And we're all supposed to have personal disaster plans, right? Like our earthquake kits so we can shelter in place?"

Genevieve did not have an earthquake kit, but she knew Thomas and Philip did; Philip was practical that way.

Thomas was nodding along. This was an encouraging sign.

"OK," he said. "That almost makes sense."

"That's it," Genevieve said. "That's all I wanted to ask. If I seemed like something was really wrong with me, what would you do? Have a Genevieve's-lost-her-mind disaster plan."

After she did her banking, Genevieve hit the grocery store for Diet Dr Pepper and a stack of off-brand low-calorie frozen entrees.

Once she'd put away her groceries, she popped in a workout DVD and flogged herself through 30 minutes of cardio and 30 minutes of resistance-band work. She hated working out; always had. She generally relied on lack of appetite and nervous energy to keep her clothes from getting too tight. But exercise was supposed to be good for mental health, and she was willing to explore any avenue that might keep her sane.

She'd just finished 300 calories of tasteless chicken and pasta when D called with the update from her sister-in-law.

"Marta says you're fine," D said. "She says people put legally unenforceable crap in those severance deals and you shouldn't worry about it."

"Good to know," Genevieve said. "What do I owe her?"

"She gave you the friends and family discount of 100 percent off," D said. "So, you blew me off before lunch, but really, what's the deal with Julien?"

Genevieve dumped the remnants of her dinner in the trash and washed her fork. "We're working together, that's all."

"You seemed pretty excited when you sent that email last night."

"I know," Genevieve said. "But then I woke up this morning, and realized how silly I was being."

"This is really disappointing," D said. "Because if you're not going after Julien, neither of us has any prospects. Want to watch TV? It'll be good practice for when we're fighting over the remote at the old folks home."

They spent a couple hours on the phone watching the trashiest reality shows they could find, hooting at the ridiculousness of it all.

Soon it was pushing 11 p.m. in Texas; D had an early morning and needed to get to bed. They'd said their goodbyes and were just about to hang up when D surprised Genevieve.

"Gen, would you ever think about moving back here? I know it's not as cool as LA," D said. "But there's all this arts stuff going on downtown, I mean, that's what I hear. I only go down there for Mavericks games. But there might be a job for you. It's just... you moved to California for Pete, and then when that went belly up, you had your job at the museum, and now that's gone. I just wondered, when you're done with the thing you're doing for Julien..."

"Honestly, D, it hadn't even occurred to me."

"You could stay with me as long as you wanted," D said. "I know it's hotter than hell here, and you hold it against Texas that boys in Wichita Falls wouldn't ask you out, but..."

"That's not true!"

"I think it is, actually, you just don't like to admit it," D said. "But Gen? There's nobody here for me to hang out with! All my girlfriends are on their third babies! I end up going out with these girls who are 26! I'm the cow out in the field with the heifers!"

Genevieve laughed. "You're not a cow, D."

"Well, you're right about that," D said. "Just think about it, OK?"

After she hung up with D, Genevieve decided to email Carol that she'd stop by the museum Monday to wrap up the severance paperwork.

When she signed on, waiting there was a message from the email address *TRISTANDIED*.

The message consisted of one word:

STOP

CHAPTER FOURTEEN

GENEVIEVE THOUGHT a long time about how to handle the email.

Alerting Henry Lazare and Julien Brooks would be the logical step, but Genevieve was reluctant. She didn't think she had the whole picture of what was going on with the Lazare cousins, and until she did, she wanted to hold her cards close. For all she knew, one of them had sent the email, although it had come to her personal address, not the one she'd used to do business with them.

In the end, Genevieve decided to wait and see what happened next.

She spent the next few days cleaning her apartment and looking for job leads to pursue when the Lazare project was done.

Julien called her Sunday evening to discuss another trip to the Getty. She couldn't think of a way out of it; she'd already agreed. "How about I meet you at your house around 10:30," she said. "I have a couple errands to run first."

Genevieve didn't require a wardrobe consult Monday. She went with black pants topped by a sweater in a shade that hovered somewhere between green and yellow. Hardly anyone but redheads and strawberry blondes could wear the color, which meant that she frequently found it on clearance racks.

She did one last check of her inbox before she left and was relieved to see her mystery correspondent had not weighed in. Carol had, though. She said that things in the museum were "unsettled this morning," and that she would leave Genevieve's severance package with the guard at the security desk.

❏

Genevieve pulled up in front of Julien's house at 10:25. He was sitting on the top step of his porch, drinking coffee and reading the paper.

Her trip to the Hilliard had been quick. The severance package had been waiting as promised, and she had worked through it quickly before handing it over.

The museum was in an uproar, although that wouldn't have been obvious to anyone who wasn't familiar with its routines.

She would have asked the guard on the desk what was up, but she didn't recognize him; he must be new. His name tag said "Darren." Two temporary guards were hovering near the entrance. The Hilliard occasionally hired temps to work special events, but Genevieve had never seen them there on a regular day. She'd have to ask Thomas what was going on.

Julien signaled to Genevieve that he was taking his coffee inside and pointed toward his car. He intended to drive again, it seemed.

"Good morning," he called when he came out the side door of the house. "Glad you had an errand this morning. Gave me a chance to drink my coffee on the porch."

Genevieve had resolved to be professional and not get

sucked into small talk, but she wasn't sure how to do that without being rude. "The yard's very pretty. It must have been a lot of work," she said.

"Erica's project," Julien said, unlocking the car.

"Did she like to garden, then?" Genevieve asked as she buckled in.

"No," he said. "She's a landscape architect."

That would explain Cohen and Associates. "Very impressive," Genevieve said.

She meant the yard, but tallying up in her head what she knew about his personal life, it could apply to his relationships, too – a landscape architect and a doctor so far. He apparently liked his women formidable.

"The house was going to be an investment. Fix it up, use the yard as a lab for Erica, so she'd have something to show clients, then flip it," Julien said. "But I love the house, so I stayed when we split."

For the rest of the drive, he told her about the renovation, including a hilarious and self-deprecating story about refinishing the floors. Apparently his remodeling expertise was limited to demolition.

The librarian at the Getty's main desk was a 20-something man with horn-rimmed glasses that were either cutting edge or hopelessly outdated. Genevieve couldn't decide which.

He wasn't going to let them breeze past as they'd done on the first visit. He insisted on looking over Genevieve's research credential.

"So," he said, with a self-important squaring of his shoulders as he handed back her card, "you're with the Hilliard."

Genevieve froze. "Yes, well," she began.

"Yeah," Julien said, taking her arm, "and we're way behind schedule. You should have seen the 405 today! What a mess!"

The librarian gave Genevieve a long look but didn't say anything more.

Once they had moved out of sight of the desk, Julien released her arm and smiled. "Always act like you know what you're doing."

Genevieve was glad to be in the library, which saved her from having to make conversation with Julien. He seemed the same as ever – relaxed, cheerful. If he was messing with her head, he really was very good at it.

It took them less than two hours to finish the material available on the shelves, hitting nothing but dead ends.

"I'll have to fill out requests for the rest," Genevieve said, closing the last journal. "Why don't I drop those off and we can grab lunch while they get things out of storage?"

They ate on the patio again. It was warm in the sun, and Genevieve pushed up the sleeves on her sweater. She tasted her salad, added pepper, tasted again and added salt. Julien was nearly done with his sandwich.

"Take your time," he said. "Don't hurry just because I inhaled my lunch. I run in the morning, so I'm usually starving by noon."

"I run too – but just to get out the door on time."

Julien laughed. "I do five or so easy miles. Keeps me in shape. I like to eat."

Genevieve's phone rang, and she scrambled to fish it out of her bag and check the display. It was Thomas.

Julien gave her one of those "go ahead, take it" gestures, so Genevieve hit the answer button.

"Are you ready for the scouting report on Julien a.k.a. Jay Brooks?"

His voice was a little loud. Genevieve, worried that Julien might have heard Thomas, walked away from the table.

"This isn't a great time," she hissed. She peered over her shoulder. Julien was engrossed in the screen of his own phone.

"Not a great time for me, either," Thomas said.

Suddenly he was drowned out by the ear-splitting wail of a siren, and Genevieve held the phone away from her ear.

"What was *that*?" she asked when the sound subsided.

Julien looked up at her. She moved a few feet farther down the patio.

"I'm outside," Thomas said. "A fire truck just went by. That's one of the things I need to talk to you about."

"Is something on fire?"

"No, why I'm outside." Thomas seemed impatient, and Thomas almost never was impatient with her.

"You're kind of all over the place here."

She could hear him take a deep breath and let it out. "It's been an upsetting day. Sorry. You're so paranoid about anyone at the museum knowing whom you're working for, I thought I'd better not make this call from my desk."

"I don't really think it's fair to say I'm paranoid," Genevieve said.

Julien's head snapped up.

"OK, whatever," Thomas said. "Here's the scouting report. My friend says Jay Brooks is an excellent graphic designer, very easygoing and fun to work with but also a pro, will deliver what you need on time."

"That's great," Genevieve said, "but it's not really what..."

"I *know*," Thomas said. "I had to figure out how to get what you wanted, so I said that the person looking for the recommendation might have to divulge sensitive business information. My guy said: 'If I had to put my life savings in a paper bag and hand it to someone to hold for a weekend, I would give it to Jay, and when I came back, I wouldn't even count it.' "

"Oh," Genevieve said. In a way, she'd been hoping his friend would say Julien Brooks was as trustworthy as a rattlesnake. That would have made things a lot simpler.

"He hasn't seen him lately, but they used to go to some of the same parties. Did you know he used to be married? My guy didn't like the wife *at all*," Thomas said.

"Yeah, I knew that. Thanks for checking, Thomas," Genevieve said. "You said it's a bad day, and Carol told me it was an unsettling morning. What's going on?"

"Philip and I heard this morning that we got turned down for the mortgage."

"What happened? I thought you said at lunch it was all but approved."

"It was," Thomas said. "Then our guy called and suddenly there's a red flag on my file, and even he doesn't seem to understand what's happened. I have *outstanding* credit."

"I'm sure you do," Genevieve said. "It will all get straightened out. Probably just some glitch."

"That's not all. Bill, one of the guards, collapsed last night and is in the hospital."

"Oh no! I know Bill," Genevieve said. "He was always really nice. What happened?"

"One of the other guards found him back by the admin area. They think he had a stroke and hit his head."

Genevieve glanced up. Julien was pointedly checking his watch. "That's awful. I hope he'll be OK. Thanks for doing that thing for me. I have to go now, Thomas. Don't worry about the house. I'm sure everything will all work out."

"What was that all about?" Julien asked when she returned.

"A friend having a bad day." She reached for her water

glass, and Julien's eyes followed her arm. He frowned. She looked down.

A thumbprint-shaped bruise was visible on the top of her arm. She tugged her sleeve down.

"Why don't you finish your lunch and we'll get back to work?" Julien said.

Genevieve picked halfheartedly at her grilled chicken salad. The lettuce was wilted, and she wasn't really hungry anyway. She folded her napkin neatly next to her plate. "I'm done."

◻

The man with the funky glasses was now handling special requests – just Genevieve's luck.

He pushed a stack of journals and books she'd asked for across the desk. "What are you looking for, if you don't mind my asking? Your requests seem really broad." He studied Genevieve from behind his glasses. "If you could be more specific, I could point you in the right direction. We're here to be resources."

Something about him put Genevieve off. "I'm deliberately casting a wide net," she said.

"What's wrong now?" Julien asked when she got back to their table.

"That librarian with the glasses is asking a lot of questions," she whispered.

Julien pointedly scanned the room. "I'm guessing he doesn't get to talk to many attractive women. You're probably the highlight of his week."

Genevieve responded by burying her head in a journal. She would not be drawn into flirting with Julien Brooks.

The librarian with the glasses was still there when

Genevieve went back for the rest of her requests. He sat with his back to her, phone to his ear. He looked over his shoulder, whispered something and promptly hung up.

Shuffling the papers on his desk, he peered up at her through those strange glasses. Definitely nerdy, not fashion-forward, Genevieve concluded.

"So, is there a particular French romantic painter you're interested in," he looked down at her request forms, then back up at her, "Ms. Genevieve McKenna?"

Genevieve noticed a film of sweat on his upper lip. What was up with this guy?

She tried for her best noncommittal smile. "Like I said, I'm casting a wide net."

He nodded nervously and headed back toward the storage area.

To her relief, a different librarian delivered the material she'd requested.

By the time she and Julien had finished the stack of journals pulled from the special collections, Genevieve had come up with a couple footnotes worth further investigation but hadn't had any "aha!" moments.

▯

"Did you find anything useful?" Julien asked as they pulled out of the parking lot.

"A couple footnotes I can follow up on, but nothing significant," Genevieve said. "Right now, we've got the fact that the drawing bears his signature and is dated 1840, and the fact that the Hilliard lists it as an acquisition from a private collection in 1979. In between is a big blank."

He gave her a hard look over his sunglasses. "And it was hanging in my family's apartment in Paris in 1939."

"Unfortunately, that's second-hand information, no help from a provenance standpoint," Genevieve said. "I can start from the beginning and work forward – Lazare drew the study and try to figure out who had it next. I can start at the end and work backward – the Hilliard has it and try to figure out who gave it to them. I can even start in the middle and work in either direction. But right now I only know the beginning and the end for sure."

"Henry's going to want to know your plan," Julien said. "I can tell you right now that 'following up on footnotes' is not a winning answer."

"I know," Genevieve said, trying hard to keep her temper under control. "But he needs to understand that these cases take time. I'll put together an email with some..."

"Henry hates email."

"Fine. I'll call him in the morning and we can hash out..."

"Henry's not really a guy you call to hash things out with."

Genevieve grabbed the door handle as Julien executed a tricky lane change. "Great. How do you suggest I handle this?"

He downshifted as traffic slowed, then again as it ground to a halt. "Might as well hash out the options with me while we sit here."

Genevieve ran through some ideas in her head, discarding a few, turning others over to see whether she could spot the flaws.

"Genevieve?"

"I'm thinking. Here's an idea. You swear an affidavit relating your mother's story and go to the Hilliard. They could ask what the donor – if he's still alive – has on the provenance, which would give us a place to start."

Traffic still wasn't moving. Julien twisted in his seat to look at her. "Didn't you just tell me my mother's word was basically worthless?"

His words stung. In her effort to be cool and professional, had she been that harsh?

"I certainly didn't mean to say your mother's word was worthless. From a provenance standpoint, it's not sufficient, that's all."

"So why would the Hilliard act on it?"

"It would be the right thing to do," Genevieve said.

"This boss you couldn't stand, he would do the right thing when we had no proof?"

"I found him intimidating," she said, "but that doesn't mean he's not an honorable person. You shouldn't let me prejudice you."

"He said your work wasn't important," Julien said. "That makes him a jerk in my book. So where does that leave us?"

"We could look for your family's wills," Genevieve said.

"Is that something you do online? Henry's ex who did all the genealogy told me a lot of records have been digitized," Julien said.

"For wills, I think we have to hire someone in France," Genevieve said. "The system is pretty complicated. I need to do more homework on that."

"Here's what we'll do, then," Julien said. "I'm going to call Henry," here he held up a hand to forestall Genevieve's protest. "You want to let me deal with him. I'll tell him your research has yielded some things for follow up and that you're putting together the documentation for the next step, which is researching the family wills in France. See how much better that sounds?"

He was right, Genevieve had to admit. It did sound better.

CHAPTER FIFTEEN

G ENEVIEVE'S PHONE RANG at 7 the next morning, setting her heart pounding.

Early morning calls always did that to her. Her father was in good health as far as she knew and had seemed fine when she saw him at Christmas, but he was over 60 now, and she worried.

She hurried to check the display. It was Christine, her mother's college roommate, calling from Chicago.

Genevieve hit the answer button. Christine never could keep time zones straight.

Christine launched into what seemed suspiciously like rehearsed remarks. She'd received Genevieve's thank-you note, the card was so beautiful, who was the artist, she was so glad Genevieve liked the earrings. She seemed to be working up to something.

Genevieve, who desperately wanted coffee, wished Christine would get to the point.

"I chatted with your dad a couple weeks ago, and he told me the museum had to cut back," Christine said, finally getting there. "I was surprised your card didn't mention your job."

Jack McKenna and Christine Jensen had been comparing notes? This was news to Genevieve. She wondered whether her thank-you had arrived just as Christine was fishing for an excuse to call her.

"I didn't know you'd heard about that. I'm doing OK," Genevieve said, eager to reassure Christine. "A lawyer hired me to research a looted art claim for his family."

She told Christine about *Study for Tristan and Iseult*, the fate of the Lazare family, and how the drawing resurfaced at the Hilliard.

She guessed she must have gone on a bit, because Christine had fallen silent.

"Sorry, Christine. Probably more than you wanted to know."

"No, it's just odd. I guess these people must be pretty famous, but..."

"Well, really they aren't," Genevieve said. "Why do you say that?"

"Oh, just that you and your mother would both be interested in them, so I guess they must be a big deal, but I've never heard of them otherwise. I don't think they have any Lazare paintings at the Art Institute," Christine said.

"My mother was interested in Théodore Lazare?"

"More the gallery, I think," Christine said. "And then, when she started getting sick, she got sort of fixated on the brother who disappeared during the war."

Genevieve had been pacing her kitchen, debating opening a Diet Dr Pepper for the infusion of caffeine, but now she sat down at the bar.

"What? All anybody ever told me was that she had a breakdown."

"Hang on."

Genevieve heard a click, a sharp intake of breath, and then a relaxed exhale. Christine had gone for her cigarettes.

"Well, your mom's parents didn't want her to go so far away to school," Christine began. "They wanted her to go to some Texas school that cranked out ministers' wives and old-maid librarians. She never did fit in with her family."

"Because she was adopted," Genevieve said.

"It wasn't just that she was adopted," Christine said. "The way they talked about her, Genevieve! They wanted a redhead because their daughter who died had red hair, and they went to an orphanage in Louisiana to get your mom. They *shopped* for her, like you would curtains to match your sofa. She hated that.

"I think she was always struggling to find herself," Christine said. "But she loved college. We'd walk to the cafe in town for coffee, and we'd meet all these oddball characters. Everybody loved your mother. One of the regulars was always telling her that she looked like something from a painting."

"It sounds like she was happy," Genevieve said. "What happened?"

"I don't know how it started," Christine said. "I'd wake up in the middle of the night, and she wouldn't be in her bed. It wasn't like when you were in school. We had curfews. She wouldn't tell me where she went. And it wasn't a boyfriend, either.

"She carried around these notebooks and was always scribbling in them, and she started talking about this David Lazare all the time. I mean, *all* the time."

Genevieve cradled her head in her hand. Where was this going? "How did she know about him?"

"I have no idea," Christine said. "Honestly, until you brought him up, I always thought maybe he wasn't real."

Another click, another sharp intake of breath. Another cigarette. "One night I came back from the library and found her in our room, well, frantic is the best word I can think of. She kept saying that David was in danger, why wouldn't he listen, and a bunch of other stuff I didn't really understand. It was frightening.

"I got her calmed down and asleep, somehow. And then I snuck out early the next morning and called her parents in Wichita Falls."

She sighed. "I never told anybody that before, that I was the one who called her parents. She thought it was the school, and I let her think that. They sent her to that hospital. The doctors said she had delusions. And then it was in and out of hospitals, until, well, you know the rest."

I don't know anything, Genevieve thought.

"What was in those notebooks? Did you ever look?"

"No! That would be like reading someone's diary, wouldn't it?"

Genevieve heard a clinking noise. Was Christine pouring herself a drink? What time was it in Chicago, anyway?

"Your dad may still have some of her things," Christine said. "You won't remember this, but after she died, I sorted through her belongings. Your dad couldn't face it. I saw some of her college books. They were in that cedar chest."

Genevieve could picture the cedar chest, although she'd never once lifted the lid. She didn't go into her father's room. "Were the notebooks there?"

"I'm not sure. You should ask your dad."

"We don't really talk about her."

"I know that. But maybe you should. Listen, I have to go open a window before Hal gets home from golf, or I'm going to catch hell for smoking in the house."

□

Genevieve sat in her PJs awhile, trying to think of a plausible reason that both she and her mother would become interested in the same art gallery in Occupied Paris and someone would send her a catalog from that gallery.

Nothing came to her.

She checked just to make sure she hadn't imagined the whole exchange with Christine, but no, there it was in her phone log – a 37-minute conversation with a number in suburban Chicago.

She took a shower and got dressed, hoping that would help fire her synapses.

Maybe Galerie de l'Étoile was more famous than she realized and these connections weren't such a big deal, like the way she always seemed to meet someone from Texas any time she ran errands in her Cowboys T-shirt.

She opened her laptop, intending to see how many search-engine hits she could find for Galerie de l'Étoile, but her inbox was open, and an email caught her eye. The sender this time was *ISEULTDIEDTOO.*

The email read:

WARNED U. WONT U BE SUPRISED WHEN U GO OUTSIDE. SOUND SLEEPER?

Ignoring the impulse to correct the spelling, Genevieve sprinted out her front door. In her tiny courtyard, she did a slow 360, trying to spot anything amiss.

She opened the courtyard gate and scanned the driveway to her left and parking pad to her right. Then she noticed the broken glass.

"Damn!"

She was barefoot; she'd need shoes to investigate further.

She'd just shoved her feet into her flip-flops when her

phone began to ring. She grabbed it as she headed out the door and checked the display. *Jay in LA*.

She *really* needed to edit that.

"Hello?"

Cautiously Genevieve edged closer to the shattered driver's window of her Camry. How had she managed to sleep through that?

"Hey, I just had breakfast with Henry," Julien began.

"Great."

"Jeez, you haven't even heard what he said yet," Julien said, clearly annoyed.

"Sorry. I just discovered somebody broke my car window last night."

"Oh, that sucks. Did they get your stereo?"

Genevieve took a step closer and poked her head into the jagged hole where the window had been. She recoiled and let out a shriek.

"Genevieve? Are you OK?"

She turned just in time to see Mona, who had slipped out the front door, jump onto the low wall surrounding the courtyard.

"Mona! Get back inside! Get! In! The! House!"

"Genevieve? What's happening?"

"He left a dead fish in my car, and now my cat is outside," Genevieve said. She lunged at Mona, who scampered along the wall, clearly under the impression this was a game.

"Why would someone stealing your stereo leave a dead fish?"

"He didn't steal my stereo," Genevieve said, swiping at the cat. "I'm pretty sure the fish was the whole point. He did say he warned me. Mona!"

Genevieve hung up and reached for the cat just as she leapt off the wall and into the brush behind it.

Once she made it into the brush, Mona decided the game was more terrifying than fun. The territory between the rear of the apartment and the retaining wall at the back of the lot had remained undiscovered for a reason.

Genevieve was worried she might lose the cat for good if she let her out of her sight, so she plunged into the no-man's-land after her. But the farther she followed Mona, the more the frightened cat retreated.

Eventually, Genevieve decided a different strategy was in order. She sat with her back against the wall and waited, then waited some more, hoping the cat would relax and come to her.

That was exactly what she was doing when she heard a car speed up her driveway, a parking brake jerk and a door slam.

"Genevieve! Genevieve?"

"Behind the house," Genevieve called in a voice she hoped was loud enough to be heard but not so loud it would further alarm Mona. "And please don't yell."

Julien rounded the corner and pulled up short. "What are you doing?"

"Trying to coax my cat into the house. What are you doing here?"

"Well, let's see, I called you, got something about a broken window, then a shriek,   something about a dead fish, then you said 'he warned me' and hung up. Sounded ominous."

He took a knee at the edge of the building despite the fact, Genevieve noticed, that he was wearing a very nice pair of pants. "What's the deal with the cat? She got herself out here, right? Can't she get herself back in?"

"You don't know anything about this, so just shut up!" Genevieve snapped.

Julien's eyes widened.

"I'm sorry," Genevieve said. "It's just a really, really, really bad morning."

"Tell me how to help," Julien said.

"Could you go in my laundry room – you have to go through the closet in my bedroom – and get her bowl and a can of food? Salmon is her favorite."

Julien stood and brushed off his knee. "Be right back."

Genevieve leaned her head against the wall. Was snapping at Julien a worrisome symptom? She never talked that way to anyone. Her grandmother had a rule: "We don't say 'shut up' at our house," and Genevieve had always thought it was a good one.

And then there was the fact that just a few days ago she thought Julien Brooks might have planted a gold pendant in her apartment to make her think she was crazy; now she was giving him the run of the place.

Julien returned with Mona's bowl and a can of salmon cat food.

"Thanks," Genevieve said. "Could you maybe go around the corner where she can't see you? Men make her jumpy sometimes."

"Lot of that going around," he said, disappearing around the side of the building.

Mona's ears pricked up when Genevieve opened the can, but she remained stubbornly out of reach. Dumping the food in the bowl, Genevieve put it down and retreated to sit and wait.

Julien sat, too, his back at a 90-degree angle to Genevieve's.

"Want to walk me through what went on this morning?"

"Thank you for coming," Genevieve said. "You didn't have to do that."

"Actually, I did," Julien said. "You scared the hell out of me. You said someone had warned you? Who warned you? About what?"

Genevieve sighed. She had hoped to keep this information to herself, but in her panic, she had tipped her hand. She told him about the two threatening emails.

Julien listened to her retelling without interrupting, even though she knew it was a little disjointed, leaving out, as she did, the strange dream-like experiences, the heart-shaped pendant and the conversation with her mother's college roommate.

"So that's everything?" he asked when she was finished.

"Yes," Genevieve lied.

"And let me get this straight – the first message came when?"

"It was... well, I'd have to look to see when it was sent. I saw it the day after you came by and we had Thai food."

"Which was last week."

Genevieve could see where this was going. "Right."

"And you didn't think to pick up the phone, or forward the email, or tell me about it during the six or so hours we were together yesterday?"

"I know it seems strange."

"Well, that wasn't the word I was going to pick, but yeah," Julien said. "Henry's really not going to like this. What were you thinking?"

Mona advanced a few paces toward the food, her nose twitching.

"Good kitty, Mona," Genevieve said. "Mmmm. You know you want some."

"Genevieve?"

She closed her eyes and tried to concentrate. This was a very bad time to be without coffee.

"I wasn't sure whether to take it seriously. There really wasn't any threat. It just said 'stop.' Obviously I didn't know he'd follow up with another email and the dead fish. I wasn't sure it was worth mentioning."

"Like you weren't sure that gallery catalog was worth mentioning."

Genevieve had no idea how to respond to that.

"Look, I get that you worked for the Hilliard for a long time," Julien began, his voice soothing. "Even though your boss was a jerk, you probably still have friends there and you might feel conflicted, and I respect that, but..."

Genevieve cut him off. "My loyalties aren't divided. And who says this is someone at the museum? This doesn't really strike me as the kind of thing an art historian would do."

"Well, good," Julien said crisply. "That's good to know. Is the cat eating yet?"

Mona had just taken her first tentative bite.

"In fact, she is."

"Excellent. Grab her, and let's go inside." Julien stood, dusting off his pants. "You can call Henry and explain this, because frankly I'm at a loss here."

CHAPTER SIXTEEN

MONA DID NOT APPRECIATE being grabbed by the scruff of the neck and hauled roughly away from her food.

First she growled, and when that display of displeasure did not result in her immediate release, Mona let loose a stream of urine that soaked Genevieve's T-shirt and capris as she carried the cat around the corner of the building.

Genevieve firmly deposited Mona inside the apartment and slammed the door.

She told herself that someday this would make a funny story: There was a guy she really wanted to impress, but then she decided she didn't trust him and withheld important information, and it all ended with her humiliated and reeking of cat pee.

Julien wrinkled his nose. "That smells really nasty."

Genevieve sighed. "Cat pee is the worst. I have to take a shower and wash these clothes. Or maybe burn them. I picked a bad morning to be without coffee."

"I need to run some errands," Julien said. "I'll wait in your courtyard when I get back."

Genevieve locked the front door behind him.

She stripped out of her dirty clothes, dumped them in the washer and turned the dial to the hottest setting.

She took a shower, washing her hair for the second time in a couple hours. She changed into a clean T-shirt and jeans and put her wet hair up in a clip. She'd never felt less attractive in her life.

Then she hustled to her living room, grabbed her laptop off the bar and hurried back to her bedroom. Julien was going to want to see the threatening emails, and she had to make sure there wasn't anything in the inbox from D, whose subject lines often appeared to be taken straight from the cover of *Cosmo*.

Mercifully, there was nothing embarrassing in her inbox. Genevieve checked her trash and sent mail just to be sure and cleared her cache just to be safe.

Her computer housekeeping complete, she opened her front door. Julien was leaning against her courtyard wall, texting. Next to him on the wall was a coffee.

"I'm no longer disgusting," she said. "It's safe to come in."

He smiled, then handed her the coffee. "Non-fat latte."

"Wow," Genevieve said, touched by the gesture. "That's very nice. And a really good guess."

"You left your Starbucks cup in my car the other day," he said.

"Ah. Sorry about that."

He spotted her laptop on the bar. "Do you mind showing me these emails?"

"Not at all," Genevieve said.

Julien strode across the room. "Henry's sending a guy, he called him a security consultant, but I think he's basically a private detective who works divorce cases for him. We're not supposed to touch anything on the car until he gets here."

"You called Henry?"

"I know what I said," Julien said. "But I couldn't make you do it after the morning you've had. That would just be mean."

□

Julien looked at both emails, opening the headers and doing something Genevieve didn't understand. He forwarded copies to himself. She sat at the bar next to him, drinking her coffee and offering no opinions.

"This isn't the same email address I have for you," he said.

"No, you have the one I use for business, Lost Art Investigations."

"So we have to figure out how this person got your personal email address," Julien said.

Just then, an instant message popped up.

D: Watched Troy on demand last nite

D: You were right re Brad Pitt in skirt :-)

"Oh, that's going to be really distracting," Genevieve said, reaching for the computer. "D gets on between appointments and it's stream of consciousness. You can't just close the chat window; she'll keep opening new ones. I have to answer her."

Was it her imagination, or was Julien a little slow sliding the computer over?

Unfortunately, Genevieve couldn't type fast enough to derail D.

D: You didn't mention HOT SEX SCENE with him and princess girl they captured

Gen: Stop. Not a good time

D: WHY HAVE YOU NOT GIVEN ME THIS DVD FOR XMAS? BDAY? FRICKIN LABOR DAY? YOU ARE SUPPOSED TO BE MY BEST FRIEND

Genevieve began to blush. Julien laughed out loud.

Gen: Ppl looking at my screen, not a good time

D: Also right re YCLI and older brother actor

D: too bad he dies early

D: and keeps CLOTHES ON

D: oh, whos looking at your screen?

Gen: explain later

D: K, bye call me

Genevieve closed the chat window and buried her face in her hands. At least D had used the shorthand YCLI – your current love (or lust) interest – rather than Julien's name.

"Sorry about that," she said, sliding the computer back toward Julien.

"Don't be," he said. "That's pretty much the highlight of my day so far."

Genevieve wasn't sure what she expected from a security consultant, but it wasn't this.

The man in her courtyard looked like a salesman on a golf outing – medium height, medium build. He had black hair, cut very short, shot through with gray. He wore khakis, a polo shirt and a windbreaker.

"Melvin Dixon," he said, offering his hand. Genevieve showed him inside.

Melvin motioned her toward the sofa. "Why don't you sit." It wasn't really a question.

Genevieve complied, and Julien took a seat next to her. Melvin grabbed one of the bar stools. He put it in the middle of the room, facing them.

"So, you're working for Mr. Lazare, and you received a couple anonymous emails, and then this morning found your car vandalized and a dead fish inside?"

Genevieve nodded.

"Have you called the police?"

"No. I'm sorry. My cat got out, and then..."

Melvin pulled a notebook and pen out of his jacket pocket. "It's fine. Good, actually. Something like this – basically vandalism – LAPD isn't going to want to f... um, mess with it. Best to handle this kind of thing off the books. Trust me, I know. I spent 20 years on the force."

Somehow, she didn't think conserving police resources was his primary concern.

"Walk me through the whole thing," he said, and so she did, starting with the first email.

She didn't think this was much help, but Melvin was taking lots of notes. "How about cars you didn't recognize parked nearby lately, anything unusual on the street?"

Genevieve closed her eyes, trying to recall. "Nothing. Well, the lights for the driveway are off, but that's not unusual. The tenant in the front house keeps messing them up. I've called the landlord."

"Call him again," Melvin said. "Now, you have no idea what time this happened? You didn't hear anything?"

Genevieve shook her head.

"No alarm on the car?"

"It didn't seem worth it to get it fixed," Genevieve said. "The car's got 200,000 miles on it."

Melvin stood. "I'll want to take a look at the computer, but let's go outside now."

The three of them walked out, and Melvin spent a few minutes circling the Camry taking photos while Julien and Genevieve leaned against the courtyard wall.

"Your cousin has this guy on the payroll?"

Julien shrugged. "Some divorces get really ugly, I guess."

When he was done with his photos, they trooped back into the apartment. Julien and Genevieve sat on the sofa again. Melvin resumed his spot on the bar stool.

"How many people are aware of your work for Mr. Lazare?"

Genevieve thought about that. "My father in Wichita Falls, and my best friend in Dallas. My godmother in Chicago found out this morning, but after the window was broken."

Melvin didn't bother to write any of that down. "Anyone here in Los Angeles?"

"We've been to the Getty library twice for research. Someone there might have had their curiosity piqued. Oh!" She turned to Julien. "Remember that librarian yesterday? He kept trying to get me to tell him what I was working on."

"I don't think that guy had anything to do with this," Julien said.

"But he kept looking at me."

Julien caught Melvin's eye and gave a little shake of his head.

"Honestly, I think he was just checking you out, Genevieve. He seemed harmless," Julien said.

Melvin seemed to accept Julien's assessment. "So there's no one else in LA who knows about this?"

"Oh, my friend Thomas," Genevieve said. "Duh."

Melvin pulled out his notebook. "And who is this Thomas?"

"He works at the Hilliard, and..."

Julien interrupted her. "Is that the guy on the phone yesterday? Seemed like that call got kind of heated. Didn't he tell you that you were being paranoid?"

Suddenly Genevieve realized how this must look to Melvin.

"Thomas had nothing to do with this, he..."

Julien glanced at the bruise on the top of her forearm. Genevieve covered it with her other hand.

"He's a very good friend. Run any background check you want. Do you need his full name and address?"

Melvin took down the information. "Who else at the museum should we be looking at?"

"This is not how museum people operate," Genevieve said. "They're snotty about people's credentials and gossip about their research methods. They don't leave dead fish in cars. We've stumbled into something else. I just don't know what."

Melvin chewed thoughtfully on the end of his pen. "Any chance this is directed at you, and your work is a red herring? Do you have an ex-husband, ex-boyfriend, current boyfriend, anybody like that you might have mentioned this project to? No shame if you do – lots of women have an asshole ex-boyfriend."

Genevieve's temper flared. "Yes, I have an asshole ex-boyfriend. But I haven't talked to him in six years."

"OK, OK. I had to ask." Melvin closed the notebook. "That just leaves the computer."

He walked over to the bar. To Genevieve's surprise, he unplugged the computer and began wrapping up the cord.

"Um, what are you doing?"

Melvin kept his back to her. "I'm going to have to take this for a few days to do some forensics on it. We'll get it back to you just as soon as we can."

Genevieve shot Julien a look. He seemed just as surprised as she was.

"Like hell you are!"

At that, Melvin turned around.

"All my financial information is on there, I need it for my work, and... well, I don't think you have any right to take it," Genevieve said.

Melvin exchanged a look with Julien. "I'm going to have to discuss this with Mr. Lazare," he said.

"Discuss all you want," Genevieve said. "My computer stays here."

Julien cocked his head toward the door. "Melvin, could I have a word?"

Melvin followed Julien out into the courtyard. Genevieve pointedly locked the door behind them. Then she took her computer into the bedroom, where she inched open a window to eavesdrop.

"...but knows about those characters? The MO doesn't add up," Melvin said.

"But why would she?" Julien said.

Why would she *what*, Genevieve wondered.

Melvin was speaking again. "The boss says..." Genevieve strained to hear as they moved away from the courtyard. "Just be objective..." They were too far away; she could no longer hear them. Frustrated, she waited.

After about 10 minutes, she heard one set of footsteps coming back toward her apartment, then a knock on her door.

She buried her laptop in her underwear drawer and went to the living room.

"Yes," she called through the door without opening it.

"Melvin left. It's just me," Julien said.

Genevieve thought for a moment, then grabbed her keys and slipped out into the courtyard, locking the door behind her. She crossed her arms over her chest.

"I didn't know he was going to do that," Julien said.

"I'm not letting that guy take my computer."

"No, I told Henry that," he said. "I have copies of the emails – that's all they need. That was bullshit. So, here's the peace offering: a guy is coming to sweep up the glass, fix the window and detail the car, courtesy of Henry. Melvin already bagged the fish and took it with him. While the mess gets cleaned up, why don't I take you out to lunch?"

Genevieve gestured toward her outfit. "I'm not really dressed for it."

"I know tons of great dives where you'll fit in just fine," Julien said.

Genevieve considered his offer. "Hang on," she said.

She went back inside, and returned a few minutes later with her laptop in her bag.

They went for Korean barbecue. Julien noted the laptop bag, which she took into the restaurant, but he didn't say anything.

"So here's something I'm wondering about," Julien said as he dug into his food. "We know this guy, whoever he is, can't spell. But does he know his literary references? The email addresses he's using – do Tristan and Iseult both die?"

"Depends," Genevieve said. "It's one of those medieval tales with a bunch of variations. The one constant is that they're eternally in love – in some versions they're under a spell, in other versions they mistakenly drink a potion. But they can't be together, because she has to marry his uncle, the king. I think Tristan always dies, but not Iseult. She does in the opera, though."

"No version where they live happily ever after?"

Genevieve shook her head. "No."

She hadn't had breakfast, but Genevieve found that she wasn't hungry. She felt overwhelmed and confused, and more than anything, she wanted quiet and time to process what was going on.

Julien noticed that she wasn't eating. "Don't like it?"

Genevieve shrugged and pushed her plate away. "It's good. I'm not hungry."

Julien finished his lunch and carefully wiped his hands on his napkin.

"I'm on your side, you know that, right? You seemed to have it under control, but for the record, I wasn't going to let Melvin walk out of there with your laptop."

"Thanks."

"Henry swears he didn't tell him to do that. Just cop instincts, I guess," Julien said.

Genevieve managed a smile. "Thank you for making sure my window got fixed and the mess cleaned up. I know that's you, not him."

"Least we could do."

The waiter approached with drink refills, but Julien warned him away with a subtle shake of his head.

"Look, Genevieve, I don't know you very well, obviously," he said. He glanced away. "Although sometimes it seems like I do, weirdly... Anyway."

He took a deep breath and continued. "It seems like maybe you have a lot going on in your life right now." His eyes slid to the bruise on her arm.

Genevieve reflexively covered it with her hand. "I know you're worried I'm dating some abusive jerk, but I'm not. I'm not dating anyone."

That last part was unnecessary. So why had she mentioned it?

Julien waited. Perhaps for an explanation of the bruise on her arm? Genevieve didn't have one that made sense.

Seeing that none was forthcoming, Julien continued.

"Even when you land another gig right away, a layoff is stressful, and it's OK if you need to take some time to catch your breath. I think I told you earlier, I had breakfast with Henry this morning. One of those annoying power breakfasts, on his turf."

That would explain Julien's switch from his usual casual look.

"I told him we're at a point where we just have to let some inquiries play out. If it makes you feel any better, the whole Luca Brasi thing this morning with your car convinced him you're on the right track."

Genevieve frowned. "The whole *what* with my car?"

"The dead fish? Luca Brasi? *The Godfather*? No? I guess gangster movies aren't your thing. More swords and sandals?"

He gave her a sly grin, then turned serious. "I mean, if someone's warning you away, you must be on to something, right?"

"I guess," Genevieve said. "I just wish I knew what."

_____

CHAPTER SEVENTEEN

A LOT OF WHAT JULIEN SAID made sense. She was under a lot of stress. Maybe she needed to take a step back.

Or maybe she needed to push forward.

Genevieve opted to push forward. Did her mother's notebooks from college survive? What was in them? She knew only one way to find out.

She started pricing tickets to Texas.

The cheapest last-minute deal was more than $900. She gulped, put it on 24-hour hold, and called D to make sure she could handle a houseguest.

"Gen! Who was looking at your computer?"

"Julien," Genevieve said.

"Ooopsie," D said. "Good thing I used the secret code!"

"Yeah, D, you really need to be careful with the IM thing. So, I need a favor," Genevieve said.

"Name it. It's yours."

"There's some stuff stored at my dad's house I need for a research project. I have a week or so off in this thing I'm doing for Julien, so now's a good time. Can I stay at your house on the way there and back? It would probably be..."

To her relief, D interrupted. "Gen, you can stay at my house for as long as you want, any time you want. You know that. And please don't tell me you bought a really expensive last-minute ticket when I'm up to my ears in flight coupons I can't use because I don't have a frickin' boyfriend to go anywhere with."

Once D had booked the flights, Genevieve emailed Julien to say she'd be out of town for a few days. She told him she'd continue to work on the issue of researching French wills.

She talked to Thomas, who agreed to feed Mona and promised he'd guard the door with his life. Genevieve could only hope the cat's outdoor adventure had taught her a lesson.

Thomas told her he'd dropped off the heart pendant with his friend who would give an expert opinion on its age and origin. She forwarded him the photos of the Lazare brides and asked for a ruling on whether it was the same piece.

She waited until evening to call her father. After the initial exchange of how-are-yous? and I'm-fines, she got to the point.

He was happy that she was coming, surprised by the timing. "Is everything OK, Genny?"

She had debated how to broach the topic of her mother's belongings. She'd even made notes before she dialed.

"Christine sent me a book from their school, and it made me wonder about Mom's time at college. Christine thought you might have some of her things still?"

Her father seemed taken aback. He was silent a moment, then cleared his throat. "Anything of hers is in the cedar chest – I thought you knew that. Of course you're welcome to go through it."

This was the answer Genevieve had been looking for, so why did it fill her with such dread?

"I'll stay with D tomorrow and be at the house around lunchtime day after. Is that OK?"

"That's fine." He seemed befuddled. "But what's the rush? Why do you want to look now?"

Genevieve was ready for this question. "Oh, Christine got me curious, and I have a break in my schedule now. I don't know when I'll get an opening again."

She wasn't telling the whole truth, and she felt bad about that. But she rationalized that telling her father everything would just worry him.

❑

After the requisite plane change in Albuquerque, Genevieve arrived in Dallas just after 6 p.m. She picked up a car and eased into the rush hour traffic, headed for D's house in the northern suburbs.

When Genevieve was growing up, she and her father had gone to Dallas every year for the State Fair. Back then, Dallas seemed crowded and terrifying. Life in LA had altered her perspective. The traffic seemed light and the city full of wide-open spaces. She passed block after block of big-box retail and parking lots that seemed to go on for miles.

D's street was lined with two-story brick houses, each fronted by a patch of lawn and a spindly tree. The homes reminded Genevieve of women she saw in some LA neighborhoods, who all went to the same hairdresser and tanning salon and boutiques – slight variations on the same theme.

She parked and was hefting her suitcase when D came flying out of the front door. She was still in her work clothes

– chic black pantsuit and four-inch heels. Genevieve didn't know how anyone could walk in those, let alone run.

D wrapped her in a tight hug.

"I am SO glad to see you! I'm taking you out for Tex-Mex and margaritas! I'm going to get you drunk and make you tell me *everything.*"

Genevieve told D a lot over dinner, but not everything. In fact, she restricted herself to one margarita so that she wouldn't be tempted to talk about the strangest things in her life.

Back at the house after dinner, D decided that Genevieve needed to raid her closet so that Julien would "get a little variety" the next time he saw her.

"Men like variety," D pronounced.

Genevieve settled on the bed while D hauled clothes out of a walk-in closet nearly as large as Genevieve's apartment.

"I don't know that I'm going to be spending all that much time with him," Genevieve said. "The next step is to hire a researcher in France, so I'll mostly be dealing with Julien over the phone. Anyway, how would I get this stuff back to you?"

"Look at this closet! All I do is shop on the off-chance I'll get a date! I won't even miss any of this stuff!" D tossed Genevieve a slim black skirt. "I know you have black skirts, but try that. It might be a little tight, but tight isn't always a bad thing."

Genevieve stood and dutifully wriggled out of her jeans.

"Oh Lord, Gen. You have got to buy some new undies."

Genevieve zipped the skirt "No one's going to see my underwear."

D put her hand on her hip. "You know what those undies say? Those undies say you aren't even trying."

"I think we've established that I'm not really trying, D." Genevieve looked over her shoulder at the mirror. "I can't wear this. My butt looks huge." Genevieve stepped out of the skirt and put her jeans back on.

D burrowed deeper into the closet. "What about Julien?"

Genevieve flopped back on the bed. "What about Julien?" She arranged some of the pillows behind her. "Why do you have so many pillows?"

D tossed an armful of clothes on the bed. "You do realize that every time we talk, 80 percent of it's about Julien, right?"

Genevieve smoothed the fringe on a pillow. "That's because art history bores you, and I don't understand pharmaceutical sales."

D waited. She loved to talk, but she also knew the value of well-placed silence.

Genevieve wilted. "I don't remember the last time I met somebody this interesting, and funny, and nice and..."

"And who made you think 'mmm-mmm, I want me some of that?' "

Genevieve nodded and scooted over to make room for D on the bed.

D slapped Genevieve playfully on the knee. "So what are you going to do now?"

"Honestly? Nothing. It would just be too weird."

D tossed a pillow at Genevieve's head. "Wrong answer. So far wrong, you can't even see right from where you are."

Genevieve rolled onto her side and propped herself up on one elbow. "This is an important job. I need to concentrate. I can't be acting like I'm 13." She flopped onto her back again. "This is hopeless."

"Why is it hopeless? I've seen the guy, Gen, and yeah, he's hot," D said. "But he's not out-of-your-league hot. And in

Vegas, he was clearly very into you."

"Was he into me in Vegas? Now it's like that never happened," Genevieve said. "He's different now."

"Sure he's different. There's a chance for something real now. Do you flirt with him? You have to give him something to work with, you know," D said patiently, as if she were talking to a 10-year-old.

D got up to put the rejected skirt back in the closet. "Gen, at some point, you have to get over Post Pete Traumatic Stress Disorder."

"I *am* over it, D."

"Could have fooled me," D said. She flashed her most wicked grin. "You know, the best way to get over a man is to get under one."

"D!" Genevieve flushed bright red.

"Gen, you know I love you. But I do not want to be sitting here when we're fanning ourselves through hot flashes still trying to motivate your butt," D said. "Get out there and take a chance! You're like one of those football teams that runs it into the middle of the line all the time. Open up the offense, girl! Play to win! Don't just play not to lose!"

"Defense wins championships," Genevieve said solemnly.

D laughed. "Seriously, Gen, we're getting to the age where everybody's a little dinged up. It doesn't matter as much as you think."

"I don't know, D, you don't seem too dinged to me."

"Well, I'm not doing so good on having four kids, am I?" She pulled a blue blouse off a hanger. "Maybe I should've stuck with genial-but-otherwise-useless Lanny."

D was such a relentless optimist, it had never occurred to Genevieve that she spent any time on regrets. "You really think about him?"

D tossed the blouse at her. "Try that on. Maybe I'll only have three kids or two or whatever. It's too early to give up. You hear me?"

Genevieve buttoned the shirt D gave her. It was a deep shade of blue, almost purple, and had a low neckline. "I hear you," she said.

"Oh, I'm liking that," D said. "The color is great with your eyes. It just hangs on me, but it really shows off that cleavage of yours. Now, I'm thinking you need a push-up bra with that." She looked hard at Genevieve. "Please tell me you have a push-up bra."

Genevieve examined herself in the mirror. "Too sexy for work." She started to unbutton the shirt, then stopped and buttoned it again.

She turned to D. "Isn't it?"

Genevieve left D's at 10 the next morning, carrying away the blue shirt and lots of advice, much of it unsolicited.

It took Genevieve little more than an hour to hit the vast emptiness of the North Texas plains. She'd neglected to pack CDs, so she found a country radio station and soon was singing along, even with songs she'd never heard before. She felt like she was slipping back into her childhood.

At noon, she pulled up at her father's house, a nondescript brick rancher on a nondescript street. They'd moved in after her mother died, and even though Genevieve lived in the house for 10 years, she had no real affection for it. It was just a house.

The door opened and a spaniel came bounding down the porch stairs, followed by her father. "Hi, honey. I'll get your bag. Ranger! You let her be!"

Genevieve studied her father for signs of age, but he looked fine – tall, broad-shouldered, fit. He hugged her. "Sure is good to see you, Genny." He even smelled the same as ever.

He hefted her suitcase and slammed the trunk shut. "How was the drive?"

"It was fine." They'd been having this conversation ever since she left for college.

He ushered her into the house and took the suitcase to her bedroom. "I went ahead and carried the cedar chest in here," he said. "Light's better."

He shooed the dog out of the room. "Go on Ranger, git!" Her father lingered in the doorway. "Do you want some lunch? I could fix us sandwiches."

"Lunch would be great," she said.

They sat in the kitchen and made small talk about the aging remnants of the McKenna clan over turkey sandwiches on wheat bread, washed down with iced tea.

Eventually, her father stood to clear the table. "I imagine you want to get to your project. I'll clean up."

Genevieve's old room was less cluttered than it had been when she was growing up, but otherwise looked much the same. Lavender walls. White curtains with a lavender floral pattern on the lone window.

Genevieve pulled a pillow onto the floor and settled next to the cedar chest. The lid creaked as she opened it, and its distinctive smell filled the room.

She pulled out a handmade, dark-green sweater. Did her mother knit? Genevieve closed her eyes, trying to picture her mother wearing it, but came up empty. She held the sweater to her nose, but all she smelled was cedar.

How could she have so few memories of her mother? There ought to be more than sitting on the sofa in a rectangle of late afternoon sun, looking at art books.

Next up was a plastic garment bag, bunched up at the corners to fit into the chest. Inside was the ivory lace sheath dress her mother had worn to be married.

Under the garment bag were photo albums. The first held pictures from her parents' small wedding and their honeymoon in New Orleans. Another had photos of their first house, her mother in maternity clothes.

Genevieve was dismayed when she surveyed the next layer – a high school diploma and yearbooks. Was there nothing from the year away at college?

A knock startled her. Her father stuck his head inside the room. "I need to go to the hardware store, Genny. I'll put the dog out so he doesn't bother you."

Stillness settled over the house. Genevieve went back to her work.

She lifted out a stack of books. *Anne of Green Gables. Black Beauty.* She opened *My Friend Flicka.* It was inscribed, "For Grace. Christmas, 1959."

She was near the bottom of the chest now. A pair of white gloves. A blank postcard of the Alamo. A battered shoebox, its lid held in place with a rubber band.

That was it. The chest was empty.

Genevieve took the lid off the shoebox. Then she sat back on her heels and sent a silent "thank you" to Christine.

The first thing in the box was a photo of her mother and Christine, arms wrapped around each other, surrounded by fall foliage. There were letters from her grandmother, addressed to her mother at college. And, at the bottom of the box, two 5 x 8 notebooks.

Genevieve wasn't sure what she'd been expecting, but she wasn't prepared for what she found in the notebooks.

There were no dates and no organization. Her mother had jotted down fragmented thoughts, sometimes just one or two words.

Familiar but not. Why do I know a painting I have never seen? From a book and I just don't remember?

Make a sketch next time, right away.

Genevieve sighed in frustration. She'd been foolishly hoping the notebooks would explain everything, something like: **Oct. 1, 1968: A professor told me the most fascinating story about a family in Paris.**

"Genevieve, you're an idiot," she said aloud.

Below the note about making a sketch, her mother had started to draw a head. She had put a lot of effort into getting the mouth right; Genevieve could see the eraser marks.

He says I look like girl in the painting.

That sounded familiar. What had Christine told her? One of the regulars at the cafe in town told her mother she looked like something from a painting.

Again last night. Christy noticed.
Where was I she says.
Where was I????

Here was something else that made sense to Genevieve. Christine had said her mother was sometimes gone in the middle of the night. But her mother didn't know herself where she had gone?

The next page gave Genevieve a jolt.

> **Must go, he says. No choice.**
> **Do I dream these things? No. Real.**

Her mother had underlined the last word so heavily that the paper had torn.

Genevieve turned the page and dropped the notebook as though it were on fire.

She was looking at a sketch of Julien.

But wait. This was a sketch of an adult. Was Julien even born in 1968? How could that be?

She picked the notebook up with shaking hands and examined the sketch. The man had Julien's eyes, but the nose was different – broader than Julien's. The mouth was off, too.

Genevieve thought back to the day they had sorted through old photos from Paris and realized that the man in the sketch wasn't Julien.

It was his uncle, David Lazare.

But David Lazare had been dead for decades when her mother drew this. How could her mother have sketched him?

From a photo? But where would she have seen a photo?

Genevieve traced the line of David's mouth.

I'm crazy, she thought. Just like her.

A wave of heat convulsed her body. The light in the room grew very, very bright, and then it began to fade.

A dark room, the wood floor smooth beneath her. She
feels, rather than sees, a shift beside her. Someone else is
here. Panicked, she tries to rise. A hand rests on her arm.
Be calm, it seems to say.
She hears voices, somewhere far below. They are indistinct
at first. They come closer. Sharp, guttural. German.
The grip on her arm tightens. Footsteps are coming closer.
Her heart hammers in her chest. Sweat springs up on her
face, under her arms.
The footsteps pause, then click away. The voices become
indistinct again.
She exhales, and so does the person next to her.
The hand remains on her arm. Time passes – impossible
to say how much. Ten minutes? An hour? She doesn't know.
Scudding clouds, the moon breaks through, the room is
bathed in light. She knows this room.
The man leans close to her ear and whispers one word:
"Neuschwanstein."

CHAPTER EIGHTEEN

A DOG BARKED INSISTENTLY, and Genevieve opened her eyes.

She was sitting on the floor of her old bedroom, the contents of the cedar chest spread around her.

She stood and stretched. Her legs were stiff. How long had she been sitting on the floor? The light in the room had grown dim. The winter sun was nearly down.

She walked into the hall. It was quiet inside, but she could hear the dog outside.

Genevieve went to the kitchen and looked out the window. Her father was in the fenced yard, playing fetch with Ranger.

She opened the door and stepped out. "Hey, Dad."

Her father pulled the stick from the dog's mouth. "There you are. Where'd you go?"

Genevieve was puzzled. "What?"

The dog was jumping, trying to pull the stick from his hand. "I poked my head in when I got back from the store and you were gone. Your car was here. Figured you went for a walk."

The back of her neck prickled, and she shivered.

"I think I'd better get a sweater," she called over her shoulder as she went inside.

Genevieve walked into her bedroom, shut the door and leaned against it.

☐

She hadn't been in this room when her father opened the door earlier?

What had Christine said? Her mother would be gone in the middle of the night, and she wouldn't say where?

Because she didn't know where, just as Genevieve couldn't say where she'd been – only that she'd been *somewhere*. It didn't feel like sleepwalking or a dream or a hallucination. It felt real, just as her mother had written in her notebook.

Did that mean she was mentally ill, like her mother?

Suffering the same delusions her mother had? What were the odds of that?

What about the pendant in her apartment? And the handprint on her arm?

Those were real.

What if her mother wasn't mentally ill? What if this was something else entirely?

She heard her father's footsteps in the hall. "Genny? I thought maybe we'd go get a steak," he said. "Do you still eat steak after you've been in California all this time?"

Genevieve stepped out into the hall and tried her best to smile. "Of *course* I still eat steak."

☐

At the restaurant, Genevieve was preoccupied with thoughts of her mother. There was so much she wanted to ask her father, but she didn't want to reopen old wounds. And she didn't want to worry him. He'd had enough of that in his life.

After they ordered, her father set his reading glasses aside and looked at her. "Christine seems to think we need to talk about your mother. Is that why you're here?"

Genevieve sat back against the hard wooden booth, stunned. It was unlike her father to be so direct. She hardly knew where to begin.

"Did you ever hear her talk about people named Lazare?"

This was not a question her father expected. He shook his head. "I don't know that name. Who are they?"

"That's the family I'm working for. Christine said Mom talked about them when she was at college."

"I'm not going to be able to help you much there," he said. "I didn't know your mom until she came back here. She never talked about college."

"What did she talk about?"

The waitress delivered their salads, giving her father time to consider her question.

"She'd get interested in something. A painter. An author, anything. She'd read all about them. She'd want to know their whole story. Some people found that strange. I liked that. Most people just pay attention to what's right in front of them."

"What was it like when she was getting sicker? Did she ever go off somewhere, and you didn't know where she'd gone?"

"Not that I remember. Now, during the day, while I was at work, I don't know what all she did." His tone became urgent. "Do you remember her leaving you alone?"

"No, I don't remember anything like that. Did it happen?"

Relief eased across her father's face. "Not that I know of," he said. "Your mother worried about it a lot, though. She was afraid that she'd lose track of you, I guess."

"What exactly was wrong with her? I've never known."

"The doctors couldn't ever agree," her father said. "It's not an exact science, like diagnosing cancer or something. I know at the very beginning, when she left school, they told her folks she had grandiose delusions."

"When she was getting bad, did she know something was wrong with her?" Genevieve asked. "Was she scared?"

Her father put down his fork. "Your mother was scared every single day. Some days weren't as bad as others, but nothing I could do or say ever made it better."

He looked tired, and Genevieve regretted that she'd brought it up. But she needed to know.

She stared at the table, trying to think how to ask the question. "Do you think that's why she did it, so she wouldn't have to be scared anymore?" She glanced up, almost afraid to see her father's reaction.

"Genny, I know what the police said, what everyone thinks. But a part of me has always had a hard time believing your mother set that fire," he said.

"The medicine they had her on, it dulled her." He stopped and rubbed his weather-beaten hands over his face.

"She had a lawn chair out there, and she'd put the door down when it was cold, sit out there with that old stray cat. I didn't want her smoking in the house, didn't want you around it. The garage wasn't safe, though. I had rags and paint out there. Gas for the mower. Sometimes, I wonder, well, maybe she just dozed off, and it went up before she had a chance to get out."

Genevieve had spent more than 25 years thinking her mother committed suicide. This was the first she'd heard that her father harbored any doubts.

"You think it was an *accident*?"

"Oh, Genny, I don't know." His voice cracked. "Maybe I just want to believe that, because it's easier."

"You never said anything," Genevieve said. "Well, nobody ever said anything about her."

"Folks said you'd do better if I just let you get over it," her father said. "Everybody said, 'Let it alone.' " His voice lowered to a hoarse whisper. "And I just felt so guilty, you know, because it was my fault."

"Your fault?"

"Making her smoke out there. It wasn't safe."

Genevieve thought she might be sick. She threw her napkin on the table and pushed out of the booth. Her father stood, calling after her, as she stumbled toward the restroom.

"You OK, baby? You need a glass of water?"

A motherly African-American woman washing her hands at the next sink eyed Genevieve in the mirror as she splashed water on her face.

Genevieve tried to work up a smile. "I'll be OK. But thank you."

When she returned to the dining room, her father looked as miserable as Genevieve had ever seen him.

"I let the girl clear your salad," he said when Genevieve slid into the booth. "I hope that's OK. They're holding our dinner. Your steak's going to be a little past medium rare, I'm afraid."

"That's fine. Sorry I bolted like that."

Jack McKenna shook his head slowly. "I don't blame you. I guess I always knew you'd react that way, which is why I never wanted..."

"Dad." Genevieve put her hand on his wrist. "I don't think it's your fault. That's not why I got upset."

"No?"

"No," Genevieve said. "Do you know why I always thought we never talked about Mom?"

Her father held up a hand to stop her long enough for the waitress to deliver two skillets holding charbroiled steaks and leathery baked potatoes.

Once the waitress had moved off, he motioned for Genevieve to continue.

"Do you remember these people from church... oh, I can't remember their name. She taught Sunday School, and they lived in that white house down by the junior high with the wagon wheel in the front yard?"

"The Childresses?"

"One time after Mom died, I was in the bathroom at church," Genevieve said. "Grandma let me go by myself, which was a big deal, and I was in the stall, and Mrs. Childress and somebody else were in there, and they started talking about Mom."

It would have been the fall after her mother died, because she and her father were living in town, not at the farm with her grandparents, and the weather was cool enough that she was wearing tights. She was having trouble wrestling them back up, which was why she had been in the stall so long.

"They were talking about what a shame it was about Mom, and then Mrs. Childress said, 'Well, the real problem is, *she never should have had that little girl.*'"

Her father stared back at her, not comprehending her point.

"I thought we never talked about Mom because it was *my fault.* I thought having me made her worse."

Her father shared stories over dinner, ones Genevieve had never heard before. These were the good memories, the Grace McKenna she could barely remember.

They drove home in silence. Genevieve was struggling to absorb a lot of new information: about her mother, her father, herself.

There were practical questions troubling her, too. These episodes she kept having – what were they? What did they mean?

The word Neuschwanstein, at least, she recognized. It was a town in Germany, home of a castle where the Nazis stored artwork they'd looted from conquered countries.

Her father pulled the truck into the garage and shut off the engine.

"We should have had this talk a long time ago," he said quietly. "I'm sorry for that."

She patted his arm. "It's OK, Dad. I'm just glad we had it."

He took a deep breath. "I hope you won't think I'm out of line here, Genny. I know you're grown up, and I need to let you live your life. But there's one more thing I want to tell you." He unbuckled his seatbelt and turned toward her. "Your mother played her cards pretty close to the vest, even with me. I see a lot of that in you.

"Don't cut yourself off from people who care about you and want to help," he said. "That's the one piece of advice I'd give you."

Genevieve exchanged "goodnights" with her father and returned to her bedroom, thinking about his advice. Who wanted to help her?

She changed into PJs, turned down the covers and put the notebooks on the bedside table. She lifted the pillow from the floor and noticed something white peeking out from under the bed. She bent to retrieve it.

It was a crumpled white handkerchief bearing the monogram DL. Had that been in the cedar chest? Genevieve wasn't sure.

Twenty-four hours earlier, this discovery would have buckled her knees in terror.

Her world *had* tilted on its axis, she realized.

Genevieve settled into bed with her mother's notebooks, eager to read past the sketch of David Lazare that had frightened her so.

This time, she examined the likeness calmly. Was he the man who had whispered "Neuschwanstein?" She closed her eyes, trying to recall.

It was no use. She didn't get a look at him, only a vague sense of his presence.

Some pages in her mother's notebooks were filled with nothing but questions, as though she were trying to recall specific details. Others contained statements, but Genevieve couldn't tell whether these were things her mother knew or whether she was merely guessing.

Gallery records burned Impossible to keep track

That didn't make sense. The Nazis were sticklers for records.

Genevieve opened the second notebook.

Again last night I brought something back this time

For the first time since she was a little girl sitting on the sofa looking at art books, Genevieve felt a kinship with her mother. She turned the page to find out what her mother had brought back, but there was no indication.

Suddenly the notebook's tone shifted dramatically. Her mother's handwriting became messy.

He is betrayed – he must be warned

Then:

Trying and not working
Try <u>harder</u>
Can I save him?

CHAPTER NINETEEN

GENEVIEVE HAD JUST FINISHED gassing up for the drive back to Dallas when her phone rang.

Jay in LA. Damn. She *still* hadn't edited that.

"Good morning," she said, maneuvering into the rental car.

"Hope I didn't get you at a bad time," Julien said.

"Just give me a second to do the hands-free thing," Genevieve said, switching her phone around. "All set."

"I wanted to give you an update," Julien said. "Whoever sent the emails is more sophisticated about covering his tracks than Melvin expected, so it's taking more time."

Genevieve fiddled with the cruise control, setting her speed slow enough to avoid a ticket but fast enough to keep her from being run off the road. Cruise control was a necessity; after years on congested LA freeways, the wide-open Texas roads tempted her to drive 90 mph.

"Well, that's disappointing," she said.

"I know. Maybe you should extend your trip, give Melvin more time."

"I'm supposed to fly back day after tomorrow," Genevieve said. "D always says I can stay as long as I want, but nobody really wants a houseguest for more than a couple days, do they?"

"Seems like you two could pop some popcorn and have a Brad Pitt movie marathon."

"Oh, stop it," Genevieve said, but she was laughing. It felt good to laugh.

"I have an update for you, too," she said. "I read up on French wills. They're archived by the name of the notary, which is why they're complicated to research."

"What kind of crazy system is that?"

"These are your people, not mine," Genevieve said. "Anyway, we're going to need the address where they lived. I think you have to search by arrondissement."

"Listen to you. Your French accent isn't so bad."

Genevieve smiled. "Thank you."

"A *little* Texan, maybe," Julien said. "I can get the address – they owned the same building for forever. What else will we need?"

"To get records less than 100 years old, you'll have to prove you're a direct descendant, so you'll need your birth certificate, your mother's birth certificate and probably her death certificate."

"No problem."

"Here comes the part that might be a problem," Genevieve said. "I priced hiring researchers."

She gave him the range, figures she'd found so shocking she'd spent two hours verifying them.

"Whoa."

"I know. When I get to D's, I'll email you the links. Maybe you can call them and negotiate a better price. I didn't think I'd get very far with my Texas-accented French."

"At those prices, we should just fly to Paris and do it ourselves," Julien said. "Is your passport up to date?"

"I'm sure Henry's *totally* going to go for that," she said, laughing.

"I can be very persuasive," Julien said.

"Here's another avenue," Genevieve said. "After the war, what happened with the gallery? It never reopened?"

"Not that I know of."

"Was anything ever recovered from the pre-war inventory?"

"No idea," Julien said. "Where are you going with this?"

"Well, I think I told you that the Nazis had several looting efforts underway, and one outfit was the ERR, which was in charge of confiscating Jewish property. A lot of the stuff it took ended up at Neuschwanstein, in Germany."

"So you want to tack on a trip to Germany after Paris?"

"Oh yeah, let's do the Grand Tour," Genevieve said. "No, seriously, the U.S. set up a bureaucracy to deal with all the cultural artifacts. The 'Monuments Men,' they were called during the war. There might be something useful in the records."

"That sounds like a great idea," Julien said. "But please tell me you aren't working the whole time you're there."

"As if D would let me get away with that."

Julien laughed. "How did you two end up best friends, anyway?"

Genevieve started telling him the story, he asked a few questions, and before she knew it, 50 miles had flown past.

◻

Two more days in D's company proved to be just about the right amount. Genevieve persuaded her to go to the sculpture museum, which D pronounced "not as boring as it sounded," and in return, Genevieve allowed herself to be dragged to the mall for new underwear and, yes, a push-up bra.

When she retrieved her car at LAX, it still retained the faint smell of lavender left behind by the thorough post-dead-fish scrubbing. It was almost as if the whole thing had never happened.

But it had, of course. A couple days of drinking wine and shopping and nodding along at D's proposed romance stratagems didn't change the fact that Genevieve had a complicated project to sort out. And the Lazare research was, in many ways, the least of her problems.

A reminder was waiting when she got home, propped up on her bar: a manila envelope from Thomas.

Genevieve left her suitcase in the living room and sat at the bar to open the envelope.

Mona jumped onto the adjacent bar stool and rubbed her head against Genevieve's elbow, purring.

"Yeah, don't think you get off so easy," Genevieve said.

She tipped the envelope upside-down on the bar. Out fell a few sheets of folded paper and a plastic bag containing the gold pendant.

She unfolded the note from Thomas.

Gen:

Hope you had a swell time with D and she didn't hook you up with any rednecks. Mona was a good kitty and did not try to bolt once.

Here is your pendant with a copy of the long-winded, overly complicated analysis I got from my friend.

Short version: Florentine in origin, mid-1800s.
He has a couple theories on the craftsman
(read note for details). He thinks it matches the
necklace in the photos but doesn't want to say
that 100 percent without more time to study.
To answer your question, he doesn't think it's a
fake, but if it is, he is certain no one could find
a replica this good in the short time frame you
describe.
You didn't ask for an appraisal and he didn't give
one, but I get the impression this thing ought to
be in a safe-deposit box, not a Ziploc.
Your landlord left a note on your door, said he
was working on the lights. Hope that makes
sense to you.
Call me when you get home.
xo,
Thomas

Well, if Julien Brooks *had* dropped a piece of jewelry in her apartment to mess with her head, at least he'd gone with the real thing, not a replica.

Genevieve checked the time. It was only 10:30. She would leave Thomas a message on his cell phone, and maybe he'd call her on his lunch break.

She was surprised when Thomas picked up.

"I was just going to leave you a message to call me back when you can," Genevieve said. "I know you don't like to talk at work."

"I'm not at work," Thomas said. His voice was small and quiet.

"Are you home sick?"

"I'm home. I'm not sick. Exactly. We're having a... Oh, Gen, I think Philip's going to lose his job."

"Oh no! Thomas! What's going on?"

"I can't believe this is happening," Thomas said, his voice cracking. "Someone sent an email to Philip's boss saying that he's gay."

"Wait a minute," Genevieve interrupted. "His boss didn't know that?"

"It's been kind of a don't-ask, don't-tell deal. Philip has to go to a meeting with his boss tomorrow. He's with a lawyer right now to find out about his options."

"But they can't actually fire him, can they?"

"I think they can, because the hospital is technically affiliated with a church."

Genevieve had never heard her friend sound so defeated.

"Thomas, I'm so sorry. Why would anyone send an email like that?"

"I have no idea. Just to be malicious? This is just the worst week ever," Thomas said. "Bill the security guard is in a coma, did I tell you that? I tried to call for an update this morning, but only Malcolm's allowed to give out information, and he's at an offsite meeting all day."

"How can I help you and Philip? If he's brushing up his résumé just in case, I could proofread it," Genevieve said, desperate to do something helpful.

"I'll tell him, but he's just like you. He doesn't like to ask for help. He wouldn't even let me go to the meeting with the lawyer," Thomas said. "He's going to shut everybody out and make us stand around helplessly and watch him suffer."

Genevieve gulped. "Is that what I do?"

"Oh, Gen, I'm sorry," Thomas said. "That came out wrong. Don't listen to me. I'm having a really bad day."

Genevieve wheeled her suitcase into her bedroom to unpack and start her laundry, but her mind kept returning to what Thomas said. Did she shut people out? Cut herself off, as her father put it? What had D said? That she needed to start playing to win instead of playing not to lose?

When Julien called around 11 – "just checking in," he said – she surprised herself by inviting him over.

"I need to show you some things I've been working on," she told him.

Genevieve's regret set in almost as soon as she hung up. What was she going to show him? What part of this could she hope to explain?

She'd start with her mother's interest in David Lazare, she decided. She had her mother's notebooks, and she could tell Julien what Christine had said. Documentation and an eyewitness account – if only this were a question of provenance, she'd be on solid ground.

She read over the expert's pages regarding the pendant. Thomas was right; his friend was a windbag. Still, that was more documentation. She scanned the pages into her computer and printed a copy for Julien.

She straightened up her apartment and gave Mona an extra helping of food as a bribe to behave.

Then she brushed her hair, freshened up her makeup and changed into a knee-length black skirt, white T-shirt and soft gray cardigan. Her theory: If she was about to say something that sounded crazy, it was best to look as presentable as possible.

Julien knocked on her door right on time, and when she answered, he offered her a huge smile and a latte.

"You must have caught the first flight this morning," he said. "Figured you could use some caffeine."

"Good call," Genevieve said, taking the cup and ushering him in.

Julien scanned the room. "Where's the cat from hell?"

"Asleep on my bed in an induced food coma," Genevieve said. "But she's not really so awful. You saw her on a bad day."

Julien raised an eyebrow. "If you say so."

Genevieve steered him toward the bar, where she'd set up folders with the various things she wanted to show him.

"I talked to Melvin," Julien said. "He said he thinks the fish might be easier to trace than the emails."

He settled onto a chair, unbuttoned his cuffs and rolled up his sleeves. His shirt had alternating stripes of olive-gray and camel that brought out the warm tones in his skin. He had a great eye for choosing colors that flattered him, she'd noticed, yet he never gave the impression of being a clotheshorse.

Genevieve rounded the bar into the kitchen. "You want water or anything?"

"I'm good," Julien said. "I'm glad you wanted to get together today, because I have something to tell you, too, and I *really* wanted to tell you in person."

She'd never seen Julien this ebullient. It made her nervous.

Julien pushed out the other bar stool with his foot. "Sit."

Genevieve sat.

"I talked to Henry this morning about how expensive researchers in France are. I had to listen to him go on about the French work ethic and two-hour lunch breaks." He made a yap-yap-yap gesture with his hand.

"But here's the important part: I told him, 'Henry, for that kind of money, you should send Genevieve to Paris, because you *know* she's going to work hard.' And he said, 'You are right about that.'

"So, there you go. The idea is planted. He didn't say yes, but he didn't say no." Julien beamed at her. "Now, what did you want to tell me?"

CHAPTER TWENTY

SOME OF WHAT I'm going to tell you will sound crazy," Genevieve began. "But please just let me get to the end."

"Sure," Julien said, settling back in his chair.

"OK, last week, my mom's college roommate called me from Chicago, and... Wait. Maybe that's not the best place to start."

Genevieve thought for a moment. "Oh, actually, it's as good a place as any. Christine called me, and I told her about this project, and she said that freshman year, my mom talked about Galerie de l'Étoile and David Lazare."

"Really? How did she know about my family?"

"I don't know," Genevieve said. "Christine didn't know."

"Oh! I get it," Julien said. "You think somebody sent you the gallery catalog because they knew about this thing with your mom?"

Genevieve had been so preoccupied with other things that this connection hadn't occurred to her.

"I don't know," she said. "Maybe."

"I was supposed to listen, and I've already interrupted you," Julien said, gesturing for her to continue. "I'm sorry. Go on."

"Christine told me that my mom kept kind of a journal, and she thought maybe I would find some answers there.

That's one of the reasons I went back to Texas, to see if I could find these journals."

Julien's expression was mildly puzzled, nothing more. So far, so good. Genevieve prepared herself for the harder part.

"My mom, um, she... she went to this women's college in Pennsylvania, and she was only there a year. Well, not even a year. She had a breakdown and left school. And, um, she struggled with what they thought were mental health issues and... I told you, I guess, that she died in a fire, but, um, I didn't tell you that it was ruled a suicide."

"Wow. That's awful," Julien said. "I'm sorry."

His expression was kind, but Genevieve could tell he couldn't quite figure out where she was going with this.

"Christine told me my mom was sort of fixated on David Lazare. When I went through her notebooks, there was a lot of stuff about him, including a sketch."

Genevieve opened the folder that held her mother's notebooks and turned to the sketch.

"That's pretty amazing," Julien said. "I guess she must have done it from a photo? Where did she get a photo, I wonder?"

Genevieve closed the notebook and placed her palm on the cover. She didn't want Julien to start leafing through it and see her mother's frantic scribbling. Grace McKenna had been dead for a quarter-century, but Genevieve still felt protective.

"Christine described several instances where she would wake up and my mom would be missing from their room. My mom describes those times as incidents where she..." Genevieve paused here to take a drink of her latte. "My mom believed that she was physically in, um, another place and time. Like, the 1940s. Where she, um, at some point encountered your uncle."

"Whoa."

"I know, it sounds crazy," Genevieve said. "But it would account for how she could draw such a good likeness of him."

Julien's eyes widened. "Genevieve, you don't really think that."

"At some point, my mom became consumed with trying to warn David that his life was in danger. She believed she could save him."

"That's a sign of what? Schizophrenia?"

"According to my dad, the doctors then said she had grandiose delusions. But by the time she died, they had diagnosed a bunch of different things and tried different treatments. Like my dad said, it's not like there's a blood test or any definitive way to make a diagnosis."

Julien put his hand on her arm. "Genevieve, what happened to your mom is really sad, and I'm sorry you went through that. But I don't see where this is going."

Genevieve fiddled with the folder where she'd placed the pendant, stalling for time. If she stopped here, Julien would think she'd over-shared about her mother's illness, nothing more. Would that be so bad?

Why had she chosen Julien Brooks as her confidante, anyway? Why not her father or Christine? She told herself that she was trying to spare them painful memories of the difficult path they'd traveled with her mother, but was that really true?

She'd just spent several days with D, her best friend, a woman who knew everything there was to know about every pharmaceutical on the market. Even with a crisis of his own at home – actually, two crises now – Thomas would try to help if she asked.

But no, she had chosen Julien, who was now watching her, waiting.

Genevieve turned her chair to face him head-on.

"A few weeks ago, I had a weird... Well, I thought it was a dream. No. I should back up. First I had the strange thing that happened at the casino. You saw that."

Julien frowned. He didn't like where this was going.

"I had this sensation of things sort of sliding out of focus and this bright light above me, and then it was like... I snapped back to where I was. Then it happened again later that night. The light was the same, and I was..."

She paused. She would not tell him that she was naked.

"I was in a room with bright sunlight streaming in, and I was looking at a bare wood floor, and my sense was that I was holding a pose. For an artist. Like I said, I thought at first that it was a dream, although it didn't exactly feel like a dream."

Julien sat up straighter and crossed his arms. Not a good sign.

"It happened again a few days after that. It was the same room, same light. A man was holding my arm and trying to force my hand open, to take something, and I wouldn't do it. I heard something clatter to the floor, and I looked down, and I saw this glint of something gold."

Genevieve pushed up the sleeve of her sweater. "A couple days later, I noticed these bruises." The marks had faded to a sour yellow.

"Then Mona was batting around something on the floor, and I swept behind the sofa, and I found this."

She pulled out the plastic bag holding the gold pendant.

"It was right after you'd been to my apartment, that night we had Thai food, and at first I thought you put it there, because I'd seen you looking at the watercolor."

"Why would I..."

Genevieve didn't let him finish his question. "I thought maybe you were trying to mess with my head. So I asked my friend Thomas to find someone who knows jewelry to take a look."

She pushed the copies of the academic's notes toward him. "He says it's Florentine in origin, mid-1800s. It's not a knockoff. I looked at it against the photos, and I think it's the pendant those generations of Lazare brides wore, the one your mother told you Théodore Lazare originally bought."

Julien opened his mouth to say something, then stopped.

"When I was at my dad's house, he went out while I was going through my mom's stuff. I was looking at the notebooks, and at first none of it made sense, and then I got to the sketch. I felt everything sort of start to slide, and then I felt like I was somewhere else, it was nighttime, and someone was there next to me, and I was scared, and there were voices. They sounded German. They moved away, and then it was like the clouds cleared and moonlight streamed in and I could see that it was the same room. The man said one thing to me, he said, 'Neuschwanstein,' which is why I think maybe some of your family's stuff was sent there."

The words had poured out in a rush. Genevieve paused and took a deep breath.

"And then I sort of came back to myself. I was back in my old bedroom. I went out to talk to my dad, and he asked me where I'd gone. He said he came home from the store and looked for me and I was gone. And later that night, on the floor in the room, I found this."

Genevieve pushed the handkerchief across the bar toward Julien. His silence unnerved her, and she began to fumble through the assembled folders.

"I made copies of the notes from the academic who looked at the pendant," she said. "Here, those are for you. And the pendant – I think that belongs with you, obviously. I didn't have time to copy my mom's journals, and I don't really want to let those go, but I can do that tomorrow maybe, and..."

Julien gathered up all the papers she shoved at him, squared the corners, and tucked them into one of the folders. He took the pendant from the plastic bag and dropped it into the breast pocket of his shirt.

"Is that everything?"

His tone struck Genevieve as cool, almost amused.

"I guess so. Yes."

"OK, then." He stood.

"OK then?"

"Look," he said, "I don't know who put this whole idea together, but I have to hand it to you, except for the last 15 minutes or so, you people are pretty good."

Genevieve stood, alarmed. "What do you mean?"

"I'm kind of surprised you got past Henry, because he said he vetted you before he hired you, and he's as cynical as they come," Julien said.

He ran his palm along his jaw, grinned ruefully.

"But I'll admit it, you suckered me pretty good. You people did your homework. Put you in my path in Vegas and knew what to hit me with: gorgeous woman, smart, funny, a little bit vulnerable. Geez, even a redhead. Did you know, or was that just luck?"

He looked Genevieve up and down. "Wait, are you really a redhead?"

Genevieve recoiled as if she'd been slapped.

Julien crossed the room in a few long strides, the folder tucked under his arm.

He stopped at the door. "It's a pretty good con. You even managed to get *me* to come up with the idea of sending *you* to Paris. And then I guess you'd find new leads to pursue so you could keep billing us, huh? But you lost me with the time-travel thing, or reincarnation, or whatever it is. I don't believe in that science-fiction crap."

CHAPTER TWENTY-ONE

AFTER JULIEN LEFT, Genevieve curled up on her bed, still in her clothes. Mona gave her the evil eye but grudgingly made room.

Genevieve stared at the wall, thinking about her mother.

She always said the only thing she remembered about her mother was sitting on the sofa after school, leafing through art books.

But that was a lie – a lie she told others, a lie she told herself.

She remembered afternoons when her mother would retreat to her bedroom and close the door. Genevieve's father would come home from work and ask, "Where's your mom?" Genevieve, engrossed in a *Brady Bunch* rerun, would just shrug and point.

She remembered whispered, urgent phone conversations and then her grandmother would arrive, cheerful and bustling, to pack Genevieve's suitcase. She remembered going into her parents' darkened bedroom to say goodbye to the woman curled up on the bed. Sometimes her mother would squeeze Genevieve's hand and say, "Sorry, baby. Be good for Grandma."

What had her mother believed, in the end? Did she see herself as a person with an unusual ability, misunderstood and persecuted?

Or did she think that the doctors were right, that she was delusional?

And which would be worse?

Did she wish, as Genevieve did, that she'd never mentioned anything to anyone?

What was done was done. Genevieve had learned her lesson.

Julien Brooks, she vowed, would be both the first and last person she would share this secret with.

But what to do now?

Obviously, her contract with the Lazare descendants was finished. Would Henry demand she return the money he'd paid so far? She could make a case that she'd earned it. She'd done the preliminary legwork and put together a blueprint another researcher could follow. But if he wanted his money back, she wouldn't fight him. Her Hilliard severance check would arrive soon; she could use that to pay Henry back.

Then what? What probably made the most sense, she realized, was moving back to Texas. D would let her stay in the guest room as long as she needed, and there always seemed to be jobs in Texas, albeit at minimum wage. Selling Monet posters and Mondrian mouse pads in a museum gift shop wasn't the best use of her master's degree, but she wouldn't starve.

How would she explain to D what had happened, though? To her father? To Thomas?

It was too overwhelming to think about. Genevieve closed her eyes.

□

Her phone woke her around 4 p.m. She wandered out to the living room to find it and checked the display. It was Thomas.

She let the call go to voicemail, powered the phone off and went back to bed.

When she woke up again, her apartment was dark. Genevieve turned on the lamp and checked the time. It was nearly 8:30.

She briefly considered changing into her PJs and turning in for the night. But she was hungry – her last meal had been a muffin at the Dallas airport.

Genevieve got up, moved a load of clothes from the washer to the dryer, fed Mona again and grabbed her laptop. She was thinking pizza rather than Thai.

Sitting cross-legged on the bed, she debated whether to check her work email. Would Henry Lazare fire her via email, or would he call? She decided not to check; what was the point in finding out she was fired at 8:30 at night? It could wait until morning.

Instead, she clicked over to check her personal email to see whether there was anything from Thomas. She felt bad about avoiding him. Not bad enough to turn her phone back on and call him – she wasn't ready for contact with the world just yet. But she did want to see whether he'd sent an update about Philip's situation.

There was nothing from Thomas, just the usual spam and an email from *NoJumpingFromBridge,* which was the name of her neighbor's band.

Genevieve opened that one, thinking it would be an update about the lights along the driveway, perhaps an apology for turning them off. But no – her neighbor said he was in Cleveland on tour, an important package had been delivered to his house, and could Genevieve please retrieve it and hold it in her apartment until he came home? He didn't want it to sit on the porch overnight.

She hit the reply button, intending to tell her neighbor no, she would not retrieve a package. But he'd helped her and Philip maneuver her sofa into the apartment while Thomas called out unhelpful instructions, and he'd once knocked on her door to let her know she'd left the Camry's lights on.

She hit the cancel button.

Sighing, she put on shoes and grabbed her keys.

It was a moonless night, and Genevieve carefully picked her way down the driveway in the dark. The wind was up, and she shivered, wishing she'd grabbed her jean jacket.

A palm frond skittered down the street, which was empty. Whenever she went back to Texas, Genevieve got a lot of comments about the glitz and glamour of LA, but her little corner of it was pretty quiet at night.

She cut across the lawn and up to the neighbor's porch, scanning for signs of a package. There was nothing. No package, no sticky note from the delivery company, nothing but a Chinese takeout menu rubber-banded to the doorknob.

She pulled that off with a satisfying thwack and stomped across the lawn and then back up the driveway, composing in her head the email she would send to her neighbor, who A) inconsiderately interfered with the outside lights – in defiance of the landlord's directives, which B) compromised her safety and then C) asked her to retrieve a package, which D) he hadn't even bothered to verify had arrived. Said email would contain many bullet points, she decided, and make her neighbor feel very, very bad.

It wasn't until she got to the gate for her courtyard that she noticed the light above her door – which was on a timer – was dark.

Before she could process that, a man grabbed her from behind, one arm wrapped around her chest, the other hand clamping over her mouth before she'd even formed the thought to scream.

Frantically, she tried to remember what she'd learned in the self-defense class she and D took in college. Was this the Bear Hug or the Rear Neck Grab? Was she supposed to sink her weight or turn and strike?

The man began dragging her backward, and Genevieve's instincts took over. Her left arm was pinned, but her right was free. She opened her mouth and bit down on the man's hand as hard as she could. In that first startled moment, he relaxed his grip just a little, and she drove her elbow back into him.

She knew she was supposed to aim for his windpipe or his groin, but it was dark, and she had no idea how tall he was. She was fighting blind. She did a half-turn, hoping to get enough of an angle to drive her fist – and her keys – into his groin, but he was ready for that. He grabbed a handful of her hair and yanked, causing her to yelp in pain.

He wrapped his arm around her throat this time. She remembered the self-defense instructor's grim face as he described a woman's limited options against the Choke Hold.

She tried jabbing her keys against the man's thigh, but it had no effect. He began to drag her again; it appeared he planned to take her into the brush behind the apartment.

If only she'd had the Camry's alarm fixed! Then she at least could have hit the alarm button on her car key, which might have attracted someone's attention.

With reserves of strength she didn't know she had, Genevieve drove her keys again into the man's leg, bit his hand, twisted in his grasp, anything to gain room to maneuver. In the struggle, she dropped her keys.

He tightened his arm around her throat, and Genevieve saw a bright light.

So this is how it ends, she thought.

But then the man turned, and she realized that the bright light was a pair of car headlights climbing her driveway. Genevieve could hear the engine coming up the grade.

The man flung her against the courtyard wall and took off around the corner of her building as Julien's silver Audi appeared.

Genevieve's head hit the corner of the concrete wall with an audible crack, and she immediately felt a warm trickle down her neck. She put her right hand up to stanch the flow and sank to the ground.

Julien jumped out of the car, leaving the door open, and ran toward her.

As he stood over her, illuminated from behind by the light from his car, she raised her left hand in supplication.

"Please don't hurt me."

□

"I'm not going to hurt you. Wait here."

He ran around the corner of the building but returned quickly. "No sign of him. Let's get you inside."

"I dropped my keys," Genevieve said.

"OK, hang on." Julien pulled out his phone and began to use it as a flashlight, sweeping it around the pavement near her. The light passed over a spot of blood, paused, came back. Julien brought the light up to her face.

"Shit."

"I hit my head," Genevieve said. "I think it's bleeding? Maybe a lot?"

"It's going to be OK." Julien looked around, then began unbuttoning his shirt, the same one Genevieve had admired earlier that day. He shrugged out of the shirt, balled it up and handed it to her. "Use that," he said.

Genevieve accepted the shirt wordlessly and pressed it to her head.

Stripped down to his T-shirt and jeans, Julien walked a circle around her, then reversed course, expanding the perimeter. "Maybe the keys are in your purse? He took it, right?"

"I didn't have it. He was dragging me that way, around the back..."

Julien stopped, shook his head. "What am I doing?"

He raised his phone and dialed 911. He gave her address to the dispatcher. "The woman who lives here, a man grabbed her outside her apartment. He... Hang on."

Crouching next to her, Julien looked her in the eyes. "Genevieve, can you describe him? Clothes, hair color, anything?"

"No. I didn't see him at all. He was behind me."

"She didn't see him," Julien said into the phone. "I only got a glimpse. Dark shirt, dark pants... No idea. I couldn't see. Maybe 5-11? A little stocky."

Julien stood and scanned the area. "He ran... northeast, I think. Yeah, northeast." He listened for a few beats. "Yeah. OK."

He scrolled through his phone and dialed another number.

"I'm at Genevieve's. A guy just tried to drag her..."

Julien paused, listened. "No, I didn't follow... She hit her head and she's bleeding. She dropped her keys and we can't... I can't tell... Uh-huh. The one by the door? OK."

He ended the call and dropped back down into a crouch next to Genevieve.

"I called the police and Melvin. If we can't find the keys in the next couple minutes, I'm going to break a window and we'll get in and see what's up with your head, OK? Just hang on a minute." He patted her knee. "You doing OK?"

Clutching his shirt to her head, Genevieve peered up at him. "Why are you here?"

"Let's find those keys," Julien said.

Genevieve watched as he walked back and forth, sweeping the phone's light on the ground before him. Her head was throbbing, and her thoughts were jumbled.

What had just happened? And what was Julien Brooks doing at her apartment?

It was all too confusing. Genevieve closed her eyes.

She heard a jingling sound and opened them again. Julien was standing over her, keys in hand.

"Success," he said. "How do you feel about standing up?"

Genevieve braced one hand against the wall behind her and began to rise.

"Go slow," Julien said, taking her elbow.

They made their way carefully, crunching through broken glass from the light over her door. Julien flipped through her key ring with one hand, keeping the other on her arm to steady her.

"It's the one with the square head," she said. "What are you doing here? You think I'm a con artist."

Julien fitted the key into the lock, and the door swung open.

"Yeah, about that," he said. "I was wrong."

Mona took one look at them and raced into the bedroom, skidding as she took the corner.

"Let's look at your head in good light," Julien said. "Maybe the bathroom?"

Her knees sagged a little when Genevieve saw herself in the mirror. Blood had soaked the top of her cardigan and splattered over her chest. Her neck was smeared red.

Julien caught her elbow and met her eyes in the mirror. "Are you lightheaded or just reacting to the blood?"

"There's a lot of it."

"Hang onto the sink with your other hand there," he said. "You're not going to fall, OK? I'm right here."

That was true. Even with the bathroom door open, they had less than three feet to maneuver in.

Julien took off his watch and tucked it into the pocket of his jeans. Reaching around her, he turned on the water, pumped soap into his hands and washed them. He grabbed a clean towel and washcloth from the rack behind him and threw them over his shoulder. Slowly, he peeled away the shirt she'd been holding to her head and dropped it to the floor.

Genevieve watched in the mirror as he took her head in his hands and gently tilted it side to side.

"What made you decide you were wrong? About me?"

"Let's tackle one thing at a time," Julien said, "I need to figure out where the blood's coming from, but it's matted in your hair, and your hair's so thick, it's hard to see your scalp."

He tilted her head forward, so that Genevieve was staring down at the sink. "We need to rinse the blood out so I can see what I'm doing."

"Kitchen sink would work better," Genevieve said. "We can use the sprayer."

With an assist from Julien, Genevieve shed her blood-soaked cardigan and grabbed a towel to wrap around her shoulders.

In the kitchen, she bent awkwardly over the sink, her hair falling forward. Julien tested the water temperature, the muscled forearms she'd admired so many times now just inches from her face. She closed her eyes.

"Let me know if it's too hot."

Wielding the sprayer with his right hand, he slowly worked his left hand through her hair, rinsing away the blood.

Under different circumstances, Genevieve thought, it might have been sensual.

Then the spray found the laceration on her head, and she winced.

"Oh, there it is." Julien rested his hand on the back of her neck.

He turned off the water and gently pulled her hair aside with both hands. "It's not so bad, actually. Still bleeding a little, but that might be from the water. It's not deep – you don't need stitches."

He held a washcloth to her head, and when he was satisfied the bleeding had stopped, he washed the cut. Then he dabbed it with antibiotic ointment he found in her medicine chest, chiding her because it was past its expiration date.

Genevieve was blotting her wet hair with a towel when someone knocked on her door.

"That'll be the cops," Julien said.

CHAPTER TWENTY-TWO

I T WASN'T THE POLICE at her door. It was Melvin. When she saw him, Genevieve picked up her laptop, walked to her bedroom and loudly closed the door. She still hadn't forgiven him for trying to confiscate her computer.

She flipped the lock on the door and stripped out of her damp, bloodstained T-shirt. Blood had soaked her bra, too. Disgusted, she took that off, and then her skirt. At least it was black – she had some hope of salvaging it.

She felt strangely numb. What she really wanted to do was put on her flannel PJ pants and a tank top, pull the covers over her head and go to sleep. Instead, she changed into a tee from a long-ago Lyle Lovett show and her most faded jeans, and topped the whole ensemble with a ratty Texas Tech hoodie, size XL, that she'd liberated from a boyfriend's closet in college.

The next step would be dealing with the bloody laundry. Before she could contemplate it, though, came a tentative knock on her door.

"You OK?" Julien asked.

She sighed. "Just changing clothes. Be right out."

Genevieve blotted her hair again and ran the towel over her face before tossing it on the sodden heap of clothes.

She found Julien cleaning the counter with anti-bacterial wipes he'd found under the sink. She stood for a moment watching his shoulders move under his T-shirt as he worked his way around her small kitchen.

"Oh, good, I was going to suggest you wrap up in something warm," he said when he saw her. "Melvin's outside taking a look around. I know he's not your favorite, but he's going to want you to walk him through what happened. You feel up to answering questions?"

"I will if you will." Genevieve was a little surprised at how pugnacious she sounded, but Julien took it with good grace.

"Fair enough," he said. "I am really sorry about earlier."

Genevieve pulled out a bar stool and sat.

"I was just about to suggest that," Julien said.

"So, you realized you were wrong when..." she said, gesturing for him to continue.

Julien leaned back against the counter. "Do you want to get into this right now? I'm a little worried you're in shock."

"I would rather talk about this than think about what just happened," Genevieve said. "Humor me."

"OK," he said, shrugging. "I called Henry before I hit the bottom of your driveway, all 'where did you find this woman, what do we know about her?' " Julien made a stern face.

"He said you were recommended by someone he trusted, that Melvin had vetted you and his assistant could send me the file. Then he put his assistant on. I hate it when he does that."

Genevieve frowned. "Who recommended me?"

"He didn't say. You don't know?"

"No idea."

"I was on the phone with Henry's assistant, and I was stuck in traffic, and I asked her to look up this academic. I figured you – or somebody – made him up. But he really exists. Then I thought, he's either in on the scam, or he's just some schmuck whose name is being used and he ought to be warned. So I called him."

"The guy Thomas contacted?"

"Right. Who went on for 20 minutes about Florentine craftsmanship. Totally sincere. And I thought, 'They're scamming this guy too.' "

Julien stopped his narrative and watched Genevieve. "You look pale," he said. He looked at her hands, which were resting on the bar. "Your hands are shaking."

"I'm hungry. I was getting ready to call for a pizza before this happened."

"When's the last time you ate?"

"I had a muffin at the airport in Dallas."

Julien opened her refrigerator, his face registering surprise at its contents. "Which was how long ago?"

Genevieve thought about it. "I don't know. I can't do the math."

Julien banged the refrigerator door shut and moved on to her cabinets, opening and closing them.

"Don't bother," she said. "There's nothing here."

"Seriously?" Shaking his head, Julien crossed back to the fridge, pulled out a carton of orange juice and checked the date. "Expired yesterday. Probably won't kill you." He found a glass and poured for her. "Drink that," he said.

"In my defense, I have been out of town," Genevieve said. She sipped the juice. "So you talked to the pendant guy."

"Right, and when I got home, the file from Henry's office was waiting in my email. So he did do the homework. I was at my computer, thinking... thinking... And I realized I still had the pendant in my shirt pocket.

"I blew the old wedding photos way up, and it did look like the same necklace. So then I'm thinking, well, she saw the photos, and then they had a good replica made."

"Except the guy says it's not a replica."

"Yeah," Julien said. "There's this jeweler in Beverly Hills, my parents used them for everything, and I... well, anyway... They're kind of the family jeweler. So I ran the pendant up there, and they're not experts on Florentine craftsmen, but they know what's old and what isn't, and what's real and what isn't. They say it's the real deal.

"I'm driving home from there thinking, 'what other thread can I pull, because I just have to find the right one to make the whole story unravel,' " Julien said. "So I called your mother's old roommate."

Genevieve nearly spewed orange juice across the kitchen. "How did you find her?"

"You said her name, Christine," Julien said. "I went through the file Henry sent, and I found a Christine Jensen in Chicago you used as a reference for your first apartment in LA, a lease you signed with Peter somebody."

Genevieve blanched.

"Melvin *is* a private detective," Julien said. "I told Christine who I was, and I got basically the same story you told me. And then I felt like a total shit."

He stopped there. "That's not an easy story to tell, and I accused you of making it up. That was heartless, and I promise you, I'm not heartless."

"No, I don't think you are."

She'd met Julien Brooks less than a month before – how could she know that? But she believed it.

"I tried calling to apologize, but it kept going to voicemail. I figured you were ignoring me, and I didn't blame you. But then

Melvin called. He'd managed to track the guy who sent the last email a little bit online, and he is into some sick, scary stuff."

"Scary how?"

Julien didn't answer. "I started thinking about you not answering your phone for hours, and what Melvin told me about this guy, and I got a bad feeling." He shrugged. "The next thing I knew, I was in my car."

"I'm lucky you got here when you did," Genevieve said.

The short-term physical and emotional anesthetic that adrenaline provided had begun to wear off, and she started to cry. "If you hadn't showed up..."

"But I did." Julien started around the bar toward her. "And you're..."

A knock interrupted him, and Julien rerouted to the front door. "Will you please talk to Melvin? He's trying to help."

Genevieve recounted everything for Melvin. She even fetched her laptop so he could see the email that had sent her to the neighbor's porch.

Melvin suspected someone had spoofed her neighbor's email address to lure her out.

He pressed her for details about her attacker, but Genevieve couldn't name a single physical characteristic.

She propped her elbow on the bar and rested her head on her hand, tired to the bone. "I'm going to have to go through this all again with the police, aren't I?"

Julien pulled his watch from his pocket and checked it. "Where *are* the police? I called them an hour and a half ago."

"Let me make a call," Melvin said, stepping outside.

He was back a few minutes later. "Dispatch coded the call as a failed purse-snatching." He held up a hand to forestall

Julien's protest. "I know. Bottom line, they're not going to get anybody out here tonight."

"Well, that's just great," Julien said.

"Budget cuts," Melvin said with an air of resignation. He exchanged a look with Julien. "Did you tell her what I found online?"

"General outline," Julien said. "Not details."

"Would you two stop talking over my head? I've already been in a choke hold tonight," Genevieve said. "How much worse can whatever you found online be?"

Julien pulled out the other bar stool and sat.

"Let's start with what I found tonight: a path through the brush behind your building, going up the hillside," Melvin said. "I'd say somebody's been spending some time up there, watching you."

Genevieve dropped her head into her hands.

"I don't like this apartment," Melvin said. "No alarm, the security lights inoperable, all this brush where someone can hide."

"You still haven't told me what you found," she said. "This afternoon?"

Melvin and Julien exchanged another look, and Julien nodded.

"I shadowed him online for a bit," Melvin said. "In the time I observed him, he looked at sports websites, porn and images of mutilated animals. The animals especially worry me. In police work, that's considered..."

Genevieve held up a hand to stop him. "I've heard enough."

"I don't know what the man who grabbed you tonight was after," Melvin said. "Maybe it was just a scare tactic, but I think we have to operate on the assumption that he meant you real harm. I don't believe you're safe here."

Genevieve's shoulders sagged.

"There's a hotel we use regularly when we need to park a client in a very secure environment," Melvin said.

"What about Mona?"

Melvin looked to Julien, clearly confused.

"The cat," Julien supplied helpfully. He turned to Genevieve. "What do you usually do? Did she go to Texas with you?"

"She stayed here, and Thomas fed her every day."

"So why not leave her here," Julien said, "and then we'll worry about the rest tomorrow?"

"Leave her here? With a guy who likes to mutilate animals watching my apartment?"

Realization dawned on Julien's face. "Well, what about one of those kennel places?"

"This late at night? I don't even know if they're open."

"Could your friend Thomas keep her for you?"

"His partner Philip is allergic."

Julien looked at Melvin, whose expression clearly said, "You're on your own, pal."

He ran his hand through his hair. "What if I took her to my house – just for tonight – and then we figure out a better plan tomorrow? She won't do anything disgusting, right?"

If she hadn't been so tired, Genevieve might have thrown her arms around him in gratitude. "What happened the other day was really out of character."

"I'll go make a call to the hotel," Melvin said.

CHAPTER TWENTY-THREE

TO GENEVIEVE'S RELIEF – and complete shock – Mona went into her carrier without protest.

"You're quiet," Julien said when they'd been on the road about 10 minutes. "Are you OK?"

"Just thinking," Genevieve said. "What would that guy..." She shivered. "You know what, I don't want to think about it. Please distract me."

"I'm glad you didn't need stitches in your head," Julien said. "I had to do that once, about 10 years ago. I was surfing, and..."

Julien's funny story about his surfing accident segued into a story about how he'd wrecked his knee playing pickup basketball, and soon they were pulling into his drive.

Genevieve took the cat carrier while Julien brought in a cardboard box with Mona's food and bowls.

"Hang a right," he said, closing the side door with his foot. "We'll set her up in my office."

Edging past the washer and dryer, Genevieve turned into a short hallway. The tile of the laundry room gave way to wood floors.

"Bathroom on your right," Julien said. "Office is the next door."

Genevieve glanced into the bathroom as she walked by. The floor was marble and the fixtures looked new. A dark blue towel hung precisely on the rack.

She followed the hallway's slight bend to the left and turned into the office. A long built-in worktable covered two of the walls, forming an L. There was a high-end Mac desktop, a laptop, a couple different printers and some other equipment Genevieve didn't recognize. Papers and sketchpads were stacked in an empty space between equipment. File cabinets were lined up under the worktable. On the wall opposite the door was a sofa upholstered in dark green fabric.

Julien kneed an expensive-looking office chair up against the worktable and put down the box of food.

Mona began to meow piteously. "I'll go get the litter and stuff from the car," Julien said.

Genevieve sat on the floor to unzip the cat carrier. Mona stuck her head out, sniffing the unfamiliar air. Sensing no immediate danger, she slunk out and climbed into Genevieve's lap. Genevieve buried her face in the cat's fur and closed her eyes, trying very hard not to think about the man outside her apartment.

"Genevieve?"

Julien was standing in the doorway. "I was thinking – do you want to stay here tonight? The couch pulls out."

Genevieve looked up at him and nodded.

"I'll get your suitcase and call Melvin."

Once Julien returned, she unpacked Mona's things and rolled her suitcase into the closet.

It was small, but shelves and racks made maximum use of the space. Sports gear took up most of it: a basketball, a wetsuit, and several pairs of running shoes in various states of wear. Crutches leaned against the back wall.

The stucco walls of Julien's office were painted terra cotta and bare except for a framed photograph of an empty white lifeguard's chair, which hung above the sofa. Genevieve squinted at the writing on the matte. "Cape Cod National Seashore, 2000."

She let herself out, shutting the door to keep Mona in, and went to look for Julien.

The hall was painted the same terra cotta and held more framed photos – all landscapes, no people. Genevieve wondered whether Julien had taken them.

A few steps down the hall was an open doorway to the living room. Ahead lay the door to what must be Julien's bedroom. She turned toward the living room, which she'd glimpsed before with its brown leather sofa and long wall of books and the giant TV.

The dining room was a small alcove off the living room. She'd seen Julien there one morning through the bay window, drinking his coffee. The table had elaborately carved feet, and against the wall was an old-fashioned sideboard of dark, heavy wood, a change from the clean lines in the rest of the house.

She heard the side door open, and Julien walked down the hall toward the office. He called her name.

"In here," she said.

Julien appeared from the hallway.

"You have a really great house," Genevieve said. "It's really..." She tried, and failed, to come up with an appropriate adjective.

"Thanks," Julien said. "Let's see about getting you something to eat."

"That would be great," Genevieve said. "Anything that delivers this late is fine. Chinese, pizza, I'm not picky."

Julien picked up one of the dining room chairs and carried it into the next room.

"Come in here," he said.

Genevieve followed him. They were in the kitchen, which was clearly the showpiece of the house.

The refrigerator was high-end stainless steel. The countertops were marble. Tall cabinets, painted white, flanked the sink. Through the glass fronts, Genevieve could see dishes neatly stacked.

Opposite the refrigerator was an ancient gas range. A rack full of expensive-looking pans hung above it.

"Wow," Genevieve said. "I think my grandmother had that stove."

"It's from the 1940s. It's original to the house," Julien said.

He pointed to the chair. "Sit there. Talk to me while I cook."

"You don't have to do that. Takeout's fine," Genevieve said.

Julien opened the refrigerator and surveyed its contents. "I like to cook."

He pulled a large pot down from the rack above the stove, then hesitated. "I'm thinking pasta. Please tell me you're not one of those weight-obsessed LA women who won't let carbs past her lips."

"I love pasta," Genevieve said. She glanced at the clock on the microwave. "But it's so late. You don't have to make all this work for yourself."

He ran water into the pot, put it on the stove and lit the flame. "Cooking for a beautiful woman is never too much work. I think that's an Italian proverb or something."

"Maybe, but you're cooking for a bedraggled woman," Genevieve said.

"Oh, it's not so bad," he said, making a show of looking her over. "You just have a little bump on the head. Venus de Milo is missing her arms, and men still think she's beautiful."

"That's because she's topless," Genevieve said. "They're looking at her breasts."

Julien laughed, and Genevieve suddenly felt better.

"Am I in the way here? I'd offer to help, but I'm useless in the kitchen."

Julien was at the counter, chopping something, his back to her. "You're fine. Red sauce OK? Do you eat meat?"

"I am a total carnivore."

He turned on another burner, pulled down a skillet and put chopped garlic and olive oil in the pan. A pungent odor soon filled the kitchen. "Why don't you cook?"

"My grandmother tried to teach me. She used to say she didn't know how I expected to get a husband if I couldn't fry chicken."

Julien smiled as he went to the refrigerator, then the pantry around the corner for more ingredients.

"That smells great," Genevieve said. "Where did you learn? Did your mom teach you?"

"My mom hated to cook."

He added sausage to the pan, broke it up with the back of a spoon and let it cook a bit before adding a can of chopped tomatoes.

"When I turned 21, I got a little bit of money my dad left me. After I finished college, I took it and went to Europe. I learned there."

"Oh, so you backpacked for a summer, stayed in hostels, that sort of thing?"

Genevieve had never known anyone who had actually done this. It wasn't really the sort of thing Texas Tech grads did, at least not in her era.

"Sort of, except I stayed for a year and a half," Julien said.

"I spent a lot of time in Italy and discovered I really liked cooking. I kept it up when I came home because..."

"It made you a hit with the ladies?"

Julien laughed knowingly, and Genevieve wondered how many women had perched on this chair while he made dinner.

While the sauce simmered and the pasta cooked, he told her a funny story about missing three consecutive trains to Milan because he was talking to a woman – but not the *same* woman. It kept Genevieve entertained and focused on something other than what had happened at her apartment earlier.

"Almost done here," he said, finally. "Does your head hurt? I'm wondering if it's safe for you to have wine." He tested the pasta.

"I'll take my chances," she said.

He bobbed his head at her. "Glasses are in the sideboard. Get one for me, too. This smells too good not to eat."

"Time to make myself useful?" Genevieve said, taking her chair back to the table. "This is an amazing sideboard."

"It was my mom's," Julien said. "And the table. It's the only furniture of hers I kept."

Genevieve poked her head around the corner. "These OK?" she asked, holding up two glasses.

Julien was at the sink draining pasta. He glanced over his shoulder. "Perfect."

"What else can I do?"

"Go sit," he said. "I'll be right there."

He came through the doorway a couple seconds later, two bowls of pasta balanced on one arm and a bottle of wine in the other hand. "Here, pour the wine," he said.

"You waited tables," she said, observing how he carried the food.

"Summers in college," he said, returning to the kitchen.

"You must have totally cleaned up on tips," Genevieve said.

Julien came back with cutlery, a wedge of Parmesan and a grater. "Why do you say that?"

"You have a lot of personality," she said. Then she surprised herself by adding, "And that smile."

On cue, he smiled, although more to himself than her. "Any waitressing on your résumé?"

"In grad school," she said. "I was too shy to really hustle tips. I'd get the orders right, be quick, and then I'd still get bad tips. My feelings would be *so* hurt."

He leaned back, opened a drawer of the sideboard and retrieved two napkins, handing her one. "You remind me of my high school girlfriend," Julien said. "She had that same shy thing, but totally smart and funny once you got to know her."

Genevieve took a bite of the pasta. "Oh God," she moaned. "This is really good."

"Better than takeout?"

She nodded, too busy eating to talk.

When she'd finished the first glass of wine, Julien poured her a second. About halfway through it, she put it down, suddenly feeling uncomfortable.

"What are we doing? Twelve hours ago you thought I was a con artist."

Julien frowned. "Genevieve, I said..."

She ignored his protest. "And you spent all afternoon, how did you put it? Pulling threads on my story, trying to find the one that would make it all unravel? And now I'm at your house eating dinner and... what? Pretending that didn't happen?"

Julien picked up her bowl and carried it to the kitchen. "I'm sorry. Earlier, it seemed like you wanted to be distracted. I'm trying to help."

"I appreciate that," Genevieve said. "But are you still trying to make the whole thing unravel?"

Returning to the dining room, Julien pulled out a chair and sat across from her.

"Do you believe me? Do you think I'm telling the truth?"

Julien looked her in the eye and took a long time answering.

"I think you believe you're telling the truth."

"That's not the same thing."

"No."

"So what does that mean? You think I'm delusional or something?"

"No," he said, shaking his head. "It's like in *The Matrix*, the part where..." He stopped. "You saw *The Matrix*, right?"

"I don't really like science fiction."

Julien began to laugh.

"What?"

"You don't see the irony?"

It was late, and she'd had a very bad day. "*You* don't like science fiction! Today at my apartment you called it crap!"

Julien checked his watch. "Yesterday, actually. I didn't say I didn't like it. I said I didn't *believe* it. But forget *The Matrix*, that's not the point. Here's the point: It's possible to suspend disbelief and hang with something because you want to see where the story goes. And that's how I feel. I want to see where the story goes."

CHAPTER TWENTY-FOUR

G ENEVIEVE WOKE UP slightly after 9 a.m., sore all over, with a hungry cat staring at her from Julien's worktable.

She fed Mona, then listened carefully. The house seemed quiet. Was Julien still asleep? As she started to open the door, she noticed the note slipped underneath.

Went to the gym. Help yourself in the kitchen.
Fresh juice in fridge.

She showered and dressed quickly. In the mirror, she noticed the beginning of a bruise on the side of her neck. Another was developing on her wrist. Her head was tender where she'd hit it, but washing her hair didn't reopen the cut. Her injuries could have been worse. In many ways, she'd been very lucky.

She was grateful when she got to the kitchen and saw that Julien had made coffee before he left. She poured herself a cup.

At first she didn't see any orange juice in the fridge, but then she spotted it: a small glass pitcher on the top shelf. By fresh, he meant fresh-squeezed. She poured a glass and took a sip. It was delicious.

She found skim milk and doctored her coffee. He also had two kinds of beer and an open bottle of white wine. On the top shelf were eggs and butter – French, by the look of the package. In the crisper, she found leaf lettuce, two other greens she didn't recognize, broccoli, apples, pears, oranges and carrots. The door rack held three kinds of mustard, club soda, tonic water, wasabi paste and capers. Wasabi paste? Capers?

She grabbed an apple and headed around the corner to scrutinize the pantry.

Four kinds of pasta. Three types of rice. Olive oil. Canola oil. Sesame oil. Five vinegars. More spices than she'd ever seen, including a few she'd never heard of. She found cereal and shut the pantry door, chastising herself for snooping.

She was pouring a bowl of cereal when she heard her cell phone in the other room. She dashed down the hall and picked it up on the third ring. It was Thomas.

"I'm sorry I didn't call you back yesterday," she said, carrying the phone to the kitchen. "What's happening with Philip? How did his meeting go?" Genevieve began hunting through the drawers for a spoon.

"He's suspended with pay for now."

"Can they do that?"

"The lawyer says yes," Thomas said.

"How's he doing?"

"He's not really saying. What's all that racket?"

"Oh, sorry," Genevieve said. "Looking for a spoon. I can't figure out where Ju..."

Genevieve stopped herself. "So, how are *you* holding up?"

"As well as can be expected," Thomas said. "Let's back up to the part where you can't figure out... what was the rest of that sentence?"

Genevieve filled him in on the previous day's happenings, or part of them, anyway, leaving out the confession that had prompted Julien to label her a con artist.

When she finished, Thomas was quiet for a long time. Then he said, "Do you want to come stay here? We can't have Mona, because she makes Philip sneeze, but you can stay on the sofa. It sounds like Mona's going to have to go to a kennel anyway."

Genevieve had been avoiding that thought. She'd boarded Mona once, when her apartment had to be tented for termites. Mona had come back with an upper respiratory infection that took two vet trips to clear up, and she'd been skittish for months afterward, hiding under the bed at any loud noise.

"Thomas, things are so tough for you right now, I don't want to impose."

When Julien returned from the gym, Genevieve was standing at the kitchen counter, finishing her cereal and staring out the window.

He was wearing a long-sleeved T-shirt and jeans, his hair still wet. He'd showered at the gym.

"Hey," he said. "Something wrong with the dining room?"

"What?"

"Eating standing up in the kitchen?"

"Oh. Sorry. I do that at home."

Genevieve turned from the window, empty bowl in hand.

Julien took it from her with one hand and gently brushed her hair away from her shoulder with the other. "You feeling OK? Your neck is bruised."

"I just talked to Thomas," she said, watching as Julien washed her bowl and spoon. "I could have done that."

"Don't worry about it," he said. "How's your friend?"

"It looks like his partner is losing his job. He offered to let me stay there, but things are clearly tense right now, and I do not want to be in the middle of that. They have really different styles of handling problems," she said.

"That'll get you every time," Julien said.

Genevieve wondered if he was speaking from personal experience.

Julien lifted the coffee pot, sniffed what was left, made a face and dumped the dregs down the sink. "You know, I was thinking, you could just skip the hotel and stay here."

"I don't want to inconvenience you," Genevieve said.

Julien put the coffee pot in the dish drainer and turned to face her, his arms crossed over his chest. "Actually, I feel better having you here where I can keep an eye on you. Seems safer."

"I feel safer here with you, too."

Genevieve knew she probably shouldn't admit it, but it was true. Despite everything that had happened the day before, she'd slept just fine knowing that Julien was only 20 feet away.

"I guess I'd better get to work finding a kennel for Mona, then," she said. "The last place I took her totally stressed her out and sent her home sick."

"Henry will pay for the best," Julien said gently. "The client I was seeing in Vegas has a dog-walking business, and he used to live here. I can see if he knows someplace good."

"OK," Genevieve said, acknowledging that he was trying to be helpful.

"I need to get some work done. Is the coast clear in my office?"

"I'll get my laptop," Genevieve said, starting down the hall.

"Do you want me to take Mona to the living room with me?" Julien followed her to the office and stopped in the doorway. Mona was asleep on the sofa. "Leave her," he said.

□

Genevieve set up shop at Julien's dining room table. She knew she should focus on finding a place to board Mona, but the task so depressed her that she just couldn't face it. She decided instead to send D a long update email.

D was online. She replied quickly via instant message.

D: How did he look stripped down to his T?

Gen: Some guy grabs me and that's your first question?

D: OMG are you OK?

Gen: Yes

D: Praise Jesus! So, how does he look in a T?

Gen: Like he works out

D: What did you wear to dinner?

Gen: jeans, Tech hoodie I swiped from Matteo soph year

D: u r frickin' kidding me

Gen: No

D: hopeless. pls dress cuter tonite

Gen: I remind him of a high school girlfriend. Good or bad?

D: Depends. Did he sleep with her?

"Genevieve? Could you come here a sec?"

She hurriedly closed her laptop. "Be right there," she said, dreading whatever stunt Mona must have pulled.

Mona was seated on Julien's worktable, one paw on his arm, head-butting his shoulder.

"What is she doing?"

"She wants you to pet her. Sorry. I'll take her out to the living room."

She scooped Mona up and was immediately rewarded with a loud purr.

"Why don't you hang out back here?"

"Sure, let me get my laptop." She put Mona down firmly on the sofa, hoping the cat would take the hint.

When Genevieve returned, Mona was back on the worktable, staring intently at Julien.

"I think she's decided she likes you," Genevieve said.

Julien shook a finger at the tabby. "So you think you can charm me, is that it?"

Genevieve was halfway through the online reviews of pet boarding facilities when Julien said, "Oh, here's my guy in Vegas emailing back."

He read silently, scrolling up and down the screen.

"Where does he recommend? I'm looking at places right now," Genevieve said.

"He doesn't recommend boarding a cat unless there's no other option because it stresses them." He turned his chair around to face her. "Which I guess you tried to tell me."

"Well, kind of."

"So it appears you're both staying." He checked his watch. "Do you want to go back to your place for your car? If we go now, we can beat the traffic."

▢

While Genevieve packed for a more lengthy stay away from home, Julien sat in her courtyard with the front door propped open and made calls.

Some of the calls were clearly clients. She heard Erica's name once. He also talked to someone named Claire, although whether she was a client, a friend, a girlfriend or his dentist, Genevieve had no idea.

He seemed to be laughing a lot, and Genevieve felt a stab of jealousy. Who were these women he always seemed to be talking to? Were they all architects or pediatricians or something equally impressive?

Listlessly, she began to sort through the clothes she had chosen, suddenly hating all of them. Maybe D was right. Maybe she did dress like an old lady.

Deciding she needed a pep talk, Genevieve took her phone into the laundry room and closed the door. But of course D didn't pick up, and she didn't answer Genevieve's text, either. It was maddening how D could be counted on to pop up with an inappropriate instant message when Julien was right there, but now that Genevieve wanted to talk about him, D was unavailable.

Genevieve walked out of the laundry room to find Julien frantically pacing around her bedroom.

"*There* you are. I was worried."

"I was just getting some stuff out of the laundry," Genevieve said, hoping he wouldn't notice she was empty-handed. "What's up?"

"I just got off the phone with Henry. I hope your passport is up to date. What happened last night convinced him we're onto something. He wants us to go to Paris."

CHAPTER TWENTY-FIVE

H ENRY WANTED THEM to go to Paris, but Henry did not want to pay last-minute prices.

The proposed timeframe for the trip sent Genevieve into another paroxysm of angst about hotels and kennels, but Julien assured her they would be fine at his house, the time would fly by.

He was right. It was fine. She quickly adjusted to his schedule, making sure that she was showered and dressed and had the pullout bed in his office put away by the time he was back from his run or the gym.

He worked on his regular projects, and Genevieve focused on the research ahead: first the Lazare family wills in France and then the wartime records of the U.S. Monuments, Fine Arts and Archives section housed in the National Archives outside Washington, D.C., where they'd stop on their way home.

Sometimes they were in different rooms, and sometimes Genevieve sat on the office sofa with her laptop. In the evenings, he cooked dinner or they went out. One night, when Genevieve was feeling particularly cooped up, they went to the movies.

Twice Julien had plans that took him away in the evening. Both times she made plans of her own with Thomas, meeting him for dinner and getting the latest on Philip, who was still in limbo at work, and their mortgage application, which still hadn't been approved.

The first night, Julien was already home watching a basket-ball game when she returned from dinner.

The second night, Genevieve was back before him. When she heard Julien come in, she was in bed, talking to Thomas, who insisted he would stay on the phone with her until Julien was home. She was trying very hard not to look at the clock.

It was almost midnight.

□

On the last afternoon before they left for Paris, they returned to Genevieve's apartment so she could get more clothes.

It took her longer than she expected to pack, and Julien suggested getting an early dinner and waiting out the worst of the traffic.

They were sitting at a sushi bar, watching the chef go through his routine, when Genevieve sensed someone hovering behind them.

"Jay," a woman said. "I thought that was you."

She was almost as tall as Julien, with short blonde hair. She wore a skirt that stopped well short of her knees, boots, a red tank, a leather jacket and no obvious makeup except for red lipstick. She was absolutely gorgeous.

Julien turned. "Hey, Meg." He stood, and after a long pause said, "Genevieve McKenna, this is Meg Lev..."

Meg didn't let him finish. She gave Genevieve a cool smile that started at her mouth and didn't quite make it to her eyes. "Genevieve? Would you excuse us?"

Surprise registered on Julien's face. "Hang on, Meg," he said.

"That's fine," Genevieve said. She headed to the bathroom. Whatever this was, she didn't want to be in the middle of it.

At the 10 minute mark, Genevieve decided Meg must have had enough time to say whatever it was she so urgently needed to say.

She'd guessed wrong, though. As Genevieve reached the end of the hallway, she could hear Meg and Julien at the bar, just around the corner.

"I'll take care of it when I get home," Julien said. "I've said I'm sorry, Meg. I'm not sure what else you want from me."

"So you think 'sorry' fixes it?"

Julien sighed. "That's not what I'm saying. I made a mistake. I admit that – always have. I feel terrible about it. But why is this all on me? You weren't up front about what you expected."

"Oh, perfect," Meg hissed. "You just put it all on me."

"C'mon, Meg." Julien's voice softened. "I wish I could undo this. I hate that I hurt your feelings."

Meg cut him off. "You are such an asshole sometimes, you know that? Just find my fucking earrings, OK? When I left them, I didn't realize I wouldn't be back. You probably have a whole drawer full of jewelry that belongs to women who've been told you're done with them."

Genevieve caught sight of Meg's back as she strode out of the bar.

Julien wore a hangdog expression. "Hey," he said as Genevieve took her seat. "Sorry she was rude to you."

Genevieve waited to see whether he would continue.

"We used to work together, and then we had a thing," Julien said, "which didn't end so well."

They were sitting side-by-side now, elbows on the bar, both looking straight ahead.

Julien sipped his beer. "On-again, off-again. Messy. I don't know how much you heard, but I'm not as bad as she makes me out to be."

"That sounds like a country song," Genevieve said. " 'I'm Not As Bad As She Makes Me Out To Be,' from the album 'Please Don't Listen To My Exes.' "

"OK, that's funny," he said, bumping her elbow. "You're good."

"I could go on," Genevieve said. "My ex-boyfriend gave me tons of material."

"Sorry to hear that."

"Long time ago," Genevieve said. "I'm lucky – I don't run into him. I hope you don't run into her very often. She seems formidable."

"She is when she's mad," Julien said. He stared at his beer, turned it on its coaster. "We were friends for a really long time. Seemed like we'd make a good couple."

He took a drink. "But we didn't. I keep ending it and then getting pulled back in. Well, you probably got the gist of it."

He swiveled to look at Genevieve. "Why am I telling you this?"

Genevieve shrugged. "I'm a good listener?"

"You are," he said. "And I guess I don't want you to think I'm awful. I really don't want to get that look I got in Vegas again."

"What look you got in Vegas?"

He laughed. "At the coffee place? When I asked where you were going to gamble that night? You looked at me like, 'Who is this sleazy dude?' Like I'd just handed you my room key and told you to meet me upstairs in 10 minutes."

Genevieve blushed to the roots of her hair. Fortunately, the chef chose that moment to put their sushi in front of them.

"Meg didn't even know about this place until I brought

her here," Julien said. "Seems like I should get custody of my favorite sushi restaurant."

Departure day was a flurry of last-minute activity. Genevieve put in a final call to the pet-sitter, who patiently listened to instructions she'd already received in person and by email. Julien made sure all the documents were ready.

Soon it was time to leave. Genevieve gave Mona one last pet and then they were out the door and into the cab.

At the gate, Genevieve eagerly dived into the book she'd brought for the trip. She was already hooked on the tale of a rare manuscript in Sarajevo when the boarding announcements began.

"This is us," Julien said, shouldering his backpack and picking up Genevieve's carry-on bag.

She followed him onto the plane, still reading, barely taking in her surroundings until they stopped and Julien dropped her bag into a seat.

"What are we doing up here?" Genevieve whispered, expecting a flight attendant to herd them back to coach.

"These are our seats," Julien said. "Why are you whispering?"

"Henry wouldn't pay for last-minute tickets, but we're in first class?"

"This is business class, actually." Julien put his hand on her elbow. "Step in so people can get past."

Genevieve stepped in, but she didn't sit. "But..."

"But what?" Julien shot her an exasperated look. "I'm 6-4, and my knee's been scoped twice. I can't fly overnight in coach. Most people would be happy to sit here. I'm not understanding the problem."

Reluctantly, she took her seat. It was, she had to admit, very comfortable. "I completely understand why you need more room, but I could have flown coach."

That earned her another look from Julien. "I'm not going to fly business while you're in coach. Who would do that? Other than a total asshole, I mean."

"Well, since you put it that way."

Genevieve busied herself settling in, not wanting Julien to see her face. She and Pete hadn't traveled much together, because she rarely could afford her share of the trips he liked. But when they did, he regularly flew first class while Genevieve flew coach.

"If it makes you feel any better, we're flying coach on the way home," Julien said. "So enjoy this while it lasts."

□

Genevieve woke with a start. She looked around, trying to get her bearings. Sunlight peeked around the window shade.

She stretched and looked for Julien. His seat was empty. Craning her head, she spotted him in the aisle near the galley, sipping coffee and chatting with a flight attendant who was standing, Genevieve thought, just a little too close.

Genevieve unbuckled her seatbelt and grabbed her carry-on. In the dim bathroom light, she surveyed the damage of the overnight flight.

There was a crease across her right cheek, probably from the pillow. Her hair was straggly. D would pronounce her a "fright."

She'd stayed awake a long time reading. Julien, a seasoned transatlantic traveler, drank two glasses of wine and took an antihistamine with dinner. He fell asleep two hours into the long flight.

Julien was back in his seat when she returned, reading a computer magazine. Other than a one-day growth of beard – which Genevieve thought looked damned attractive – he seemed no worse for wear.

A second cup of coffee had appeared. Julien handed her the coffee and powdered creamer when she sat down.

"Bonjour. I have to warn you, the coffee's awful," he said.

She doctored the coffee and took a sip, then grimaced. He was right.

"At least it's hot," he offered. "You want to discuss a plan for the day?" He seemed to be bursting with energy.

"Sure," she said, feigning more enthusiasm than she really felt.

"We land a little after 11. Once we get to the hotel, we should drop the bags and then get lunch."

Genevieve was content to let Julien worry about these details. "That sounds fine."

"Now, the trick to avoiding jet lag is not to nap, no matter how sleepy we feel."

Genevieve was sure that was for her benefit.

"There's no point trying to get started on the wills today. By the time we got there and got in our requests, it would be practically closing time. I think we should go see where the gallery used to be."

"That sounds good."

"Natural light helps reset your body's clock," he said.

She had no idea he was such a jet-lag expert.

Julien picked up on her mood. "If I'm annoying you, you can just say so. You seem groggy. Did you stay up reading your book?"

"It's really good," Genevieve said. "It starts with this manuscript in Sarajevo and then traces it back through time."

"You're going to be jet-lagged," he said. "Don't say I didn't warn you."

After they landed, Genevieve found herself herded here and there by Julien without much registering.

Finally, they were out of the airport and into a cab. Genevieve sank back into the warmth as Julien negotiated with the driver.

She wondered whether she would be able to see any of the famous sights on the drive. Julien had explained to her the route they would follow into the heart of Paris, but she was fuzzy on the details. She was fuzzy in general.

"Genevieve!"

"What's wrong?" Julien was shaking her arm.

"You were sleeping."

"I was not."

"You were," he said. "You can't nap. You'll have jet lag the rest of the trip."

A flash flood of irritation breached Genevieve's internal levees. "I'm dying here."

"Lack of sleep never killed anyone."

"Right, because your body wouldn't let that happen," she said. "You'd just FALL ASLEEP. People who are tired fall asleep. And I'm really, really tired."

"Well. The whining is a new development."

Genevieve sighed. It sounded melodramatic, even to her. "Fine. I'm whining. But your lecturing me about jet lag is really tiresome. So there."

The cab driver turned up the radio.

They rode in silence for a few minutes, and then Genevieve shifted restlessly in the seat. "I'm totally awake now. That should make you happy."

"Ecstatic."

More silence.

"*Un tiran*," Julien said.

"What?"

"In French. Call me *un tiran*." He smiled. "Despot. Tyrant."

Genevieve ventured a smile. "Is that an apology?"

"Yes. I would have offered it sooner but I couldn't think of the word."

"What does that make me?"

"I knew you'd ask me that." He leaned toward the driver and rattled off a question in French, ending with the words "wah, wah, wah," uttered in an exaggerated tone.

The driver nodded and responded.

Julien sat back, satisfied. "*Pleurnicheuse.* Whiner."

"I did not sound like that."

"No, of course not," Julien said. "Sometimes one has to exaggerate to communicate across the language barrier."

"I thought you spoke perfect French."

Julien threw up his hands and said something in French. The driver laughed.

"What was that?"

"Roughly translated, 'I surrender.' "

The cab deposited them in front of a white stone building on a quiet street. Genevieve stood gaping as Julien dealt with the driver. The buildings, even the trees – everything was just as she'd imagined it would be.

Julien chatted with the young woman at the reception desk as Genevieve explored the lobby.

"They've got two rooms ready now on the third floor, if we'd like to go ahead and get settled," Julien said, waving

Genevieve back over. "Or we could leave the bags and come back later; she may have something on four then."

The thought of a hot shower was very seductive. "I vote we check in now," Genevieve said.

"The only thing is…" Julien was distracted by the young woman, who was batting her eyelashes and leaning over the desk in a way Genevieve thought was very unprofessional.

"I swear I won't nap. I just want a shower."

He handed her the keys and smiled at the clerk. "Go look at the rooms, choose which one you want. I'll be up in a minute with the bags."

They met in the lobby 45 minutes later. Genevieve's shower had given her a renewed burst of energy. She was downstairs ahead of Julien.

He smiled as he cleared the last step. The edges of his hair were wet – he'd showered too, and shaved. "Feeling better? Ready to go?"

"It really is true," Genevieve said as they walked outside. "The light in Paris is different from the light anywhere else."

"Just wait until you see it at night. You're going to love it."

CHAPTER TWENTY-SIX

IT WAS SUNNY and unseasonably warm, and Julien decreed they would walk rather than take the Metro.

"My goal is to keep you moving," he said. "I'm afraid if we lose momentum, you'll collapse."

Walking was fine with Genevieve, who was terrified of the Metro. She hadn't confessed that to Julien, worried it would make her seem like an unsophisticated hick.

He steered her left outside the hotel. "The woman at the desk said there's a good cafe around the corner."

"Was she recommending it for lunch or suggesting you meet her for a drink later? I thought her eyelashes might fall right off, the way she was batting them," Genevieve said.

"We can walk the other direction and go someplace touristy." Julien halted in the middle of the sidewalk, but his expression was playful.

Genevieve resumed walking, and when Julien didn't budge, she grabbed his elbow and dragged him along. "I'm sure the cafe recommended by your new best friend is excellent."

When they got there, Genevieve froze in the doorway, suddenly daunted by the unfamiliarity of it all.

To her relief, Julien took charge. Soon they were settled at a table and had ordered, the waiter hardly grimacing at all at her French.

"This is all the way I'd imagined it would be, only better," Genevieve said, taking in the dark wood bar and tile floor, the street scene outside. "I can't quite believe I'm here. I hope I won't embarrass you by gawking at everything."

"Gawk away," Julien said with an expansive wave of his arm. "It's fun to be here with someone who thinks it's new and exciting. Although I can't believe an art history major never made it to Paris. Didn't they have study abroad at your school?"

"They did," Genevieve said. "I signed up to do a six-week summer course in Europe. My dad and I worked out a deal to split the cost, and I got a second part-time job."

"What happened?"

"Right before the deadline to send the money, the woman my dad was dating pulled me aside and asked was I sure I wanted to go, because she was worried I'd get to France and be miserable and it would be a waste of money. She said my dad couldn't really afford it but didn't want to say no. Then she said – I'll always remember this – 'You shouldn't expect people to spoil you just because of your mother.' "

Julien frowned. "Please don't tell me you let her talk you out of it."

"I let the deadline pass and then told my dad I decided I didn't want to go."

"What happened to the girlfriend?"

"Oh, that's the worst part," Genevieve said. "She and my dad broke up because she wanted him to take her to Hawaii for her 40th birthday, and he wouldn't do it."

Genevieve couldn't believe she'd volunteered that story. She'd never told her father why she'd backed out.

Julien had already finished his lunch and ordered coffee. "The opportunity never came around again?"

"If I go on vacation, it's generally with D. She likes resorts and drinks with umbrellas in them," Genevieve said. "Why is it you've never seen the building where your family lived even though you've been to Paris?"

Julien took a sip of his coffee and leaned back in his chair.

"The first time I came to Paris, I was 14 and not happy to be on vacation with my mother. That was the summer I was very diligently trying to win over Rachel... What was Rachel's last name?" He stopped, ran his hand through his hair.

"Well, anyway. I wanted to be back in LA chasing Rachel, not trudging through the Louvre. I was pretty sullen company. Mom saved the old neighborhood for the end of the trip.

"There was a family from Minnesota at our hotel with a son and a daughter about my age, and I'd been hanging around with them – the girl was very cute. They were doing the day trip to Versailles, and I persuaded Mom that I really wanted to go. She surprised me by saying OK. So she went to see the old neighborhood alone, and I kissed the girl from Minnesota in the gardens at Versailles."

"Forgetting all about Rachel in LA?"

Julien caught the waiter's eye and asked for the check. "Well, I remembered her when I got home."

"But you've been to Paris since then, haven't you?"

The bill arrived, and Genevieve dug in her bag for her credit card. Julien waved her off. "Get the next one," he said.

"I came with Erica, but she was miserable, so we cut Paris short and took the train to Normandy. I thought she might like it better."

"Miserable in Paris?"

"Too many museums, too much sitting around, too hard to get in a good run."

Julien picked up his coat and held Genevieve's out to her. "Ready?"

Julien didn't consult a map, just set off walking, and soon they were in the heart of the 8th arrondissement.

A series of turns took them away from the busier roads, and then they were in a quieter area lined with four-story buildings that housed cafes and boutiques at the street level.

"Number 28," Julien said, pointing to a storefront across from them. In the window, a bright scarf adorned an otherwise naked mannequin, a minimalist and effective display.

Julien waited for a car to pass, then started across the street.

"We're going in?" Genevieve scurried to catch up.

A bell dinged as they pushed through the door, and the woman behind the counter looked up.

She appeared to be in her 40s, her dark hair caught in a very chic ponytail, a dramatic streak of gray radiating from one temple. An eggplant-colored shawl was tossed casually over her shoulder, and she wore lipstick in a matching shade.

"Bonjour," Julien called to her, giving her his best smile.

The woman came out from behind the counter, and Genevieve wandered off to browse while Julien worked his magic.

Genevieve had promised D a souvenir. She tilted her head, did the Euro-to-dollars calculation on some earrings and backed away.

She drifted back to look at scarves as Julien and the woman chatted. She heard him introduce himself and saw him pull a sheaf of papers from his jacket. He was probably showing the woman that his mother had been born at the address.

The scarves, she quickly discovered, were no closer to her price range than the earrings. The patterns were beautiful, though. She took the corner of one between her fingers and closed her eyes at the luxurious sensation of the silk.

"Not really your colors."

She opened her eyes. Julien was at her elbow, grinning. She let the scarf drop. He was right – the pinks and oranges were wrong for her.

"Feel it," she said. "It's amazing."

"I'm sure it is," Julien said. "But I have something even more amazing."

He dangled a key in front of her. "Want to see Théodore Lazare's studio?"

"What did you do?" she whispered, leaning past him to look at the clerk, who was busy with a laptop at the counter.

"They use it for storage."

Genevieve looked again at the clerk. "She just handed you the key?"

He waved to the clerk as they left the boutique and turned the corner into a tiny courtyard Genevieve had missed when they came up the street.

Julien fitted the key into the lock of a heavy wooden door at the back of the courtyard, gave it a shove and shooed Genevieve ahead of him. She climbed a narrow flight of stairs, made a left, climbed more and came to a landing.

"That's the apartment where my mother lived," Julien said. "Madame LeGrand – the woman in the store – said the couple who lives here now is on vacation."

"You two got very chummy," Genevieve said.

Julien poked her in the back. "Keep climbing. Three more flights."

The stairs narrowed after the first landing, and Julien had to duck at each subsequent turning. Genevieve was warm and a little out of breath when they came to the last door.

Julien reached around her to unlock it, and Genevieve was conscious of his arm against hers and his breath on her hair as he struggled with the lock. Finally it gave, and he pushed the door open.

Genevieve stepped into the small space, and Julien ducked through the low doorway right behind her.

"Oh wow," Julien said.

The room, like the storefront below, was narrow and deep. But high windows on three sides flooded it with bright, warm light that accentuated every nick and scuff on the bare wood floors. It was empty except for a half-dozen boxes pushed against one wall.

Genevieve hastily unbuttoned her coat and shrugged it off, warm from the climb but also feeling vaguely uncomfortable.

She knew this room.

Keeping her back to Julien, she walked to one of the windows and looked out at the blue sky and Paris rooftops. She closed her eyes.

Bright light flooding in. Scuffed wood floors.

Yes, she knew this room.

Julien peered over her shoulder. "OK view," he said, turning away from the window. "But this room. This light. Wow."

Genevieve, her eyes closed, leaned her head against the window and took deep, even breaths, trying to slow her heartbeat.

"This is unbelievably cool," Julien said. He strode around the room, oblivious to Genevieve's discomfort. "My great-whatever uncle worked here. Probably sketched *Study for Tristan and Iseult* right here. Painted here. And OK, he wasn't one of the greatest of his century, but still. It happened *here*."

He took off his coat and tossed it onto the pile of boxes against the wall.

"I'm going to move in. What do you think?"

Julien touched her elbow. Genevieve steeled herself and turned around.

"Desk right here," he said. "Bed over there. That's it. What else do you need in life, really?"

Genevieve tossed her coat onto the boxes with his. "Sounds like you're set, then. Madame LeGrand downstairs will be so pleased to have you as a neighbor."

Julien laughed. "I can't believe they haven't figured out how to turn this into an apartment. Isn't this an amazing space? I don't want to sound all California, going on about energy, but this place has something. Don't you feel it?"

"Yes," Genevieve said. "I definitely feel it."

□

After Julien returned the key, they did some upscale window-shopping and strolled back toward their hotel.

Genevieve's lack of sleep was catching up with her, and even Julien didn't seem so energetic now that the light was fading.

"We should grab dinner, even though no French person would eat at this scandalously early hour," he said.

They ducked into a cafe Julien remembered from his last trip, and Genevieve practically sleepwalked her way through a dinner of roast chicken and, at Julien's insistence, two glasses of white wine.

Then they walked out into the Paris night. Genevieve gasped. "It's so beautiful!"

"I told you that it was even better at night," Julien said. "If you want, we could walk up the Seine a little."

Genevieve nodded eagerly.

Sightseeing boats moved slowly down the river, their reflections rippling in the water. "I'm going to spend this whole trip being amazed every five minutes," she said.

Just then, a gust of wind whipped around them. "It's beautiful, but I'm freezing." Julien pointed toward a red M sign. "Let's take the Metro back."

Genevieve balked. "I'm not that cold."

"Well, I *am* that cold," Julien said. "And suddenly pretty tired myself."

"Can't we just walk?" she wheedled. "It will wear me out and help me sleep."

"You seem barely upright as it is. Your eyes were closing while we were waiting for the check," Julien said. "Do you really want to walk 20 more minutes in the cold?"

Genevieve stared at her feet. "I'm sort of terrified of the Metro."

"Really? Why?"

"I don't even know," Genevieve said. "Because I don't know what you're supposed to do? Worried I'll get lost? I can't even explain."

Julien took her arm. "Well, we're not walking everywhere, and we're not taking cabs. I promise you, it's not that bad."

He propelled her to the Metro station and down the stairs. Once inside, he showed her how to buy a ticket and board.

"Was that so bad?" he asked as they settled into their seats.

The train lurched forward, and Genevieve grabbed the edge of the seat. Her heart began to pound. The rattle of the machinery seemed deafening. She closed her eyes as the car picked up speed.

After what seemed like an eternity, the car began to slow. She opened her eyes and started to stand, but Julien put his hand on her arm. "We're the next stop."

She lowered herself toward the seat with a sigh.

"You really are scared, aren't you? I thought you were exaggerating." He patted her arm.

Once she was back at the hotel, Genevieve thought about sending D an update. But she couldn't face the idea of going to the lobby to use the wifi. Instead, she yawned her way through brushing her teeth and slept her first night in Paris with the bedside lamp still on.

CHAPTER TWENTY-SEVEN

GENEVIEVE WAS AWAKE and in the breakfast room by 8. Julien was already there, talking on his cell phone. Genevieve looked at her watch and tried to do the math. Wasn't it the middle of the night in LA?

"Oh, good," he said into the phone as Genevieve approached. There was something in his voice that Genevieve couldn't quite figure out. Then it dawned on her. He was talking to a woman.

"Well, that's great." Another pause. "Yeah, me too. OK. Bye now."

Julien didn't seem bothered that she'd overheard his call, cheerfully asking her how she'd slept and telling her about his morning run along the Seine.

Genevieve had brought her laptop down and was surprised to find a response from the grad school classmate she'd emailed to ask about academics with expertise in the French romantics.

Her classmate recommended that Genevieve get in touch with a Dr. Suzanne Marchand in Paris and had attached a copy of the woman's latest paper. She'd also copied the professor on the email. Dr. Marchand had replied and listed when she was available.

Genevieve double-checked the calendar – the professor was free that morning.

"There's a professor here one of my grad school classmates thinks could help us. Today at 10:45 is the only time she has free," Genevieve said to Julien.

Julien checked his watch. "Didn't you tell me we have to fill out a bunch of forms at the archives and put in requests before we can see anything? Why don't we do that and then go see this woman?"

"I wonder if it's too late to make an appointment? I guess I'll email her."

"Your aversion to calling people is silly," Julien said. "Give me the phone number."

Genevieve gave him the number and went to the front desk to print Dr. Marchand's article. She hated to go into a meeting without doing background reading.

Then it was back to the breakfast room to finish her coffee and croissant before they headed off to the Metro.

Their ride was longer than the one the previous night and required a change of lines. Genevieve clung to the seat as they lurched from stop to stop.

"Maybe you should bring the novel that kept you up half the night on the plane," Julien said.

Genevieve shook her head. "I can read on planes, but I think this would be like trying to read in a car. It would give me a headache. Talk to me. Distract me."

Julien thought a moment. "OK. Tell me something about you I don't already know. Something you're really good at. Off the top of your head. Quick."

"I can't think of anything."

"Oh, c'mon. If I said 'tell me something you're really bad at,' you could have told me ten things like that," Julien said, snapping his fingers.

"That's true," Genevieve said. "So I'm good at being self-deprecating. Now tell me something you're bad at."

"Ha. OK, I'm going to let you get away with that, because it's funny. I can't bake decent bread. I like to improvise, and baking is more like chemistry. Your turn. Tell me something else about you I don't know. Build from what I told you. Quick."

"Um... chemistry. I enrolled in a chemistry class in college that was way over my head," Genevieve said. "I had to drop it, and the prof was really mean. Your turn."

"OK. Science classes... Hmmm. Should I tell you that I slept with my biology TA?"

Genevieve, thrown off stride, gaped at him. "Did it help your grade?"

Julien laughed and shook his head. "No."

"Did you think it was going to?"

"Nah, I just thought Sheila was cool," he said. "Ready? This is where we change lines."

While Julien waded through paperwork at the National Archives, Genevieve settled into a chair to see what she could glean from Dr. Marchand's article. It was in French, and as a result, it took a bit for her to get the gist of it. When she did, she realized that her grad school classmate hadn't really done her a favor.

"Ready to go?" Julien came hustling toward her, shrugging into his coat. "If we walk fast, we should be in time to see the professor."

Genevieve hung her head, embarrassed. "I should have known better than to ask this classmate for help – she never did like me. I just got done reading Dr. Marchand's article. Her area of expertise is re-evaluating 19th century courtesans in feminist terms."

Julien paused, one arm in his coat, one out. "You're not serious."

"Afraid so," Genevieve said, waving the printout. "I should have read it before we scheduled. I guess we can't just blow the meeting off, can we?"

"When I called, I told her Théodore Lazare was my great-great-whatever uncle and she didn't act like it was odd we'd want to talk to her," Julien said. "And you're right, it would be rude not to show."

Genevieve put on her coat. "If this is horrible, I'm never going to hear the end of it, am I?"

Julien just smiled as he held the door for her.

☐

Genevieve had pictured Suzanne Marchand as a dotty academic with messy hair, pasty skin and a fraying cardigan.

She was wrong.

Marchand was 40 at most. She was tall and impeccably dressed in a crisp gray suit with a white blouse unbuttoned perhaps one button too many.

She beckoned them into her office, giving Genevieve a quick up-and-down that left her feeling very much the hick from Wichita Falls. Then she did the same with Julien, staring at him with a frankness Genevieve found startling.

Julien greeted her with his most charming smile and a few words in French. Then he said, "I wonder whether we could proceed in English, for Ms. McKenna's benefit?"

"But of course. Now, Mr. Brooks, tell me, what is it about Théodore Lazare that brings you and your assistant all this way?" She smiled. "I am at your service."

Genevieve wasn't sure what galled her more – the blithe assumption that she was the assistant, or the blatant flirting with Julien.

"Ms. McKenna is the researcher," Julien said, gracefully handing the reins to Genevieve.

Suzanne Marchand's smile slipped a little. "My apologies. How can I help?"

"I read your most recent article," Genevieve began, "and I know you've done considerable work on 19th century courtesans..."

"Yes, it's remarkable how they were able to manipulate the patriarchy to their benefit," Dr. Marchand broke in. "And so many of the courtesans were associated with the noted artists of their time, an inspiration to them."

Julien raised an eyebrow at Genevieve. If the whole half-hour progressed like this, he would never let her forget it.

"Now, Théodore Lazare had little to do with courtesans," Dr. Marchand said, as though this were a mark against him. "Although his personal life was not without intrigue."

"So you've researched him?" Genevieve pulled a notebook from her bag.

"Not specifically," the professor said. "But he was the subject of much gossip in the letters of the era."

"Really?" Julien said.

Dr. Marchand leaned toward him, flashing a bit of cleavage. "He was thought to be devastatingly handsome, did you know?"

Julien smiled, a little too smugly, Genevieve thought.

"What was the gossip about?" Genevieve asked.

"A love affair," the professor said. "A young woman from a very good family. There was the issue of his... milieu." She paused awkwardly. "You understand?"

"Because he was Jewish, you mean," Julien said.

Dr. Marchand shrugged. "The times," she said.

"Her parents forbade it. The gossips hint that they continued to meet in secret. We know Lazare's brother sent him to Florence. Perhaps to forget the girl? The story goes that he came back with a gift for her, a necklace, which she refused to accept."

Genevieve and Julien exchanged a look.

"They say she is the model for two paintings. The first is *Pyramus and Thisbe*, which is in the Louvre. Thisbe is partially nude, but Lazare obscured her face. It's also said he used her in *Tristan and Iseult* but showed her face. Lazare's brother took control of the painting and refused to exhibit it. Because of the scandal?"

"Who was this woman?" Julien asked. "What happened to her?"

"That I cannot tell you," Dr. Marchand said. "The letters were coy. Lazare, of course, went off to Morocco and did those Eastern paintings, which were not very good – if you'll forgive me saying so – and then caught some fever and died."

The professor discreetly checked her watch. "And that is all I can tell you of Théodore Lazare."

"Did he leave letters? Or perhaps his brother?" Genevieve hadn't given up the idea of a trove of Lazare letters in some dusty Paris archive.

Dr. Marchand shook her head. "I do not believe so."

Genevieve and Julien stood to leave. Dr. Marchand shook hands with Genevieve and then Julien, holding his hand for just a beat too long.

"Tell me, have you seen *Pyramus and Thisbe*? No? You really must. It is so beautiful, so full of longing. Most sensual."

Then she switched to French, exchanged a few more sentences with Julien, and showed them out.

□

"Well, that was a waste of time," Genevieve said when they were back on the sidewalk.

"Was it?" Julien said mildly, scanning the street.

"Do you want to go back? I'm sure Dr. Marchand can make more time for you." Exasperated that Julien wouldn't look at her, she tugged on his sleeve. "What are you looking for, anyway?"

Julien's eyes traveled down to her hand on his sleeve, then back to her face. "Why are you mad at me?"

Genevieve dropped her hand. Busted.

"It's annoying that a feminist academic thought I was your assistant," she said. "And she was flirting with you, which was weird, and then she switched to French at the end."

Julien had resumed scanning the street over her head, and it was all Genevieve could do not to stamp her foot. "Sorry, am I boring you?"

"There it is!"

"There what is?"

"The restaurant the professor recommended." Julien smiled down at her. "At the end? When she was speaking French?"

He waited for a break in the traffic, then grabbed Genevieve by the wrist and pulled her across the street.

On the opposite sidewalk, he let go and walked a few doors down to a cafe, holding the door for her. Inside, he signaled the waiter that they would be two for lunch and chose a table.

Julien settled into his chair and shed his coat. "So, your complaints, in no particular order: Perhaps she assumed you were my assistant because I made the call? But yes, I can see that would be upsetting."

The waiter arrived with menus. Julien ordered water, glanced at the menu and put it aside.

"On the switch to French: She thought she insulted me with the reference to my family being Jewish. English isn't her first language. I accepted her apology, thanked her for her time, asked her where we should get lunch."

The waiter returned with their water. "Do you know what you want? She recommended the mussels."

Genevieve hadn't looked at the menu. "That sounds fine."

Julien ordered, and the waiter left.

"So what does that leave?" Julien took a long drink. "Oh, right. She was flirting. Don't know what to tell you. I like talking to women. Women seem to like talking to me. I believe you, on occasion, have talked to me in a way that might have counted as flirting. When you aren't mad at me, that is."

Genevieve began to blush.

"Did you really think it was a waste of time? I guess it didn't help with the provenance research," Julien said. "But I thought it was interesting. I never knew any of that about him."

Relieved to be on safer ground, Genevieve looked up, hoping the red in her face had faded. "You're right that it doesn't really help, but it was fascinating."

"You did know the part about the necklace, though," Julien said. "That day in your apartment, you told me..."

Watching Genevieve's face, he fell silent.

"You really hadn't heard that story before."

"No."

"And yesterday, in the studio, when I was going on about the creative energy or whatever, you said you felt something too. What did you feel?"

Genevieve stared out the window. The wind had come up, and people on the street were turning up their coat collars and adjusting their scarves.

"Genevieve?"

"It felt familiar."

□

They spent a frustrating afternoon battling French bureaucracy and an arcane record-keeping system.

Late in the day, though, they had a breakthrough: Julien found a severe-looking archivist in her 60s who proved surprisingly susceptible to his charms. With her help, they were able to identify the notaries who had witnessed four generations of Lazare wills and formulate a plan for the next day. Their progress had been glacial, but Genevieve felt confident they'd have better luck on Day Two.

As she watched Julien bid adieu to the archivist who'd proved so helpful, she realized something she'd overlooked before: Julien didn't turn on the charm only for women who were conventionally attractive, and he didn't do it simply when he wanted something.

She'd seen him chat up an overweight teenage ticket-taker at the movies, an elderly woman in a wheelchair in the LAX security line and a lot of women in between. It was true: He liked talking to women, and women liked talking to him. He seemed to find something interesting in nearly every woman he encountered, and women above a certain age or outside certain parameters of attractiveness weren't invisible to him.

When they left the archives building, Julien surprised her by leading her toward the Seine, not toward the Metro station they'd used that morning.

"Where are we going?"

"Back by a different route," Julien said.

Once they had boarded the Metro, Julien turned to her and said, "OK. Pyramus and... Thisbe? What's their story?"

Grateful that he had found another ruse to distract her, Genevieve gave him the abbreviated version.

"Another pair of star-crossed lovers, this time from Roman mythology. Supposedly Shakespeare based Romeo and Juliet on them."

Genevieve closed her eyes for a moment, shutting out the clatter of the Metro and recalling the details.

"I'm not sure why – probably family opposition – but they meet in secret. One night Thisbe's waiting at their spot, and she's startled, I think by a lion."

"Wait, did you say a *lion*?"

"I think it was supposed to be in Babylon or something," Genevieve said. "Anyway, she's startled, and she runs, but her veil is torn, maybe by a thorn? So Pyramus shows up, finds the bloody veil, thinks Thisbe is dead and kills himself. Then she comes back and finds his body and kills herself."

"Another happy ending," Julien said.

"Well, art imitates life," Genevieve said, "and for a lot of history, people didn't choose who they married. It was arranged. Falling in love pretty much guaranteed an unhappy ending."

The Metro stopped, and Julien motioned her to her feet. "This is us."

"Really? Now where are we going?"

"It's a surprise," Julien said. "But we need to hurry."

Julien hustled her to the left outside the train. Genevieve finally saw a sign.

"The Louvre? But what time does it close?"

Julien glanced at his watch. "We have 45 minutes."

"You expect me to see the greatest collection of art in the world in 45 minutes?"

"We're not here to see the whole thing," Julien said, "just *Pyramus and Thisbe*."

CHAPTER TWENTY-EIGHT

J ULIEN HAD TO WORK his magic at the ticket booth, which was closing when they arrived.

But work it he did, and then he and Genevieve walked as fast as they could – running being strictly prohibited – toward the salon where *Pyramus and Thisbe* was displayed.

Genevieve kept falling behind, mostly because she'd catch a glimpse of something she'd always longed to see and linger, just for a moment.

Finally, Julien firmly grabbed her hand. "We'll come back. I promise."

A guard tried to shoo them out, but Julien just waved and kept going, a man on a mission. They turned one last corner, and then they were there.

The painting's background was some sort of ancient tomb. Genevieve remembered that, from the story.

Pyramus sprawled in the foreground, a white veil splotched with blood clutched to his lifeless chest.

Thisbe sat on a stone bench, turned away from his body, one arm raised to cover her face as she wept. Her diaphanous blue gown fell away from her torso, revealing one pale breast, and the fabric caught between her knees, showing her bare thigh and calf.

Genevieve had seen representations of the couple in art before, but never anything like this. Théodore Lazare's Pyramus and Thisbe clearly had not been meeting in secret to exchange demure glances and chaste expressions of courtly love.

"Wow," Julien said.

He took a step back from the painting. "My mother dragged me all over France to see Lazare paintings, but I am sure I never saw this. I would remember this."

"Maybe she didn't think it was appropriate for a 14-year-old boy?"

She took a step back, too. She'd initially focused on the figures in the painting, because they were so compelling, but the light was interesting, too. Thisbe seemed to be captured in a stream of pure moonlight.

"The light's really unusual," Genevieve said.

"It's good, isn't it? I've always thought he was mediocre," Julien said. "But this – this is actually good, isn't it?"

"The composition is good, his colors are beautiful, the light is extraordinary, but mostly, it's so *alive*. Or she is, anyway."

"To have had that" – Julien gestured toward Thisbe – "and lose it. Devastating."

Genevieve gave him a hard look.

"What?" Julien's eyes widened. "Oh, not in a 'damn, she's hot' kind of way. Give me *some* credit."

Julien took Genevieve's arm and pulled her closer to the painting. "Doesn't it seem suffused with..."

"Um, *yeah*," Genevieve said.

Julien laughed. "Well, obviously. But not *just* sex. Although..."

"Oh. My. God," Genevieve said.

"Oh. My. God. That's right," Julien said. "But my great-whatever uncle loves that woman. You can see it. You can feel it. He loves her in a burn-you-up-and-leave-you-in-ashes kind of way. And when she's gone, he's going to be like Pyramus there, and he knows it."

Julien shook his head.

"Poor bastard."

At breakfast the next morning, Genevieve faced an irate email from D complaining that she had been in France for "THREE FRICKIN' DAYS" without sending a single update.

And it was true. The first night, Genevieve had tumbled into bed before 8 p.m., too jet-lagged to email. The previous night, she and Julien had gone to the Louvre, and then to dinner, where they talked for hours.

They compared notes on growing up in single-parent households. Julien, who had no grandparents and only a handful of distant cousins, had constantly battled his mother's neediness. He sympathized, given her past, but it irritated him nonetheless. He talked frankly about the painful realization, in his 20s, that much of his mother's unhappiness had been caused by his father's affairs.

Genevieve told him something she'd never spoken aloud, not even to D: How well-intentioned matchmaking efforts on her father's behalf had terrorized her as a child. She'd lie awake at her grandparents' house, knowing her father was on a date, visualizing a future in which he'd move in with a new wife and leave her behind.

It was liberating to talk about it. She'd given up the idea that anyone would ever understand. Pete had accused her of playing the "dead mother" card too often.

How could she summarize the last couple of days for D in an email?

"Everything OK?"

Julien was looking at her over his coffee. "You're sighing a lot."

"A demanding email from D," she said. "I've been negligent about updating her. Which reminds me, I haven't heard anything from Thomas – about Philip's job, the guard in the hospital, nothing. I need to email him."

Julien checked his watch. "Make it quick. If we get what we need today, we can sightsee tomorrow."

Genevieve was already writing to Thomas. "And shop. I have to get D a souvenir."

When they got to the archives, Genevieve and Julien found themselves at odds.

Julien wanted to look for his grandfather's will, and his reasoning was solid. Laurent Lazare's will could place *Study for Tristan and Iseult* in the hands of the family on the brink of the war.

Genevieve wanted to look first for the will of Henri Lazare, the artist's brother. She hoped for an orderly chain of possession, all documented, with no gaps.

Rather than argue, they agreed to proceed with the idea of meeting in the middle. Genevieve could tell that Julien hoped to make a race of it, one he expected to win.

By the time they broke for lunch, neither had made much progress. The records were handwritten and hard to decipher. Genevieve had to take a break every 20 minutes and stare at the ceiling to avoid eye strain.

Midafternoon, Julien discovered he'd been given the wrong volume of records and went stomping off in search of the correct one.

Shortly after that, Genevieve stumbled upon a faster way to zip through the records, and within a half-hour was frantically waving Julien over.

She'd found Henri Lazare's will, dated 1865.

They scanned through the pages until they found mentions both for the drawing and the painting *Tristan and Iseult*. The last listing was followed by a sentence that Genevieve couldn't quite make out, an admonition of some sort. She could read the *ne* and *pas*, but the handwriting and French grammar conspired to baffle her.

When he saw what she'd found, Julien slung his arm around her shoulder and pulled her close, burying his face in her hair.

"Yes!" he whispered.

"What does that line say?" she whispered back, pointing.

Julien squinted at it. "It says 'not to be shown in public.' That squares with what the professor told us, that Henri was worried the painting would cause a scandal."

When Genevieve returned from getting certified copies of the will, Julien was packing up their things.

"Closing early today," he said, shrugging. "Some kind of strike, I think."

On the Metro, Genevieve couldn't stop chattering about their find.

"Now that I've figured out this faster way to sort the records, maybe we can find the other three wills tomorrow morning, and we could sightsee in the afternoon," she said. "What would you like to do?"

"I'll see whatever you want," Julien said. "I'll even drag myself through the Louvre again."

"It's so hard to choose," Genevieve said. "The Louvre, the Impressionists at the Musée d'Orsay – the Impressionists were my first big art crush, you know? Or Montmartre. Could we maybe do that now... What?"

"It's great to see you having so much fun," Julien said. "You forgot to be scared on the Metro. Here's our stop."

They walked to the hotel, but Julien paused at the entrance, pulling her aside to let another guest pass and leaning one arm against the building above her head.

"I promised to pick something up for a friend," he said. "I think I'll do that now."

Genevieve's face must have registered her disappointment. She'd hoped they were going to drop off their things and explore the city before dinner.

"Why don't you scan what we found," Julien said. "Send that to Henry. When I get back, we'll have a drink and then let's have a nice dinner on Henry's tab. Did you bring something dressy?"

Genevieve nodded.

"Good. Wear it tonight."

Genevieve scanned the documents and sent them to LA, then hurried up to her room to prepare for a night out.

What should she wear? She pulled D's blue blouse from its hanger. Was it cut too low? Maybe it was too wrinkled. She hung it up, then pulled it out again. She held it against her chest and studied the effect in the mirror.

The color was nice. She could steam the wrinkles out.

She checked the time. When would Julien be back? He

hadn't said how long his errand for his friend would take. What friend? What errand?

She checked the time again, did the math, and pulled out her cell phone. She'd bought a limited number of international minutes before the trip, and so far she hadn't used any of them.

"Hey, D. Can you talk?"

"You're calling me? That means things are either going really good or really bad."

Genevieve held the receiver away from her ear. D sounded as though she was in the hallway, not halfway around the world.

"Today we found a letter that proves Julien's family had the drawing, at least in 1860-something."

"Don't bore me with the art history," D interrupted. "How's it going with Julien?"

"We're going out to dinner, and he asked me if I brought anything dressy," Genevieve said. "Last night, we talked and talked, and walked along the Seine, with all the lights, and D? I like him so much. But I'm nervous."

"Gen, sounds like it's going great! Sometimes you make life way more complicated than it has to be," D told her, not unkindly. "Now, what are you wearing?"

She changed three times, but in the end Genevieve wore D's blouse. She paired it with a black skirt and heels – the only pair she owned. They'd been a last-minute addition to her suitcase.

Julien was waiting at the bottom of the stairs. He was wearing a white shirt, collar open, and black pants and a jacket. Genevieve could tell that he'd just showered and shaved.

"Hey, you're taller," he said when she cleared the last step. He looked her up and down. "I don't think I've ever seen you in anything but flats."

Julien took her coat and held it open for her. Genevieve thought that was a gallant gesture, helping a woman with her coat. It was one of those old-fashioned manly things, like carrying a handkerchief.

Outside, Genevieve instinctively turned toward what she had come to think of as "their" Metro stop. Julien caught her elbow.

"Other way," he said.

"Are we walking to dinner?" She wondered whether she would regret the heels.

"Let's get a cab," Julien said.

They started with drinks at a bar somewhere on the Right Bank. Julien managed to snag a seat for Genevieve, and he stood with one arm draped on the back of her chair. It was hard to hear each other over the jazz combo and the other patrons. When Genevieve spoke, Julien watched her face intently. When he wanted to be heard, he leaned close to her ear. Genevieve was drinking a French apértif, something Julien had recommended. The effect was intoxicating.

After an hour, or maybe two – Genevieve lost track – they walked down the street to dinner. Warm light spilled out of the restaurant's big windows and onto the sidewalk.

"I think I'm underdressed," Genevieve muttered as they walked in. After the din of the bar, the restaurant seemed quiet as a church.

"Ridiculous," Julien said. "You look fantastic."

Genevieve took stock of the people around her. The other patrons all looked very French and very sophisticated. And very rich.

"I might be in over my head," she said. "This is a long way from Wichita Falls."

"Is that such a bad thing?"

It didn't take long for Genevieve to realize this probably would be her most memorable meal ever. The food was amazing – the tastes seem to explode in her mouth. A different wine arrived with each course, and for the first time, she began to see the alchemy involved in pairing food and wine.

They drank wine and sampled from each other's plates. He told her a funny story about eating snails. She told him about ordering a shrimp dish on a date and being horrified to find that the shrimp, in a cream sauce, still had the shells attached. She'd eaten hardly anything, terrified of making a mess.

They were laughing about that when Genevieve noticed a man two tables over staring at her. She quickly lowered her head and stifled her laugh.

"What's wrong?"

"I'm too loud. There's a man over there staring at me," she whispered.

Julien sneaked a look.

"You're right," he said. "He is staring at you." He leaned over the table and whispered, "Why wouldn't he? You're the most beautiful woman in the restaurant."

Genevieve blushed to the roots of her hair.

"Oh, here we go with the blushing," Julien said, leaning back in his chair. "You kill me with that – every time. You *do* know that, don't you?"

Genevieve felt her face grow even hotter.

"No, you don't know it," Julien said. "That's part of your charm."

Genevieve hazarded a look up. He was smiling at her affectionately.

"Beet-red face," she said. "Yeah, that's *totally* charming."

"A woman who doesn't realize how beautiful she is? *Very* charming."

She tried to hold his gaze but couldn't. She looked nervously off to the side.

"Especially from LA, where so many women are workin' it all the time," he said.

"But you have to tell me, Genevieve." He paused. "You know, I like it better in French." He said it again, softening the G, stressing the first syllable – Jhan-vee-ev. "How can you *not* know you're beautiful?"

"There are plenty of beautiful women in here," Genevieve said. "He must be looking at my hair. I swear, sometimes it's like having a neon sign on your head."

Julien leaned his chin in his hand, listening. "You don't like being a redhead?"

"It attracts attention. When you're a kid, people call you Carrot Top and stuff, and when you're older... " Here she faltered.

Julien raised an eyebrow.

"Some men have a weird thing for redheads," Genevieve said, dropping her voice to a whisper.

Julien cleared glasses from the space between them. He reached out and ran one finger along the back of her hand. "How *interesting*," he said, his eyes intent on her face.

Genevieve hoped he didn't see her shiver. She blushed furiously. Again.

He leaned back in his chair. "You know, the first girl I ever kissed had red hair. Her name was Jessica. It was at my friend Jon's bar mitzvah. I was 13."

Genevieve's blush receded. She liked it when Julien talked about himself.

"Your turn," he said, as a waiter cleared the remains of their dinner. "First kiss?"

"Me? Danny Foster. Out at the lake."

"And you were how old?"

"Fifteen. No, wait. I drove. So I was 16."

"No one kissed you until you were 16? What was *wrong* with those boys in Wichita Falls?"

□

Like everything else, dessert was amazing. Julien ordered after-dinner drinks, then had the waiter whisk hers away and bring something else when she didn't like it.

Three sips into that drink, Genevieve set her glass down a little unsteadily and excused herself.

Genevieve studied her face in the ladies' room mirror, carefully applying lipstick.

What was it about drinking that made your face more interesting, she wondered?

A man she met at a conference once told her she looked like Botticelli's Venus. He described her skin as "alabaster" and her hair as "molten flame." It was an improvement over the words the boys back in Wichita Falls used, things like "pasty" and "orange."

What would people back in Wichita Falls say if they saw her now?

"You're drunk," she told her reflection, answering her own question.

Did she say that out loud? She looked around, relieved to see that she was alone.

She adjusted her neckline. Thank God for D. Thank God for push-up bras.

Julien did the half-rise thing as she returned to the table. Such lovely French manners.

"Ready to walk a bit?" he asked as they left the restaurant.

"All the way back to the hotel?" Genevieve really was going to regret the shoes.

"Not quite yet," he said. "I have a surprise."

CHAPTER TWENTY-NINE

With her hand tucked in the crook of Julien's arm, they set off. It was a beautiful night, chilly but not cold, a full moon illuminating the city.

They made a left and then another left, onto a quiet street that was vaguely familiar. Then Julien stopped at a door and produced a key from his pocket.

"What are we..."

"Ssshhh." He put one finger to his lips as he worked the key in the lock.

The heavy street door swung open, and they stepped into a dark courtyard.

"Be careful. The stones are uneven," Julien whispered as he guided her across the courtyard to a second door.

"Are we supposed to be here?"

"I seem to have a key," Julien said.

The second door opened, and Genevieve realized where they were. The stairs to Théodore Lazare's studio beckoned.

Genevieve began to climb. Then Julien closed the door, eliminating the light from the courtyard, plunging the stairwell into darkness.

"Hang on," he said. He reached out for her, his hand landing in her hair, which he patted reassuringly.

Genevieve heard rustling, and then the narrow path up the stairwell was lit by the glow from Julien's cell phone.

Genevieve concentrated on navigating the stairs, a task made more difficult by her heels and the drinks she'd consumed.

"How do you have a key?"

"Ssshhh," Julien whispered, inches from her ear. "Don't attract the gendarmes."

Genevieve stopped, and Julien nearly plowed into her.

He put his hand on her shoulder. "I'm kidding. It's fine. Keep going."

They reached the top landing and engaged in an awkward ballet as Genevieve tried to move so Julien could unlock the last door.

"Just stay there," Julien said, reaching around her to press his phone into her hand. "Hold the light for me."

Genevieve inhaled, smelling sunshine, clean cotton and bright Texas skies – in the middle of a dark Paris stairwell.

Julien worked the key in the lock, his head right next to hers.

"What *is* your perfume?" He turned his face into her hair and breathed in. "I know it, but I can't come up with the name. I've been trying to think of it since I met you."

"I don't wear perfume," Genevieve said.

"Really?"

The lock clicked, and the door to the studio opened.

"Oh." Genevieve stepped into the studio, which was flooded by moonlight streaming in the big windows. "It's the light."

Julien spread his arms wide. "I thought about what you said about the light in the painting, and I realized this had to be the place."

Genevieve walked to one of the illuminated rectangles in the center of the room and turned her face up to the pure, white light. "Beautiful," she said, sighing.

"Yes."

"But warm," she said. She unbuttoned her coat. The climb from the courtyard had overheated her, and the attic was stuffy.

Julien crossed to her. "Let me take that."

Genevieve slipped out of it. Julien took it to a pile of boxes on the far side of the room. Then he shrugged out of his own coat, taking a moment to fold it before crossing back to her.

"You still haven't explained how you have the key," Genevieve said.

"I came to see Madame LeGrand this afternoon," Julien said. "I told her about *Pyramus and Thisbe* and asked if we could see the studio at night to see if it was the same light."

He reached for her wrist and held it.

"So naturally she gave you the key," Genevieve said. "Who wouldn't?"

"I did a little shopping first," Julien said, "to soften her up." He pressed something into Genevieve's hand.

"What's this?"

Julien shrugged.

Genevieve held the package up to the light. It was a small roll of fabric, tied with a ribbon. She unfastened the bow and unfurled a scarf.

"You needed a souvenir," Julien said. "This suits you better than the one you looked at the other day. Blue, a little green, and that violet that's exactly the color of your eyes."

Genevieve always heard that she was impossible to shop for. Her father bought her books from her wish list; D gave her gift cards. Christine occasionally hit the mark, but she missed plenty, too. Julien? He'd made a perfect choice the very first time.

He looped the scarf around her neck, lifting her hair to nestle the silk against her skin.

"There," he said, admiring the effect. "Yeah. Thisbe's got nothin' on you."

"It's beautiful. I..." She meant to say "thank you," but instead, Genevieve leaned up and kissed him.

Julien was initially startled. He drew back, just for an instant. Then he returned the kiss, twining his fingers in her hair and angling her head back. She wobbled a little in her heels. Julien wrapped one arm around her waist and steadied her against him.

Genevieve's heart began to hammer in her chest. Suddenly the room seemed airless and much too hot. She pulled away, gasping and overwhelmed. Julien relaxed his grip on her waist.

"Maybe we..." Genevieve searched Julien's face. His eyes were on hers, an intensity she hadn't seen before glittering there. "Maybe we should go?"

Julien adjusted the scarf around her neck, fingered a strand of her hair, ran his thumb across her lower lip. "Should we?"

He kissed her. It began slowly, then built. Genevieve felt suspended in that white rectangle of light, timeless, weightless, as though this space existed separate from the rest of the world.

A buzzing sound startled her, and she stumbled away from Julien, nearly falling. He caught her arm.

"It's my phone," he said. "It's just my phone."

Genevieve put her hand to her chest, gasping, and discovered that the first three buttons of her blouse were undone. When had *that* happened?

Once he was sure she wasn't about to topple over, Julien walked to the boxes in the corner of the room and rummaged in his coat until he found his phone. He silenced it.

Genevieve buttoned her blouse while his back was turned and tucked in a spot where it had popped loose from the waistband of her skirt.

"Julien?" He was in a dark corner of the room, his back to her. "We should go."

He nodded once and picked up their coats.

Two streets over, Julien waved down a cab, and Genevieve sank back into the seat, a little dazed.

He leaned forward to give the driver the hotel address, sat back, then leaned forward again to add something.

"What was that last part?"

"I told him to go by the Arc de Triomphe," Julien said. "You should see it at night."

Genevieve leaned her head against Julien's shoulder, and he shifted to put his arm around her.

"You called me Julien," he said.

"Hmmm?"

"Just now, up there," he said. "You called me Julien."

"Oh!" Genevieve pulled back to look at him. "I did?"

"It's funny, because you never call me anything," he said. "When you need to get my attention, it's always 'hey' or 'oh' or 'um.'"

Genevieve felt her face begin to color. "That's so rude. I'm sorry," she said, biting her lip. "It's just, in my head, for some reason, you're Julien, but I know you hate it."

"I don't hate it," he said. He put his hand on her chin and gently turned her head away from him. "You're missing the sights."

The Arc de Triomphe, brilliantly lit, loomed ahead and to the left.

"I hated it when I was a kid," Julien said, his face next to hers. "But the only person who calls me that since my mother died is Henry, and, I don't know... When you did it, it was kind of nice."

They rode in silence for a few minutes, enjoying the view. Then Julien told the driver to turn back toward the hotel.

Genevieve rested her head against his shoulder again. "So, just to be clear, I'm allowed to call you Julien? I don't have to call you Jay? Or Hey? Or Oh?"

Julien put on a serious face, made a show of considering it. "I think you are allowed to call me Julien. Yes. Definitely." He pulled her closer. "If you kiss me."

When they reached the hotel, the cab driver coughed discreetly to get their attention.

Julien paid him and held the hotel door open for her.

They walked up the stairs and down the hall. Genevieve stopped outside her room and faced Julien.

He leaned his arm against the wall above her head. They stood like that for a few minutes, eyes locked. He toyed with a strand of her hair. "Genevieve," he said. Then he said it again, in French.

His phone buzzed, and he rolled his eyes in exasperation.

"Go ahead," she said. "I can wait while you check it."

He looked her in the eye and smiled. "Big day tomorrow. We'd better call it a night, don't you think?"

Of course, she thought. That was the smart thing to do.

"Right," she said, fumbling with her key. "I'll see you in the morning."

Julien put his hand under her chin and just brushed her lips with his. "See you then," he said.

◻

Genevieve couldn't remember whether her limited international calling plan included text messages. She didn't really care.

She turned on her phone and typed a message to D.

Gen: Back from dinner. wore heels

D: Yay! Fun?

Gen: I think I love him

D: Haha. Just how much did you drink?

D: Gen?

D: Haha right?

D: Gen?

CHAPTER THIRTY

G ENEVIEVE WOKE UP the next morning expecting a hangover. But she felt fine. Terrific, even. And hungry.

She hurried through her shower and got dressed, at the last minute adding her new scarf to her outfit, her favorite lavender twin set and a pair of black pants. The scarf was even more beautiful in daylight, the colors just right for her. Julien had a good eye.

To her surprise, Julien wasn't waiting in the breakfast room off the lobby, a small, arched space with stone walls.

Genevieve thought that maybe he was feeling great, too, and decided to push his morning run an extra mile or two. Or perhaps he'd rushed out to accomplish some romantic last-minute gesture, like buying flowers.

Genevieve ordered a café au lait and snagged a fruit-filled pastry and a cup of yogurt from the buffet.

Then, making sure she was seated with her back to the wall where no one could peer over her shoulder, she sent D an email update: the drinks at the bar, dinner, the attic, the scarf, the cab ride back, all of it.

She had just hit the "send" button and was beginning to wonder whether she ought to call up to Julien's room when he appeared in the doorway. He scanned the room, and she smiled when he finally spotted her.

"There you are," she said as he dropped into the chair opposite her. He hadn't shaved, which Genevieve thought gave him a slightly roguish look that was very attractive. "Did you run an extra couple miles or something?"

Julien winced. "God, no. I slept in. I feel like hell."

"I feel great," Genevieve said, beaming at him. "I couldn't believe how hungry I was after that big meal. You should try those fruit-filled things; they're really good."

Julien flagged down the waitress for coffee. Genevieve checked to make sure her email to D had gone through and clicked over to the account she used for work.

"I got an email back from Henry, and you said Henry hates email!" she said. "But he saw the documents I sent yesterday, and he said, 'Excellent progress.' That's a huge compliment from him, right?"

"Sure," Julien said. He wandered over to the buffet, surveyed the offerings and came back with a plain croissant. He picked at a corner of it.

"Do you think I should fill Henry in on the whole thing about not displaying the painting in public? I didn't get into the Dr. Marchand interview with him."

Julien tentatively sipped his coffee, carefully set his cup down and pushed away the plate that held his croissant. He sighed.

"Look, Genevieve..." He sighed again. "I think we probably got a little ahead of ourselves yesterday."

"I guess we can wait until we find the rest of the wills to update him. I just thought he might be interested in the story about your great-whatever-grandfather trying to keep the painting under wraps."

"Genevieve."

Genevieve had already hit the "reply" button. She hit "cancel" and looked up.

"I'm not talking about what you told Henry yesterday," Julien said. "I meant last night."

Then he smiled. Kindly. To soften the blow, she supposed.

"Oh."

She looked back at her computer screen, desperate to think of a way to salvage some shred of dignity. What would D do?

D would brazen it out, that's what D would do. She would make it all a big joke.

"What was in that after-dinner drink anyway?" she said. "The last thing I drank that hit me that hard was served out of a 5-gallon Home Depot bucket at a house off-campus with a couch on the front porch and a ping-pong table in the dining room."

This was a lie. When she went to those parties in college, she was the designated driver.

Was Julien buying any of this? She had no idea. She studiously avoided looking at him.

"Genevieve, I don't mean... I just think..."

"It's fine," Genevieve said. Another lie. "I totally understand." Also a lie. "Shouldn't have happened." That, at least, was true, she supposed.

She shut her laptop, a little harder than she meant to. "The good thing is, nobody knows but us. Well, and the driver. But I'm sure we can count on a French cabbie to be discreet. We'll just say it never happened, and that's the official version."

She slid her laptop into her bag. "There's a lot to get done today. If you'd like to finish your breakfast, I'll just go on, and you can catch up with me at the archives."

"Genevieve..."

"I can manage the Metro on my own. I'm sure I won't get lost." She was rising now, trying to put on her coat and pick up her bag all at the same time. She couldn't get out of the room fast enough.

Julien stood and grabbed his own coat. "Hold on. I'm coming with you."

The Metro was crowded, forcing Julien to stand and allowing Genevieve to avoid conversation with him. As they walked to the archives, they passed a group of protesters, and Genevieve asked Julien to explain their signs. She could read the signs well enough and understood that they were demonstrating against government cutbacks. But she preferred faking illiteracy about current events to another conversation about what had happened between them.

What *had* happened? Genevieve tuned out Julien's political commentary and ran through the entire evening in her mind, trying to find the point at which things had turned, the thing she'd done wrong. Nine hours ago Julien Brooks could hardly keep his hands off her, and now it was all a mistake. What had she done?

At the archives, Julien returned to his task from the day before: trying to find his grandfather's will. Genevieve concentrated on those of his great-grandfather and great-great-grandfather.

Fortunately, in a library it was perfectly acceptable to ignore someone, and that was exactly what Genevieve did, until Julien pulled his chair over to hers.

"I'm dying for coffee," he whispered. "Want to take a break?"

Genevieve didn't even look up. "No thanks. I'm fine."

"There's a place right across the street," Julien said. "Won't even take 15 minutes."

"You go," Genevieve said. "Take your time."

She suspected he would; Julien was probably eager to avoid her, too.

When he'd been gone 10 minutes, she switched over to the carrel where he'd been working. His grandfather's will was the linchpin to the family's claim to the drawing, and so far it had eluded Julien. Maybe she'd have better luck. And if she showed Julien up in the bargain, well, that would be OK, too.

She managed not to crow with delight – but just barely – when she found Laurent Lazare's will. Julien apparently had not been using the speedier method she'd figured out, even though she'd explained it to him.

She quickly paged through the will looking for references to *Tristan et Iseult*, but when she reached the end, she realized there would be no shortcuts. She'd have to read the whole thing, slow as she was with her rusty French.

When Julien returned, she was on the second page, having just worked through the bequest to Georges, Henry Lazare's grandfather. He got money but no property from his father's estate.

"What's up? You're in my chair," Julien whispered.

Genevieve showed him what she'd found.

"You *found* it? Wow. You're good."

"I haven't found the listing of the art," Genevieve said. "The will started with the bequest to Georges, which was complicated."

"Just scan for '*Tristan et Iseult*,' " Julien said.

"I did," Genevieve hissed. Realizing how she sounded, she moved aside to make room for Julien. "You should probably take over. You're faster."

He began to move briskly through the pages. "Provisions for my mom's education. Several paragraphs about the gallery."

Julien read for a minute, turned back a page, read again. "Well?"

"It's not here," he said.

"What?"

He ran his finger along a line from the will. "It says, 'the apartment and all its contents, including furnishings and works of art.' "

"No," Genevieve said. This could not be happening. Surely the universe would not heap personal *and* professional humiliation on her in the same day. "Maybe there's an addition, another page."

"It ends here." Julien showed her the last page. "The drawing's not mentioned. We struck out."

"Excuse me a minute." Genevieve grabbed her bag and headed to the bathroom. She needed to compose herself.

She locked herself in a stall and sat for a minute with her head in her hands, breathing in through her nose and out through her mouth, trying not to cry.

She'd started the day so happy – how could everything have gone to hell before lunch?

Well, whatever the reasons, she couldn't very well hide in the bathroom all day. She unlocked the door and went to wash her hands.

In the mirror above the sink, she noticed the scarf, which she'd forgotten she was wearing. She looked like a total idiot. She whipped the scarf away and immediately felt guilty. It wasn't the scarf's fault. Folding it carefully, she put it in her bag. One more deep breath, and then she pushed the door open and went back to face Julien.

He was waiting by her chair, his backpack zipped and ready to go, his coat folded over his arm. He offered her a wan smile.

"I guess the silver lining is an afternoon free. What would you like to do next?"

Genevieve pulled out her chair and sat. "I'm going to stay and look for the other two wills."

She wasn't sure what to make of his expression. Surprise? Annoyance? "You don't have to do that," he said. "Look, I know this is a setback, but we still have those records in D.C."

"I *do* have to do it," Genevieve said, loud enough to earn her a shushing from another patron. "I'm staying."

Julien dropped down into a crouch so that he was at eye level with her. "Can we talk about this outside?" he whispered.

"There's nothing to talk about."

"Humor me," Julien said. "Please?"

Genevieve waited just long enough to make it clear that yes, she was humoring him, before gathering up her things and following Julien out of the room.

He led her down a flight of stairs and into a small courtyard. The sky had clouded over since they arrived, and the air seemed chillier. Genevieve pulled her coat tight around her.

"Look," Julien began. "I know you're angry with me, and that's..."

"I'm not angry with you," Genevieve said.

Julien stopped, looked away, took a deep breath.

Then he started over. "I realize you're disappointed, but that's no reason to go through some pointless exercise..."

"It's not pointless."

Julien stopped again. Took another deep breath.

"It's your last afternoon in Paris. Wouldn't you rather go see something? What about the Impressionists at the Musée d'Orsay, all those paintings you used to look at in books with your mom when..."

"Please don't do that." It came out more plaintive than Genevieve intended. Shock registered on Julien's face.

This was the worst part. She'd shared memories, little bits of herself, because she wanted to let him in. But to Julien, it was simply information, just conversational currency to be dropped the way he might leave the small change on the bar after he'd paid the tab.

Don't tell people things. The worst people would use her secrets against her, and even the best people would be careless with them. Hadn't she learned this lesson in first grade? Why did she always make the same mistakes?

"Don't do what?"

Genevieve recovered, squared her shoulders. "Please don't try to talk me out of this. Maybe I can fill in some gaps in the drawing's provenance. It's not pointless to me."

Julien ran a hand through his hair, clearly frustrated. "The thing is, I have to leave, at least for a little bit."

"I'm fine on my own here," Genevieve said, striving to sound as pleasant as possible.

"I have to take the key back," Julien said.

"Of course," Genevieve said, trying to keep her face neutral, desperate not to blush at the memory of the previous night. And then an idea occurred to her.

"As long as you're going there..."

She opened her bag and pulled out the scarf, held it out to Julien folded neatly in her palm. "I've been thinking maybe you'd like to return this."

Julien's shoulders slumped. "I thought you liked it?"

"It's beautiful," Genevieve said. "It's just, under the circumstances..." She continued to hold the scarf out, but Julien wouldn't take it.

"It was very thoughtful," she said. "But I'd feel so much better if you took it back. I know you must have a bad case of buyer's remorse. Just take it back. Please."

"Genevieve." Julien shook his head slowly. "Genevieve, let's go get some lunch, have a glass of wine and really talk about this. And I don't mean the scarf, which I am not taking back, so put it away."

Genevieve put the scarf back in her bag.

"I had a huge breakfast. I'm not interested in lunch," she said. "I'll get back to my research now." She shouldered her bag and turned to go inside.

Julien caught her arm. "Genevieve, please. I'm sorry. I know I'm making a mess of this. I... look, let's just go sit down somewhere and..."

"You were perfectly clear this morning," Genevieve told him. "I don't want lunch. I don't want to walk around Paris with you, and I most certainly don't want to have a conversation that is only going to make me more embarrassed than I already am. The nicest thing you could do for me right now, honestly, is just leave me alone."

CHAPTER THIRTY-ONE

GENEVIEVE LEFT the archives a little before 4 in the afternoon with a consolation prize: copies of four generations of Lazare wills.

Emile Lazare, nephew of the artist, mentioned the drawing and painting by name in his will and repeated his father's admonition that the painting *Tristan and Iseult* should not be displayed in public.

Emile's son Daniel, Julien's great-grandfather, listed "two works by the artist Théodore Lazare" among his possessions. That was less definitive, but still helpful, especially in the context of the earlier wills. She'd managed to do a little, then, to document the drawing's history.

Julien, mercifully, had stayed away.

She planned to squeeze in some souvenir shopping for D when she left the archives, but she had no guidebook, not even a map. She'd been relying on Julien to help her navigate Paris, which now seemed ridiculous.

When she walked outside, the skies were low and threatening, and she was daunted by the prospect of wandering without a plan. Much better, she decided, to take the Metro back to the hotel and regroup. Perhaps someone at the front desk would have a helpful suggestion.

She also needed to figure out a plan for dinner, something close to the hotel where she could eat on her own and not feel conspicuous. She'd skipped lunch, and now her head was pounding.

Beyond dinner loomed the prospect of a flight with Julien the next day to Washington, D.C. How long could she avoid conversation by reading her book, watching a movie, feigning sleep?

And after a day in the archives in Washington would come another long flight and then, perhaps the thorniest problem of all: what to do when she got back to Los Angeles. Staying at Julien's house was unthinkable. She couldn't go back to her apartment.

As she climbed the stairs from the Metro, the skies opened up. Naturally, she had no umbrella. She turned up the collar of her coat and trudged the two blocks to the hotel, arriving wet and thoroughly depressed.

She shelved any thought of souvenir shopping. Instead, she went up to her room for a hot shower and a good cry.

□

The hotel had a happy hour in the breakfast room. Genevieve wasn't happy and didn't want a drink, but she needed to get online, so she took her laptop and headed downstairs.

Genevieve accepted a glass of Perrier and took a hunk of baguette and a few sweating slices of cheese from the picked-over remains of the happy-hour spread.

She had an email waiting from D, a response to the one Genevieve had sent that morning, before Julien had come downstairs and completely rearranged her thinking. Genevieve didn't have the heart to open it.

Instead, she created a new email to D and typed a short message:

J said this morning it was a mistake. Nightmare.

Call you tomorrow from DC.

I am such an idiot.

Once that was sent, she emailed Thomas, letting him know she'd failed to find the proof she needed in Julien's grandfather's will and asking for an update on Philip's job situation and their mortgage.

"Mind if I sit?"

Julien had his hand on the chair opposite hers, waiting for a response. She hadn't even seen him come in.

"Hey," Genevieve said. She gestured toward the chair. "Go ahead."

D always did say she lacked the rudeness gene.

He'd changed clothes since she'd seen him last, and it looked as though he'd just showered and shaved.

Julien seemed tired, and maybe a bit wary of her, which she supposed made sense. She had asked him to leave her alone the last time he'd seen her.

"I found the other wills," she said. "I was just getting ready to email Henry."

"That's great," Julien said.

Before she could click over to the email account she used for work, something popped up in her personal account. The sender was *TristanTriedToHide*.

"Oh no," Genevieve said. Her heart began to pound. She opened the email, gave a little cry of alarm, and slammed her laptop shut.

"Genevieve, what is it?"

"Another email," she said, fighting the tide of panic and nausea rolling over her.

Julien reached for her laptop, but Genevieve pulled it toward her. "No!"

Then, aware that people were staring, she lowered her voice. "I don't want you to read it."

"Why?"

"It's horrible," Genevieve said quietly. "It's some kind of sex-slave thing."

Julien's mouth was set in a grim line. "Give me the computer." He stretched his hand across the table. "I'll forward the email to Melvin. We need to figure out how this guy got past the filters we've set up."

Genevieve reluctantly slid the laptop over to Julien. "Is it bad that I hope Melvin catches him instead of the police, because then there aren't so many rules?"

Julien shook his head. "I was just thinking the same thing." He took the laptop and waited, his hand on the closed lid. "Do you want to be here while I look at this?"

When Genevieve returned from the bathroom, the laptop was back in front of her chair, closed up tight, the menace contained.

Julien stood and pulled her chair out for her.

"I had to set up some fairly elaborate filters," he said. "I put a note on your desktop to explain."

"Thank you," Genevieve said.

"I don't think that guy has any idea where you are," Julien said. "He's just throwing stuff out there, trying to scare you."

The room was chilly; Genevieve ran her hands over her arms trying to warm up. "Anonymous emails are just so chickenshit."

Seeing Julien smile, she said, "I know, that's the Texan in me coming out, but it *is*. Like the person trying to get Philip fired. I mean, if you really have such a problem with someone's personal life that you think they should lose their job over it, at least put your name behind it, you know?"

"You lost me there," Julien said, frowning. "Is this about your friend Thomas and his partner?"

Genevieve gave Julien a synopsis of Philip's situation, how an anonymous email to his boss had put his job in jeopardy.

"Did you mention this to Melvin?" he asked.

"No, why?" Then realization slowly dawned on her. "But why would someone... He doesn't have anything to do with... Oh no." Genevieve slumped back in her chair. "I got Philip fired by poking around on this, didn't I?"

"It may just be a coincidence," Julien said. "Either way, it's not your fault."

Genevieve often comforted herself with the idea that she had experienced the lowest point of her life early, when her mother died, and that her emotional trajectory had to be – *had to be* – upward from there. Some days, though, that theory was sorely tested.

"The worst part is, he's going to be fired for nothing," Genevieve said. "I'm just blundering around, causing all this damage, and I can't prove anything."

"Genevieve, please stop," Julien said. He reached across the table for her hand, then thought better of it and pulled back. "What my grandfather did or didn't put in his will is not your fault. None of this is a reflection on you."

Genevieve hugged her arms tighter across her chest.

"Are you too cold?" Julien began to shed his jacket, but she waved him off.

"Let's go get some dinner," Julien said, trying a new tack. "You'll feel better after you've eaten."

"I had something from the spread here. I think I'll just go to bed," Genevieve said. "The flight's early, and I'm tired."

Julien eyed her plate, which held two pieces of cheese, now stiffening around the edges, one clearly untouched, the other missing only a small bite. "That's not a real dinner. You didn't have a real lunch, either."

Genevieve was about to invent a story about how she'd gone out, but something stopped her.

"I checked in on you," Julien said, "around 1:30. You seemed busy, and OK, so I didn't bother you. But you didn't have lunch."

"I was working," Genevieve said. It sounded defensive, even to her.

"Look, I understand..." Julien started, then stopped. He took a deep breath.

"Would steak frites appeal to the carnivore in you? I know a place, it's really loud. Great people-watching. You can just sit back and be entertained."

He was offering her dinner on her terms. Just food, no conversation.

When she didn't answer right away, Julien stood. "You've had a bad day. Dinner will make you feel better. I promise. Let's go up and get our coats."

Genevieve stood and followed him up the stairs.

In her room, she opened up her laptop to power it down and save the battery.

There were two notes on her desktop. The first, as Julien described, explained the new filters on her email account.

The second was just below an instant message window from D, who must have messaged while Genevieve was in the bathroom.

D: He whaaaaa?
          TOTAL A-HOLE MOVE!!!!!

Julien's note below was succinct:

She's right. It was.

Genevieve tried – and failed – to work up righteous indignation that Julien had read her instant message from D. It
was right there on her screen, and he saw it only because he
was dealing with that horrible email.

Mostly, she was just too tired to be mad.

Julien seemed tired, too. As they rode the Metro to dinner,
he told her that he'd gone for a long run in the afternoon,
"trying to clear my head," as he put it. He'd also been caught
in the rain.

When they reached the restaurant, Julien looked in the
window and then craned his head up to double-check the
address. Only three tables inside were occupied.

"My friends who were here in September said it was
packed every night." He turned to Genevieve. "Do you want
to try somewhere else?"

"Maybe it's the weather," Genevieve said, and, as if on cue,
light rain began to fall. "This is fine. Let's just eat."

Julien kept the conversation afloat for 10 minutes, asking
her about the wills she'd found that afternoon. But there
wasn't much to tell, and they soon lapsed into silence.

The quiet was punctuated only by cutlery clinking against
plates and the low hum of a TV over the bar tuned to a soccer
match. Julien turned once or twice to check it out.

"Who's playing?"

"What?"

"The game," Genevieve said. "Or match or whatever. Who's
playing?"

"No idea," Julien said. "I don't follow soccer."

"I would have figured you for a fan," Genevieve said. "Liking soccer is a thing now, isn't it?"

Her old boss Malcolm followed soccer and insisted on calling it "football." Genevieve considered that the height of pretension, unless a person came from a country where the sport was popular.

Julien seemed bewildered by the conversation's turn. "I think it's boring. All that running around, and at the end the score's still zero-zero half the time. I don't see the appeal."

His phone buzzed. Julien pulled it from his pocket, checked the screen and silenced it.

With that one gesture, Genevieve suddenly understood everything.

Their embrace in the attic – which, Genevieve had to admit, seemed headed somewhere far more serious than mere kissing – ended when Julien's phone buzzed.

When they stood in the hallway outside their hotel rooms and Genevieve was weighing whether to ask Julien into her room or wait to let him make the move, Julien's phone buzzed.

She knew that Julien had been on a date before he came to her apartment the first time, and he'd been out twice during the time she was staying with him. But she'd dismissed the idea that he was involved seriously with someone. What woman wouldn't notice that her boyfriend had a female houseguest for so long or would tolerate it without wanting to check it out?

But maybe Julien's girlfriend had an especially demanding career and was used to not seeing him much. Maybe she traveled for business.

Maybe she was just trusting.

Genevieve thought of all the times she'd called Pete when he was supposedly working late or was on the road. All the times he didn't pick up. All the explanations. Turned the ringer off and forgot to put it back on. The restaurant was loud. Battery ran out of juice.

"You can step outside and return that," she told Julien. "It's fine."

"It's not important," Julien said.

"Really, go ahead," Genevieve said. "I've been..."

No. She would not tell him that she'd been the woman on the other end of that call. *Don't tell him things.* Why was this so hard for her to remember?

"You've been what?"

"I don't know what I was going to say," Genevieve said. "I'm really tired. Please, just go return your call."

"It was an automated thing from the airline," Julien said. "Probably just a gate change or something."

Was he lying? Genevieve couldn't tell. He would have to be pretty smooth at it, she guessed, to keep a relationship afloat while pursuing other women on the side.

Another blinding flash of insight. She put down her fork, her appetite gone.

Had Julien pursued her? Or had she pursued him? He was a flirt, it was true, but hadn't he essentially told her it was meaningless? Hadn't she noticed that he engaged every woman between the ages of 16 and 86 pretty much the same way?

She'd kissed him first.

He'd been surprised, and his first reaction was to pull back. He'd come down to breakfast the next day determined to deliver a clear message that this couldn't go any further, because he wasn't available.

The trouble with opening up the offense, as D had encouraged her to do, was that sometimes your receiver was covered.

□

They headed back to the Metro about the same time a political demonstration broke up, and a noisy crowd hurtled down the stairs behind them into the station.

As Genevieve was buying her ticket, the train pulled in.

"Perfect timing," Julien said.

Genevieve went through the turnstile and boarded the car. She looked back. Julien wasn't behind her.

Fighting traffic, she headed back up the aisle and looked out. Julien had been caught behind a clump of protesters.

A signal sounded. The doors were about to close.

"Wait for me on the platform at Chatelet," Julien called.

The car was jammed, and Genevieve couldn't find a seat. She was stuck in the middle of a noisy group, people talking over her head, gesturing.

Genevieve couldn't tell whether they were all on the same side, energized by the march, or whether she was trapped between opposing factions. Had any of the protests in France turned violent?

Taking deep breaths, she tried to calm herself.

Then she thought about the email. What if the man who sent it followed her to Paris? What if he was right here, on the Metro?

She could feel a wave of heat building inside her. The car picked up speed, and her stomach lurched. The noise seemed deafening.

The shaking of the train seemed to intensify, and the voices around her grew louder. How many stops to Chatelet? Wasn't there a map of the route on the wall?

She ducked under the arm of a man next to her, hoping to make her way to the map.

Suddenly the car was plunged into darkness.

Bare wood floor. Moonlight streaming in.

A man next to her in the dark, breathing.

He moves away. Toward the stairs.

She should stop him, warn him. It isn't safe.

She opens her mouth to protest.

The door to the stairs creaks open, and he turns to her.

She raises her hand, gestures for him to stop.

But she can see, in his face, that there's no point.

He already knows. He shakes his head, smiles sadly.

The door closes, and he is gone.

CHAPTER THIRTY-TWO

PEOPLE STIRRED around Genevieve. The train slowed as it came toward a station.

The sign came into view: Chatelet.

Genevieve staggered down the aisle and out to the platform. She took a deep breath, tried to get her bearings. She felt dizzy.

A familiar face swam into view.

"There you are," Julien said, his voice sharp. "Where the hell have you been? I've been waiting at least 15 minutes. How did you end up on a train *behind* me?"

He stopped. "You look awful. Are you OK?"

Genevieve wobbled and lost her balance. Julien caught her hand to steady her, but it was so slick with sweat that he let go and grabbed her sleeve instead.

"You're clammy. Are you sick? Wait, did someone..."

She shook her head. "No. But I think I'm going to pass out."

Julien propelled her to a bench, where Genevieve sagged down. She felt his hand on the back of her head, pushing.

"Put your head down," he said, then rested his hand on her back. "Get it lower than your heart."

Genevieve complied, knowing that she looked ridiculous but not really caring.

After a few minutes, her head began to clear. She tried to sit up straight.

"Go slow," Julien said. "We're not in a hurry here."

"I'm OK," she said. "Let's go back to the hotel. People are staring at me."

Julien didn't move. "You disappear on me, and now you want to go back to the hotel?"

Genevieve had never felt so utterly defeated. Julien expected an explanation, and she didn't have one, not one that he would believe.

She stood. "Can we please just go?"

"I was on the train right behind you. You should have been waiting for me on the platform. Where were you?"

"I don't know," Genevieve said.

"What do you mean, you don't know?" Julien rose to his feet.

A couple carrying a large sign turned to stare, but Julien ignored them.

"Did you ride a stop too far? That doesn't make sense – you would have doubled back from the other direction. Did you get off a stop too early? That doesn't make sense either, because you would have just boarded the next train, which would have been the same one I was on. Where have you been for the last 15 minutes?"

"I don't know," Genevieve said. "I got on the train, and then I... I don't know."

Julien dropped back down onto the bench. "Was this like what happened to you before? Where you blacked out or whatever and thought you were somewhere else?"

Genevieve sat, too. She was too tired to make up a plausible story. "Yes."

"But it doesn't make sense," Julien said. "Even blacked out, you would still be on the same train. I mean, the laws of physics are still in effect."

He looked at Genevieve. "Aren't they?"

She shrugged.

He ran a hand through his hair. "This is messed up."

"Yeah."

A train rattled into the station, and a large group got off, carrying banners and chanting. Julien waited for them to pass, their slogans echoing down the tunnel and then out into the night.

"All the times this has happened to you before, you said there was a room. It was the studio, wasn't it?"

Did it really matter now what she told him? Probably not. Genevieve nodded.

"I went back there today, before I returned the key," he said.

She turned to look at him. "Why?"

"I wanted to see it one more time, in the daylight," he said. "I wanted to see what it felt like without you there. It wasn't the same. But it wasn't normal, either."

"Meaning what?"

"I think it means I sort of believe you." He closed his eyes, rubbed his hands over his face. "And I'm having a hard time wrapping my head around that. I'm a guy who doesn't believe in... I don't know, pick something most people believe in. I don't have a lucky number. I think astrology is bullshit. I don't even exactly believe in God the same way most people do. But I believe this. What sense does that make?"

"None," Genevieve said.

"Yeah, that's right," Julien said. "None."

He turned so that he was facing her fully. "Genevieve, last night, in the attic..."

She put a hand up to stop him. "I really don't..."

"I know you don't want to talk about it," Julien said, halting as another train pulled in, disgorging another noisy group.

"We can't do this with protesters parading by." He held out a hand to her. "But we have to talk about it. C'mon. Let me buy you a drink."

They found a quiet spot a block or so away. Under different circumstances, Genevieve would have been reveling in the very Frenchness of it all – the tile floor, the small cafe tables, even the world-weary man behind the bar.

She immediately excused herself to the restroom. She wanted to wash her hands and freshen up after her misadventure on the Metro, and she also wanted to steel herself for the conversation ahead.

Julien had ordered her a glass of red wine, and it was waiting when she got back. She didn't even take a drink, just sat down and launched into what she'd decided needed to be said.

"About last night: I owe you an apology. I'm sorry."

Julien choked a little on his wine.

"*You're* sorry?"

"I wasn't seeing how much of this is my fault. But I kissed you first."

"That's true, you did."

Genevieve felt her face begin to color, but there was nothing to do but keep going. "You're seeing someone, right?"

"What?"

"Please don't..." She'd started to say, "*Please don't lie.*" How many times had she said that to Pete?

"Please don't feel like you need, I mean, I would feel better if you would be straight with me," Genevieve said. "I've been the woman on the other end of those calls."

Julien's face registered nothing but confusion. "I'm sorry, what calls?"

"At dinner just now, last night in the attic, in the hall at the hotel."

"What are you *talking* about?" Pulling his phone from his pocket, Julien put it on the table between them. "Air France called during dinner to offer me an upgrade. The two calls I got last night were from a client who forgot I was out of town. You want to check the call log?"

Genevieve pushed the phone back toward him. "I'm not grilling you, for God's sake." She recognized this tactic. Pete had used it. He'd shift the focus onto her so he wouldn't have to answer her questions.

"Look, I knew you were out with someone before you brought my wallet by, and then when I was at your house, you were out late, and I'm just saying, I get it now, I understand."

"No, you don't understand," Julien said. He tipped his wineglass back and took a generous drink.

"The woman you're asking about, I've seen her exactly twice," he said. "We met for drinks, and that would have been it, but she called me with an extra ticket to a concert, and that takes guts, so I said yes. She's very nice, but there's nothing there."

"Oh." Genevieve felt like an idiot.

"If I were seeing someone, we wouldn't have been up there last night," Julien said. "I have a lot of faults, and I admit I've screwed up here, but I'm not *that* bad."

Genevieve turned her head away and watched the bartender methodically wipe down glasses.

"Please don't hide behind your hair," Julien said. "I'm trying to talk to you."

She straightened in her seat and looked him in the eye.

"I am *so* sorry about this. When I came down this morning and saw how happy you were, I knew this was going to be hard, and I was so mad at myself," Julien said. "And then when you didn't want to talk about it, I went with that. But I shouldn't have, because that was taking the easy way out."

He took a deep breath. "Genevieve, I can't do this, and not because I'm seeing someone. I can't be with someone who..."

"Someone who's crazy?"

Irritation flashed across his face. "If you're crazy, then I'm crazy, too. And why do you do that? It's like you can't wait to let me finish a sentence, you have to say it first. To prove you know what I'm thinking? Because I don't think you do, actually."

Genevieve sat back, stung. He was right. It was a bad habit. If the conclusion was something negative about her, she wanted to be the one to say it. That made it hurt less, somehow.

"I'm sorry," she said. She waved her hand over the table. "You have the floor. I'll listen until you're finished. You can't be with someone who..."

Julien drained his wine and put the empty glass on the table.

"Who makes me feel... This seems like a compulsion, like you have some kind of power over me."

Stunned, Genevieve put a hand to her chest and began to protest. "But I..." Then she remembered that she'd promised to let Julien talk.

"Last night was..." Julien stopped, then threw up his hands. "I can't even come up with a word to describe it. I mean, I had your shirt halfway off, and I don't even know how that *happened.*"

Genevieve felt the color begin to creep up her face.

"Maybe you had it totally under control and I'm the one who..." Julien shook his head. "Seriously, if my phone hadn't rung, that would have ended on the floor with clothes everywhere and me wondering *what the hell*? Wouldn't it?"

Genevieve put one hand over her eyes. Her face was now burning.

"I'm making it sound like it's all about sex, and it's not," Julien said. "That's what I mean – I can't even explain it. God, that blushing *kills* me."

Genevieve raised her hand. "Can I say something?"

"God, yes," Julien said. "Please do."

"Do you think I'm trying to manipulate you or something? Because I'm not."

Julien caught the eye of the barman. "Do you want another glass?"

Genevieve tipped the half-glass she still had left toward him. "I'm fine."

The barman shuffled over to refill Julien's glass. Julien murmured "Merci," and waited for him to leave.

"I don't think you're *trying* to do anything," Julien said, smiling. "That's the thing. You can't help it. You make me believe things I can't believe. And even when you're doing something that annoys me, like interrupting, you're just..."

Aware that she'd promised not to interrupt, Genevieve waited for Julien to finish the sentence. She was just... *what*? Everything he'd said so far made it sound suspiciously as though he felt about her the way she felt about him. So what was the problem?

She watched as Julien's smile faded.

"I can't do this. I can't get pulled into something over-powering like this. The last few years – changing careers, my mother, the divorce – life's been too hard already. I want to keep my life really..." He extended his arm like a referee signaling a first down. "Simple. Straightforward."

Julien paused and took a drink. "I am *so* sorry that I didn't have this realization sooner, because I know I jerked you around and hurt your feelings, and I never wanted to do that. I will make that up to you. I promise."

Genevieve sat still, thinking.

"Genevieve? You can talk now."

Could she promise Julien that a relationship wouldn't be complicated? She knew the answer was no. If her father had it to do all over again, if he knew the misery to come, would he still go inside the bank and cash a check for $10 – all he could afford – just so he could talk to that pretty redhead in line?

"Genevieve?"

She smiled her bravest smile. "That's probably the smart decision."

Was it her imagination, or did Julien's shoulders sag, just a little?

They sat quietly for a few minutes, nursing their drinks.

Then Genevieve sighed. Time to move on. "Well, I guess the thing to do is keep things professional and maintain a certain amount of distance. You should call the airline about that upgrade."

"We've discussed this. I'm not doing that."

"You don't have to jam yourself into coach to make a point. My ex-boyfriend upgraded all the time. I'm used to it," Genevieve said, then immediately regretted it. More personal information. She really needed to stop that.

Ignoring Julien's frown, she said, "The point is, this is a

business relationship. Treat me as you would any other colleague."

"I was hoping for something more like friends," Julien said. "I promise you, I'll be a great friend. You can count on me. I'll do anything for you."

He looked down at his hands. "And the physical attraction – who knows? Maybe it'll burn itself out. It happens."

"You might be right," she said, "but it won't if you flirt with me."

"Fair enough," he said. "If I'm crossing the line, you just have to tell me."

CHAPTER THIRTY-THREE

After Paris, Washington seemed grimy and depressing. In Paris, the bare tree branches seemed architectural. In Washington and its suburbs, they just seemed bare. Remnants of a recent snowstorm were piled along the edges of the pavement, like trash swept to the curb after a parade.

Genevieve and Julien were booked into a hotel on the University of Maryland campus. It would take them only a few minutes to get to the National Archives the next morning.

Once they'd checked in and the elevator deposited them on their floor, Genevieve looked left, then right, trying to decipher which direction led to her room.

"You are seriously jet-lagged," Julien said, nudging her with his elbow. "This way. You're right next to me."

In her room, she took a shower and changed into her pajamas. She flicked through all the TV channels twice. Nothing looked interesting.

She called the cat-sitter in LA and got an update on Mona, who seemed to be enjoying her vacation from her owner just fine.

D was expecting an update, and Genevieve had promised to call. But she knew a phone call would last hours and leave her in tears. She saw that D was online and took the easy way out.

Gen:	Long talk last nite
D:	And?
Gen:	Friend zone
D:	What the WHAT???
Gen:	Relationship too complicated, life's been too hard already. etc.
D:	I call BS on that. He wants you. You don't have to take no for an answer.
Gen:	Yes, I do. Need to sleep now.

It was after 11 p.m., but she didn't *feel* sleepy. She decided to call Thomas. She needed to hear the latest on Philip, and maybe Thomas would have art-world gostsip that would put her to sleep.

He picked up right away. "Gen? Are you still in Paris?"

"No, Maryland." She pulled the second pillow from the other side of the bed and propped it behind her. "We're hitting the MFFA records at the National Archives tomorrow. What's new with Philip?"

At Julien's urging, she'd sent Melvin details about the anonymous email that had led to Philip's suspension from work. She hoped he would conclude it was unrelated to her research. Until she knew for sure, she didn't want to mention it to Thomas.

"I gather the lawyers are wrangling. He doesn't tell me much."

"Thomas, I'm sorry."

"Thanks. How are you? You don't sound so good."

"Jet-lagged," Genevieve said, "and blue that Paris didn't turn out better. Could we yak awhile? Please tell me you have juicy gossip, or if you don't, could you maybe make some up?"

"Oh, Gen, have I ever." Thomas was playing up the drama, probably for her benefit. She loved him for that. "Did I tell you about the woman in Newport Beach who bought a $12,000 sculpture and then tried to return it to the gallery because it didn't match her coffee table?"

"I've heard that one," Genevieve said.

"How about the publicist in San Francisco who..."

"Hit reply-all on the email where she described a reporter as having the artistic sensibilities of a New Jersey mob wife?"

"Well, how about this one," Thomas said. "Word is the Kaufman deal is oh-eff-eff."

Billionaire Edward Kaufman owned the largest private art collection in the United States. His announcement a few years earlier that he was leaving it to a small, private university had been an art-world blockbuster.

"What happened?" she asked.

"My source says there was a blow-up over the architect for the museum the school was supposed to build," Thomas said.

"So who gets the collection now, according to your source?"

"No one knows. But Malcolm *has* been at all these mystery meetings lately."

Genevieve laughed. "Remember when you thought he was interviewing for a job in Florence, and it turned out he was visiting his in-laws in Florida, who you insist are *not* wealthy shipping magnates even though everyone else says they are?"

Thomas let out an exasperated sigh. He never liked it when she played devil's advocate.

"As if you'd ever let me forget," he said.

"What would the Hilliard even do with the Kaufman collection? There's no place to put it."

"They could start by getting rid of that hideous Kandinsky," Thomas said.

"You are completely wrong about that painting," Genevieve said. "It's fantastic."

They spent the next 15 minutes picking apart the Hilliard collection, a parlor game they'd played many times. Soon, Genevieve was yawning.

"Have I put you to sleep?"

"Yes," Genevieve said. "Thank you."

Genevieve's eyes snapped open at 3:22 a.m. She was wide awake.

She grabbed her laptop, thinking maybe she should give D a more complete report on the Julien situation.

Genevieve launched her email program, then shrieked and scrambled off the bed, dumping her laptop to the floor.

Suddenly she heard a banging, and Julien's voice. "Genevieve?" He was pounding on the door that connected their rooms. "Open the door!"

Genevieve fumbled with the deadbolt. Julien pushed past her and scanned the room. "What happened?"

Genevieve could barely get the words out. "He killed my cat."

Julien whirled to look at her. "What?"

"He cut her head off. He sent a picture." She pointed shakily at her laptop, which was lying on the floor next to the bed.

Julien retrieved it. "You've got to stop opening these emails." He sat on the bed and adjusted the screen. "Oh, ugh."

"I didn't click on it," Genevieve said. "It was just there." She hugged her arms across her chest. "How could this happen? I talked to the cat-sitter before I went to sleep and she was just there and Mona was fine."

Julien looked up from the computer. "When did you talk to her?"

"I don't know," Genevieve said. "It was maybe 6:30 in LA?"

"This isn't Mona." Julien patted the bed next to him. "Come here. I'll show you."

"I can't look at that again," she said.

"I'll cover up the gruesome part," Julien said. "Come here."

Genevieve reluctantly sat next to him. He had his hand over the top part of the screen. All she could see was the lower half of the cat's body in the photo.

"You talked to the cat-sitter around 6:30 in LA, and Mona was fine," Julien said. "This photo is taken in afternoon sunlight. The sun's down by 6 this time of year."

Genevieve looked again. "Mona's sort of beige on her belly. That cat's white."

"It's some sick photo he found online," Julien said. "He's trying to scare you."

"Oh God," Genevieve said. And then she began to sob.

She leaned her head against Julien's shoulder. He hesitated for an instant, then put the computer aside and wrapped both arms around her.

"This is so dumb," she sobbed into his chest. "Why am I crying now?"

"No idea," Julien said, his chin against her forehead.

The sobs began to subside, and it was only then that Genevieve realized Julien wasn't wearing a shirt. She pulled away. "I need a Kleenex," she said.

Julien was sitting across the room at the desk when she came back from blowing her nose.

"I'm sending this to Melvin." His fingers clicked rapidly on the keyboard. "Tomorrow we'll set up a new address and you can selectively give it out, and I mean, seriously, five people can have it. This has got to stop."

"I'm so tired." Genevieve plopped down on the edge of the bed. "It's like I'm too tired to sleep. I'm sorry I woke you up."

"I was watching cartoons," he said, eyes trained on her laptop. "It's jet lag."

"Would you watch cartoons with me for a little bit?"

He exhaled slowly. "Sure."

She clicked on the TV. "Can you see from there?"

Julien looked at her for a few beats. Then he got up. "Give me a second," he said, disappearing into his own room.

He came back pulling a T-shirt over his head, another in his hand. He tossed it to Genevieve. "That one's clean," he said.

She looked down. She was wearing pajama pants and a thin, white cotton tank top. "Oh," she said, embarrassed. She pulled Julien's T-shirt on. "I'm sorry."

Julien sat up against the headboard, stretching his legs out, keeping two feet of space between them. "Not as sorry as I am."

When Genevieve woke again, it was 6:46 a.m.

She was on top of the covers, curled up in Julien's T-shirt, a spare blanket draped over her. The TV was off, and the door to the connecting room was shut.

Julien was gone.

She showered and met him in the lobby a few minutes before 8. He was reading the *Washington Post* and drinking takeout coffee. He had a latte and a muffin ready for her, which she gratefully accepted. He said nothing about what had happened in the middle of the night. She decided to let it go.

The Archives building was tucked amid woods on the edge of campus. Genevieve supposed it was pretty when the trees had leaves. But on a gray day in March, it seemed forbidding.

In France, Genevieve had known what she needed to find. Here, she didn't even know whether any documents on the artwork looted from the Lazare family existed.

She decided to start with the reports filed by the monuments officers in the field. She thought that would give her the best overview. Julien would look through records of confiscated property in France.

She discovered a trove of memos written by James J. Rorimer, who had been at Neuschwanstein and gone on to a long career at the Metropolitan Museum of Art in New York.

She began to grasp the huge task the men at Neuschwanstein had faced. The castle and its grounds held thousands of looted objects. Some carried identifying marks from their original owners. Others had been tagged by the Einsatzstab Reichsleiter Rosenberg, which confiscated Jewish property in France.

After a couple hours, Julien came to sit with her. "Any luck?" she whispered.

"I'm not sure what I'm looking for," he said. "What are you looking at?"

"I'm reading memos. It's funny how many really bad typists there were. You see all these strikeovers and mistakes," she said. "They found a good typist at some point. You can tell it's the same person, because there's 'sfm' in lowercase letters at the bottom of the memos."

"One of the women working here told me the Nazis created an index card for everything, and they have the records here," Julien said "Do you think I should look at those?"

"The ERR files?"

"Eizen-something Rosenberg," Julien said. "Is that ERR?"

"That could be really good. I can't even imagine how many boxes that is. Maybe I should come look with you?"

"They're on microfilm. She said she'd show me this afternoon," he said. "If I need help, I'll come find you."

After a quick lunch, Genevieve went back to her boxes of memos; Julien went to look at microfilm.

By midafternoon, her attention began to flag. She was tired, depressed about Julien, and no closer to finding what she was looking for. All she really knew was that the Monuments Men faced a daunting task, generated lots of memos and eventually found a good typist.

Henry Lazare was really going to be impressed.

Julien was probably chatting with some attractive archivist who actually knew what she was doing.

Genevieve stared out at the barren woods, brooding.

She realized she'd sold the landscape short. The weak daylight slanting through the trees cast interesting shadows. She imagined what a gifted photographer could make of the scene.

"Well, duh," she said aloud. She was a visual person. She needed visual stimulation.

□

Genevieve was sitting at a table with photos from Neuschwanstein spread in all directions when Julien appeared at her elbow looking equally discouraged.

"Nothing," he said. "I mean, it was educational. I learned how the Nazis put a code of letters and numbers on the back of the artwork and then created an index card for it. But I didn't find a card for the drawing."

He looked down at the photos. "What have you got here?"

"I decided I needed visual stimuli."

"Did you find anything?"

Genevieve shook her head.

"Maybe this guy is your perfect typist," Julien said, picking up a photo. It showed three men in uniform crammed into an office. Two in the foreground were looking at a painting. A third man was seated at a desk with a typewriter in front of him.

Genevieve slid down so that the back of her neck rested against the top of the chair. She stared at the ceiling tiles.

"I don't know what I expected to find," she said. "I don't even know what I'm looking for."

"I don't know either," Julien said. "I mean, you're going through boxes of photos, so you can learn what? That the unit at Neuschwanstein had a great typist named..." He flipped over the photo. "Private Stimson F. Miller?"

Genevieve, who had been counting ceiling tiles, sat up so abruptly that she almost tipped over her chair.

"What did you just say?"

Julien looked at the back of the photo. "It says 'Lt. Commander James J. Rorimer, Sgt. R.J. LaRue and Pvt. Stimson F. Miller.' "

"Stim Miller?"

Julien put the photo down. "You *know* this guy?"

"He's on the board of the Hilliard."

CHAPTER THIRTY-FOUR

AT 10:30 THE NEXT MORNING, Genevieve and Julien were in a cab headed to Henry Lazare's house. It felt good, although disorienting, to be back in the California sunshine. They'd left their hotel in the predawn hours for an early flight, spent nearly six hours in the air, and yet it was still just midmorning in LA. Genevieve had to fumble in her carry-on for her sunglasses. It seemed ages since she'd needed them.

She was nervous about meeting Henry for the first time and wished they weren't going straight from the airport. She was tired of all the clothes in her suitcase and felt bleary after the flight. But Henry had insisted on meeting right away, and at his home, not his office.

He lived in a sprawling Mediterranean-style house in a quiet corner of Brentwood. Huge hedges and an electronically controlled gate screened it from the street.

"This is quite something," Genevieve said as the driver piled their luggage on the circular driveway. "I wish I could have cleaned up first."

Julien had been uncharacteristically quiet on the ride. "Don't worry about it," he said as he stepped up to the massive wooden door and rang the bell. It echoed for what seemed like minutes.

A tiny woman in a blue dress opened the door. "Oh, Mr. Julien, hello," she said.

Julien greeted her warmly. "Hello, Anna."

She stood back from the door. "You can leave the luggage in the hall," she said. "Mr. Henry is on the way from the office. You should wait in the library."

They followed her down a long hallway and then turned left through a pair of heavy wood doors.

The books in Henry Lazare's "library" were confined to two low shelves that flanked a stone fireplace. A pool table anchored the middle of the room. Opposite the fireplace was an old-fashioned wooden desk, nearly as big as the pool table, with an arrangement of cracked leather club chairs in front of it.

A small landscape of the Dutch school hung on the wall behind the desk, and Genevieve moved in for a closer look.

"I'd love to know the story on this painting," she said. "How long has he had it?"

"As long as I can remember," Julien said. "When I was a kid, Henry's dad was always calling me in here to lecture me. 'Julien, your mother was disappointed you got a B in Algebra. Your mother was upset to find music by a group called the Dead Kennedys in your room. Your mother says you've been staying out past curfew,'" he intoned solemnly. "I just wanted to shoot some pool."

Genevieve looked away from the painting. "That is a nice table. Solid slate, I bet."

"Are you an expert at pool table provenance, too?"

"D and I were dorm champs freshman year. Took down a couple really cocky rednecks, and oh, were they mad,"

Genevieve said. "Although D ended up dating one of them later."

"You're a pool shark?" Julien asked, incredulous.

"My dad taught me, and D grew up with all these brothers," Genevieve said. She backed a couple paces off the painting. "He's got this hung too high. Is Henry really tall, like you?"

Julien laughed. "Want to shoot pool while we wait?"

Before Genevieve could respond, the doors opened and Henry Lazare strode into the room, trailed by Melvin.

Genevieve's first thought was: My God. He's shorter than me.

She caught Julien's eye. He smiled and shrugged.

Henry Lazare's suit was impeccably tailored but failed to conceal his figure flaws: short legs, rotund belly. He looked like a well-dressed penguin with an expensive haircut.

He held his hand out to Genevieve. "Nice to meet you finally." He clapped Julien on the arm.

"Let's get this show on the road," he said, waving them toward the club chairs and seating himself behind the massive desk. Melvin hovered off to one side, his back to the wall.

Genevieve detailed what they'd found in the archives in Paris and Maryland, keeping her presentation concise. Julien had coached her during the flight, and she was grateful. She might have been tempted to meander otherwise. He'd done a good job anticipating Henry's questions.

When she finished, Henry leaned back in his chair, which Genevieve saw now was on a small platform to give him the illusion of height. "We don't have enough to go to the museum yet, is that what I'm hearing?" he asked.

"It would be one thing if we were sure the museum would deal in good faith," Genevieve said. "But we can't count on that. The response we've provoked – from someone – is completely out of proportion to the value of the drawing."

"You have a theory about that?" Henry asked.

"It has to be something that involves a lot of money. Why go to all this trouble? Maybe the drawing doesn't matter, but the route the drawing took does. Maybe it leads to other, more valuable things looted from your family," Genevieve said.

Out of the corner of her eye, she noticed Julien sitting with his chin propped in his hand, staring at her with something that looked suspiciously like admiration.

"Who knows what artwork could be out there?" she continued. "We've got no eyewitnesses, no business records to reconstruct the inventory of the gallery."

Julien took this opportunity to jump in. "Where are we on the threats, Henry?"

Henry turned to Melvin. "Yes, Melvin, let's get an update on that, since my cousin felt the pressing need to call me in the middle of the night about that."

Confused, Genevieve tried to catch Julien's eye, but he ignored her.

Melvin stepped away from his spot against the wall.

"Still working on the emails, but it's different ISPs. Might even be two different guys. Neighborhood canvas turned up a lady the next street over who works at home, some kind of writer, although it sounds like she mostly stares out her window all day. She saw an unfamiliar black SUV in the neighborhood a couple times. Another guy thought he saw..."

Genevieve found herself zoning out, looking at the landscape above Henry's desk as Melvin went through the information he'd gleaned from her neighbors.

"I also found a bag from a fish market in Glendale in the scrub behind the apartment. I'm hoping to call in a favor and get that run for prints, but that takes time."

His report concluded, Melvin perched on a corner of the massive desk.

"What about the anonymous email to my friend's boss? Is that related?"

Melvin and Henry exchanged a glance.

"That's going to be hard to trace without a copy of the email," Melvin said.

Henry weighed in. "If your friend has legal counsel, it's probably best that we coordinate through him. Or her. Can you get the name?"

Genevieve had been hoping to avoid that conversation, but it looked as if she wasn't going to have a choice. "I'll talk to Thomas this afternoon," she said.

Melvin's phone buzzed, and he pulled it from a case attached to his belt and checked it. He and Henry exchanged another glance.

"The main thing is, you've been safe with Mr. Brooks, and there's no reason to think that won't continue to be the case," Melvin said.

Genevieve took a deep breath and looked at Julien. He was staring pointedly in the other direction. "Actually, I need to take you up on the offer of a hotel. I've already stayed too long – it's an inconvenience for someone who works from home."

She and Julien had argued about this for roughly half of their nearly six-hour flight.

"You can't do your work at Starbucks, Julien? Every other quote-unquote self-employed person seems to," Henry said.

Genevieve winced at how sharply Henry spoke to Julien.

"This is my decision. He's very graciously offered to keep my cat for me," Genevieve said.

"Her mind's made up, Henry. Good luck trying to change it," Julien said.

Henry raised an eyebrow but said nothing. Instead, he picked up a phone on his desk and asked the housekeeper to call a cab.

The meeting was breaking up, but the cab wouldn't arrive for a few minutes, and Genevieve had an idea. She excused herself to wash her hands.

When she returned, she summoned her best smile for Henry. "That's a very nice landscape. I understand it's been in your family a long time?"

Henry cast a quick glance over his shoulder. "As long as I can remember."

"I hope you'll forgive my saying this," Genevieve said, channeling her best Texas manners, "but it's hung just a little too high."

Julien suppressed a smile, but just barely. That smile turned to surprise, though, when Genevieve stood and walked behind Henry's desk.

"Maybe I could show you? Would you two help me?" She looked at Julien, then Melvin. "Is this wired into the security system, or could we take it down?"

Shocked but game, Julien sprang to his feet.

Melvin peered behind the painting. "Not wired. It really should be, boss."

Henry had swiveled his chair around to watch. He waved his hand, granting permission. Julien and Melvin each grasped an edge of the painting and removed it from the wall.

"Now bring it down about six inches," Genevieve said. She

stepped back. Then she moved forward, putting her hand under one corner. "Maybe just a little higher," she said.

She repeated the process of stepping back, then put her hand under the other corner and raised the painting a bit.

Returning to Henry's side, she said, "See, isn't that better?"

"If you say so," Henry said.

The housekeeper knocked once and stepped into the room. "Your cab's here."

In the cab, Julien gave the driver his address, then turned to Genevieve. "What the hell was that? Were you trying to make me *jealous*? Trust me, Henry is not your type."

Genevieve was tired and cranky, but she did her best not to respond in kind.

"Oh, please," she said, clapping her sunglasses on. "That was research."

"Research?"

"That's a very nice painting. And by nice, I mean significant, and worth a lot of money."

"Really? I've always thought it was ugly," Julien said.

"I was sitting there looking at it, and I was thinking, well, it makes sense that Henry's father would have had something that nice," Genevieve said. "Your family was in the gallery business for generations, after all. But here's the thing."

Julien waited.

"That's exactly the kind of thing the Nazis would have stolen," Genevieve said. "And then I thought, well, maybe Henry's father bought it after he came to the U.S. But you told me that side of the family was never really interested in art."

"Where are you going with this?"

"Didn't you tell me there was always tension between your mother and her oldest brother?"

"Neither of my parents had anything good to say about him. Why?"

I wasn't adjusting the height of the picture," Genevieve said. "I was feeling the back of it. In the lower left corner, there's an erasure – you can feel the roughness."

Pushing his sunglasses up, Julien rubbed his hands over his face. "Which means what?"

"You'd need an infrared camera to tell for sure, but I think there was a code there at one point. I think that painting was looted, and I think Henry's grandfather got it back. I wonder whether Henry knows more about looted Lazare art than he's telling. Why didn't he want to go to the museum with this? And why doesn't Melvin ever want us to call the police?"

At Julien's house, Genevieve started a load of laundry and played with Mona, who seemed not to have missed her at all.

Julien gathered up the mail the cat-sitter had left on the dining-room table and disappeared into his office.

He'd been surprisingly defensive about her suggestion that Henry might be playing a double game. He thought his cousin treated him like a 15-year-old and was often guilty of behavior that Julien characterized as "dick swinging." He did not, as it turned out, believe his cousin was truly dishonest.

He rejected her idea that Henry had somehow engineered their original meeting in Las Vegas. "Conspiracies always have too many moving parts. The simplest explanation is usually the right one."

Genevieve wasn't so sure, but she didn't want to press the issue. "Just friends" was proving difficult to navigate; she saw no need to make things harder.

They'd already argued over her desire to go straight to a hotel. She'd agreed to go to his house only because she wanted to see her cat and she needed clean clothes.

She decided to try to arrange lunch with Thomas, which would serve two purposes: She could get the name of Philip's lawyer, as Henry had requested, and she could take a break from Julien.

Thomas was reluctant when she called, because he thought he'd been gone from the office too much lately. "Even when I'm here, I'm completely distracted," Thomas said.

"I wouldn't ask if it weren't important," Genevieve said. She checked the time. "Can you meet me at our usual place at 12:30?"

"It's gone out of business," Thomas said. "I went to get takeout Monday and there was a sign on the door."

"But it always seemed so busy," Genevieve said. "Well, what about the cheap coffee place?"

There was a long silence, but Thomas finally relented. "OK, 12:30."

Genevieve went back to Julien's office and tapped tentatively at the door to get his attention. He was sitting at his worktable, staring intently at the computer screen.

"Hey, I'm getting ready to leave for lunch with Thomas," she said.

"OK." Julien stretched his arms above his head and then picked up his keys, wallet and sunglasses.

"What are you doing?"

"You want to move your car so I can get mine out of the garage?"

"No. You are not coming with me," Genevieve said. "This conversation is going to be hard enough, and Thomas doesn't even know you."

Julien stood. "You don't go anywhere alone. Didn't we just discuss this from the East Coast to the Mississippi this morning?"

"I won't be alone, I'll be with Thomas," Genevieve said. "In the middle of Santa Monica, at high noon, practically."

"I'll wait across the street if you want, but I'm driving you there. No debate."

"You're impossibly stubborn, you know that?"

Julien edged past her. "I was just thinking the same thing about you."

THE CHEAP COFFEE PLACE was a deli tucked into the bottom floor of a rundown 1950s office building around the corner from the Hilliard.

Genevieve and Thomas liked it because it was inexpensive, the Greek family that ran it was nice, and the only other museum employees who went there were the guards.

Genevieve ordered her usual turkey sandwich and one the way Thomas liked it, and secured one of the two tables outside. Julien took one of the three counter seats inside. She thought he was being ridiculous, shadowing her, but he would not be deterred.

While she waited for Thomas, she said hello to some Hilliard guards dropping by to pick up sandwiches – Romesh and Keisha and some guy she didn't know whose badge said "Darren." She had just finished catching up with Keisha, who was always one of her favorites, when Thomas showed up at 12:40.

"I had trouble getting away," he said as he dropped into a chair. "Was Keisha telling you about the guards' latest grievances?"

Genevieve had zero interest in that topic, but she let Thomas tell her how Darren, who was new, had managed to get on day shift, how Victor, who had been bounced back to nights, had conspiracy theories about Bill's accident, and how all the guards were nervous about a sudden influx of temps.

Eventually, Thomas ran out of steam. "But you didn't call me to catch up on Hilliard gossip," he said. "What's up?"

Genevieve pushed the remains of her sandwich away. "I need the name of Philip's lawyer," she said.

"Are you thinking of suing the Hilliard?" Thomas asked, clearly surprised. "I think this guy specializes in sexual-orientation cases."

As gently as she could, Genevieve explained about the anonymous emails she'd received and their possible connection to Philip's situation.

She produced a pen and piece of paper, and Thomas wrote down the lawyer's name for her.

"What I don't understand," Thomas said, "is why anyone would think getting Philip fired would make any difference."

"I don't understand either," Genevieve said. "Maybe they want you distracted by this so you can't help me, although I'm not sure how you *could* help me."

Thomas crumpled his napkin and tossed it on his plate. "I really do not want to think anyone at the museum is mixed up in this. Assaulting you? Sending you pictures of dead cats and sexual threats? What the hell is wrong with people? It's a drawing. By a minor French romantic, for God's sake. If nothing else, you'd expect museum people to know it's not worth it."

"Somebody thinks it's worth it," Genevieve said.

Thomas scooted his chair toward Genevieve and leaned close. "So, I don't want to alarm you, but there's a guy at the counter who's been watching you the whole time we've been here. Don't turn around."

"I don't need to," she said. "Dark hair, grayish-green shirt? That's Julien."

Thomas swiveled his head around. "*That's* Julien? Oh my. He's a tall drink of water, isn't he?"

"Just friends," Genevieve said.

"That sounds definitive," Thomas said.

"Sadly, yes," Genevieve said. "How are things with you and Philip?"

Thomas smiled. "Better, I think. We're going to try couples counseling, which is probably just him humoring me, but that's a good thing, right?"

◻

Julien joined her outside after Thomas left.

"Your secret agent skills need work," Genevieve told him. "Thomas spotted you."

"I want people to know someone's watching out for you," Julien said. He pushed aside the plate that held her half-eaten sandwich. "Was your lunch not good? The moussaka was outstanding. Too bad this place is closing."

"It's closing?"

"That's what the guy at the counter said. New owner bought the building and they're losing their lease."

"Our other favorite lunch place closed, too. Just over there." Genevieve pointed out the building. "Thomas tried to go Monday and there was a sign on the door."

"Did you get the name of his boyfriend's lawyer?"

Genevieve showed him the piece of paper.

"How did the news go over?"

"Thomas doesn't think it makes any sense, either. The drawing just isn't worth that much. I keep coming back to the idea that the drawing must lead somewhere else, but I can't think... Oh."

"Oh?"

Genevieve reached for her phone. She scanned the area around her and then quickly called Thomas.

"Yes?" he answered.

"Restoration?" Genevieve said.

Then she hung up without saying another word.

"That was cryptic," Julien said.

"Just a thought," Genevieve said. "Probably nothing. He'll know what I mean."

Genevieve shouldered her purse, and they started toward Julien's car.

"Thomas said he and Philip are going for couples counseling. He seemed happy about that."

"Ah, so they can learn all about 'when you X, I feel Y,' " Julien said. Then, seeing Genevieve's expression, he said, "One session. Erica refused to go back."

Genevieve pondered that bit of information while they waited for the light to change. "Thomas and I always called this corner 'Coming Soon,' because there was always some plan to tear down this apartment building and build something fancy here, and then it always fell through. We'd be like, 'Oh, I saw Keisha and Romesh at Coming Soon on the way back from lunch.' "

Julien pointed to a notice posted on the wall around the mock-Tudor complex. "Looks like Coming Soon is finally coming – that's demolition paperwork."

Genevieve walked over for a closer look. "The whole time I worked here, the neighborhood was dead, because it's too far from the water and too far from the Promenade, and now something's finally happening. Figures."

□

After three loads of laundry, many pets for Mona and an early dinner with Julien, Genevieve was back in Santa Monica, checking into a hotel. It catered to a wealthy clientele, one that valued its privacy and, therefore, its security.

Genevieve tried very hard not to gawk as Julien wheeled her suitcase inside.

"This seems a bit much."

"I think one of the top guys keeps Henry on retainer for his divorces," Julien said.

Upstairs, he took a tour of her room, checking the closets and testing the locks on the balcony doors. "These stay locked," he said. "You can enjoy the view from inside."

"I'm on the third floor! What can happen?"

Julien shot her a look that suggested he would tolerate no argument.

"Don't open your door unless it's me. Not for maintenance, not for housekeeping, not for room service. Nobody."

This struck Genevieve as over the top. "What if I get hungry?"

"The minibar is stocked," Julien said. "Knock yourself out."

"What if I want something other than $15 chocolate-covered pretzels?"

"If you decide you need a burger at 1:30 in the morning, call me, and I will get you a burger at 1:30 in the morning. If you decide you need anything, I don't care what it is – ice cream, tampons, whatever – call me and I will get it. Do not open this door."

"Yessir."

Julien didn't much care for her tone, it seemed. "The hotel was your idea."

They were both exhausted, and it would have been easy to lapse into an argument. But Genevieve decided instead to focus on the fact that Julien, tired as he was, had just offered himself up as her butler in order to keep her safe.

"I know you're just looking out for me," she said, walking him to the door. "I promise not to call you because I want a pint of Cherry Garcia."

Then she shut the door behind him, put on the deadbolt and the chain, and steeled herself for a task she'd been dreading: a phone call to D.

D was not happy, not happy at all, that Genevieve had abandoned Julien's house for a hotel.

"Well, there goes my frickin' action plan," she said.

"Which was?"

"Tiptoe down the hall, slip into his bed naked, let nature do the rest," D said. "Tell me again why he slammed on the brakes?"

Genevieve sighed. It was tricky to explain without divulging why she made Julien so uncomfortable. "I think he's been through a really hard time in his life lately."

"But wasn't that awhile ago? Aren't he and the ex all chummy?"

"I know he had a relationship after the divorce that got really messy, too," Genevieve said.

"Maybe I should call him and give him a kick in the pants," D said. "What do you think?"

"If you call him, I will never speak to you again."

"Except to ask me to be your maid of honor!"

Genevieve picked up the TV remote and clicked through the channels. "Is there anything good on? What are you watching?"

"That house-buying show. Girl is 24 years old, Daddy's giving her the down payment, and she's all 'I have to have stainless and granite!' Please!"

"You have granite counters," Genevieve said.

"I'm over 30, and I saved up my own down payment," D said. "OK, so back to Julien, how about this for an action plan? If he insists he has to go everywhere with you, tomorrow you tell him you need to go shopping."

"Because everyone knows men love to shop."

"First stop, panties and bras," D said. "Since he's so concerned about letting you out of his sight, you make sure he sees when you saunter over to where they keep the 38Ds..."

"That's not what I wear!"

"He doesn't know that... yet," D said. "You make sure you pick one that's leopard print or something trashy, and a lacy black one, hold them up, like you have to study them from every angle, maybe even hold them up against your chest. Then you walk *real* slow to the dressing room..."

"You've done this, haven't you?"

"Because my 32As are such a selling point? Please. Now, I *might* have dropped by Vicky's once when I was at the mall with Tad and I needed a new black thong."

"Which one was Tad?"

"I only went out with him a couple times," D said. "He lived clear over in Euless? Did I not tell you about him? The music minister?"

"You took a minister shopping for a *thong*?"

"He ran like a scalded cat," D cackled. "Said he'd wait for me down at the Christian bookstore."

Genevieve could hardly stop laughing. "I thought sales was about knowing your audience."

"Well, I misjudged him," D said. "Don't you make the same mistake with Julien. Now, I gotta go, because I have Brazilian Butt Lift class at 6 tomorrow. Keep me posted!"

Five minutes after she finished her call with D, Genevieve's phone rang.

"Hey," she said. "I was just thinking, could I get some tacos from Tito's?"

"Very funny," Julien said. "What have you been up to?"

"Talking to D. She thinks I should make you take me shopping tomorrow."

"What do you need?"

"Nothing," Genevieve said. "It's punishment. Because you swerved, as it were."

"Ah. I'm thinking it might have been a mistake to get on D's bad side. Do I need to avoid the state of Texas from now on?"

"It might not be big enough for both of you, and it's pretty damn big," Genevieve said. "So, what have you been doing tonight?"

"Catching up on work, mostly. Erica's business website was glitchy, so I had to fix that. One of these days I'm going to have to build her a new one. She had some stuff added to my original design that's not very compatible."

Genevieve walked to the windows that overlooked the ocean and pulled up a chair. "Why didn't she just have you add the stuff?"

"We weren't speaking to each other at the time."

"But I thought you get along," Genevieve said, then immediately regretted it.

"We didn't always," Julien said. "There was a stretch..."

"You don't have to tell me this," Genevieve said. "I don't want to pry."

"I don't think it's prying if I'm volunteering," Julien said.

Genevieve pulled the other chair over so she could prop up her feet. "Well, I guess if you're talking, I'm listening."

"The crazy thing is how fast it all went south for us," Julien began. "Erica's really independent and single-minded, and I loved that about her. When she wanted to quit her job and start her own business, we knew it would be hard, but I was on board. I took on a lot of freelance work on the side to keep money coming in. Then my mom got sick, and I was completely overwhelmed. And it seemed like Erica just pulled away, like all she wanted to think about was her business and her triathlon training. If I asked for help with my mom, she resented it, acted like I was being needy."

Genevieve listened as Julien took a deep breath.

"She thought I was changing the rules, and she didn't want the rules to change. She thought I needed to suck it up, get through it, and then Mom would die and everything would go back to normal. But I felt like she didn't have my back. And to me, that's the point of being married, knowing that someone's always got your back.

"So I wanted a divorce. That part was amicable. My mom died, and then... Well, let's just say Erica and I said things we shouldn't have and leave it at that. It got pretty frosty for a year or so. But we're past that."

"That sounds really hard. I'm sorry," Genevieve said. She stared out at the Pacific. "I'm glad you told me."

"I was sitting here, feeling bad about snapping at you today," Julien said. "Do you need to go shopping tomorrow? Because I'll take you."

"No, I don't have anything to do tomorrow. I feel like I should do something. I just don't know what. Maybe a good night's sleep will give me an idea."

"I'm kind of a zombie, too. Maybe you can hang out here tomorrow and convince your cat not to sit on my scanner," Julien said.

"Just push her off," Genevieve said.

"Oh, she's fine," Julien said. "I think she just misses you."

He sighed. "She's not the only one."

CHAPTER THIRTY-SIX

THOMAS CALLED first thing in the morning, waking her up.

"Restoration," he said. "Theoretically, your question would be?"

Genevieve thought about how to phrase things. She didn't want to put Thomas on the spot. "Theoretically, if, say, a drawing, had restoration work done, would there be a record? Would photos be taken?"

"The museum keeps a master list of all restoration work," Thomas said. "Additionally, there's a restoration file specific to each work, and in that file would be the details of the process used and so on. It's typical to take photos. Does that help?"

"Maybe," Genevieve said. "Thanks."

Her next call was to Julien. He was at her door an hour later, latte in hand.

He'd been up since 4:30, he said, and had already been to the gym. "I'm still trying to get my time zones straight," he said.

From there, it was back to Julien's house, where he worked and Genevieve, for lack of a better plan, read everything she could find online about Stimson Miller while the information from Thomas rattled around in the back of her mind.

She was desperate to do something – anything – to advance their case, but she was out of ideas. What was worse, her failure now wouldn't just be a professional flop. She would be letting Julien down.

For lunch, they walked a few blocks to Culver City's downtown and ate at a barbecue restaurant where Julien was a regular. The waitresses were clearly sizing Genevieve up, and she wanted to tell them, "Hey, we're just friends."

Julien's phone rang during lunch. "My friend Brent," he said. "Mind if I take this?"

"Go ahead."

Julien walked out with the phone pressed to his ear.

She watched through the window as he leaned against a bike rack, chatting. At one point, Julien caught her eye and smiled at her, and Genevieve wondered, for one selfish moment, whether she didn't need new bras after all.

Julien ended the call and came back inside.

"Everything OK?"

"Yeah, he had an extra ticket to the Lakers tonight, but I told him..."

"And you're not going?" Seeing that he was tempted, Genevieve pressed her case. "I'll be tucked in tight at the hotel, remember? We can get my mail this afternoon, and then I'll spend tonight getting caught up. I need to do expenses for Henry. Call your friend back."

□

Julien dropped her at the hotel after an early dinner. Genevieve tackled her stack of mail and pile of receipts. She'd just finished the paperwork when Thomas called.

"Did you know," he said, "that *Study for Tristan and Iseult* had restoration work in 2000?"

"Really?"

"Did you know – no, I'm certain you didn't – that the restoration file is missing? Isn't that a coincidence?"

"What?" Genevieve almost dropped her phone.

"What made you ask me about restoration?"

"Julien's cousin has a painting that I think was looted and returned – I felt an erasure on the back where I think the Nazis coded it," Genevieve said. "That made me wonder whether there had been anything on the drawing, and whether anyone had ever taken photos."

Thomas was quiet for so long that Genevieve thought he might have hung up. But then he asked, in an oddly jaunty tone, "So, does Julien go everywhere you do now, or what's the security procedure?"

"He's at the Lakers game tonight, and I'm holed up here like a princess in a tower," Genevieve said.

"Oh, that's even better," Thomas said. "I'll call you back in an hour."

Even better than what? Genevieve wondered.

A little more than an hour later, she admitted Thomas to her room, though if he hadn't called ahead, she would have been reluctant to unchain the door.

Thomas, one of the most stylish dressers she'd ever known, was wearing a gray cotton work shirt and matching pants. A black baseball cap was perched on his head. He carried a plastic shopping bag.

"Did you just come from a costume party?" Genevieve looked into the hall, checking to see whether Philip was there in a SpongeBob suit.

"On a scale of one to 10, how mad are you at the Hilliard?"

Genevieve considered his question. "I don't know. Seven?"

"Well, if someone there did this to Philip, I'm at 11," he said, thrusting the bag toward her.

Genevieve looked inside. It contained an outfit like his.

"You need to make a quick decision. We don't have much time."

Clutching the bag, Genevieve backed up and sat on the bed. "What am I deciding?"

"Do you remember Jerrold?"

"The guard with the freckles, served in Iraq? Sure," Genevieve said.

"He was a medic," Thomas said.

"OK." Genevieve wasn't sure where this was going.

"He's the one who found Bill. He doesn't think Bill fell and hit his head. He thinks somebody hit Bill in the head. He found him in the hall outside the room where they keep the files."

Genevieve took in this information. "So Bill interrupted someone taking the file on the drawing?"

"Jerrold has a new job, and tonight's his last night. They're having cake for him, and you know, the cameras might not be monitored so closely for a little bit. And if some temp guards were to wander over to the East Gallery..."

"You are not suggesting stealing *Study for Tristan and Iseult*."

"Of course not. We're just going to look at it."

"There are cameras everywhere. You think uniforms will fool anyone? You *work* there. I worked there."

"You know how it is – to most white folks, all black men look the same," Thomas said. "Now, for you, my redheaded friend..." He reached into the bag, under the uniform, and produced a curly, platinum blonde wig.

"No."

"You can put it in a ponytail," Thomas said. "What can I say? I had a drag phase."

□

They found a parking place four blocks from the museum and waited on the loading dock. Thomas handed Genevieve a pair of latex gloves. "Try to keep your hands in your pockets," he said. "Keep your head down so the bill of your cap shields your face."

Genevieve had no idea how long they waited – she had no watch, and Thomas insisted that she leave her phone at the hotel.

Finally, a door creaked open, and a hand beckoned them in.

Thomas and Genevieve stepped inside a small receiving area. Jerrold closed the outside door behind them and led them down a short flight of stairs.

"Congratulations on your new job," Genevieve said. "Where are you headed?"

"Costco," the guard said over his shoulder. "Better health plan. I got kids."

At the bottom of the stairs, Jerrold swiped a card in front of an electronic eye. He opened the door for them, then turned and left.

Genevieve looked around, trying to get her bearings. They were in a hallway that ran behind the galleries. Its utilitarian appearance – concrete floor, cinderblock walls – gave no hint of the treasures on the other side.

"Thomas," she hissed, "this is a secure area! I wasn't even allowed down here when I was on the payroll!"

She heard a noise ahead and froze. Footsteps sounded on the hard floor, coming toward them.

Genevieve looked around for someplace to hide. Behind her was a locked door. Ahead was almost certainly a security guard.

Suddenly a beam of light focused on Thomas.

Genevieve thought she might faint. Would Julien bail her out? Hadn't he said he'd do anything for her?

A security guard strode into view, flashlight trained on them.

"Hi, Victor."

"Hi, Thomas." Victor nodded at Genevieve as he swiped his card and opened the door. The three of them walked quickly through the darkened East Gallery until they came to *Study for Tristan and Iseult*.

"The lock's disabled," Victor said, donning a pair of cotton gloves. "You got, like, five minutes. That's it."

"Well, let's have a look," Thomas said.

With a man on each corner, they carefully removed the drawing and held it a few feet away from the wall. Genevieve circled behind them.

The back of the drawing was blank – no surprise. She clicked on a small flashlight Thomas had given her and bent down for a closer look.

Suddenly, Victor's radio crackled to life.

"Vic, what's your location?"

"Ned. Dammit," Victor said. "Thomas, can you hold this thing?

"Nervous Ned? Gen, take that corner," Thomas said.

Genevieve stuffed the flashlight in her pocket and took a corner of the drawing while Victor keyed the "talk" button on his radio. "Ned, what's up?"

Ned's voice came back. "Is anybody supposed to be in the East Gallery? On Camera 12, I just saw a pair of feet go by."

"Shit," Thomas said.

Victor held out his hands and made a calming gesture. He depressed the "talk" button again. "Probably one of the temps, lost and looking for the john."

"Had weird shoes on," Ned said.

Victor, Thomas and Genevieve all looked down at her black ballet flats. She'd had nothing in her hotel room that remotely resembled security-guard footwear.

"We need to get you guys out of here," Victor said. "Nervous Ned wasn't supposed to be on the camera booth."

He keyed his radio again. "Yeah, Ned, I don't know where they're getting these temps. Buncha amateurs. Keisha said one girl last week showed up in FMPs."

Victor looked at Genevieve and shrugged apologetically.

Ned's voice came back. "Think I ought to send Luis up?"

Victor spoke into his radio. "It's just one of the dumbass temps took a wrong turn. Tell you what, I'll come and relieve you on the cameras, and you can go have a piece of Jerrold's cake. I'll be there in two minutes. Sit tight."

"Here's what's going to happen," Victor said to Thomas and Genevieve. "We're going to hang that thing back up."

"We didn't get what we need," Thomas said.

"Too late," Victor said. "You two are going to mill around here for a couple minutes, looking lost, give me time to get to the camera booth. Then you are going to walk out that way, past that big picture of the naked lady." He pointed toward the West Gallery. "You know the one I mean?"

"Yes," Thomas said. Genevieve was too frightened to speak.

"There's a door there the guards leave unarmed so they can take smoke breaks. Anybody asks, you're going out to smoke."

Thomas began to protest. "Not unlocked, just unarmed, so you can push it open from the inside without setting off the alarm," Victor said.

A door clanged somewhere in the distance, and Genevieve jumped.

"Anybody catches you, I got no clue how you got in here, you understand?"

"Just one thing," Genevieve said.

"No, I'm serious, you get caught, I don't know you," Victor said.

Genevieve pointed to the breast pocket of Victor's uniform. "If we're going on a smoke break, we need smokes."

Victor and Thomas rehung the drawing, then the guard handed Thomas a pack of Marlboros and a lighter and hustled away.

Another door clanged, even closer this time.

Genevieve began to walk toward the West Gallery, but Thomas held her back. "We're supposed to wait," he said.

A radio crackled somewhere in one of the upper galleries, its noise drifting down the big central staircase. Thomas and Genevieve exchanged a look.

"OK, walk," he muttered under his breath. "But not too fast."

He shook a cigarette from Victor's pack and put it in his mouth, unlit.

The radio seemed to be getting closer. "Gloves," Genevieve muttered.

She peeled her own gloves off and stuffed them in her pants pocket as she and Thomas passed under the atrium between the East and West galleries.

"Hey!" a man's voice called out. "Where you guys going?"

Thomas waved the pack of Marlboros behind him. "Smoke break." Genevieve had never heard his North Carolina accent so pronounced.

"Wait up," the man called.

"Walk faster," Thomas whispered.

They passed through the big doors into the West Gallery, and Genevieve could see the red exit sign, the only thing illuminated in the dark room. She focused on the sign.

She and Thomas were practically running now, swerving past a big sculpture, heading for the exit, hoping that Victor was right and the door wasn't armed.

The gallery doors behind them opened.

"Hey, I said wait up," the man behind them called.

They reached the exit door, and Thomas pushed it open with his elbow. "I don't think we can just keep walking," he whispered to Genevieve. "We'll smoke a cigarette and try to figure out how to get rid of this guy."

Genevieve passed through the doorway and Thomas followed her out onto a 6 x 6 concrete platform. It was screened from the street by a hedge and held nothing but a plastic garden hose caddy and an overturned trash can.

"I don't know how to smoke," she said.

"Seriously?"

Cupping his hands against the breeze, Thomas lit the cigarette in his mouth and handed it to Genevieve. "Just hold that," he said, "and don't say anything."

He pulled another from the pack and lit it for himself. Genevieve watched as he inhaled deeply. Clearly, Thomas knew how to smoke.

She heard a radio crackle on the other side of the door. Genevieve sat on the overturned trash can and turned away from the door. She concentrated on holding the cigarette, willing her hand not to shake.

A man stepped out. "Hey, I was calling you guys," he said.

Inspired by the way Thomas had summoned his North Carolina accent, Genevieve channeled Lisa Ann Lewis, the meanest of the mean girls in her high school. "EXCUSE me," she said. "We get a 10-minute break, OK? So we're taking our break, OK? If you got a problem, go find whoever's in charge and talk to them, OK?"

"You don't have to get all pissy," the man said. "I was just going to tell you there's cake in the break room."

The door clanged shut.

Thomas took another deep drag on his cigarette, then stubbed it out against the building and stuck it in his shirt pocket. He gestured for Genevieve to hand hers over, and he repeated the procedure.

They squeezed through the hedge, hopped onto the lawn and walked back to the car. They were quiet until they were safely buckled in and driving away.

"Did you know the cheap coffee place is closing? The counter guy told Julien," Genevieve said.

"I'm losing all my lunch places," Thomas said. "Could you see anything? On the drawing?"

"No," Genevieve said.

"Maybe with an infrared camera," he said.

"I'm not going back for that," Genevieve said. "We're going to be all over the security cameras, aren't we?"

"Maybe. Maybe no one will look. Maybe I should just waltz in tomorrow in broad daylight and take the provenance file for the drawing." Thomas drummed his fingers nervously on the steering wheel as he waited for the light to change.

"Thomas, no. I'll find some other way."

"It's probably gone anyway."

"I can't believe I did that," Genevieve said. "I can't believe you did that." She twisted in her seat. "Why did you do that?"

"The same reason you did," he said. "Love."

□

Thomas wanted to walk her up to her room, but Genevieve told him she'd be fine – the elevator wouldn't move without a room key to activate it. She handed over the cap and wig at a stoplight a block from the hotel, gave him a half-hug in the driveway, and told him she'd call him.

The lobby was deserted, but Genevieve followed Melvin's instructions to be aware of her surroundings. No one followed her to the elevator.

She looked both ways when she left the elevator, but the floor was empty. Just before she put her room key in the door, she checked again to make sure no one was behind her. The coast was clear.

Genevieve inserted the key in the lock, heard the electronic whirr, saw the light go green, and clicked the handle open. She walked into the room and shut the door. She reached for the light. Home free.

A hand grabbed her arm, and a man growled close to her ear.

"What the hell do you think you're doing?"

CHAPTER THIRTY-SEVEN

G ENEVIEVE FELL BACK against the door and blinked as Julien turned on the light. "Jesus Christ! You scared me to death! What are you doing in my room?"

"What am I doing in your room? What the fuck are you doing *out there*?"

"Don't you swear at me!" Genevieve snatched her arm away.

"What did I tell you?" Julien stabbed his finger at the door behind her, his face inches from hers. "Don't open the door. Don't leave this room."

"I'm not a prisoner. I..." Genevieve inhaled. Why did he have to smell so good?

"You what?"

Genevieve closed her eyes, inhaled again, opened them. "I can't think with you two inches from my face."

She pointed to the chairs overlooking the balcony. "Go sit over there."

Julien didn't move for what felt like a very long time. Finally, he backed up a few steps, shaking his head.

"You. Are. Something." He retreated across the room and sat. "This far enough away?"

"Yes. Thank you," Genevieve said. "How did you get in here?"

"Henry's friend had the manager give me a key. I tried calling you after the game, and when you never picked up, I got pretty worried. Then I saw your purse and phone here..." Julien's voice trailed off. "I was just about to call Melvin and tell him we needed to go into search-and-rescue mode."

Genevieve ran her hands over her head and shook out her hair. The wig had been hot and itchy.

"Could you please not do that?"

"What?"

"That thing with your hair," Julien said.

She dropped her hands to her sides. "I had no idea you were going to call me. I didn't mean to worry you."

Julien looked her up and down as though seeing her for the first time. "What are you wearing?"

"A security guard uniform. It's really not very comfortable, and it's kind of a long story," Genevieve said. "Can you wait two minutes while I change?"

"I'll wait," Julien said. "But please don't come out in that tank top you had on the other night."

In the bathroom, Genevieve changed into jeans and a sweatshirt. She brushed her hair but resisted the temptation to touch up her makeup.

When she emerged, Julien had opened the doors to the balcony and was leaning on the rail, looking out at the Pacific. Genevieve watched him for a moment, wondering what might have happened if they'd stayed two people who met randomly at a coffee shop. Would they have made a connection? Would it have worked?

"Hey," she said.

Julien turned away from the view and came inside. He shut the heavy glass doors and locked them, then sat.

Genevieve took the other chair. Julien waited, his hands on his knees.

"The drawing had restoration work done in 2000, and there should be a file on that, but there's not," Genevieve said. "Thomas looked. It's missing."

"I hope this story isn't going where I think it's going," Julien said.

"Right after I started working on this, one of the Hilliard guards was found injured. They thought he had a stroke and hit his head. Tonight, Thomas told me the guard who found him was a medic in Iraq, and he thinks someone hit Bill in the head."

"Do *not* tell me you were at the museum tonight."

Genevieve tried to keep her voice as normal as possible. "There was a going-away cake for one of the guards, and Thomas had it all arranged."

"Good God, Genevieve! If anybody saw you, do you have any idea how much trouble you could be in?" Julien got up and stalked across the room.

"The only people who saw us were two guards who knew we were coming," Genevieve said. "Well, one other guy saw us."

"What is wrong with you?" Julien whirled to face her. "You could get arrested! Why would you risk that?"

"Because I need to do something!"

"And you thought breaking into the museum was a good idea?"

"We weren't breaking in. You're not listening to me," Genevieve said. "All we did was look at the back of the drawing. We were inside less than 10 minutes."

Julien rolled his eyes. "Ten minutes or two hours – you think that's really going to make any difference, legally?"

Genevieve slumped back in the chair. "No. But I had to try *something*. The restoration file is gone for a reason. If we'd had a little more time, or an infrared camera..."

Julien shook his head wearily. "What are you talking about?"

"I think the drawing's like the painting at Henry's. I think there's probably an erasure on the back where the Nazis coded it, and that was documented when the restoration work was done. Which is why somebody made the file disappear. You could see it if you took infrared photos."

"Even if we had these infrared photos," Julien said, "would that prove it was ours?"

"It would prove it was looted," Genevieve said. "That would be progress."

Julien sat and pulled his chair toward Genevieve so that their knees were touching.

"I appreciate your dedication to your job, Genevieve. I do. And I'm sure Henry does, too. But neither of us wants you to get arrested, or worse. Do you understand?"

Henry? He'd met her exactly once. Oh, she understood. She understood all too well what Julien was doing.

That didn't mean she had to let him get away with it.

Genevieve looked Julien square in the eye. "It doesn't really have anything to do with dedication to the job," she said. "I want to do this for you."

"I know," he said. "But what am I going to do if anything happens to you? How would I live with that?"

She really hadn't considered it from his perspective.

"If we can't be together," Julien said, "can we at least do our best not to hurt each other?"

It wasn't what she wanted, but Genevieve knew it was all she was going to get. "I'm sorry I scared you."

"I'm sorry about the swearing," Julien said. "I worked in a newsroom too long. You get immune to it. It wasn't directed at you."

He scooted his chair back. "Tell me everything you and Thomas did, start to finish."

Genevieve ran through the entire episode, from the time Thomas called until the time he dropped her off.

As soon as she was done, Julien was up and walking around the room, poking his head into the bathroom and opening the closet door.

"OK, here's what happened," he said. "You were taking a bath – that's why you didn't answer when I called."

He pulled a plastic hotel laundry bag from the closet and put it on the bed. "Give me the uniform and the gloves. Actually, you know, you'd better give me the shoes, too."

"Why?"

"I'm going to get rid of it all, that's why," Julien said. "Let's just hope Thomas has enough sense to do the same."

When Genevieve woke up the next morning, she called Julien first thing, as instructed. He was at her door an hour later with a latte.

He was quiet, almost brooding. She tried to ask him once what he'd done with the things he'd taken away from the hotel room, but he simply gave a little shake of his head.

Genevieve was in a mood herself. She'd slept poorly, endlessly replaying her decision to go to the museum with Thomas. Julien was right, of course. It was dangerous and ill-considered. Worse, it had gained them nothing.

And what did she have to look forward to? Another day spent sitting around Julien's house with nothing to do but toss balled-up pieces of paper for Mona to chase and surf the Internet hoping for inspiration to strike.

Once they had finished breakfast and were back in his car, Julien surprised her by heading away from his house.

"Where are we going?"

"Nordie's Rack," he said. "We need to get you some new shoes."

Julien had confiscated her ballet flats. The result was that she was hopelessly overdressed for a day spent lounging at his house: black skirt, white T-shirt paired with a pale blue cardigan, and the heels that she'd taken to Paris.

"Not that you don't look great," Julien said.

He turned out to be surprisingly helpful in the store, scouring the top rack of the size sevens and persuading her to try a funky black wedge she might have overlooked otherwise.

She changed shoes in the car, putting her heels in the shopping bag.

"Now what?" It was only 10:30, and she had nothing to do.

"Do you want to hit the bookstore? I could put the hammock up for you," Julien said. "You could just hang out, lose yourself in a novel."

"I don't want to lose my..."

Genevieve's phone rang. She fished it out of her bag and checked the display.

"It's Thomas."

"Be really careful what you say," Julien said.

"I will," Genevieve said, hitting the answer button. "Hey, Thomas. We're in the car. I'm going to put you on speaker."

"Oh," Thomas said. "Who's we?"

"Julien and I."

"Well, I was just running out to the cheap coffee place and thought I'd share the latest museum gossip with you."

Something in his tone seemed forced. Genevieve shot Julien an alarmed look.

"Do you remember Jerrold, the security guard? They had a going-away thing for him in the break room last night, and I guess people were trading off responsibilities and doing jobs they don't normally do. Somehow somebody hit the wrong button and erased all of the security video from last night. Can you believe it? What a screw-up!"

Genevieve exhaled; she hadn't even realized she was holding her breath. Julien smiled, ever so slightly, and offered her a fist bump.

"Wow, that is a screw-up," Genevieve said.

"I thought you'd like that one. Oh, and remember the thing I told you about the Kaufman collection? My friend says the deal is truly off and the new home will be announced next week. Remember, you heard it here first."

Genevieve laughed. "I will remember that, if, in fact, it ever actually happens."

Thomas laughed too. It was good to hear him laugh. "I'm at Coming Soon, and there's a demolition notice on the wall. Could it be that Coming Soon is really coming?"

"I'll believe it when I see the wrecking ball," Genevieve said.

She and Thomas said their goodbyes and hung up. Julien turned down his street, waving to a neighbor who was walking a dog, pulling over and motioning to another driver to go ahead at a spot where it was difficult for two cars to pass. A house was under renovation, and a dumpster for construction debris was parked in front, restricting the traffic flow.

As he turned into his driveway, an idea came to Genevieve, and she put her hand on his arm.

"Do you know how to search property records?"

CHAPTER THIRTY-EIGHT

"Property records?"

"Someone's buying up property around the Hilliard," Genevieve said. "Coming Soon has a demolition notice, the cheap coffee place lost its lease because of new owners, and Thomas said our other favorite lunch place closed."

"It's Santa Monica, Genevieve," Julien said. "Property gets developed."

"But it's not the good part of Santa Monica," Genevieve said. "And this thing about the Kaufman collection..."

"I thought he was leaving it to some little college nobody ever heard of – I remember reading that in the paper."

"Thomas heard they had a big fight over the architect and now he's looking for another home for it," Genevieve said. "And if the Hilliard's in the running..."

Julien looked at her over the top of his sunglasses. "Do you really think the Hilliard's in the running?"

"I know it sounds crazy," Genevieve said. "Why would he pick a third-tier museum like the Hilliard? But why would he pick some little school nobody ever heard of? And if the Hilliard were getting it, it would need room to expand."

Julien put the car in reverse.

"Thank you," Genevieve said.

"Once you've destroyed evidence of a felony for someone, a property records search isn't such a big thing," Julien said.

◻

First they went by the building that had housed her favorite lunch place and noted the address. Then they went by the cheap coffee place, wrote down the address and bought takeout coffee.

Their next stop was Coming Soon. When they got there, Genevieve studied the demolition notice dubiously. "What of this info do you think is useful? Samby Properties. What kind of name is that?"

Julien pulled out his phone and snapped pictures of the notice. "There," he said. "Now you don't have to write down any of it."

"Hey, Gen!"

Startled, Genevieve looked up to see Keisha, one of the Hilliard guards, greeting her. She was accompanied by Romesh and the new guy Genevieve had met a couple times.

"Oh, hi," Genevieve said.

"You're looking good, girl," Keisha said. The comment was directed at Genevieve, but Keisha was 100 percent engaged in sizing up Julien. "Real good."

"Thanks, Keisha," Genevieve said. "I was in the neighborhood and thought I'd get coffee. Can't believe something's finally happening on this corner."

When the guards had moved down the street to the coffee place, Julien said, "This notice came from the city. Let's go over to Santa Monica City Hall and see what we can find."

At city hall, Genevieve hung back and watched Julien work his charm. A woman there saved them a trip to county offices, calling and confirming that Samby Properties also bought the other two buildings near the Hilliard.

Unfortunately, the information about Samby Properties was scant.

Genevieve and Julien sat on a low wall outside city hall to plan their next move. "Looks like a holding company," Julien said, studying the copies they'd received from the city. "They file their paperwork with the state, not the county, so it's all in Sacramento."

"Do you know anybody who can look that stuff up?"

"Well, Meg's good at it, but she's not going to do me any favors," Julien said.

"Did you ever find her earrings for her?"

"You heard that, huh?" Julien sighed. "You probably think I was a real shit to her."

Genevieve held up one hand to forestall him. "Does it really matter?"

"Actually, yeah," Julien said. "I care what you think. It's not like I hooked up with her and then blew her off. She told me she just wanted to keep it casual, because obviously we don't work as a couple, and then a day later she's on the phone yelling at me because I broke some unwritten rule of the new arrangement. That's when I told her I was done with her. It wasn't a great choice of words, I admit that."

"That's messed up."

"It was," Julien said. Then he laughed. "What is it about you that makes me want to tell you everything?"

They sat for a moment, Julien swinging his long legs against the wall, Genevieve thinking.

"Do you know how Stimson Miller made all his money after the war?"

"Stimson Miller, the typist? I'm going to say he opened a chain of secretarial schools," Julien said.

Genevieve laughed. "Real estate development. I read up on him yesterday, while you were working. On paper, he doesn't seem like a bad guy."

"Other than he probably gobbled up miles of orange groves for strip malls, you mean?"

"Well, other than that," Genevieve said. "He gives away boatloads of money, and not just to the Hilliard."

Julien snorted. "Shall I run down the list of absolute bastards who sit on the boards of big charities? What else did you learn about Stimson Miller?"

"He was married to the same woman for more than sixty years," Genevieve said. "She died last year. He has a daughter. He lives in Malibu." She turned to Julien.

"Want to drive up and look at his house?"

□

Julien agreed to a drive past Stimson Miller's house ("You know it's going to be behind a big wall, right?") but wanted lunch first.

After lunch, they hit the Pacific Coast Highway, headed north. The day was edging from cloudy to sunny. A mist hovered over the ocean, turning it a deep shade of blue.

As they passed the manicured campus of Pepperdine University, Genevieve said, "It's amazing that anyone could go to school someplace so beautiful."

"Texas Tech wasn't beautiful? Where is Texas Tech, anyway?"

"Lubbock," she said. "Where did you go to school?"

"Cal. Where I majored in disappointing my mother."

"Oh, it can't have been that bad."

Julien laughed. "I went off the rails for a while. My high school girlfriend dumped me freshman year. She went to school back East and discovered I wasn't the only guy who was ever going to think she was cool."

He turned, and the car climbed a steep road.

Genevieve looked back to see the Pacific glittering in the afternoon sun. Except for one SUV, they had the road to themselves. "Oh wow," she said. "It's gorgeous."

Julien smiled. "The Golden State."

"So what happened after the big breakup?"

"I responded, naturally, by going to parties, getting mediocre grades and seeing how many girls would sleep with me," Julien said.

"I'm guessing the answer was, a lot," Genevieve said.

Julien merely shrugged.

"Guys like you terrified me in college," Genevieve said. "I never even had a boyfriend until I was a sophomore."

"Which raises serious questions about Texas men," Julien said. He tossed his phone into her lap. "Check the map – how many miles to Stimson Miller's house?"

The car hugged the edge of a narrow two-lane road. On one side was a steep drop down to the canyon floor.

"Hard to believe this is so close to LA," Genevieve said. "It feels like the middle of nowhere."

Behind them, a battered Jeep Cherokee slowed and turned, and a black SUV sped up behind them.

Julien glanced up in his rear-view mirror. "Jeez, buddy, back off."

The SUV inched a bit closer. It was now only a car length behind them.

Julien glanced in his mirror again. "What is it with this guy?"

A car passed going the other direction, and the SUV backed off. But as soon as the passing car had disappeared around a curve, the SUV picked up speed.

Genevieve sneaked a look in the side mirror. Her stomach lurched.

"Didn't Melvin say one of my neighbors had seen an unfamiliar black SUV?"

Julien glanced at her, then up at the rearview mirror. "There's roughly a million black SUVs in LA, Genevieve."

The SUV driver sped up again. He was half a car-length behind them. Genevieve took another look. "Does this seem like regular tailgating to you?"

"Melvin's in my phone, under M. Call him."

Genevieve picked up the phone. "No service."

"Try yours."

Genevieve bent down and pulled her phone from her purse. Before she could dial, though, she was suddenly thrown forward, smacking her forehead against the Audi's dash. The phone tumbled from her hand.

"Shit!" Julien put his hand on her shoulder, just for a second, before grabbing the wheel with both hands again. "Are you OK?"

"I hit my head, what just..."

"He bumped us," Julien said. "Did you get the phone?"

Genevieve looked down. "I dropped it. I think maybe it went under the seat?" She started to bend down to search for it.

"Don't do that! You could snap your neck. Forget the phone. Sit back."

"This is crazy," Genevieve said. "What's he doing?"

"Trying to force us over the side of the canyon would be my guess."

Genevieve turned to gape at him just as Julien took a curve very fast, throwing her hard to the right.

"I always figured I'd have a heart attack and be discovered dead on the kitchen floor by the cleaning woman," Julien said, not looking away from the road. "So, this is an improvement. At least I'm not alone."

"Is that supposed to be funny? Because it's really not."

They were on a particularly curvy stretch of the road, which made it hard for Julien to maintain his speed. Genevieve glanced back and saw that the SUV was only two feet off the bumper. The driver's face was close, close enough for Genevieve to make out his features.

"Jesus, I know that guy! He's a guard! At the museum!"

The SUV crept closer still.

"What should we do?" Genevieve grabbed Julien's phone from the console and checked the display. Still no service.

The road straightened a bit, and Julien floored the accelerator. The Audi shot ahead again.

"I have an idea," Julien said. "Erica and I used to train up here sometimes, if I can just remember the spot..."

"What are you going to..." Genevieve turned around to check on the SUV. It was gaining again. "He's catching up! If anything happens to me, my poor dad..."

"Genevieve, we're going to be OK," Julien said. "Just stay calm. Is your seat all the way back? Check the button, it's on the side."

"What difference..." Genevieve fumbled for the button and pushed it. The seat didn't move. "It won't move."

"That means you're as far from the airbag as you can be. You need to hang on, because I'm going to..."

At that moment, Julien jerked the wheel hard to the left. The car squealed across the blacktop and bumped onto a gravel cutoff.

The SUV tried to follow, but the turn was too tight, and its center of gravity was too high. Genevieve watched over her shoulder as it rose on two wheels, wobbled and then began to roll over with a tremendous groan.

When she turned her head, she saw Julien's biceps straining as he fought to steer them to safety. But the road angled sharply downhill, it was gravel, and it was narrow.

"Shit," Julien said.

And then the tires lost their grip on the gravel, and the car left the road.

Genevieve screamed as a tree filled the windshield.

CHAPTER THIRTY-NINE

THEIR EYES MET, and then Julien yanked the steering wheel hard to the right, insuring that the driver's side would take the brunt of the impact.

The collision was deafening, a sickening combination of splintering wood, cracking glass and shrieking metal.

The car immediately filled with smoke. Genevieve began to cough and was desperate for fresh air.

The window on Julien's side was spiderwebbed with cracks; the door, crumpled. His body was slumped to the right. His eyes were closed, and blood was trickling down the left side of his face.

Genevieve gave a little involuntary cry and strained for his right hand, which rested – palm up, not moving – on his thigh.

She put her thumb on his wrist. His pulse was strong.

Julien's eyes opened, and he began to cough.

"We have to get out," Genevieve said. "Something's on fire."

Julien reached out and turned the key, shutting off the car. He sniffed the air. "That's from the airbags. Are you OK?"

Genevieve strained for the seatbelt button. "I can't get out. Are you OK? You're bleeding."

Julien pressed his left hand to his eyebrow and winced. "Yeah," he said.

His seatbelt gave easily. "Let me try yours." He pushed on the release button and tugged on her belt, popping it loose.

"Your eyes look a little unfocused. Don't try to get out," he said. "I'll open your door for some air."

He leaned across Genevieve, his right hand braced on her seat, his body pressed against hers. He hit the door handle, Genevieve gave a shove with her foot, and the passenger door sprang open.

"Look what I found," Julien said, leaning down to retrieve something from the floor. He came up holding her phone. "You've got two bars."

First, Julien called 911. Next, he got Melvin's number from his own phone and called him.

Then they waited.

It was peaceful, in a way. Julien found napkins in the console and pressed them to the cut on his head. He leaned back, his eyes closed.

Genevieve's head hurt. But other than that, she thought she was OK.

"I saw what you did," Genevieve said.

Julien didn't open his eyes. "What did I do?"

"At the last minute," Genevieve said. "You swerved."

Julien shrugged.

Genevieve felt compelled to go on. "That night you lost me on the Metro, I was back in that attic, with... well, I'm pretty sure it was your uncle. He was leaving, and there was some kind of danger, and I thought 'I have to warn him,' and then he looked at me, and I realized, he already knew. He knew, and he was going anyway."

Julien opened his right eye – the left was beginning to swell – and looked at her.

"I'm pretty sure that when he died, he knew it was coming, and he went anyway, because he believed in what he was doing, and because he was brave."

Julien closed his eye again.

"I feel bad, because when you said you would do anything for me, I thought that was one of those bullshit things people say, like, 'it's not you, it's me,' or 'we'll always be friends.' But now I know that you meant it, because you just... you *swerved*. And I know this happened because I wanted to drive up here, and now your car is wrecked, and I feel terrible about the times I've been mad at you, and the way I've messed everything up, and I'm so sorry I kissed you in Paris and made everything weird between us, and..."

"Genevieve?"

"Yes?"

"Please stop talking."

Julien's head was tilted back against the seat, a trail of blood marking the left side of his face and staining his shirt.

"Oh. OK. Sorry."

"And don't be sorry you kissed me in Paris," Julien said.

"No?"

"No." He opened one eye again. "Right before we hit the tree, the last thing I thought was, 'damn, I wish I'd turned off my phone that night.' "

In the distance, a siren wailed.

The fire and rescue guys had to walk in because the SUV rollover was blocking the turnoff. They evaluated Genevieve and decided she could get out of the car. Julien pretzeled himself out the passenger door behind her.

Julien and Genevieve assured everyone they were fine to walk out to the main road. Then Genevieve walked 10 feet and fainted.

When she came to, she was lying in the sparse grass next to the gravel road, her head cradled in Julien's lap. Someone had draped a blanket over her.

She was game to try the walk again, but the professionals insisted she needed a gurney, which meant waiting for another ambulance. The first was already gone, whisking the SUV driver to the nearest spot where a helicopter could land.

Genevieve could hear the whap-whap-whap of the chopper echoing down the canyon.

While they waited, Julien got a bandage on his forehead and the worst of the blood cleaned off his face. The police had questions, and Julien squeezed her hand under the blanket to tell her he would do the talking. She closed her eyes and let him.

The gurney ride was bumpy. When Genevieve complained, only half-joking, that they were making her carsick, one of the EMTs handed her a bag designed for that contingency.

It was a good thing, too. When they wheeled past the crushed SUV, its tan upholstery sprayed red with blood, she threw up.

Genevieve and Julien rode together in the ambulance. She was strapped to the gurney with an IV in one arm. He sat on a bench beside her, holding her other hand.

At the hospital, though, they were quickly separated, despite Julien's strenuous protests. A nurse helped her change into a gown, and then Genevieve was taken for a CT scan and an x-ray of her spine, two more gurney rides that made her sick.

She was feeling very alone and pathetic when the curtains around her ER bed parted and Thomas poked his head in.

Genevieve, her eyes brimming with tears, held out her hand to him, and Thomas grasped it.

"I'm so glad you're here," she sputtered. "Did Julien call you?"

Thomas squeezed into the small space and pulled the curtains closed behind him. "Carol came by my desk and said you two had been in a wreck and I should get over here. Are you OK? You have a really nasty bruise on your forehead."

"They're doing neurological checks. Hitting your head twice in a month is a bad idea, apparently. My eyes were unfocused, and I passed out."

Thomas leaned close and looked carefully at her. "They seem OK now. Do you need anything?"

"Can you find out what's happening with Julien?"

Thomas went off to do battle with the health-care bureaucracy and came back to report that Julien was getting a CT scan of his own.

While they waited – for test results, or doctors to appear, or *something* to happen – Genevieve filled Thomas in, including her suspicions that Stimson Miller was buying up property around the Hilliard and that the driver who tried to run them off the road was a Hilliard guard.

"What? Let me check with my sources." Thomas pointed to the sign prohibiting cell phone use. "Be right back."

When Thomas returned, he was brimming with information.

"Your wreck is the talk of the museum. Malcolm was forced to issue a memo," he said.

Thomas tapped on his smartphone screen and then intoned, in his Malcolm impersonation: "You may have heard that our former colleague Genevieve McKenna was involved in a car accident. She is being treated at the hospital. We'll pass along further information when we have it."

Thomas gave her his best conspirator's grin. "Now here's where it gets interesting. Keisha says that Darren, the guard you thought you saw, didn't come back from lunch. One of the other guards heard Darren was in an accident. And Keisha, being Keisha, buttonholed Malcolm and asked if it was true that Darren was the other driver."

"Go Keisha," Genevieve said.

"Indeed," Thomas said. "Go Keisha. Keisha says Malcolm told her Darren may have been stalking you." He frowned. "Did you two even work there at the same time?"

Genevieve shook her head, although it hurt to do it.

"Well, when Keisha tried to press Malcolm on it, he said he had to run because he had to take his son to his guitar lesson," Thomas said.

He paused for dramatic effect. "But get this. Keisha heard him tell someone else he was leaving early because he had to take his daughter to ballet."

Genevieve sat up in bed. That *really* made her head hurt. "Tabby."

"Excuse me?"

"Malcolm's daughter. Tabitha – Tabby, right?"

"Yes," Thomas sniffed. "Awful name."

"And his son's name is Sam."

Thomas looked over his shoulder, alarmed. "Should I find a nurse?"

"No," Genevieve said. "Find Julien. I know this sounds crazy, but you need to repeat this message, word for word. Tell him to call Melvin, and tell him Samby – S-a-m-b-y – is Malcolm Stewart. His kids are Sam and Tabby."

CHAPTER FORTY

G ENEVIEVE SPENT the night in the hospital for observation.

Julien got four stitches and was cleared to go home, but he didn't. He spent the night on an uncomfortable recliner in Genevieve's room, sleeping as best he could with people waking her every two hours.

Melvin called at 9 a.m. to say that Darren Lister, an ex-con who never would have passed a background check for a security guard job and didn't know Tristan and Iseult from Homer and Marge Simpson, died in surgery. According to Melvin's LAPD sources, he was a regular at the bar where Malcolm Stewart watched soccer.

Thomas called at 9:15 to report, breathlessly, that an emergency board meeting was in session. Lawyers accompanied by armed (armed!) guards were carrying boxes out of Malcolm's office. Rumors of embezzlement, sweetheart land deals and a scheme to land the Kaufman collection were sweeping the office.

At 10 a.m., Henry knocked on the door, asking, "Everybody decent?"

When Julien let him in, Henry handed him a bouquet of yellow roses. "Those are for her. Jeez, you look like hell."

"Thanks, Henry. Good morning to you, too."

Henry had a point. Julien had a shiner and needed a shave. And he was still wearing his bloodstained shirt, because by the time the hospital had moved Genevieve out of the ER and into a room, it was so late that he wouldn't have been allowed back in if he'd left.

Henry held a tray of coffees and had a shopping bag looped over his arm. He put the coffees down on the bedside table, pried one loose and handed it to Genevieve.

"Latte," he said. "Carol tells me that's your drink."

"Who the hell is Carol?" Julien asked.

Henry handed a coffee to Julien. "Black for you. I left bagels and danishes at the nurses station. Go grab something before it's gone."

Genevieve sat up – very carefully, because her head was pounding – and took a sip. "Carol, as in Malcolm Stewart's assistant Carol?"

"Lovely woman," Henry said. "Met her at temple. My inside source." He winked at Genevieve. "We'll all have to get together for dinner soon."

Then he turned to Julien. "Julien, the patient needs a cheese danish, I think."

Julien sighed and stalked out of the room. Like a teenager, Genevieve couldn't help thinking.

Henry pulled up a chair. "The bag here has clean clothes and toiletries. Carol packed up your room at the hotel last night."

"Thank you," Genevieve said, practically swooning at the idea of her own clothes.

"I owe you an apology. I didn't know this would be dangerous," Henry said. "I guess Malcolm Stewart had all his ducks in a row for a big score with the Kaufman deal, and he couldn't allow any bad publicity over looted art to scuttle it. The working theory is this Darren Lister was roped in to keep up the harassing emails and keep an eye on you, but then he took his job a little too seriously."

"Kind of hard to believe that's it," Genevieve said. "I hoped we were on the trail of all the missing Lazare art."

"Hard to believe," Henry echoed. He smoothed his tie.

She looked at him over her coffee. "That De Momper in your library, you should have someone do an infrared examination. I think you're going to find vestiges of markings on the back indicating it was looted and recovered."

Henry smiled. Because he'd been caught out? She couldn't tell.

"Are you pitching me on a search for the rest of our artwork?"

Before she could answer, Julien came in bearing a danish for her and a bagel for himself.

Henry patted her arm. "We'll talk about this later."

□

The doctor released Genevieve that afternoon with a pain-killer for her headache, a muscle relaxant for her stiff neck and the suggestion that she have someone keep a close eye on her for a few days.

The doctor also gave her a referral for a neurologist, because something "unusual" had been spotted on her CT scan. No, not a tumor, the doctor hastened to add when she saw Genevieve's alarmed expression. Just an "anomaly."

"I've never seen anything like it," the doctor said. She flipped through Genevieve's chart. "But you didn't indicate a history of neurological symptoms, so it's probably nothing."

Julien raised an eyebrow, which Genevieve ignored.

The thought of packing and transporting herself and Mona home seemed daunting, especially so close to rush hour. So when Julien insisted on taking her to his house, Genevieve acquiesced without a fight.

Spending the night there seemed like the easiest thing all around. They were both exhausted, and his car was totaled. He could drive her Camry while she was at his house.

Once she'd settled into the guest room, she made the obligatory calls to her father and D, assuring them both that she was fine.

Henry had Greek food delivered, which Genevieve thought was sweet and Julien, for his own reasons, thought was irritating.

By 8 p.m., Genevieve was asleep.

On the second day, Genevieve rested while Julien went a few rounds on the phone with his insurance company. After Greek leftovers for lunch, Genevieve curled up at one end of the living room sofa and Julien sprawled at the other, and they whiled away the afternoon with a "Friday Night Lights" marathon. Julien had never seen the show, and Genevieve was feeling nostalgic for Texas.

Julien rallied to make dinner, and Genevieve managed to stay up until 9 p.m. before retiring to the guest room.

The third day was better. Julien felt good enough to go for a run. Genevieve woke up planning to pack up Mona and go home. But then Henry called. The Hilliard's lawyers had asked for a meeting. Henry thought they wanted to talk settlement.

□

"This afternoon?" Genevieve said when Julien told her about the call.

"You have other plans?" Julien looked up from his computer, where he was researching cars.

"I still have this hideous bruise on my forehead."

"You don't look so bad today," Julien said. "And I think my shiner gives me a rugged charm." He gave her his most rakish grin.

"This is brilliant strategy, actually," he said. "Let them see what they did. I'd like to haul the wreckage of my car and that SUV over there, too."

Genevieve shuddered at the mention of the SUV.

Julien frowned. "This is good, you know. Victory lap for you. Why are you dreading it?"

Genevieve grabbed the excuse closest at hand. "I don't know what to wear. You want to give me an opinion?"

"In my opinion, you look good in everything." He shut down the computer. "I'm going to grab a nap on the couch. Wake me at 1:45 so I can change my shirt and shave, OK?"

Mona jumped down from the worktable and sashayed out to the living room after him.

"Traitor," Genevieve muttered to the cat.

After pulling several outfits together and then rejecting them, Genevieve did what she always did in these situations. She called D.

"Hey, Gen," D boomed.

"Are you in a good spot to talk?"

"Stuck on the frickin' Tollway," D said. "If I'd known there was a wreck, I would have taken Central, where at least I'd be stuck for free. Why are you whispering?"

Genevieve eased the door closed. "Julien's taking a nap in the living room."

"I thought you were going home today," D said. "Gen, if you're not going to give him a taste of what he's missing, well, you need to do a Number Two or get off the pot."

"Ew. D, that's the most disgusting mixed metaphor ever."

"Well, excuse me for not majoring in English," D said. "But why are you still there?"

Genevieve pulled a black skirt from her suitcase and shook it out. It had been laundered since the wreck and appeared presentable.

"I'm here because we have a meeting at the museum this afternoon. And that has me completely freaked out." She lowered her voice again. "I told Julien it's because I don't know what to wear, but that's not really it. I don't *know* why."

"Really? You don't know why? You're freaked out because once this is settled you have to go *home*," D said. "No more Julien making you dinner then watching TV and going to sleep in the guest room."

"But..."

"You guys are like one of those old married couples that doesn't have sex anymore, except you skipped the part where you ever *had* sex. Which is the fun part! Why would you want to skip the fun part?"

Genevieve tried to break in. "Well, I don't think that's exactly..."

But D was on a roll. "Look, I know you think he's your soulmate or whatever. But if he doesn't want you, Gen, then, by definition, he's not the perfect guy for you."

"I don't think it's fair to say he doesn't want..."

"Oh, right, he wants you, but he's not going to do anything about it, because why again? His ex-wife was mean to him?"

"It's more complicated than that," Genevieve said.

"He's either in or he's out, Gen," D said. "Reasons don't matter. He says he's out. You seem to think that's the final word. So you need to do this meeting, and then you need to get your butt on home. Hanging around him is just going to break your heart."

Genevieve sat on the sofa. "Not being around him is going to break my heart," she said softly.

"All the time you spend with him is time you're not spending meeting somebody who could be the guy," D said.

Genevieve took a deep breath. It was hard to imagine that such a person, other than Julien, existed.

"And if you truly care about him, and want the best for him, then you want him out there trying to meet the person he can be happy with."

"Oh." Tears welled in her eyes, and Genevieve blinked them back.

"Yeah, I know," D said. "That is a First-Class, All-Expenses-Paid Guilt Trip right there. But it's true."

"D, you don't get enough credit for how smart you are, you know that?"

"I *know*," D said. "And I don't even have big boobs, so how is that fair?"

Genevieve laughed and dashed at a tear running down her cheek.

"Action Plan: Go to your meeting," D said. "Then pack up your stuff and your kitty and go home. Then call me, and we'll watch TV. Or I can put you on speakerphone and let you bawl if that's what you need. OK?"

"OK," Genevieve sighed.

"And Gen, really, after the meeting, just pack up and go. Don't have drinks to celebrate. Don't let him make you dinner. Don't wait for rush hour to clear," D said.

"But..."

"No buts," D said. "It's like getting a bikini wax. They rip that sucker off fast for a reason. Still hurts like hell, but it hurts a whole lot worse if you drag it out."

CHAPTER FORTY-ONE

W HEN GENEVIEVE, Julien and Henry arrived at the
Hilliard, they were ushered into a boardroom on the
second floor that Genevieve had never seen.

At the head of the table was the board chairman, whom
Genevieve recognized but had never met. On his left was a
man Genevieve didn't know, although she suspected he was
a lawyer. He had a pile of manila folders and a legal pad in
front of him.

The chairs next to the lawyer had been pushed aside to make
room for a wheelchair, which held a man with an impressive
mane of silver hair. An oxygen tube snaked from his nose to
a tank on the back of his chair. He wore an expensive-looking
shirt, open-collared. His neck swam in his collar like a single
flower in a too-large vase.

A young man in a polo shirt and khakis stood behind
the chair.

The lawyer stood when they entered the room. "I'm Paul
Travis, counsel for the museum. You know Mr. Landley, of
course, the chairman of the board."

The lawyer gestured toward the man in the wheelchair.
"And this is Stimson Miller."

Genevieve had seen photos of Stimson Miller in her research, but she realized now that they must have been several years out of date. The frail man in the wheelchair bore no resemblance to the tycoon she'd seen in publicity photos.

Julien cleared his throat quietly. Genevieve looked over. He was holding a chair out for her. She sat.

The lawyer shuffled the papers in front of him.

"We're here to discuss the drawing *Study for Tristan and Iseult*, which the descendants of Georges Lazare and Regine Lazare Brooks suggest was appropriated from their family in Paris in..." He shuffled more papers. "Sometime after..."

Genevieve glanced at Henry. He seemed unperturbed by the lawyer's preamble.

"We'd like to establish that the museum received this drawing in good faith," the lawyer said. "Mr. Miller, who donated the drawing, has volunteered to waive his anonymity and join us today in an effort to facilitate this process. For which we thank him." He nodded toward Miller.

Miller did not acknowledge him. The lawyer droned on.

"Questions of provenance are quite complicated and can take a long time to resolve, but the museum is committed to..."

"Actually, we can make quick work of this one."

They all turned toward Miller, whose words trailed off into a cough.

His caretaker took a few cautious steps toward him.

Miller waved him off. "I'm fine," he wheezed.

They all waited while Miller caught his breath.

"You notice I'm the only one here without a lawyer? Just Viharn, who's here to get me in and out of the car and make sure I get my meds on time."

He might be frail, but he was obviously used to commanding an audience.

"The museum told me there were questions about the drawing. Said they'd protect my privacy. But I said I'd take this meeting. Do you know why?"

The lawyer tried to regain control. "Mr. Miller, we do thank you for coming, but I think it's best if..."

"Shush," Miller said. "You know how long it takes me to get in and out of the car? I didn't go to all that trouble to sit here like a lump."

The lawyer began aligning the corners of his file folders.

"So, why am I here?" Miller continued. "I'm here because I'm an old man who's not well. And I'd like to square a few things up."

His eyes bore in on Henry. "You know how I made my money?"

"Real estate, I believe," Henry said.

Miller waved his hand dismissively. "That's the fancy explanation. I made deals, that's what I did." He leaned toward Henry. "Let's make a deal."

The board chairman tried to intervene. "Stimson, really..."

"Oh, shut up," Miller snapped.

The silence in the room was broken by one word from Julien.

"Why?"

Miller turned toward him. "Which one are you again?"

Julien stood and leaned far over the table, extending his hand. "Julien Brooks. Regine Lazare was my mother."

Miller shook his hand. "Why did you steal it?" Julien asked.

Miller studied Julien. "You want to hear the story?"

Julien sat back down. "Yeah, I want to hear the story."

□

"Toward the end of the war," Miller began, "I got myself assigned to the unit that was cataloging loot from France.

"It was quite an eye-opener for a poor boy from Bakersfield. Paintings. Sculptures. Piled to the rafters. I'd never seen so many beautiful things in my life.

"I saw the drawing one day and fell in love with it. Nothing more complicated than that. You have to understand, we'd been away from home for years, fighting our way across Europe. We felt like we'd earned souvenirs. I felt like I was stealing from the Nazis, not you people. I took it out of the frame, erased the code off the back, fudged some paperwork, rolled it up and mailed it home."

Miller smiled ruefully. "I didn't know anything about art then. If I'd known what I was doing, I might have taken something more valuable.

"When I got home, I made some deals, made some money. Married a girl with taste. I decided to learn about art.

"*Study for Tristan and Iseult* was the first piece of art I loved. But it nagged at me. It's the only thing I ever flat-out stole in my life. Not even a piece of candy when I was a kid.

"So I gave it to the museum, to ease my conscience, I guess. It never occurred to me that any of your people survived.

"Now, the lawyer there is telling the truth when he says the museum didn't know it was stolen when I gave it to them. But once this looted art thing blew up a few years ago, I told Malcolm Stewart the whole story. He said the museum was working on this provenance thing, trying to set things right. But then nothing happened."

The lawyer made a little strangled noise of protest.

"Oops," Miller said. "Guess I wasn't supposed to tell you that part."

He chuckled, and Genevieve realized that he was enjoying himself.

"So, what do you folks want?" Miller asked. "You want your drawing? I'll buy it back for you. You want your money? I'll have it appraised and pay you what it's worth."

Julien looked at Henry, who said nothing.

The lawyer spoke up. "Really, Mr. Miller, I must insist... The purpose of this meeting is to open a dialogue, not facilitate some kind of back-room deal. The family's claim to the drawing is far from meeting a standard of..."

Miller continued to talk over him. "You want to expose me as a thief? Go ahead. My wife's dead – you can't embarrass her. And my only child is an environmentalist who thinks having a developer for a daddy is as low as you can get already."

"Mr. Miller, we have to think about the precedent we'd be establishing," the lawyer went on. "There's no definitive proof of the drawing's ownership on the eve of the war and..."

"My cousin and I need to talk about it, Mr. Miller," Henry said.

Miller signaled to his aide that it was time to leave. "Don't talk about it too much. I won't last much longer."

As soon as the Hilliard contingent had filed out and the door closed behind them, Genevieve slumped in her chair. "I think I've been holding my breath for half an hour."

Henry put his briefcase on the table and hitched up his pants. "That was fun. Don't remember the last time I ended a meeting without even opening my briefcase."

"The lawyer's right," Genevieve said. "We don't really have enough proof. It would set a bad precedent for the museum. There's still a gap in the drawing's provenance and... what?"

Henry looked incredulously at Julien, who shrugged.

"Yes, she's serious," Julien said.

"Let me explain a few things to you," Henry said.

Genevieve sneaked a glance at Julien, who rolled his eyes.

"The director of this museum has just been implicated in using inside information to orchestrate a real estate windfall for himself, hiring an ex-con to terrorize a former employee and conspiracy to commit murder."

Genevieve gasped. "Malcolm tried to murder someone? Who?"

Julien laughed. "Hello? Us?"

Genevieve felt her face begin to redden. "But that wasn't actually..."

"This museum is facing a shit storm of bad publicity," Henry said. "Actually, it might be more like a shit hurricane. So they may talk a good game about precedent, but they're going to cut us a deal. The only question is whether we're going to let them dress it up as some kind of service to humanity."

"Oh," Genevieve said. "I suppose you're right, when you look at it that way."

"You realize they're going to offer you a settlement too, right?"

"Really?" Genevieve looked at Henry, then at Julien for confirmation, then back at Henry.

"Oh good grief," Henry said. "Let me give you some recommendations on counsel. If anyone from the Hilliard or the board calls you in the meantime, tell them your attorney will be in touch and hang up. Got that?"

"Just hang up?"

Henry smiled and patted her hand. "People like me eat people like you for breakfast."

There was a tap at the door. Carol poked her head into the room. "I'm here to see you out," she said.

"I'd like to take a look at our drawing before we go," Julien said.

"Follow me," Carol said. "We'll cut through the employee area."

They walked by Malcolm's office, where Genevieve had experienced the worst 10 minutes of her adult life a few months before. The door was shut, the lights off.

Several of her former colleagues looked up as she passed. One nodded at her. Another smiled and waved.

Thomas stood as she walked by his desk. He didn't say a word, just watched as she passed, her head held high.

CHAPTER FORTY-TWO

H ENRY SUGGESTED they all meet up later for a drink to celebrate, but Genevieve begged off on the grounds that the doctor had told her to avoid alcohol.

As she and Julien got in her Camry to leave the museum, Genevieve began to have guilt pangs about her plan to head home. Julien had no car, and that was her fault.

But then she remembered D's bikini-wax analogy.

"Do you want me to drop you off to pick up a rental car? Didn't you tell me there was a place on Venice close to your house?

Was Julien startled by her offer? Maybe a little.

"Sure," he said. "Good idea."

Dropping Julien off also gave Genevieve the advantage of a head start on packing. She had everything zipped up and ready to go – well, everything except Mona – within 15 minutes of arriving back at his house.

She was tempted to write a note and leave, but she knew even D wouldn't approve of that quick a departure.

With time to kill, she found herself wandering around the house, indulging in the worst kind of nostalgia, remembering the first time Julien made her dinner and the way he pretended not to like her cat.

The first night she was out of the hospital, she heard Julien's phone alarm several times during the night. He padded down the hall, came into the guest room, and stood next to the bed, making sure she was OK. Once or twice he had smoothed her hair away from her face. It was comforting, and she pretended to be asleep, because she didn't want him to stop.

What if she had opened her eyes and reached out for him?

Genevieve shook her head. This was not a good road to be on. Not good at all. D would talk her out of this kind of thinking.

Unfortunately for her, D's phone went straight to voicemail.

Genevieve sat on the guest-room sofa, tapping her foot impatiently. What about Thomas? She started to dial his number, then stopped. She had another idea.

"Genny?" Her father sounded slightly alarmed. "Is everything OK? You aren't back in the hospital, are you?"

Genevieve rubbed her forehead. Maybe this wasn't such a good idea after all.

"I'm fine, Dad. I didn't mean to worry you. Is this a bad time?"

"Hang on, just let me put the dog out," Jack McKenna said. "Go on now, Ranger. Git! No, don't stand there makin' your mind up. I said git! That's right. Good dog."

Genevieve smiled. Talking to their animals – maybe she and her dad had more in common than she thought.

"How are you feeling?" her father asked. "I've been meaning to call and check up on you, but I know how busy you are, and I don't like to stick my nose in."

Did her father really think he couldn't call to ask how she was? "I feel fine, Dad. No headache today. I do have a couple questions that might be kind of strange, though."

"Well, that's all right," he said. "Shoot."

"Did Mom ever see a neurologist?"

"Your mom saw lots of doctors. I don't really know about a neurologist."

"Do you know if she ever had a CT scan?"

"Did we have those back then?" He fell silent. "I think I'd remember that, because it would have been something pretty new, right? So I don't think so. Sorry, I can't say for sure."

"That's OK," Genevieve said. "I was just curious."

"What's this about, Genny?"

"I've been thinking about her a lot lately, about things we might have in common. Something will happen, and I'll wonder if it ever happened to her," Genevieve said. "It doesn't exactly make sense, I know."

"It's your age," her father said, his voice hushed. "Once you have your next birthday, you'll have lived longer than she did. That's got to be strange for you. I know it is for me."

He was right, of course. Genevieve had never done the math until that moment, but he was right.

"That must be it."

She took a deep breath and composed herself. "Well, I know it's your suppertime, so I'll let you go. I'm headed back to my apartment, and the traffic's going to be brutal."

"You be careful on the highway, Genny."

"I will, Dad. And Dad? It's OK to call me."

"OK, honey. I'll remember that."

Genevieve heard a car door slam. "Dad, can I ask one more thing about Mom, and do you promise to tell me the truth?"

"I always do," her father said.

"I know this is a hard question, but just take me out of the equation, OK? Pretend that I never existed, so it's not, like, a referendum on me," Genevieve said.

"I'm not really following, honey."

"If you had it to do over again, if you knew everything that was going to happen, would you still have gone into the bank to cash a check just so you could talk to that redhead waiting in line?"

Jack McKenna was quiet for a long time. Then he took a deep breath and said, "Genny, I have so many regrets about so many things. But my biggest regret when it comes to your mother is that I didn't have more time with her. So the answer is yes, I would do it all over again. And not just because of you."

□

"Genevieve?" Julien called when he came into the house. "Where are you?"

She walked into the kitchen, where Julien was pulling items from a shopping bag.

"There you are," he said. "I was thinking chicken Milanese for dinner, pasta, and you like arugula, right?" He took in her expression. "You don't like arugula. OK. No problem. I got asparagus too, just in case."

"I'm sorry, I didn't know you were going shopping, or I would have said something," Genevieve said. "I can't stay for dinner."

Julien paused with the refrigerator door open, asparagus in his hand.

"What do you mean?"

"I'm going home," Genevieve said. "I've just been waiting for you to get back. All I need to do is put Mona in her carrier and load the car."

Julien nudged the refrigerator door closed. "Did I do something wrong?"

"No," Genevieve said, mustering a smile. "It's just time for me to go home."

"Traffic's going to be awful," Julien said. "Stay for dinner. Go later."

"I really need to go now."

"If you leave now, you'll sit in the car twice as long, which means Mona has to be stuck in her carrier twice as long."

"Don't you use my cat against me."

Julien's eyes widened at her sharp tone. Genevieve turned and walked away.

OK, so the conversation hadn't started off so well. Time to try again.

"I left the key in here," she said, starting down the hall. "Oh, and there's an exhibit coming to LACMA in May that's supposed to be really good. If you're interested, I could talk to Thomas about getting us all into the preview cocktail party. That might be fun."

Julien followed her down the hall. "What are you talking about? I don't understand what's going on here."

Genevieve sighed. Why was he doing this? He acted like she was breaking up with him. They weren't a couple. Wasn't that the whole point?

"I'm going home. That's what's going on here."

"Why can't you stay for dinner?"

"Because I'll stay for dinner, and then it will be late, and I'll be tired, and you'll tell me to go tomorrow, and..." Genevieve sighed. Again.

"I don't understand why you're so angry with me all of the sudden," Julien said.

"I'm not angry." Genevieve took a deep breath. "Well, maybe I am angry. But at the situation, not at you."

"The situation?"

"Yes, the situation. Sometimes it feels like this is, I don't know, a joke the universe played on me. Like it made me think we're supposed to be together, but we're really not. And that's why you feel the way you do. Because maybe it really is a bad idea and you just see it more clearly than I do. Does that make sense?"

"Genevieve..."

"Anyway, that's why I have to go home. I can't keep spending all this time with you. It's too hard."

She dragged Mona's cat carrier into the middle of the room.

"I'm really sorry about everything bad that happened because of me," she said. "Especially your car. I know you really liked it, and now it's totaled."

"Side impact is one of the worst kind of crashes you can have," Julien said.

Genevieve rattled a package of cat treats. "Mona? Here kit-kit-kitty!"

"The front and rear have crumple zones to displace the energy from the crash," Julien said. "The sides, not so much. I know this, because I'm one of those geeks who reads the safety reports when I shop for cars. I might still buy the sporty one, but I do the homework."

Genevieve rattled the cat treats again. Why wouldn't Mona just come to her? She really didn't need cat drama on top of everything else.

"Statistically speaking, I made a stupid decision," Julien said. "I was thinking about that this morning, when I was out on my run. Why did I do that?"

Realizing that Julien wasn't just making conversation about his car, Genevieve stopped trying to lure the cat into her carrier and focused her attention on him.

"I know what you did," she said. "It was really brave. I appreciate it. I really do."

Julien took a step toward her and reached for her hand. "I realized, when it comes to you, I need to follow my instincts. And my instincts keep saying one thing: Swerve."

Genevieve was awakened by a persistent buzzing. She buried her head in the pillow and willed it to stop.

When it didn't, she pulled the pillow over her head. That seemed to do the trick. She started to drift back to sleep.

"That was Henry," Julien said from somewhere.

Genevieve turned her face toward the voice. "Henry? What time is it?"

"It's 1:38."

"Why is Henry calling you in the middle of the night?"

The pillow was lifted off her head. "Open your eyes."

"I'm sleeping."

"Clearly you're not, if you're talking to me."

Genevieve blinked. Sunlight was slanting through the shutters.

Julien, propped on one elbow next to her, grinned. "Yep, 1:38 in the afternoon."

Genevieve groaned and threw her arm over her eyes..

"I'm starving," Julien said. He leaned over to plant a kiss on Genevieve and climbed out of bed. "Any requests?"

"Coffee." Genevieve started to throw off the covers, then pulled them back up. "And clothes?"

Laughing, Julien dropped his shirt from the previous day on the bed. "There you go," he said. "Meet me in the kitchen."

Genevieve shrugged into Julien's shirt and petted Mona, who was basking in a sunbeam on the floor. She stopped in the guest room to unearth her toothbrush from her suitcase.

Then, carefully, the way one might handle a live grenade, she peeked at her phone.

Dead battery. She dug out her charger, plugged the phone in and hurried out of the room before it could power up.

She found Julien in the kitchen, mulling the contents of the refrigerator.

"There she is," he said, wrapping an arm around her waist and reeling her in for a kiss. "I'm thinking a frittata."

"Sounds great," Genevieve said. "Can I do anything? Maybe deal with the dishes from last night?"

The remnants of their 11 p.m. pasta were stacked in the sink. They never did get around to the chicken Milanese.

"Leave it," Julien said. "We'll do all the dishes at once." He pulled down two mugs and handed them to Genevieve. "Just pour us coffee and stand there looking gorgeous. Maybe I'll let you make toast."

Genevieve leaned against the counter with her coffee and watched as Julien worked, not quite believing her luck.

His phone began to buzz again. "Look at that for me, will you?" Julien said as he chopped a red pepper.

"Henry," Genevieve said, checking the display.

Julien motioned her over with his chef's knife. "Hit speaker. I guess he's going to call until I pick up."

"Hey, Henry," he called.

"I don't know how you can run a successful business if your clients can't reach you during normal working hours," Henry said.

"And yet I do," Julien said. "What's up?"

"What do I tell these people when they call about the drawing? Do you want it?"

"Do you?"

"I was in this thing to make a point and maybe have a payday," Henry said. "You're the one who cares about the picture."

Julien locked eyes with Genevieve for several seconds.

"I think the museum can keep it," he said.

Genevieve mouthed her surprise. "Really?"

"You sure about that?" Henry asked.

"But they need to turn it into an education thing about looted art," Julien said.

Genevieve wrapped her arms around Julien, and he returned the hug with his free hand.

"In other words, you're going to let them sell this as a service to humanity," Henry said.

"I'm not saying just give it to them," Julien said. "But this is a chance to tell our story to a lot of people, make people understand what happened. That probably does more to honor my mom than hanging the drawing in my living room."

"You're a good kid, Julien," Henry said. "I'll see how much I can talk them out of. Once I have the number, I'm thinking about a bonus for Genevieve."

"Great idea," Julien said.

"I'm thinking you might have a conflict of interest there."

Julien laughed. "You might be right."

"I've got some names for her," Henry said. "She needs a lawyer. But she hasn't answered her phone today, either."

"You don't say."

"You talk to her, tell her to check her messages," Henry said. With that, he hung up.

Julien smiled down at her. "Henry says check your messages."

Genevieve unwound herself from Julien with a sigh. "OK."

Twelve missed messages. Two from Henry, three from Thomas, seven from D.

"I called you a million times!" D said when Genevieve got back to her.

"I know, I'm sorry, I..."

"You stayed there last night, I know," D said. "You had dinner, it was late, and you stayed in the guest room. And you think I'm going to yell at you. Which I'm not. I mean, who knows? Maybe your way is better. And maybe there's a frickin' business opportunity out there for salons specializing in slow bikini waxes that draw out the pain. I mean, I never thought that Brazilian thing of waxing your whole hoohaw would catch on either, but I see girls at the gym who..."

"D?"

"What?"

"I didn't stay in the guest room."

"Well, if you went home, why didn't you call... oh! OH! Hang on!"

"D, what are you doing?"

"Pulling over! So you can tell me *everything*!"

"I'm not telling you anything. In fact, I have to hang up. Julien's making me breakfast. I just didn't want you to think I'd fallen off the face of the earth."

"Breakfast? What time is it out there?"

"Two in the afternoon," Genevieve said.

"Dang, girl."

CHAPTER FORTY-THREE

"SORRY IT'S SUCH A MESS," Genevieve said as she unlocked her apartment door. "If I'd known we were coming here, I would have straightened up."

In the two months she and Julien had been a couple, Genevieve's housekeeping standards – never high – had plummeted. They spent so much time at his place that anything more than minimal cleaning seemed like wasted effort.

By nearly every measure, though, it had been the best two months of Genevieve's life. The panic attacks and insomnia had disappeared, prompting D to observe that "Gettin' it regular is good for you. Nobody tells you that in Sunday School."

All of Genevieve's symptoms – including the ones she never mentioned to D – had disappeared. No more flashbacks to the studio in Paris. No more visions of David Lazare.

Encouraged by Thomas, she was working on an article about the drawing's circuitous path from Paris to the Hilliard. Stimson Miller granted her an interview before his death, recounting for the record how he'd stolen *Study for Tristan and Iseult* after the war.

The museum's board agreed to an infrared examination of the drawing, which revealed it had once been marked with a swastika and an alphanumeric code that included the letters LZ. A similar code was found on the back of the painting in Henry's library – strong circumstantial evidence to support Genevieve's theory that both had been looted from the Lazare family.

Still, she wished she had a contemporary eyewitness who could place the drawing in David Lazare's Paris apartment. Thomas told her not to let the perfect become the enemy of the good, whatever that meant.

Thomas had his hands full at the museum helping to unravel Malcolm's schemes. Among other things, he'd diverted money from the security budget, necessitating the hiring of temp guards. Then he'd taken advantage of the situation to spirit relics out of storage and sold them on the black market to help finance his real-estate speculation.

"Turns out the security is ridiculously lax," Thomas told Genevieve over lunch, with a completely straight face.

She wasn't really interested in Hilliard gossip or even in Malcolm Stewart's criminal case. Genevieve was focused on finishing her article, which she hoped would help bring in clients for Lost Art Investigations.

□

Genevieve and Julien had spent the afternoon in Pasadena with Henry's first ex-wife going through old Lazare family photos for her article, then got stuck in traffic on the 110. They were at her apartment because they saw no hope of making it back to Julien's house before the Lakers playoff game started.

"As long as you paid the cable bill, it's all good," Julien said. He shooed Mona from the prime viewing spot on the sofa, kicked off his flip-flops and put his feet on the coffee-table. Genevieve unearthed the remote from a pile of mail and handed it to him before heading to the kitchen. Mona jumped into Julien's lap and curled up.

"Do you want to get takeout during the game or go out after?" Genevieve opened the refrigerator, which – as usual – held almost nothing. "There's one beer. Want it?"

"Whatever you want," Julien said. "I'll take the beer. Unless you want it?"

Genevieve walked back to the living room and handed Julien the bottle. He grabbed her wrist and pulled her down for a kiss. "Thanks, Gen."

"You're welcome," she said.

Surveying the mess on her coffee table, Genevieve settled next to Julien on the sofa. "I might as well go through this junk while you watch the game."

By halftime, Genevieve had cleared off the top of the coffee table. She sat on the floor to tackle the lower shelf.

"I don't want to say it's been a long time since I cleaned, but I just found a Christmas card," Genevieve said. She leaned her head against Julien's thigh. "It's weird to find stuff from when I didn't even know you. I feel like I've always known you."

Julien put his hand on her head and stroked her hair.

"I'm sorry, I should only talk during the commercials, right?"

"Talk whenever you want," Julien said.

Genevieve spied a book under a pile of holiday catalogs and pulled it out. "Oh wow," she said. "I wondered what happened to this."

"What's that," Julien said absently. "C'mon, Kobe, make the pass!"

"My mom's roommate sent it to me. It's a book from their college's anniversary. There's supposed to be pictures of my mom in here."

"Oh, don't let him have that shot!"

Genevieve began to leaf through the book, wondering why she hadn't done so sooner. For a lover of vintage fashion, what could be better than historical photos from a women's college?

Finally, she found one of the photos Christine must have wanted her to see. It was a black-and-white shot of a museum outing to Philadelphia, according to the caption. Genevieve studied her mother's face, so young and untroubled, turned slightly toward the teacher.

"Oh! Julien! Oh!"

Genevieve shoved the book toward him and dashed to the bar, where her laptop was charging.

Julien dropped his feet from the coffee table with a thud. "Gen? What's wrong?"

"Look at that photo!"

He glanced at the open book in his lap. "Which photo? It's a double-page spread of photos." Julien grabbed the remote and hit the mute button. "Are you OK?"

"I'm sorry," Genevieve said. "I know the game's important, but..." She sat next to him on the couch and began scrolling through photos on her computer.

"Look at that photo," she said, pointing. "That's my mom."

"You look exactly like her," Julien said. "She's really pretty."

"Read the caption," Genevieve said.

"On an outing to the Philadelphia Museum of Art, eager acolytes gather round..." Julien paused. "Who wrote this stuff?"

"Keep reading," Genevieve said.

"Eager acolytes gather round professor Vivian Chalifoux as she..."

Genevieve found the photo she wanted and turned the screen toward Julien.

"Vivian Chalifoux, that professor? Look. She's the woman in this photo in front of the gallery with David."

"What?" Julien took the laptop from her and enlarged the photo, handing her the book so they could look at the two pictures side by side.

She had changed, obviously, in the 30 years between that sidewalk in Paris and the museum in Philadelphia, but it was unmistakably the same woman.

"Weird," Julien said.

"That would explain how my mom knew about your family," Genevieve said. She flipped to the front of the book, read for a moment, then flipped to the back.

"What are you doing?" Julien asked.

"The table of contents says there's a directory."

"She's probably dead, don't you think? She'd be really old," Julien said.

Genevieve ran her finger down the listings for C. "Oh my God."

"What?"

"Vivian Chalifoux's address is a post office box in Wiscasset, Maine. Remember the postmark on the envelope the gallery catalog came in?"

Julien picked up the remote and turned off the game.

The post office box was the only point of contact they could find for Vivian Chalifoux. Julien tried several databases, and Christine called the college for them, but every attempt to turn up a phone number ran into a brick wall.

"I think you're going to have to write her," Julien said, finally.

"And say what? If I say something about the gallery catalog, and it wasn't her, I'm going to sound like a crazy person."

But she managed to come up with something, introducing herself as the daughter of a former student and mentioning her role assisting heirs of the Lazare family of Paris in their bid to recover artwork looted during the war. Would Ms. Chalifoux be willing to discuss her memories of Genevieve's mother, Grace Knapp? Genevieve included all of her contact information, mailed the note, and waited.

The response came more quickly than she anticipated.

In a spidery hand on very good stationery, Vivian Chalifoux wrote that she would be delighted to meet Genevieve and "hear all about your adventures regarding the Lazare family."

She was home most days, she wrote, and 2 p.m. was the best time for her to receive visitors. Genevieve should choose a day and write ahead. She included directions to her house.

Genevieve read the note aloud to Julien, incredulous. "She expects me to go all the way across the country and just show up on her doorstep?"

"So it would seem."

"Is this like a horror movie, like she's trying to lure us there?"

Julien laughed. "Gen, this woman's got to be 90-something years old. I think we can handle her."

And so Genevieve and Julien flew to Boston, spent the night, then got up in the morning and drove to Maine.

Vivian Chalifoux, as it turned out, did not live in Wiscasset proper. Julien had printed out a map, but they still had to stop twice for directions.

Her road, when they finally found it, was not a road at all, but a set of well-worn tracks that bumped along in a sparse grove of trees. Through the breaks in the trees, they could see a small bay. There was not another house in sight.

The tracks petered out 100 yards from a two-story saltbox house. A narrow wooden-plank sidewalk was carved out of the scrubby, native grass.

Julien put the car in park. "Are you sure this is it?"

Genevieve pointed to a nearby outbuilding. "The guy at the convenience store said to look for the shed with the red door." The door, weatherbeaten and peeling, had definitely been red at some point.

They picked their way up the plank sidewalk, which was slick with moisture. Fog was in the process of burning off – remnants still floated over the bay.

"Look, she has a satellite dish." Julien grinned at Genevieve. "You pictured this hermit, and I bet she has a blog where she advises other retirees about day-trading in the Asian markets."

As they neared the door, Julien's foot slid off the path, landing in soft mud. He found a stick and bent over to clean his shoe as Genevieve knocked on the door.

Vivian Chalifoux was nothing like Genevieve had pictured. She was very tall, with white hair cut in a flattering pageboy. She wore tan chinos with a blue and white striped T-shirt smartly tucked in. A blue cardigan was draped around her shoulders.

Her face, though lined, was still beautiful.

"Hello," Genevieve said, offering her hand. "I'm Genevieve McKenna."

"Yes. Oh yes, so much like your mother," Vivian said, holding out her own hand, smiling.

Julien finished cleaning his shoe and tossed the stick away. Wiping his hand on his pant leg, he straightened and faced the door.

The color drained from Vivian's face, and she inhaled sharply.

"I think I wrote that I was bringing my friend with

me," Genevieve said, puzzled. "This is Julien Brooks. His mother was..."

Vivian stood back to admit them. "Regine's boy. Of course. I thought we could sit outside, by the water." She led them through the living room to a pair of French doors.

The walls of the living room were bare, painted a stark white. An old-fashioned settee upholstered in pale blue took up one wall. A wing chair faced it at an angle.

Vivian opened the French doors and led them out onto a rock terrace facing the bay. Adirondack chairs were grouped in a corner around a rough-hewn wooden table. A plank sidewalk led down to a small dock.

She waved them toward the chairs. "Please, have a seat. Would you like lemonade?"

"That sounds nice," Genevieve said. "Can I help you?"

"No, please sit," Vivian said. She went back inside, closing the doors firmly behind her.

"Did you notice that her walls were completely blank? How strange is that for someone who taught art history?"

Before Julien could reply, Vivian returned balancing a tray with two antique green glasses. Julien rose to help her. "Just take the glasses, if you would," she said.

She put the tray down on the table and angled an Adirondack chair toward them.

"The resemblance to your Uncle David gave me a bit of a start," she said. "And you, Genevieve, are just as lovely as your mother. And you're together! That's magnificent. I'm delighted it's finally all come together, and you've come to let me know."

Julien and Genevieve exchanged a look.

"What's come together?" Genevieve asked.

"Oh," Vivian said. "You don't know, then."

Vivian tapped her right hand rhythmically against the arm of her chair. "I'm trying to think how to explain all this." She settled deeper into her chair. "Well, they always say the best place to start is the beginning."

CHAPTER FORTY-FOUR

"I NEVER EXPECTED to have a glamorous life," Vivian began. "I thought I'd marry my sweetheart Gordon, a boy I'd known all my life, and we'd be the most conventional of couples. But that changed in the spring of 1938, just a month or so before my college graduation.

"We were at a dance, and I realized that I hadn't seen Gordon in a bit. I went outside to look for him, and I found him in the back of a car, *in flagrante*."

Vivian paused dramatically. "With *his* best friend."

"Oh," Genevieve said, nearly choking on her lemonade.

"Oh indeed. Such things were hardly spoken of in those days, so to say I was shocked would be putting it mildly. Though it did explain a certain lack of ardor on Gordon's part."

Genevieve shot Julien an alarmed look. Where was this story going?

"I'd no idea what to do with myself after having my plans upended. Fortunately, I had a small inheritance," Vivian said, "so I attached myself to a school chum who was traveling to Paris with an aunt and sailed shortly after graduation."

She scanned the horizon, shielding her eyes with her hand. "Turning out to be a beautiful day," she said.

"I'd been in Paris a few weeks when I met David." She stared frankly at Julien. "He was handsome like you. Though not as tall. That must come from your father."

"My mother always said I didn't get it from the Lazares," Julien said.

"David was very sophisticated, had a brilliant eye, and, well, he was just a beautiful man," Vivian said. "Though with a bit of a reputation for the ladies."

She grasped the arms of her chair. "Well, why dance around it? We became lovers. I was never so happy, although I suppose I knew deep down it couldn't last. Herr Hitler would see to that.

"By 1939, things in Europe were very tense. David knew artists and intellectuals who had fled Germany. He was certain a war was coming. And he worried about your mother. She was just a teenager, and David was responsible for her. I suppose your mother told you some of this," she said.

"She said when he sent her to England, he told her it was just to visit their friends," Julien said. "She said an American friend of his traveled with her. Was that you?"

"It was," Vivian said. "David was reluctant to send her alone. And he was determined that I leave, too."

"I took Regine to England, and I sailed home in August of '39, one of the last ships to New York. Then Germany invaded Poland, and the war began in earnest."

Vivian sighed. "I had been home a month when I realized I must be pregnant. David and I always took precautions, but my last evening in Paris, we met in the studio above the apartment, and we were quite overcome."

Julien and Genevieve exchanged a look. Vivian chuckled.

"Oh dear. Have I shocked you, children?"

"No," Genevieve said.

"I have a cousin?" Julien leaned forward in his chair.

Vivian held up her hand. She'd tell her story her way.

"As you can imagine, this was quite a predicament," Vivian said. "I cabled David – the promptest method of communication in those days, but not private, which obliged me to speak in code. I followed up with a letter, in which I was more explicit."

She stared off into the distance for a moment, then said softly, "But time was of the essence, and I didn't hear from him."

"Ironically, Gordon saved the day," Vivian said. "We struck a deal that we'd keep each other's secrets, and we did love each other, after a fashion. We eloped and moved to Seattle. We cabled our families the next summer and said 'Surprise, we have a son!' We neglected to mention he was born in March."

She smiled. "You're dubious, but Gordon was a marvelous liar. He had to be."

"You never heard from David?" Julien asked.

"A letter did catch up with me, that winter before the baby was born," Vivian said. "I've no idea what it said. I was angry. I had Gordon burn it."

Genevieve gasped.

"I know," Vivian said. "I've never forgiven myself."

She took a moment to compose herself and then resumed her story. "When the Japanese bombed Pearl Harbor, Gordon enlisted. He was killed in the war. So I was a widow with a young child to support. David and I moved..."

Seeing their expressions, she stopped. "Yes, I named him for his father. Gordon didn't mind. We lived with my mother while I did my graduate studies. Later, of course, I would learn that my great love had not survived."

She leaned forward and patted Julien's knee. "And that's the story of me and your uncle." She tilted her head. "Now tell me, how is your mother?"

"She died three years ago," Julien said.

"Did she have a happy life?"

Julien thought about that. "Not especially, no."

"So few people do," Vivian said. "No one likes to admit that."

She stretched her legs in front of her, then stood. "Would either of you like more lemonade? No? If you'll excuse me a moment, then."

Julien stood as she left.

"Wow," he said, easing back into his chair.

"That's the saddest story I've ever heard," Genevieve said. She reached out toward Julien, and he grasped her hand.

The door handle turned, and Vivian returned. She handed a bottle of sunscreen to Genevieve. "The sun here is stronger than it looks," she said, "and you've got that fair skin like your mother."

"Thanks," Genevieve said, squeezing lotion into her hand and rubbing it on her arms. "You seem to have vivid memories of my mother."

"Oh yes," Vivian said. "How could I not?"

Seeing Genevieve's confusion, Vivian shook her head. "Forgive me. You must find the way I'm telling this story infuriating."

"It's your story to tell," Julien said.

Vivian flashed a smile at him. "So gallant, you Lazare men. Let's see, how shall I proceed? Well, I suppose this is the part where Genevieve's mother enters the scene. I think she became my student in 1967, or maybe 1968."

"It was '68," Genevieve said.

"She stood out for so many reasons – a bright girl, of course, and that red hair. And it soon became clear that Grace was an old soul," Vivian said.

"My son, David, you see... David had an accident when he was 12. He fell off his bicycle and hit his head. No one wore helmets then, and it damaged his brain. Before the accident, I thought he might be an artist. Afterward, while I was teaching, David liked to spend his days at the cafe in town. The owners were fond of him, and he'd sit at the counter all day, sketching."

"My mom's roommate said they went to the cafe sometimes," Genevieve said.

"David noticed her right away," Vivian said. "The owner had strict instructions not to let him make a pest of himself, and by the same token, girls from the school were not allowed to bother him. He was a grown man with the mind of a little boy, you understand. But Grace was kind to him, and the two of them seemed to have a genuine affinity."

Vivian paused, unsure, it seemed, how to go on.

"Was it you or your son who told my mother about David Lazare and Paris?" Genevieve asked.

Vivian thought before answering. "If I said she learned of that through her own unconventional methods, would that make sense to you?"

Genevieve looked to Julien, who shrugged.

"Yes," Genevieve said.

"One day she came to my office," Vivian said. "Her head was bare, and snow was melting in her fiery hair. I remember thinking there was a metaphor there. She was frantic. She had to know: What happens to David Lazare?

"I was shocked. I hadn't heard David's name in years. I'd never confided to anyone but Gordon.

"I asked where she'd heard that name. She wouldn't answer. She kept pressing me – what happens? I tried to calm her, but she wouldn't be deterred."

Vivian closed her eyes briefly.

"She talked as if it weren't all 30 years in the past."

The sun went behind a cloud, and Genevieve shivered.

"She was back the next day, much calmer. She told me, quite matter-of-factly, of these strange experiences she'd had, the sensation of being in the studio above the apartment. I told her what I'd learned after the war, that David had died. She stood up, then, and looked me in the eye, and she said, 'I can save him.'

"You know the rest," Vivian said. "Someone alerted your grandparents. They whisked her away to some hospital. I should have done more to help her, I suppose, but I hardly knew what."

Genevieve leaned forward in her chair. "You believed her."

Vivian gave a small smile. "Joan of Arc heard the voice of God calling her to save France. And so she did. I suppose they'd say now that she was mentally ill."

"Why did you send me the catalog?" Genevieve asked.

"Christine is quite the dynamo about sending class updates. I saw in one of her newsletters that you were working at the Hilliard," Vivian said. "I was struck by the fact that you shared your mother's interest in art, and I wondered whether you were like her in other ways, and if you were…"

She looked out at the water a long time. When she spoke again, her voice was barely more than a whisper.

"I wondered whether you could save him."

Genevieve looked at Julien. How much should she tell?

"Go ahead," he said.

She got up and went to Vivian's side.

"I am like my mother. I've experienced the same things, and I've, well... I think I've encountered David."

"But you were not in time," Vivian said. It was a statement, not a question.

Genevieve put her hand on Vivian's knee. "No, I was there in time. But I don't think it's possible to change anything. I don't think he wanted to change anything. I think he already knew he would die. And he went anyway."

Vivian covered Genevieve's hand with hers.

"Well," Vivian said finally, wiping away tears with her free hand. "I'm glad to know that. Thank you." She patted Genevieve's hand. "Thank you for telling me that."

They were quiet for a few moments, then Julien said, "Where's your son now? It would be good to meet another cousin."

"My David died in '72. A seizure," Vivian said.

"Oh," Genevieve said, "I'm so sorry."

Vivian fingered Genevieve's hair, then looked at Julien.

"Together at last," she said.

"Excuse me?" Genevieve said.

"Come with me," Vivian said. "It's time you knew the rest of the story."

CHAPTER FORTY-FIVE

JULIEN STOOD and took Genevieve's elbow, helping her up. He offered his other hand to Vivian.

"Follow me," Vivian said, going inside and heading toward stairs that angled off the entry hall.

"A 93-year-old woman is inviting you into her bedroom," she said to Julien. "What do you think about that?"

Julien responded in French, something Genevieve couldn't make out.

That prompted a throaty laugh from Vivian. "You're as bad as David. He was an incorrigible flirt."

She grasped the banister and climbed the stairs ahead of them. At the top, she made a turn, took a few steps, and opened a door. She stood aside for them to enter.

Confused, Genevieve walked into the room. White curtains framed the windows, which looked out on the water. Like the living room, it was sparsely furnished. There was an antique wooden bed, topped by a white chenille cover. Next to it stood a nightstand, which held an old-fashioned alarm clock and several prescription bottles.

Turning from the bed, she looked at the opposite wall.

And there it was.

Genevieve gasped.

"Oh wow," Julien said. "She looks just like..."

"Behold *Tristan and Iseult*, by Théodore Lazare. Other than my son, and the ignorant man who framed it, you are the first people to see it since the war," Vivian said. "And yes, Julien, Iseult looks very much like your Genevieve."

Genevieve was too stunned to speak.

"Sit on the bed, dear, it's fine," Vivian said.

"It's beautiful," Julien said. "I thought the Thisbe painting in the Louvre was gorgeous, but this... Wait, how did you get this?"

"We'll get to that in a moment," Vivian said. "Shall I tell you the story of this painting? You saw *Pyramus and Thisbe*? So perhaps you recognize the model, although as Thisbe her face was obscured."

Genevieve backed up and perched on the edge of the bed.

"It's a woman Théodore Lazare was in love with, right? She rejected him, so he showed her face here to punish her, and his brother kept it under wraps to avoid scandal," Genevieve said.

"Oh my," Vivian said. "Who told you *that*?"

"A French academic pieced it together from gossip in letters," Julien said, "although she didn't know who the woman was."

"Her name is Marianne Mercier," Vivian said. "She loved Théodore, and he loved her. But their love was doomed. Her family would never let her marry a man who wasn't a Christian. Théodore's brother tried to intervene by sending him to Florence to paint, but all he did was come back with a gift for Marianne, a pendant."

"So that's why he painted her as Thisbe, and again as Iseult," Genevieve said. "Doomed love."

"Heartbreaking, as you can see from the painting," Vivian said. "She didn't reject him. They were separated by her family. And he didn't want to punish her. He painted her face so he could remember her after she left."

"Where'd she go?" Julien asked.

"Her family arranged a marriage to a man taking a government post in Martinique."

"How do you know all of this?" Genevieve asked.

"Henri Lazare wrote a letter to his son, explaining the painting's history. David showed it to me," Vivian said.

"It freaks me out how much she looks like Gen," Julien said.

Vivian put a hand to her chest. "Imagine my surprise when Genevieve's mother arrived on campus."

" 'He says I look like a girl in a painting,' My mother wrote that," Genevieve said. "Your son said that, didn't he? But he didn't mean *a* painting. He meant *this* painting."

Genevieve stood. So many things were becoming clear. "The things that happened to my mom – the flashbacks or whatever – that started after she met your son, after she met someone from the Lazare family. And it happened to me right after I met Julien."

Julien looked alarmed. "Wait a minute. I'm causing this? *I'm* the problem?"

"On the contrary," Vivian said, "I prefer to think you two are the solution."

"You lost me," Julien said.

"After I saw Genevieve's mother, I became very interested in the story of Marianne Mercier," Vivian said. "She had three daughters and two sons. Can you guess where at least one of her descendants ended up, Genevieve?"

When Genevieve didn't respond, Vivian supplied the answer: "Louisiana."

"I don't get it," Julien said.

"My mother was born there," Genevieve said.

"I thought your mother was from Texas."

"The family that adopted her was from Texas, but she was born in Louisiana."

"The adoption may make things difficult to trace," Vivian said, "but I would wager that you are descended from Marianne Mercier."

"Wait a minute. You think..." Julien began.

"Two kindred souls, endlessly circling, looking for the right opportunity, the right circumstances..." Vivian sighed. "Perhaps I'm just an old woman who reads too many novels. But that's my story, and I'm sticking to it, as they say."

"But how did you get the painting?" Genevieve asked.

"In 1946, I got a letter from a gallery owner in New York, an acquaintance of David's. He said he had a package for me," Vivian said.

"In the early days of the Occupation, David worked with a network of like-minded people to keep art out of Nazi hands. Somehow he managed to get the painting to a friend, who got it to a friend, who got it to the colleague in New York by way of Lisbon. David intended the painting to be a legacy for his child."

"But there's no record of anything. This painting just dropped out of sight," Genevieve said.

"David burned all his records, so the Nazis wouldn't know what to look for," Vivian said. "He cut the painting from the frame – how it must have pained him to do that – and sent it to me, along with a letter."

To Julien, she said, "This rightfully belonged to you, I suppose, once my son died."

She turned to Genevieve. "You must wonder, given my background, how I could countenance this, allowing the world to believe a painting is lost when it's been hanging on my bedroom wall. I took pains to hide it, too."

She crossed to the painting and adjusted the frame slightly. "I have no good answer to that. All I can say is this: It's the last thing I have that was touched by David."

"Do you still have the letter?" Genevieve asked.

"Of course I still have the letter," Vivian said, squaring her shoulders. "But you'll forgive me, I hope, if I don't show it to you. It's rather personal."

Genevieve gave a little gasp, embarrassed that Vivian had misunderstood. "I only meant that if you have the letter, that proves the provenance."

Julien put his hand on her arm to stop her. "You don't owe my family anything. David wanted you to have it, and as far as I'm concerned, it's yours. I don't think anyone needs to know about this."

He looked at Genevieve. "What do you think? Can you live with this on your conscience?"

Genevieve nodded, knowing this was one decision she would never second-guess.

"Well," Vivian said briskly, "that's settled. I'm so glad you came. It's been lovely visiting with you." She looked at her watch. "But tonight's my book club, and I really must have a nap if I'm going to be sharp. Our theme this month was erotica, and I think it's going to be a lively discussion!"

Julien threw his head back and laughed.

Twenty minutes later, they were in the rental car, headed back to Boston. Julien found a scenic spot where they could pull over, and they sat on a rock, staring out at the vast expanse of the Atlantic.

Genevieve wrapped her arms around her knees and rested her head on them.

"Are you cold?" Julien asked.

Genevieve shook her head. "I'm just really sad. It all turned out so awful for everyone. Nobody got to be happy." She began to sniffle. "I think I'm going to cry."

Julien put his arm around her.

"I'm sorry," she sputtered. "Do you think it's true, what Vivian said? About us?"

"What, that we're some kind of cosmic do-over for a couple that got wronged by the universe?"

"More science-fiction crap for you not to believe, I guess," Genevieve said.

"I don't know, Gen." Julien leaned his head against hers. "I know that when I saw you in Vegas, sitting there drinking coffee, I plugged in a laptop that was already fully charged just so I could talk to you. And it wasn't like 'Oh, I think I'll talk to her.' It was like 'I *have* to talk to her.' "

"Really?"

Julien nodded. "And I know I love you so much that I can't quite believe it."

Genevieve drew back and looked at him.

"Yeah, I really said that. I know. It's too fast." He shrugged. "But I love you."

"Julien..."

"You don't have to say it back," he said. "It's cool."

Genevieve began to laugh. "I promised myself I would wait another month before I said it."

Julien began to laugh too.

"It's marked on my calendar," she said. "You can look when we get home."

"OK, I love that, too," Julien said. He glanced around. "It's kind of deserted here. Want to climb down to the beach and make out?"

"Julien! It's cold!"

"I said make *out*, Gen."

She shot him a look. "It's too bad you didn't bring your camera," she said. "You like taking pictures of deserted landscapes like this."

"What do you mean?"

"There are no people in the photos in your house," she said.

Julien pulled his phone from his pocket. "We'll fix that. Come here." They turned so the ocean was behind them. Julien rested his head against Genevieve's and wrapped one arm around her. He held the phone out and snapped the picture.

"How did it come out?" Genevieve asked, craning her head to see.

Julien showed her the photo. "There's your happy ending."

AUTHOR'S NOTE

Not In Time is a work of fiction. Théodore Lazare never existed, nor did Galerie de l'Étoile in Paris, nor the Hilliard Museum in Santa Monica.

The Nazis did loot thousands of works of art, many of which have not been returned to their rightful owners – as recent news events have made clear.

James Rorimer and the Monuments, Fine Arts and Archives section, mentioned in passing in these pages, were real. The thieving typist I've placed in their orbit at war's end is an invention.

ACKNOWLEDGEMENTS

I'd like to thank my husband for thinking a time-traveling art detective would make an excellent premise for a novel. I'd also like to thank him for taking a job in Culver City, California, in 2006. I wrote the first two drafts of Not In Time at our dining room table in a house very much like Julien's.

My agent, Lauren Abramo of Dystel & Goderich Literary Management, saw something in the first draft of Not In Time and encouraged me to find a better ending, for which I thank her.

Dr. Sue Williams, purveyor of fine chocolates, advised me on ER protocol in cases of concussion. Barbara Morris, the pixel-packin' mama, makes my website and paperbacks purty.

My sister read every version of this manuscript and liked them all. My parents probably hit the refresh button all night waiting for this book to show up online so they could buy it first. Writing can be lonely and discouraging work, but I couldn't ask for better cheerleaders.

I'd also like to thank the stickman at the Paris casino in Las Vegas who helpfully informed me (after I hit him with the dice) that the dealers are in play.

IDENTITY

NEW JOB. NEW TOWN. NEW LIFE.
Risky Business is big at the box office, Journey is on the radio, and Sharlah Webb's luck is finally turning.

Or she thinks it is, until the day she comes home from her waitressing job to find police cars in her driveway and her boyfriend, Brian Lowry, in jail on drug charges.

Suddenly, she's got all kinds of trouble. She's broke, Brian's family blames her for his arrest, and a hurricane is bearing down on their Texas Gulf Coast town.

Even worse, Brian refuses to cooperate with the police and won't tell her why. It soon becomes clear that his secrets have put them both in jeopardy.

As the danger grows, so does Sharlah's confusion. Is Brian not the man she thought he was? Can she trust the police? Brian's family?

Should she stay put, or flee the approaching storm?

Sharlah embarks on her own search for answers. Then one fateful decision launches a mystery that will take years to unravel.

Identity: A novel of suspense, love and finding your true self.

ABOUT THE AUTHOR

Shawna Seed is a writer and editor whose work has taken her to both coasts and several spots in between, working for organizations ranging from The Dallas Morning News to ESPN.com. Her previous novel, Identity, was released in March 2013.

Originally from Kansas, she has lived in seven states and every continental U.S. time zone. She and her husband – and their two cats, Gus and Lulu – now make their home in Dallas.

You can learn more about the author at www.shawnaseed.com

Like Shawna Seed on Facebook: www.facebook.com/shawnaseedauthor

Follow Shawna Seed on Twitter (@shawnaseed)

Find Shawna Seed on Goodreads (www.goodreads.com)

Cover design: Heather Kern, popshopstudio.com

1. What do you believe happened to Genevieve during her "flashbacks?" What leads you to that conclusion?

2. Do you believe that some couples are simply "meant to be?" Or do you think that there are multiple ideal matches for most people?

3. Whom would you rather have as a best friend: Thomas or D?

4. What do you think D is short for?

5. Genevieve believes she is adrift in her life when the novel begins. Do you think Julien is adrift? Why or why not?

6. Thomas tells Genevieve that Julien doesn't seem like her type. Do you think Thomas is right? Why or why not?

7. Why do you believe Genevieve chose to confide in Julien rather than someone closer to her?

8. If a museum bought or received looted artwork in good faith, do you believe it is morally obligated to return it to the original owner?

9. Do you believe Vivian's actions were wrong?

10. Do you think Genevieve and Julien handle Vivian's actions correctly?